"IF YOU DON'T WANT TO DANCE, LET'S GO."

Marisela finished her drink, slipped her fingers into her jacket pocket, threw a ten onto the bar, and nodded toward the door. She twisted off the bar stool, but Frankie moved only to tilt his head toward hers so she'd hear him over the music and the crowd.

"How do you know I'm not waiting for someone?"

Surrendering to her instincts, Marisela drew one of her long fingernails over Frankie's angular jawline. "I don't. But you just got a better offer."

"Julie Elizabeth Leto's *Dirty Little Secrets* is one of the sexiest books I've ever read, with fun, fast writing. Fizzy as a flute of Clos du Mesnil champagne. As a guilty Latina pleasure, *Dirty Little Secrets* ranks alongside silk Eberjey negligees, Blanxart Spanish chocolate bars, and Maria Evora black soap."

—Alisa Valdes-Rodriguez,
author of *The Dirty Girls Social Club*

DIRTY LITTLE SECRETS
IS ALSO AVAILABLE AS AN EBOOK.

Dirty Little Secrets

Happy Reading!

JULIE LETO

doWn tOwn press

Naughty Girls

New York London Toronto Sydney

An *Original* Publication of POCKET BOOKS

DOWNTOWN PRESS, published by Pocket Books
1230 Avenue of the Americas
New York, NY 10020

Library of Congress Cataloging-in-Publication Data

Leto, Julie Elizabeth.
    Dirty little secrets / Julie Leto.—1st Downtown Press trade pbk. ed.
      p. cm.
    ISBN 1-4165-0162-2
      1. Hispanic American women—Fiction. 2. Tampa (Fla.)—Fiction. I. Title.

PS3612.E82885D57 2005
813'.6—dc22

                                                                2005041334

First Downtown Press trade paperback edition June 2005

10   9   8   7   6   5   4   3   2   1

DOWNTOWN PRESS and colophon are
trademarks of Simon & Schuster, Inc.

Manufactured in the United States of America

Designed by Jaime Putorti

For information regarding special discounts for bulk purchases,
please contact Simon & Schuster Special Sales at 1-800-456-6798
or business@simonandschuster.com

For my family, especially Tim, Alyssa, and Lady, who put up with the days when my head is in the clouds (or more specifically, in the book) and love me anyway.

For my friends, especially Janelle Denison, Susan Kearney, Leslie Kelly, Julie Kenner, Carly Phillips, and Vicki Lewis Thompson, who stoked the fire when I needed it and weren't shy about saying, "Go for it" or "I told you so."

ACKNOWLEDGMENTS

Writing this book came about because of inspiration from several sources, including a few of my writer friends who had the *cojones* to pursue their dreams and write the kind of heroine who can take care of herself—and anyone else she deems worthy. Special thanks to Diana Peterfreund, Kathy Carmichael, Beverly Brandt (a.k.a. Jacey Ford), and Katherine Garbera for pushing me in the right direction—even if you didn't realize that's what you were doing.

Special thanks to Anita Durand, Barbara Pollack, and Mireya Orsini for checking and double-checking all the Spanish in the book to make sure I didn't screw it up too badly. I know I at least got the curse words right. Those I remember firsthand.

I also had the courage to take a chance and do something different with this book because of the encouragement and confidence of my amazing agent, Helen Breitwieser, a true kick-ass heroine in her own right, though her style is classier than most. And of course, to the awesome editorial team at Simon & Schuster, particularly publisher Louise Burke, senior editor Amy Pierpont, and Megan McKeever, for believing in my vision and doing all you could to make sure the magic came through on the page.

And to the founders and creators of Google, without which this book could never have been written.

One

"I REMEMBER WHEN you used to stroke me like that."

Marisela Morales punctuated her pickup line by blowing on the back of Francisco Vega's neck. She watched the soft downy strands on his nape spike and knew her luck had finally turned around.

His fingers, visible as she glanced over his shoulder, drew streaks through the condensation on his beer bottle. Up and down. Slow and straight. Lazy, but precise. He toyed with his *cerveza* the same way he'd once made love to her, and for a split second, a trickle of moist heat curled intimately between Marisela's thighs. For the moment, the part of her Frankie used to oh-so-easily manipulate was safe, encased beneath silky panties and skin-tight, hip-hugging jeans.

Tonight, she'd have him—but on her terms. The hunter had found her prey. Now, she just had to bring him in.

"I don't remember taking time for slow strokes when you and me got busy, *niña.*"

Marisela sighed, teasing his neck with her hot breath one more time before she slid onto the bar stool next to his. She'd been trying to track the man down for nearly a week. Who knew Frankie would turn up at an old haunt? Since they'd parted ways, Club Electric, a white box on the outside, hot joint on the inside, had changed names, hands, and clientele a good dozen times. But a few things remained constant—the music, the raw atmosphere—and the availability of men like Frankie, who defined the word *caliente.*

Like the song said, *Hot, hot, hot.*

"We were young then," Marisela admitted with a shrug, loosening the holster strap that cradled the cherished 9mm Taurus Millennium she wore beneath her slick leather jacket. "Now, I'm all grown up."

Marisela wiggled her crimson fingernails at Theresa, the owner of the club. The way the older woman's face lit up, Marisela figured she was going to get more than a drink. *Damn.* Marisela loved Theresa as if she were her aunt, but now wasn't the time for . . .

"Oh, Marisela! *Mija,* how can I thank you for what you did?"

The sentiment was as loud as it was sincere. So she'd done a nice thing for Theresa. The world didn't have to know. Good deeds could ruin her reputation.

And a simple thank-you wasn't enough for Theresa. She stepped up onto the shelf on the other side of the bar and practically launched herself into Marisela's arms. Rolling her eyes at Frankie, Marisela gave the owner a genuine squeeze. She deserved as much. She was a good listener, kept great secrets and mixed the best *Cuba Libre* in town.

"*De nada,* Theresa," Marisela said, gently disentangling herself. She appreciated the woman's gratitude, but she had work to do.

"Anything for you. Anytime. For you, drinks are on the house from now on, okay? You and . . . your friend."

Even as she tried to be the courteous hostess, Theresa's voice faltered when her eyes met Frankie's. Marisela's ex hadn't been in the neighborhood for years. And in that time, he'd aged. His skin, naturally dark, now sported a rough texture, complete with a scar that traced just below his bottom lip. His jaw seemed sharper and his once perfect nose now shifted slightly to the right—likely the result of an untreated break. Even if he hadn't matured from a devilish boy to a clearly dangerous man, he likely wouldn't be recognized by anyone but Marisela and a few others who'd once known him well—the very "others" Marisela had made sure wouldn't come into Club Electric again, on Theresa's behalf.

"I never say no to free booze," Marisela answered. "*Gracias,* Theresa."

Theresa blew Marisela a kiss, patted her cheek, then moved aside to work on her drink. To most people, a *Cuba Libre* was just rum and Coke with lime. To Marisela, it was a taste of heaven.

"What did you do for her?" Frankie asked, his voice even, as if he wasn't really curious.

Marisela knew better. She slid her arms on the bar, arching

her back, working out the kinks in her spine while giving Frankie an unhampered view of her breasts. She didn't want him to waste his curiosity on what she'd done for Theresa; she wanted to pique his interest another way.

"Last week, *las Reinas* chose this bar as their new hangout. Not quite the clientele Theresa has in mind. Gangs aren't exactly good for business. I politely asked them to pick someplace else."

"Politely?" Frankie asked, his dark eyebrows bowed over his hypnotic eyes. "Last I remember, *las Reinas* didn't respond well to polite."

Marisela shrugged. She'd earned a great deal of respect from her former gang by choosing to bleed out. She'd used every fighting skill she'd ever learned, every survival instinct she'd ever experienced, to escape a lifelong bond to the gang. But she'd survived. Barely.

"They've learned some manners while you've been gone. Lots of things have changed. Like," she said, snagging his beer around the neck and taking a sip, "I don't settle for fast and furious no more."

Frankie didn't move a muscle. "Is that so?"

She smoothed her tongue over her teeth, then licked the lip of his bottle, careful not to smudge her ruby red lipstick. He snagged his drink back and chugged, his gaze locked on her mouth. Frankie always had a thing for her lips. Marisela thought they resembled something between Angelina Jolie and a grouper, but Frankie considered her thick, pouty flesh mighty fine. A detail she intended to use to her advantage, now that she'd found the man.

Theresa delivered her rum and Coke, tall and icy with a

wedge of lime. After another wary glance at Frankie, she left them alone.

"So you come here a lot?" he asked.

"Where else am I gonna go? This is West Tampa, not Miami. We've got one club and this is it."

"There's always Ybor City."

"If you don't mind drunks who can't dance and ridiculous cover charges. This is still the neighborhood hot spot. You'd know that if you came around more."

"I've been busy," he answered, draining the rest of his beer.

She sipped her spiked cola. "And how *was* prison?"

He chuckled, slid his beer bottle away. "Big party," he quipped. "I got out two years ago."

"Really? I hadn't heard."

He snorted. He likely knew as well as she did that the precise location and activities of all the neighborhood kids—young, old, and in between—were reported, catalogued, and reported again from the shiny vinyl chairs of Viola's Beauty Parlor, two blocks south of Columbus Drive. Their mothers both had standing appointments every weekend. And thanks to Aida Morales's devotion to the Saturday morning religion of gossip and speculation, Marisela knew precisely what Frankie had been up to over the last decade as if she'd been there herself. Gang. Prison. Dock work in Miami. Nothing too complicated.

Then a week ago, he'd shown up in Tampa uninvited and unexpected. After less than an hour in town, he'd been arrested for possession. Thanks to his parents, he'd made bail—and then he'd promptly disappeared.

Which was why she was here.

"So what have you been up to, Marisela?"

Her turn to snort. "Nothing too exciting. I did nails for a while. Worked at Wal-Mart. Graduated to Saks. Did some phone work and filing for Alberto Garcia, on the side. Now, I'm looking again."

She conveniently left out the parts his mother couldn't possibly have told him. Hardly anyone knew that her work for Alberto went beyond answering calls and shoveling papers. The owner of AAA-Able Bail Bonds had helped her out when her gang activity landed her in juvie. Instead of processing the teen and sending her on her way, he'd promised her a job. A real job. One where she'd put her fighting skills and gun experience to good use. She'd run little errands for him and trained her ass off until she turned twenty-one. Then, he'd put her in enforcement. For seven years, she'd tracked down bail-jumping bozos all across the state.

But Alberto had been careful not to send her into her own neighborhood to pick up strays. Called it a conflict of interest. So her secret life was safe. A good thing, too, since Frankie might not be so anxious to relive a little heat from their past if he knew she still carried a gun.

Illegally, but that was a fact she continued to ignore. She'd lost her license to carry and immediately thereafter, her position with AAA-Able. But she hadn't given up her piece. What the cops didn't know wouldn't hurt them, but ditching her weapon could get her killed.

"So, you're short on cash," Frankie said with a nod, his lips slightly pursed, hinting that maybe he knew more than she'd hoped.

"Who isn't?"

"Chasing deadbeats doesn't appeal anymore?"

Damn. Frankie might have been away for a while, but he obviously still had contacts. Still, she wiggled her newly polished nails, the index fingers tipped with tiny fake diamonds, and hoped to play down his knowledge of her enforcement activities. "Too hard on the manicure."

He chuckled. "Were you good?"

She sipped her *Cuba Libre,* enjoying the burst of the sweet carbonation against the smooth tang of the rum. "I'm good at lots of things."

"I remember."

Man, Frankie had some incredible eyes. Technically, they were hazel, but the flecks of green glittered as deep and vivid as fine oriental jade. Offset by his swarthy skin, his irises simmered with hot intentions—every one of which Marisela could imagine in great detail.

"Wanna dance?" she asked, flicking a glance at the dance floor. At Club Electric, the music pulsed as hard and bright as the neon lights. The minute Marisela allowed herself to acknowledge the sounds, the rhythm seeped into her veins. Her shoulders and hips rocked and her feet itched to hit the dance floor and work off some of the fiery vibe slashing between her and Frankie.

"No," he answered.

She didn't hide her disappointment, pushing her lips into a thick pout. "Why not?"

"Not in the mood."

She leaned forward, her lips inches from his ear as the crowd around them whooped and sang a chorus of "Yo Viviré," a cover of Gloria Gaynor's "I Will Survive," by Celia Cruz. "I can always put you in the mood, Frankie." She shimmied her shoulders ever so slightly. "Like no other woman ever could."

"We were young, Marisela. Didn't take much to put either of us in the mood."

She laughed, punched him in the shoulder then downed a few more gulps of her drink. A flush of warm heat surrounded her skin and she didn't know if the reaction stemmed from their proximity to the writhing masses of dancers or from being so close, and yet so far, from her first love.

Back in high school, she and Frankie had melted more than one dance floor—not to mention the damage they'd done to various backseats. He'd loved her wild ways, her innate curiosity. She'd wanted to explore the world, find her place outside the tight community she loved, but still resented. To date, she hadn't gone anywhere too exotic, but her ambitions hadn't died, even if they were harder to pursue with bills hitting the mailbox like baseball-size hail.

Even after he'd chosen his gang over her, he'd kept her secrets. He'd never popped off to his *hombres* about her sexual appetites. The worst thing he'd ever done was break her teenage heart.

Now she was about to screw him in the worst possible way. Or maybe, the best way? Didn't matter. Bottom line—she was going to royally piss him off, although for a good cause.

A very noble cause. The noblest. Marisela may have skirted the law from time to time—well, she'd actually flashed and mooned the law on one or two occasions—but give her a benevolent purpose and she could be downright patriotic. And ruthless. Not that she needed a good reason to spend a little quality time with sexy, dangerous, Frankie Vega. But lucky for her, she had a good reason all the same. He was about to jump bail and she was going to stop him.

She finished her drink, slipped her fingers into her jacket pocket, threw a ten onto the bar, and nodded toward the door.

"If you don't want to dance, let's go."

She twisted off the bar stool, but Frankie moved only to tilt his head toward hers so she'd hear him over the music and the crowd.

"How do you know I'm not waiting for someone?"

Surrendering to her instincts, Marisela drew one of her long fingernails over Frankie's angular jawline. "I don't. But you just got a better offer."

Knowing she had to seal the deal, she dropped her touch slowly down his neck, until the ruby red enamel on her nail sparkled beside the gold chain he'd worn since his confirmation. Unlike the other Cuban-American males in this part of the world, Frankie didn't dangle a crucifix or saint's medallion from the necklace. No sense in contradicting his daily activities. He wore the gold serpentine necklace flush to his dark skin, even if the links probably pinched the hell out of his chest hair every once in a while.

Marisela grabbed his open collar and with surprise on her side, yanked him to his feet. Frankie wasn't the tallest man in the world—just shy of six feet—but to her tall-for-her-genes five foot seven, he towered over her just enough so she could glance through the veil of her eyelashes when she spoke.

"Do you understand what I'm offering?"

Before he could answer, she slipped her free hand between them and cupped her palm over the bulge in his jeans. She smiled, a thrill streaking through her like lightning.

He was hard. As a rock. Thinking he'd want her again was one thing. *Knowing* stole her breath.

Like the charmer he was, Frankie seized her winded moment and kissed her. Not hot and impatient like he used to. Oh, no. The son of a bitch took his time, pressing his lips against hers like a warm iron on a silk blouse, careful not to scorch her by pressing too hard. His hands inched from her hips to her ribs, his fingers tantalizing the bared skin of her midriff with hungry, yet contained caresses.

Harvesting all her self-control, Marisela forced a step back, breaking the connection so quickly, Frankie's lips were still puckered.

He had the audacity to grin as if he'd been the one to push her away.

"Blast from the past too much for you, *vidita?*"

Marisela slipped her hands into the pocket of her jacket. Feeling the handcuffs she'd hidden there, she remembered the true purpose of this seduction.

She scooted away from her stool, away from him—knowing he had every motivation to follow. "Too much for me?" she asked, sassy and doubtful at the same time. "I'm just getting started."

Two

DAMN IF MARISELA'S ASS didn't look even better aged ten years. He pushed through the crowd to keep up with her, knowing that if he'd had any sense, he'd realize that meeting up with her tonight was no accident. Maybe Blake moved in without Frankie's answer? Not plausible. Ian Blake was desperate, but he wouldn't act haphazardly.

Still, before Frankie left town tomorrow, he wanted to make sure Blake didn't pursue Marisela for his operation. Why Frankie cared, he didn't know. The *chica* could take care of herself. But Frankie had been the one to bring her name to the table and since he was ditching the deal, he'd decided to make sure she wasn't sucked in to a dangerous, trecherous world without him there to watch her back.

And yet, he couldn't ignore the fact that she'd come to the

club armed. Maybe Blake had made contact. Maybe he'd sent Marisela to lure him back to the fold. Or was she simply being Marisela, ready to protect herself from the lowlifes he'd heard weren't too happy with her job hauling in criminals for cash? She'd tried hard to conceal her piece under that sexy black jacket, but Frankie'd become quite good at spotting guns. *¡Coño!* He didn't need this distraction!

His arrest last week had been the final straw. Yeah, he'd left Miami seriously entertaining Ian Blake's job offer, but being booked for possession five minutes after he cruised into town had changed his mind. He'd had enough of the life. Serving six years in prison for armed robbery, most of the time spent doubling as a DEA mole, had cut out the last of his cancerous obsession with high stakes thrills. Now, he just wanted to lie low until his hearing tomorrow morning, take care of business, and then get the hell out of town before he burned his *cojones* on the big trouble brewing so close to home.

Trouble that seemed to follow him wherever he went. Trouble Marisela didn't ask for. And probably didn't deserve.

Maybe he was just being paranoid. Maybe his running into his ex had been a simple stroke of good luck. And maybe Marisela's flirting was just because she was hot to trot, and for once in his hard-luck life, he was in the right place at the right time. He might as well take advantage while he had the chance. Once he left Tampa this time, he was gone for good.

Marisela waited for him at the exit, leaning suggestively against the door, one foot flat against the surface, her knee drawn up, sexy and bold. She always did have a way of broadcasting exactly what was on her mind at any given moment.

Lying and manipulating took too much time and effort. With Marisela, what he saw was what he got.

And man, he liked what he saw tonight.

He slapped his hand on the door above her shoulder, then eased forward, inhaling her spicy scent as his nose neared her neck. "You want to start right here or take it outside?" he whispered, brushing his lips across her fragrant skin.

She chuckled softly, but enough so that her breasts bounced gently against his chest. "Either way, we'll have an audience."

He ran his tongue against the cool gold of her hoop earring. "Does that turn you on?"

"Who says I'm turned on?"

In a flash, she'd ducked away from him and pushed into the thick, outdoor air. The bouncer pretended to ignore the overheard exchange, but as Frankie strutted past the oversized cue ball of a man, he caught the glimmer of lust in the man's eyes. That same hungry shine reflected in the stares of the half-dozen or so punks hanging out with their backs to the wall, swinging their Colt 45 malt liquors. He smirked, confident that Marisela not only wanted him, but that for the first time in a long while, every guy in this joint wanted nothing more than to be in his *zapatos*.

As Marisela predicted, the parking lot outside Club Electric was jammed with nearly as many hot bodies as inside. Underaged girls sat on the hoods of cars driven by boys they had no business messing with, boys with knives in their back pockets and oversize beer cans clutched in angry hands.

It wasn't so long ago that he'd been one of those jerks. In a lot of ways, he still was. But now he had the chance to jump back to a simpler time in his life—when the only thing that mattered was hot sex and cool living.

He caught up with Marisela as she approached the one-of-a-kind rust bucket his mother called her second car. Most of the time, she tooled around in the practical four-door Chevy Malibu she'd bought herself after hitting good numbers on the lottery. But to accommodate any one of her six children who often returned to the nest with one sob story or another, she kept the beat-up Impala. Frankie hadn't thought much about the car parked perennially in his mother's garage until he'd found himself in quick need of wheels to make a fast escape, his own ride impounded.

"Why does your *mami* keep this old thing?" Marisela asked, running a tentative finger over the oxidized paint of the dented outer shell.

He leaned one hip on the door, knowing he looked just as cool now as he used to back when Marisela thought he'd owned the world because he had wheels at his disposal. *"Yo no sé.* I think she's sentimental. I may have been conceived in this car," he said, half-joking. The Impala hadn't been around quite that long, though he wouldn't doubt if some of his brothers hadn't spawned a few of his nieces and nephews in that spacious backseat.

Marisela rolled her eyes, and then leaned in through the open window to inspect the interior more closely, giving him a view of her backside that made his cock tight.

No way was that move unintentional.

"What the hell are you doing, Marisela?"

She wriggled back out. He had to adjust the seam of his jeans. He didn't try to be sly about it, either. Why should he? She certainly wasn't.

"Just seeing if the old juices still flow between us," she explained.

"I could be an old man sitting in my wheelchair on the front porch and you'd get my juices flowing, *vidita.*"

Marisela stalked toward him slowly, allowing him time to appreciate every soft bounce of her unbound breasts, every swing of her sexy hips.

"Why don't you let me taste some of those juices, Frankie? I'm thirsty. Aren't you?" When she stood toe-to-toe with him, her nipples brushed against his chest. His entire body tensed, hard and electric—as if he was on the job, ready to jump, react, strike, flee.

He swiped his tongue around his lips, then yanked Marisela close and pressed his mouth over hers. In an instant, she soothed the parched thirst crackling through his body. Just as fast, they were in his car, barreling out of the parking lot and over the half-bricked city streets of the old neighborhood. She climbed onto his lap, laughing her deep, throaty laugh, kissing his ears, sucking his neck, untucking his shirt, popping buttons so she could dip her fingers into his waistband.

Several skidding turns and rolling stops later, Frankie killed the engine, allowing the momentum of the car to propel them up the driveway beside his mother's house. When he'd first hit town, he'd planned to take up residence in the tiny apartment above the detached garage, but his arrest changed all that. Instead, he'd crashed in some flea-bit motels on the port side of town, avoiding Ian Blake and his far-reaching grip. Instinct alone steered him here, to the same apartment where he'd lost his virginity to Marisela—and she to him—all those years ago.

He fished the key out of the flowerpot beside the door and by the time he turned to Marisela, she'd kicked off her boots and jeans, right there in the open air.

Lust surged and he grabbed her, not thinking about anything but feeling her naked against him. They fell into the apartment, landing half on the bed, half on the floor. Before Frankie could remove his own shoes and pants, Marisela lost her jacket and her T-shirt. For an instant, he spied the black holster she'd worn around her shoulder and waist, but the minute she crawled onto his bed, wearing nothing but pale pink panties, he willingly forgot about her gun. She hooked her hands under the lower rod of the cast-iron headboard, tested the strength of the metal with one wanton tug, then waited, her breasts round and tight-tipped, her areolas dark, her mouth slightly parted and still a blurry red from his kiss.

Frankie stopped, just for a fraction of a second, to drink in her illicit beauty. He tore off his own shirt, but swallowed a grin when her deep brown eyes sparkled with appreciation. Not much for a man to do in prison but work out, and his last job on the docks had enhanced his physique. He wasn't some scrawny schoolboy anymore—if he'd ever been.

"Jesus, Frankie. You look good," she said, slicking her tongue over her lips. He loved her mouth. He'd always loved her mouth. How it felt pressed against his skin. How she could use all that hot, wet flesh to drive him insane.

"*Vidita,* I could come right here, just looking at you."

She glanced down at her own prone and posed body, then shifted into the moonlight streaming in through the window.

"That would be a big waste, wouldn't it?"

The glow emphasized the gloss of sweat forming over her

skin. The air inside the apartment was hot, stuffy. He hadn't noticed. He glanced at the dormant air conditioner unit shoved between the window and the cracked wooden frame.

In a rush, he marched to the window, pressed buttons, turned knobs, and cursed until the ancient unit kicked to life, blasting tepid air against his naked chest. He adjusted the thermostat, breathing easier when the temperature dropped just enough to let him know the junker still worked. But the last thing he wanted to be was cool. He spun around, just in time to catch Marisela fiddling with the pillows, propping them purposefully against the slender wrought-iron bars of the old headboard.

"Comfortable?"

She snuggled into the cushions, patting and fluffing as she spoke. "Not as comfortable as I could be." When she had the bed arranged as she wanted, she stretched her arms toward him. "Come here," she said, her voice husky.

Frankie crawled across the mattress, ignoring the pop of the tight springs beneath his hand, his knee, his foot. He stopped and placed one hot, delicious kiss on her thigh. Sweet cocoa butter teased his nostrils, taunting him with hints of the musky scent he'd discover when he kissed her a little higher.

But just as he moved into position to taste her through her panties, Marisela rolled aside, quick and agile. He opened his mouth to protest, but she silenced him by pressing her now free lingerie against his face. He growled, inhaled like a junkie, and while he wondered how she'd taken off her underwear so quickly, she pinned him, her bare breasts inches from his face.

18   Julie Leto

"Screwing around with you again can't be a good idea," she said.

He gripped her around the waist, spreading his fingers so he could feel her skin so hot beneath his. He inched his thumbs upward, teasing her sweet, round breasts. Her chin dropped and her tiny tortured moans fired his lust.

"Want to leave?" he asked. He could feel her moist warmth against his thigh, could see the sharp tightness of her nipples. Her lids had dropped, but not entirely. He watched as her pupils dilated with pleasure.

She wanted him just as much as he wanted her—just like before when they were too young and too stupid to know better. Only now they were old enough to know that you take what you want when you want it—or you might lose your shot forever.

She splayed her hands on his chest, tugging gently at his chest hair. "Leave? Not right this minute, no."

She inched upward, pressing her sex against his body so that her sweet, wet lips taunted his hard cock. Frankie filled his lungs with air, hoping to keep himself still enough to do this right.

He countered her attack by stretching to capture her breasts with his mouth. He flicked his tongue over her pebble-hard nipples, loving the hot, salty taste of her skin. She tilted her neck back and sighed, the sound deep and arousing. Could he make her come right here? Right now? With only his tongue and lips? Did he want to send her spiraling so soon?

She rocked and writhed atop him, sealing their bond with slick need. *Dios,* he ached to push inside her, feel the hot heat of her flesh encasing his sex, milking him, squeezing him, tugging him toward the ecstasy he hadn't experienced in way too long. Was she still tight or would her woman's body coax him deeper, right to the sweet target that would make her scream his name? He bit and suckled until her tiny, pleasured cry squeezed him from the inside out.

He grabbed her hips, loving the blistering slide of her body over his. With her hands on the iron headboard, she pulled herself completely up, repositioning her knees on either side of his face. He grinned up at her.

"*Mi vida,* you are so hot. I have to taste you." He eyed her hungrily, then wasted no more time before slipping his tongue inside her.

She nearly bucked off the bed, so he braced her with one hand on her bottom and the other on her breast. He kneaded and plucked and licked until she came, her pulse surging against his tongue.

Almost instantly, she pushed away, panting, and if he wasn't mistaken, softly cursing.

"Marisela?"

She shook her head, her hair spilling across her eyes in damp streaks. When she spoke, her words shot out on a series of panted breaths. "Frankie, you always could make me lose my mind."

He swallowed, loving the flavor of her in his mouth. God, how he'd missed that taste. He leaned forward and took her hand in his, then pulled her back on top of him. "The power is mutual."

He stretched to the opposite side, reaching over the edge of the bed. He couldn't wait one more minute. Unable to reach the pants he'd tossed on the floor, he spat out a venomous, "damn."

The curse cleared the cloudiness from her eyes. "What?"

"I can't reach the condom."

She grinned, a little too forced for his liking, but Frankie wasn't going to let her amusement slow them down. She shifted so he could move, then wrapped her hands around his left wrist.

"I can't let you go too far away, Frankie."

He smiled, then performed the needed gymnastics to reach the jeans without leaving the bed. He didn't realize what she'd done to his wrist until he heard the all-too familiar metal click and felt cold steel press against his skin.

He dropped the rubber.

"What the fuck?"

Marisela vaulted off him, her panties reclaimed. She slipped them on, then reached for her T-shirt and gun while he tugged and cursed, a noisy clatter renting the air.

He watched her intently, somewhat relieved when she strapped the holster on, but made no move to remove her piece.

Forcing himself to calm down, he decided to revert to charm. "Okay, great joke, *vidita*. I can do kinky if that's what you want."

She tugged her jeans over her hips. "Frankie, baby, I want to try kinky with you more than you know." She grabbed her jacket from the floor and punched her arms into the sleeves. "But not tonight."

He laughed, hoping the slightly crazy sound covered the desperate metal clanks of the handcuffs. "Why not? We got all night. I'm not going anywhere."

"No, Frankie. You're definitely not going anywhere. Not until tomorrow morning."

"I have court," he said, trying to figure out what the hell was going on. "Ten o'clock. Courtroom B. What's this about, Marisela? You don't work for Alberto no more. And I haven't jumped bail."

She shook her head, rubbing her hand over her mouth as if she needed to ease the vibrations of their kisses. No matter how this played out, Frankie knew she hadn't faked her desire. No way, no how.

"This one was personal," she said.

She whipped out her tiny cell phone, punched in a few numbers, then spoke in Spanish to the person on the other end of the line.

Yes, I found him. No, you won't lose your house. Yes, he's home. In the apartment. No, I need a few minutes.

"A few minutes for what?" he demanded.

She flipped the phone shut and shoved it in her back pocket. She took a single step toward him, still well out of reach, and her face changed. While her cheeks and lips were still red and swollen, her eyes cooled. No more volcanic fire, spouting from deep within. Now, she was all business.

"I bought you some time, okay?"

"Time? For what?"

She shook her head and turned to the door, her fingers dancing over the knob as if she was reluctant to leave. "Time to power down."

¡Coño! Enough was enough. Frankie raged against the handcuffs; the old, rusty headboard couldn't hold him for long.

The minute his traitorous ex finally tore open the door, he shouted her name. "I'm going to get you for this."

She had the decency to turn and face him, though he had to stretch to meet her icy gaze. For an instant, he thought he spied regret in her eyes, but before he could speak and milk her remorse into release, she smirked, gave him a subtle salute in true *las Reinas* style, then disappeared into the night.

Three

OUT OF HABIT MORE than necessity, Marisela killed the engine and doused the lights on her fourth-hand Toyota Corolla she'd left in the parking lot of Club Electric, allowing the car to silently roll to a stop in front of her parents' house. For the entire walk back to the club and the drive home, she'd shoved down the residual lust coursing through her and froze out her regrets.

But staring at the darkened windows of the small but neat home, knowing her mother would likely meet her in the hallway, sleepy-eyed and curious about the turn of the night's events, Marisela's body vibrated. She shifted in her seat, uncomfortable, and despite her orgasm, unfulfilled. Frankie hadn't forgotten how to touch her, how to prime her, how to lure her to the ledge, even when her good sense shouted for her to run in the other direction. They could have made love all night. She could have turned him over to his parents at dawn. She could have owned a memory of her and Frankie as adults, instead of idealized re-membrances of a lovestruck girl and her macho *novio*.

Could have—but now, never would. She figured she'd better face the undeniable truth.

She leaned her elbows on the steering wheel and cradled her head in her hands. What the hell had she been thinking, going after Frankie like that in the first place? She could have just lured him outside the club, cuffed him inside the car, and deliv-ered him to his mother safe, sound and unaroused. But no, she had to play with fire. Tempt fate. Entice her own supercharged libido with the man she'd said no to only once—right before he chose his homeboys over her and walked away.

Okay, enough of that. She removed the key from the igni-tion, jolted out of the car, closed the door quietly and jogged to the trunk. Adhering to the house rule against bringing a firearm into the house, she traded her 9mm for her purse, detached the clip and engaged the lock, then stuffed the gun into a secret compartment she'd created beneath a rip in the upholstery. She secured the car with a press of a button. The car might be old, but back when Marisela had had a steady job, she'd splurged on LoJack. She managed to keep up the monthly payments by re-locating to the spare room in her parents' house for the second time since she'd turned eighteen. The first time she came back, it was after leaving the house run by the gang her parents hated. And this time, when she'd given Alberto no choice but to fire her when she lost her license to carry—and therefore, lost her great two bedroom, three roommate apartment only a bridge away from the beach.

She couldn't believe how she'd screwed up what could have been a bright future, but her pink slip had caused her parents to dedicate a whole litany of *novenas* thanking God for his intervention. They'd hated her working with criminals, even if they didn't know the full extent of her job. Just being near the jail was too dangerous, too violent.

Too damned exciting.

God, she missed it. The adrenaline. The strategy. The money.

With that thought to propel her, Marisela took off her shoes and tiptoed up the driveway. The house was dark and quiet, her father's car parked silent and cold beneath the carport. She had no desire to disturb the peace. If she was lucky, she could sneak to her room and take advantage of the "purple-headed passion" vibrator Lia had given her for her birthday. That ought to shake the last of the pent-up tension out of her body.

As if.

Marisela entered through the door from the driveway, sneaking into the kitchen with practiced stealth. She didn't need either of the two sources of light—the timer over the oven and the moonlight from the window—to make her way inside. She could traverse this house blindfolded. Or at least, blind drunk. She'd pulled that off more than once.

Wiping her feet on the kitchen rug, Marisela attempted to remove all the moisture from her skin. The house was carpeted, but like any good Latina woman, her mother had hard plastic runners protecting the light-colored shag from dirt. Moist feet tended to make a sucking noise even Marisela didn't have the grace to mask.

The same sucking noise she heard just before she rounded the corner.

A gun barrel glinted, flashed beside Marisela's cheek. With a burst of fear, Marisela grabbed the gun and yanked forward, slamming the man attached to the weapon into the plaster arch of the doorway. When the attacker sprung back with a grunt, she kicked out his knee, knocking him to the floor. She stomped his wrist, heel first and hard, dislodging the gun from his grasp. With a swipe of her foot, the weapon skidded beneath the couch. Marisela jumped back, her fists in front of her, her weight balanced, her ears trained for any sign that someone else was in the house.

She heard nothing. No one. Not even her parents. Bottomless dread threatened to drown her as she reached for the phone. But a hand shot out of the darkness, snaring her wrist. Pain sliced up her arm as a finger squeezed between her muscle and bone. The handset clattered to the floor, the plastic casing shattered, as her captor stepped out of the shadows.

"No, no, Marisela. No cops, *chiquita*. And now, no witness."

Light flashed. A deafening pop rent the air, followed instantly by an anguished scream from the guy on the floor. Then silence.

The man who'd captured her arm spun her around, and jabbed the barrel of his gun into her stomach. The warm steel was as deadly and unpredictable as the man who held her captive. The man who knew her name.

She forced stillness into every muscle of her body.

"Ooh, honey," the man purred. He rubbed the barrel up her body, sliding the gun against the undersides of her breasts, then pressed his face into her neck and inhaled through his mask, which Marisela saw was nothing more than panty hose. "You smell like you've just been fucked."

He must have been confident that she wouldn't move with the gun still squashed against her chest, because he released her wrist and used that hand to grab between her legs.

"Are you still wet with his come, *puta,* or did you clean yourself up before coming home to your *mamacita?*"

Ignoring him, she focused on what she needed. Information. A break. A chance to turn the tide. Who was he? He knew her name. He knew her. His voice sounded only half-familiar, muted by the nylon stretched across his lips. Whoever he was, he'd just killed his partner, or at least, silenced him. Had he done the same to her parents? Were they dead in their chintz and floral bedroom, their blood spilled on her mother's new mauve carpet simply because they'd invited their risk-taking, violent daughter back under their roof?

"Who are you?"

He abandoned his grinding grip on her crotch to grab her backside, squeezing her hard, but not enough to hurt. If he thought manhandling her would humiliate her into submission. . . . Marisela pushed the acerbic thought aside. She forced herself to whimper and sent a shimmy through her body so that she shook in his grasp. *Let him think I'm afraid. Let him think I'm terrified enough to do whatever he wants.*

"Someone who's wanted to fuck your ass for a long time."

He pushed her back, slamming her against the kitchen table while he worked the buckle of his jeans. The edge of the table had jammed into the sensitive small of her back and she grunted, using the pain as an excuse to turn, half-crouched, flinging her hair over her eyes so he couldn't see her face. He still had the gun aimed at her, but his grip had loosened. He wasn't going to shoot her. Yet. He was going to rape her first.

Or die trying.

He was sloppy, overconfident. Just like a man.

Through the curtain of her hair, she sighted him. Still bent low and whimpering for effect, she stamped his instep and butted her head hard against his stomach. She used his surprise and her full weight to smash him into the counter. She rose fast, smacking the back of her skull against his chin.

Light exploded behind her eyes, but she latched onto his gun hand, twisting his wrist upward until she heard the snap of bone.

His shriek echoed in her ear, adding another layer of pain to her aching body. She scrambled, retrieved his lost weapon and retreated, her back to the refrigerator, the gun aimed at her attacker. She took an instant to register the model of the gun. Cheap piece of shit. Six rounds. One spent on his partner. Two on her parents? *God, no.* But either way, she had at least three bullets left to put him down if he made one more move. If it had been fully loaded to begin with.

Clutching his broken wrist to his stomach, the intruder had dropped to his knees. "You fucking cunt!"

She bit back the urge to pump bullet number four into his thigh. Since she didn't know who else was in the house, every round had to count.

"Who the hell are you?"

"Fuck you, bitch," he grunted.

She needed to remove his mask. She needed to get the hell out of the house. But she couldn't leave until she knew her parents were safe. Maybe they were tied up, guarded by a third man, alive until the intruders had what they wanted. Only this attack wasn't a robbery. She could see the light from the DVD player blinking in the living room. The television hadn't been touched and though her father owned a business, he kept no cash in the house.

So many possibilities, she couldn't discount any. But until she knew her family was safe, she wouldn't abandon them.

She pulled back the hammer on the gun, unnecessary on the semiautomatic weapon. Still, the sound was hugely influential in getting jerks to talk.

"Take off your mask, or I'll do it for you. *After* I shoot you."

Her fingers throbbed as she clutched the gun and her heart slammed against her chest. She broadened her stance, her vision swimming with colors and shapes that, thanks to the smack on her skull, didn't really exist. Maybe she should just shoot him and take her chances that no one else would show.

He pulled off the mask and looked her straight in the eyes, his gold teeth gleaming between lips permanently split thanks to a knife slash he'd earned in prison. Nestor Rocha. A three-strike junkie she'd once picked up for jumping bail, a creep who pushed his wares on the whores that walked Nebraska Avenue, when he wasn't beating them to a bloody pulp.

"Recognize me, *caliente polla?*" he said, the shakiness of his voice nearly covered by his bravado.

Prick-tease? He didn't know the half of it.

"Yeah, from my nightmares, Rocha."

She buoyed her gun hand. If she had to make this shot, she wouldn't miss. Rocha was a killer and she had no doubt he'd like to prove his evil right here, right now.

"What do you want?"

"I told you. I want to feel my *cojones* slapping against your *culo,* bitch."

One-track mind. What a *pendejo*.

"Sorry to disappoint you, Rocha. Who's your dead pal?"

He shook his head and Marisela watched his uninjured arm drop limply to his side. For a weapon. Fuck.

She shifted right and pulled the trigger. The sound of her bullet hitting his chest popped at the same moment he fired his hidden gun into the refrigerator. When his body fell, limp on the linoleum, the gun he had strapped to his ankle dropped from his hand and spun across the floor.

She grabbed the gun and tucked it in her pocket. She leaped over him, then over his partner in the hall, a demented game of hopscotch. She ran down the hall and kicked open her parents' bedroom door.

Empty. The bed was still made. She glanced at the clock. It was nearly three in the morning, where in the hell were her parents? Even for weddings and *quinces,* they didn't stay up beyond midnight.

Suddenly sensing a presence behind her, Marisela dived across the bed, tucked into a roll that knocked the lamp off the end table, but landed her out of the line of fire. She hated to shoot blind. What if her parents had come home? What if neighbors had heard the gunshots and had come to investigate?

"Who's there?"

"Don't fire, Ms. Morales. We're not here to hurt you."

"Could've fooled me."

She glanced to her side. The window was far to her right. No way could anyone sneak up behind her again. She didn't dare look over the mattress, so she quietly flattened herself to the floor, attempting to peek beneath the bed. True to her mother's form, not even a dust bunny hampered her view. She could see two polished shoes in the doorway. One foot lifted to step forward.

"Unless you want your toes blown off, you'll back up. Slowly," she said.

In the distance, sirens sounded. Not unusual for this part of town, but not typical, either. Her neighborhood had no code of silence for criminal activity. They might not have loads of money, but the residents looked out for their own.

"Hear that? You'd best beat it," she warned. "I'd hate to have to explain three dead bodies in my house."

"I'm sure you would. I'm also sure you don't want to try and explain five."

Marisela had no head for math, but this guy sounded different. Calm. Educated. Maybe even a hint of an accent lilting the clear threat against her parents.

She came up from behind the bed, her gun pointed at his chest. He held out his hands, showing that any weapon he had was at least safely tucked away. For now.

"Who are you?"

"My name is Max."

She stood, certain that though this man looked perfectly harmless, he was likely nothing of the sort.

"Great to meet you, Max," she said, forcing the fear out of her voice. "Where are my parents?"

"Safe. For the moment."

Marisela swallowed, her vision swimming again. God, if he hurt them . . . She blinked the fog away.

"Prove it," she demanded.

He turned his palm, produced a card and tossed it on the bed. Her father's driver's license.

"That doesn't prove anything. You could have lifted his wallet."

"True. It also doesn't prove that if I do have him that he, and your mother, are alive and well. You have no choice but to believe me and take a chance. One that could save their lives."

"I could wait for the cops, let them sort out your story after they book you . . . for trespassing? Breaking and entering? Maybe a little attempted murder?"

He nodded, a tentative but practiced and eerily sharp smile on his lips. "I hate to admit I'm expendable, Ms. Morales, but the truth remains. Are your parents? I don't believe my associates can guarantee their safety if I'm arrested."

She swallowed hard. She could take care of herself. But her parents wouldn't stand a chance against professionals. Especially sloppy ones.

"What do you want?"

"There's someone who wants to make your acquaintance."

Inhaling loudly, Marisela filled her lungs, trying to tamp down the anger shooting through her veins. "Couldn't this someone have just issued an invitation? Something engraved, maybe? Little R.S.V.P. action?"

Max, nondescript in a plain, but well-fitting suit, chuckled at her sarcasm. Good. He didn't need to know she was scared spitless. This man wasn't some ordinary thug. His confidence at her inevitable compliance was tangible, and yet, he wasn't cocky. He knew what she didn't know—plus everything she did, which wasn't much.

In the darkness, she couldn't judge his hair or eye color. He bounced on the balls of his feet, which combined with her blurred eyesight, made it hard to judge his height. If she had to describe him to the cops, she wouldn't do a very good job. Probably his intention. A man like him could easily get away with murder.

"Tonight's operation wasn't supposed to include homicide."

"You should have told that to Nestor," Marisela snapped.

"We did not anticipate his killing one of our agents."

"Nestor didn't work for you?"

"His assignment was temporary. Please, Ms. Morales, my employer simply wants to speak with you," Max insisted. "He'll explain with much more detail than I am at liberty to divulge."

"And why should I believe you?"

The sirens grew louder, then seemed to fade.

"My people have diverted the police for a few moments, long enough for us to clean up and get out. If you want your parents to remain unharmed, you'll come with me."

He dropped one hand, and curled his fingers so the other beckoned her with cool politeness.

She took a step, but he chastised her with a clucking tongue. "Leave the gun. Someone will see to its disposal."

Marisela had no choice, not if he really had her parents—and she could think of no other reason why they wouldn't be tucked into their beds at three o'clock in the morning, snoring softly, oblivious to the violence that had crept into their home. She dropped the revolver on the bed and walked around slowly, slightly comforted by the feel of Rocha's tiny .22 in her pocket. Max stepped back as she approached, giving her plenty of room to walk. So far, so good. When she turned into the hallway, she noticed the man Rocha had shot was gone.

"Where?"

Max gestured toward the door. "Everything will be explained soon. Please, Ms. Morales. We haven't much time if we wish to avoid police questioning. Further delay could put your parents at risk."

Marisela nodded. A man who was confident enough to escort her away without the benefit of a gun—at least, one that she could see—probably had the experience and skill to take her where he wanted her to go with or without her cooperation.

He diverted her through the living room instead of the kitchen, so she couldn't see if Rocha had been "cleaned up" as efficiently as the guy in the hall. Outside, the street was quiet, though several neighbors peeked through drawn curtains. Marisela took a deep breath, then exhaled, hoping her parents truly were safe, praying her mother and father would be around tomorrow morning to field the barrage of nosy questions the neighbors would undoubtedly throw their way.

The minute her foot touched the edge of the driveway, an ordinary, dark-colored sedan eased to a stop in front of the house, just behind her Corolla. The back door flew open and Max hurried her inside. She barely had time to settle into the seat before the car lurched forward, quietly speeding down the street without benefit of headlights.

She stared down at herself, suddenly aware of every ache. Her arm throbbed from where Rocha had grabbed her. Her neck and skull still reverberated with pain. Her temples pounded and despite several deliberate blinks, her vision wouldn't quite clear. Still, so far as fights went, this one was rather tame. But where fists rattled her body, gunplay rattled her soul. And Marisela found her shaking hard to control.

"You put up quite a fight," Max noted, his eyes scanning the road ahead and behind them, likely checking if the police had followed.

Marisela wasn't sure if she hoped they did or not. She had, after all, shot and likely killed Nestor Rocha. Not that he was any great loss to the human race, but murder was murder.

"It was either him or me."

"An unfortunate turn of events."

"Really?" she asked, raising her voice a decibel louder than she intended. Her sarcasm must have hit the mark because he closed his eyes a few seconds longer than a typical blink.

"Errors were made. I offer my sincerest apologies."

She crossed her arms, seeing no need to hide her anger. "You can shove your apologies, Max. And for the record, if one hair on my parents' heads is out of place, I'll be shoving something a lot more painful than an apology up your ass."

He returned his gaze to the road. "I don't doubt that, Ms. Morales."

Good, because neither did she.

Four

IAN BLAKE RAISED a finger to his ear, adjusting the tiny device so he didn't miss a word.

" . . . if one hair on my parents' heads is out of place, I'll be shoving something a lot more painful than an apology up your ass."

Ian winced. He could only imagine what Marisela Morales might choose as her weapon of choice for such a reprisal. Likely something steel—and with double barrels.

One of these days, Ian was going to learn to stop underestimating women in terms of their potential deadliness. Marisela Morales's reputation had been brought to his attention by a credible source and she'd proved her abilities tonight, even if his test had never been meant to go so far. He'd had no idea the orchestrated scenario at her home would go from bad to fatal in the blink of an eye, but he couldn't change the past or alter his plan now. Too much money had been exchanged and too many people were in place.

All except for his lead operatives. But by tomorrow, he'd have cleared that hurdle as well.

"Are they on the way?"

Ian glanced at his slim, professionally blonde client, Elise Barton-Ryce, who tugged at her stylish cashmere gloves. In Boston, her fashion choice would have barely registered, a simple sign of her ultra-traditional upbringing and perhaps, the weather. But here in the Florida heat, he knew she wore gloves for one reason and one reason only. If something went awry, she didn't want so much as a fingerprint to tie her to Titan International.

Fine with him. Less than ninety-six hours after accepting the retainer from Barton-Ryce's attorney, Ian suspected he'd made a mistake in taking the assignment rather than extending a referral to another firm. Titan was one of the top investigation organizations in the country, but their business had been limited to the upper Northeast and Europe. He had operatives in place in Prague, London, Paris, Munich, Berlin, and Geneva, with satellite offices in New York, Philadelphia, Washington D.C., and Toronto.

He didn't know a damned thing about Puerto Rico or Miami, much less a small burg like Tampa. And though a few of his agents could speak Spanish, none quite looked the part enough to blend into the Hispanic culture in San Juan or perhaps, Havana. He needed new blood. But he hadn't meant to spill that blood so soon.

Ian pressed a tiny button on his lapel. "ETA?"

Max answered instantly. "Ten."

"The agents will arrive shortly. Shall I pour you a brandy?"

With a sniff, Mrs. Barton-Ryce gracefully unfurled her crossed ankles and strolled to the bar. She lifted the crystal stopper of one decanter, then another, then another, apparently disappointed with the variety of his offerings.

He remained still, an indulgent grin pasted on his face. Dealing with women such as her, with her impossible-to-please standards and air of superiority, had become old hat. She reminded him of his grandmother, his aunts, and each and every one of his female cousins, from first to fourth-removed. Had his mother lived long enough, he had no doubt her old Boston money would have caused her to show the same privileged attitudes. Even Eris, his former . . . what? lover? addiction? poison? . . . had been a snob of palatial proportion. Only his sister had managed to buck the social system of the British and American upper crust. Yet, if Brynn knew about this job and how things had so quickly turned from bad to worse before the operation had even begun, she'd be jetting back from Prague with a silver platter in her carry-on, primed to hold his severed head.

He could still turn this operation around, but as he watched Mrs. Barton-Ryce huff and abandon her quest for a suitable libation, he knew he had to change at least a part of his initial plan.

"Perhaps you should wait at your hotel. As I explained, things did not go as anticipated tonight. Ms. Morales may not be in the proper mood to appreciate the dire circumstances of your situation."

Elise drew a hand to her chest, surprise artfully etched on her perfectly smooth and botox-enhanced face. "How could she not? We're talking about the life of a child, here, Mr. Blake. Your organization came very highly recommended, but you are by no means the only firm in town."

Ian nodded. "I explained to you, madam, that Titan might not be your best choice for this operation. There are groups, some working entirely gratis, that specialize in this type of retrieval. If you'd like to go elsewhere . . ."

"No," she said, firmly, and without any hint of the desperation Ian had witnessed at their first meeting. He still wasn't entirely sure why Elise had come to him for this job, but he couldn't deny that her generous transfer of funds would stave off Brynn's interference in the business for at least another month. He needed time to fix things, make things right.

"You remain confident in Titan?" he asked one last time.

"For now," she answered.

He shook his head and stood. "No, Mrs. Barton-Ryce, that isn't enough. Once I engage my operatives, there will be no turning back. I've lost one life tonight. I won't sacrifice others unless it is necessary to obtain the objective."

She blinked several times and Ian wasn't sure if she was having trouble understanding his meaning or if she was unaccustomed to having anyone contradict her so forcefully. Likely a bit of both. She'd better get used to giving him control. He'd played the customer-service card long enough. Now, he would show her who was in charge.

"I'd kill to get my daughter back," she said.

He kept his expression benign. "I understand."

"I expect you to do the same."

With a light chuckle, he returned to his chair. The lumbar-pampering design wasn't custom leather like the one he had back at the home office in Boston, but the furniture and accessories at this makeshift office were the best his people could manage on such short notice. Before he met with Marisela Morales, he'd had to establish a presence. By morning, this office would be returned to its original state—a bare warehouse minutes from Tampa's port. And hopefully he, and his new agents, would be on board the yacht en route to Miami.

But he wouldn't gain Ms. Morales's cooperation with haughty Elise Barton-Ryce turning up her nose at her. He'd intended to use the mother of the missing child angle to further his case, but he doubted Elise would be effective with her current mood broadcasting doubt, dissatisfaction, and arrogance instead of the emotional desperation she'd shown to manipulate him into taking her case. Or else, her pride wouldn't allow her to show her vulnerabilities more than once. Ian wasn't sure which—but so long as her checks continued to clear, he really didn't care.

"Titan will do whatever is necessary. That's what you pay us for."

With a curt nod that barely displaced a single blond hair of her sculpted bob, Elise retrieved her handbag and stood, ramrod straight, waiting for him to stand and escort her to the waiting limousine. Without a hint of his frustration, he did as she expected.

Just as her black stretch sedan disappeared, he caught sight of the dark gray four-door pulling into the lot.

Ian practiced his best smile, not needing a mirror to know his blue eyes held just the right dash of charm to pique the insatiable Ms. Morales's interests. Personal and professional. Even if tonight's operation had spun out of control, Ian had learned a great deal about fiery Marisela, the street-smart woman who'd soon be in his employ.

And he intended to exploit each and every detail—hopefully, to their mutual satisfaction.

"Where the hell are my parents?"

Marisela kept her tone even, her words clipped just short enough so the sharp-dressed man in the thousand-dollar suit knew she meant business. He'd waltzed into the expertly appointed office as if he owned the place, so for the moment, she assumed he did. Max even bowed his head ever so slightly toward his boss before he disappeared outside, as if the deferential gesture wasn't required, but was a natural response to his employer's power.

"Their driver is just now finding his way back after making an unfortunate wrong turn," he answered, his voice undeniably cultured. Possibly English. Pierce Brosnan as James Bond.

"Where are they now?" she asked.

He arched a brow, as if challenging her not to believe him. "Just coming over the Sunshine Skyway Bridge. I hear the Bay is lovely at this time of the morning."

She ignored his attempt at levity and tried to wrap her mind around the idea of her parents tooling around in a slick black car instead of lying dead in some dirty alley or weighted and dumped into the murky waters of Tampa Bay. She met his gaze dead on, gauging the steadiness of his stare and despite her best efforts, noting the cerulean intensity in his pale eyes.

Either he was telling the truth, or he was the best liar she'd encountered since Sister Dominique convinced her that masturbation led to blindness. Of course, she'd been eleven then—and a hell of a lot more gullible.

"A limousine, huh?" she asked, her brow arched. People in her neighborhood rode in rented cars for two reasons—weddings and funerals. "Somebody die?" she asked.

"Other than the man in your kitchen?"

She leveled her gaze into his. He wanted to play Rocha's death against her, huh? Let him try.

She gave him the finger.

He chuckled, rounded his desk and plucked a cigar from a carved box. With a tug at his pant leg, he leaned casually on the polished edge, his buffed shoe inches from her knee. Bruno Magli. Lambskin. Probably the Rangle half boot, from the looks of it.

Damn, but Marisela had a thing for shoes. Not women's shoes, fortunately for her wallet. Give her a boot with a sharp heel or a tennis shoe built for speed and she was a happy camper. But put a pair of expensive loafers on a well-dressed man, and she turned to jelly.

Hot, melted jelly like the kind that oozed from a Krispy Kreme doughnut when she bought them right off the rollers early Sunday morning after dancing away every last moment of a Saturday night. Why this man evoked thoughts of sultry, sexy salsa and forbidden, calorie-laden treats didn't make sense.

Must have been his shoes.

She cleared her throat. "How did you get my parents out of the house so late at night?"

"The evening began quite early, actually. Didn't you hear the last minute announcement? Congratulations go out to Ernesto and Aida Morales, Hispanic Business Owners of the Year, pre-

sented by the newly endowed Fund for Economic Growth of
Greater West Tampa. The ceremony will be next week, but
tonight the winners enjoyed a complimentary meal at Bern's,
dessert and aperitifs in their legendary dessert room, and then a
moonlight drive across the Courtney Campbell causeway in a
spectacular stretch Humvee."

He rolled the cigar between his fingers and the earthy odor
of hand-rolled tobacco taunted her as she judged his every
word, the pitch of his every syllable and swing of each inflec-
tion. Was he screwing with her? Making a joke?

After clipping the edge off the cigar with a miniature guillo-
tine, a nice Hollywood touch, he smiled in a way that made her
breath catch. Okay, what the hell was going on? Sure, this man
could have walked straight off the cover of *GQ* or *Entertainment
Weekly*, but hot-stuff suits didn't usually appeal to her. Not in
real life.

Or did they? She couldn't remember the last time she'd been
in close proximity to a man like this. Maybe she needed to re-
think her choice of hang-outs. Maybe her tastes were finally
reaching upward. Or maybe the slightly overheated quiver in
her body was simply a residual effect from her interaction with
Frankie.

Or maybe not.

"Relax, Ms. Morales. Your parents have been out all night
with my associates, safe and sound."

She swallowed, forcing her off-kilter attraction to the pit of
her stomach, right beside her anger and indignation. "Safe and
sound? Can't say the same for the sanctity of their home, can
you? I mean, with a dead guy in the kitchen and another in
the hall."

He cleared his throat. "By the time your parents return from their little adventure, they'll never know their daughter committed murder just a foot from where her mother brews her coffee every morning."

Marisela scoffed, unwilling to accept even an inkling of guilt. According to Max, Nestor Rocha had been on the same payroll as he was, which all linked back to Mr. Rich Suit. She'd done nothing less than protect herself and her parents' home— which she figured he'd expected.

"You can work your guilt trip on someone else, *cabrón*. He was in my house, attacking something I love very much—my body. Don't expect regrets from me. Self-defense is not murder."

He retrieved a lighter from beside the cutter and rolled the cigar into the flame, puffing gently, patiently. Marisela wondered how much this man knew about her, wondered if his choice of smoke was meant to provoke her. Her grandfather had hand-rolled cigars in Ybor City after emigrating from Cuba. Her father, usually after dinner while he sipped an espresso, puffed nightly on a Romeo Y Julieta Reserva Real *robusto*. The woodsy, earthy odor evoked strong impressions of her childhood, her family. Her life.

What did this man want from her?

Through a silver gray haze, he eyed her with undisguised admiration. Or was it something entirely more basic?

"A tactical error on my part put you in unnecessary danger tonight," he said. "For that, I apologize."

She didn't believe him. She couldn't. Believing him meant trusting him and she wasn't about to let her primed and simmering hormones cloud her already foggy judgment. She un-crossed her legs and balanced both feet firmly in front of her, leaning her elbows on her knees. He'd interpret the move as casual. But she was ready to strike if she didn't like the more detailed version of his explanation.

"Nestor Rocha wanted me dead," she spat. "Has for a long time. How come you didn't know that? Everyone else in West Tampa did."

He nodded. "Yes, well, I don't know much about West Tampa, Ms. Morales. My initial contact here made himself scarce and time constraints forced me to move without him. Mr. Rocha was employed simply to lead us to you. We had no idea he'd manipulate the situation for his own benefit."

"Crooks and killers like Rocha don't give a damn about anyone's agenda but their own. You should choose your hired help more carefully. You're out of your league. Your 'ivy' league, if you know what I mean."

He chuckled softly. "Very good. Yes, I know exactly what you mean. In fact, my deficit in that particular area is why I need a woman with your expertise for an operation I'm putting together."

"My expertise?" she asked, a doubtful laugh in her voice. "What, you need a manicure?"

He leveled her self-indulgent grin with a steely glare. Apparently, he was no longer in the mood for jokes. *Well, hell.* After tangling with clearly unresolved attraction to her ex, killing a man in her kitchen, and then grappling with some fantasy man who clearly held her future in his hands, a little cheesy comedy could go a long way.

"No manicure, I had one Tuesday," he claimed, and she believed him. He was just the type of guy both vain enough and man enough to have his nails professionally done. "I'm more interested in your . . . natural abilities."

He hadn't said anything the least bit offensive, but Marisela felt her skin ripple with gooseflesh all the same. His pause, just before he said the word *natural,* gave the word a lurid ring. As if he knew what she'd done tonight. Not with Nestor, but with Frankie. As if he wanted a piece of the sexual action for himself.

"Sorry," she answered, ignoring how her mouth suddenly dried. "I ain't selling."

She balanced her hands on the armrests of the chair and pushed to her feet, her shoulders tensed, ready to counter any attack that might keep her here one minute longer. He matched her stance, unrestrained in his desire to meet her point for point. Did he sense how he unnerved her? Did he think pumping up the charm would lure her to play his game, whatever it was?

She didn't know his name or where he was from. Or what he really wanted. But she couldn't forget that he'd been responsible for a scenario that forced her to take a life—and yet, she experienced a familiar tug of attraction nonetheless. With this *varón* exuding sex from his expertly clipped tawny hair to the dark threads in his silk socks, how could she fight her intrinsic reaction to get busy?

By reminding herself that this bastard had her parents, that's how.

She wanted to go home, make sure her mother didn't find so much as a crocheted doily out of place, not to mention bloodstains on the new kitchen rugs with the swaying palm tree motif. But most of all, she wanted out of here before her jum-bled emotions led her into the exact kind of temptation the nuns at St. Joseph's had warned about.

"Don't you at least want to hear my offer?" He made no move to touch her, but kept her captive with his tone. He had an enticing voice to match his expressive eyes and expensive shoes. If he wasn't a politician or a gigolo, he was missing his calling. "I'm willing to pay more than you've made in your en-tire lifetime."

That stopped her. Currently out of work, Marisela couldn't ignore a chance at big money. At least, not until she heard ex-actly what he had in mind.

"To do what? A makeover?"

"You're a bail enforcement agent."

She shook her head. "Your intel is old. I *was* a bail enforce-ment agent."

"Fired, four weeks ago last Thursday, after an unfortunate plea agreement with the prosecutor's office. You allegedly beat one Rob Dalton within an inch of his life after he jumped bail, abandoning his devoted wife and their four children to skip town with his gay lover. The prosecutor allowed you to trade your license to carry for your freedom and a clean record. You accepted. A smart move."

She arched a brow, conceding the accuracy of his informa-tion.

"Sometimes I lose my temper."

"Don't we all?"

A laugh burst out of her before she could hold it back. "I'm willing to bet you never lose your temper. At least, not when people might see."

This time, he arched his brow. "You're a good judge of character."

"I try."

"You're also physically adept, formally trained in *krav maga* at the Twenty-second Street gym by an ex-NYPD sergeant named Whiskey Parker. You also have extensive informal training courtesy of a rather brawl-happy group of women who call themselves *las Reinas*. You're mentally quick, a fast draw and an accurate shot. You speak fluent Spanish with a Cuban dialect, and you need money. Other than the little problem with your temper, you're the perfect candidate for the job I'm offering—especially since without your license, you can't work in law enforcement in any capacity."

He recited the condensed version of her past and the bleak reality of her future with total confidence that he'd missed nothing—which he hadn't. Nothing of consequence, anyway. And he'd delivered the rundown in a deep throaty voice that evoked thoughts of sweaty sheets and iced champagne rather than skanky jail cells and unemployment.

She hooked the thumb of her left hand in her waistband, leaving her right hand free, just in case. "I'm a hot tamale, what can I say?"

"You're a lethal hot tamale, Ms. Morales. Which is why I'd like you to work for me."

Again, acute speculation lit his blue eyes, reminding her of the aquamarine earrings her parents' had bought her for her *quinceañera*. God, this man was magnetic. He seemed to appreciate her sharp quips and irreverent comments. And most perilous of all, he seemed to know when she was acting all that to make a point.

"Look, I still don't know who you are, much less what you do," she pointed out, desperate to regain the upper hand. "Kind of hard to make a life-changing decision without more information."

He stood, unfolding to his full height, his chest mere inches from hers. "I'm not sure that you're ready for all the details yet. You've had a trying evening."

A trying evening? More than likely, the women in his rich-ass, pampered world had "trying evenings" when the designer dress they'd chosen for dinner at the club had a rip in the hem and the maid had the night off. Yet, for all his spit and polish, she sensed a man who knew, at least by rumor, the true nature of violence, crime, and risk.

They matched stares, stances. His gaze lowered, sweeping over her in appreciation that didn't seem lecherous, and yet, taunted her. Enticed her.

"I'm not a killer," she insisted. "Despite what happened tonight."

"Mr. Rocha's job was to lead us to you, help us test your ability to stand against several men in a fight. He obviously had his own agenda."

"You might have known how he hated me if you'd checked him out with the right people. Like me, for instance," she challenged.

"No argument. And because of my unfortunate lapse in judgment spawned by a tight timetable, you now have the upper hand in our negotiation."

"You have my parents."

He shook his head. "Not for much longer. They will be home any minute. I won't use them as leverage. Doesn't exactly engender trust between employer and employee, does it?"

Narrowing her eyes, she searched his face for any sign that he was lying. She found none.

"I'm not an ex-cop or ex-military," she said. "I'm just a girl who once had a semi-interesting job and a past in a gang. Besides, I've got a rap sheet, though that didn't stop you from hiring Nestor."

"In my business, a dubious past can be an asset."

"Really? And what business is that?"

With a sweep of his hand, he invited her to sit again. He also brushed her arm with his fingers, sending a spark of electric awareness crackling around them. For a moment, Marisela considered chastising herself for allowing this man's buff body, devilish good looks, and well-cut suit to excite her so intrinsically. He'd nearly gotten her killed. He'd set her up, forced her into a situation where she'd had no other option but to kill a man.

On the flip side, toying with the sexual tension coiling between them beat the hell out of waiting in the church parking lot to be first in line for confession after what she'd done to Frankie. Not to mention Nestor.

She eased into the chair, but instead of crossing her legs casually as she had before, she kicked her heels up onto his desk ankle over ankle. With his back to the desk, she'd blocked him from moving in any direction—except backward. Retreat.

He remained still. "My company is a varied conglomerate, mostly private investigation, protection, security. We need someone like you—well acquainted with the criminal element. You know how to move in and out of their circles and you speak the language of the man I'm currently after. You're beautiful and you can take care of yourself in a fight if your backup is somehow diverted or delayed."

"You certainly think you know a lot about me," she said.

"I do, and you know it. Besides, your reputation precedes you," he answered.

"Really? Maybe yours does, too . . . of course I wouldn't know because I still have no idea who the hell you are."

"Forgive me. My name is Ian Blake."

She kept her hands folded across her stomach, a sliver of bare skin poking from beneath her midriff tee.

He took her coolness in stride. "I'm the president and CEO of Titan International."

She rolled the name around in her head. *Nothing*.

"Tell me when I'm supposed to be impressed. I wouldn't want to sound stupid for not knowing you. Or Titan International."

His grin quirked up on one side, bringing one dimple into sharp relief against his rugged jaw, smooth shaven, yet still dangerously angled. "We're one of the top private investigation firms in the country. We handle some of the business the CIA, DEA, and the FBI don't have the manpower for."

She looked around, refusing to appear dazzled by his claim. "And you have a location in Tampa?"

Ian glanced around. "In the United States, we're headquartered in Boston. This is a small, discreet satellite office, one we may or may not keep in operation after our business here is complete."

Marisela laughed. Though blindfolded before she'd left the car with Max, she'd traversed yards of hallway before arriving at

Ian Blake's private lair. If this office was small, then so was her
Jennifer Lopez butt.

"You can check us out," he offered. "Information is readily
available through various sources. I actually didn't plan to discuss the details of the case tonight."

"What? You were going to wait until after I got out of the
hospital? How kind."

"You look no worse for wear," he insisted.

She swiped a finger over the cut on the side of her mouth.
The sting had dulled and the blood had stopped seeping onto
her tongue, though she could feel the ugly swelling of moist
flesh. She didn't even want to think about what she'd discover
when she peeled off her blouse and examined her back from
where Rocha had flung her against the table. There went wearing her teeny-weeny red bikini to the beach tomorrow.

She shook her head, and felt the strain in her neck. "Yeah,
I'll bet I look like Miss America."

"I've known quite a few Miss Americas. You have entirely
more panache."

She rolled her eyes at the compliment, then forced herself to
stand. "I've got a lot more than panache going for me," she said,
eyeing him up and down with unhidden appreciation.

"No doubt. Would you like to hear my offer?"

She shrugged as if the money didn't matter. "Hit me."

He complied. The dollar amount nearly knocked her off her
feet.

At her stunned silence, he grinned. "Too little?"

She couldn't think. No one promised cash payments of
that ilk just for knocking a few heads around, maybe digging
into some dirt. Still, she had no means of comparison and

wasn't about to let this smooth talker take her for a ride. "Maybe."

His stare skewered her, but then an indulgent grin lightened the mood. "You need time to think over the compensation package. That's understandable. Take the night. I'll find you in the morning," he promised.

To regain a semblance of power, she flicked a nonexistent piece of lint off the shoulder of his suit. Marisela had her bold moments, but touching a stranger, hunk or not, without a reason, was brazen, even for her.

She broke the contact, winked, then strolled to the door.

"Just sit tight, Mr. Blake. If I'm interested, I'll find you."

Five

"MARISELA, WAKE UP! The traffic is going to suck if we don't hit the road."

Marisela rolled over, wincing as her muscles screamed in protest. Her brain throbbed in time to Lia's pounding on the door. *Dios mio.* Why was Lia here at daybreak? To torture her?

"Marisela, open the door right now or I'm leaving without you."

"Cállate!" she shouted, but the reverberation of the volume and pitch sent her flopping back into her pillow. *"Por favor, mija, cállate."*

The last part came out in a pathetic croak, so Marisela pulled the sheet over her head and whimpered.

Apparently, her friend heard the desperation in Marisela's voice and toned down her knocking to light taps.

"Marisela, your mother's getting suspicious."

With a groan, Marisela whipped off the tangled sheets. She sat up and staggered to the door, flipping the lock. Wavering, she waited for Lia to slip her skinny body inside before she crashed back on the mattress.

"Lock it," Marisela ordered.

"*Chica,* you look like shit."

Marisela forced her gaze to focus on Lia's face, pretty and perky with that certain pale shade of olive skin designed to soak up the sun from Tuscany to Sorrento. She'd tamed her naturally bushy eyebrows into sleek arches and even though their plan today included nothing more than a lazy trip to the beach, Lia's dark green eyes were as expertly lined as her mouth, which she'd tinted with a lipstick that matched the fuchsia pink swimsuit she wore underneath a sexy, white mesh cover-up.

Such perfection so early in the morning made Marisela's stomach turn. "Why are you here so early?"

"Early? It's ten-thirty. Frankie's court appearance was at ten. Didn't you call me before dawn and order me to shanghai you before he came down here and kicked your ass for whatever mysterious trick you pulled on him last night? Which, by the way, I'm still waiting to hear about in tantalizing detail."

Marisela groaned, but Lia's reminder spurred her to scramble out of bed and stumble toward her dresser. She scanned the collection of makeup, jewelry, perfumes, and assorted accessories from bracelets and bangles to toe rings and nail polish for an old discarded bottle of water, not quite ready to venture out of her room for a drink to relieve the dry, cottony coating inside her mouth. She found nothing and cursed, but Lia solved the problem in her usual no-nonsense way, retrieving a half-frozen bottle from her beach bag without being asked.

After drinking greedily, Marisela started to feel alive again.

Lia crossed her slim arms. "What happened last night?"

"My parents went out to dinner and stayed out until after three o'clock in the morning. They didn't even call. I should ground them."

Lia frowned. "That's not what I'm asking about and you know it. What happened between you and Frankie?"

Marisela blew out a breath. It was an attempt at a whistle, but her lips were still too dry. "What didn't happen last night?" She tossed the bottle back to Lia. She turned to shuffle through several bureau drawers until she found a one-piece tanksuit that would cover the bruises on her back.

"Well, you didn't sleep well, for one thing," Lia guessed.

Marisela laughed, the vibrations awakening the pain in her back. "I'm surprised I slept at all. Last night did not go as I expected."

And she wasn't even talking about Nestor Rocha or Ian Blake.

Lia dropped her bag on the cedar chest next to Marisela's bed and proceeded to untangle the sheets so she could inject her usual order into Marisela's chaotic world. "And you thought meeting with Frankie would be all business. Not so easy seeing him again, was it?"

Actually, hooking up with Frankie had been as effortless as slicing through custard with a razor-sharp knife. Marisela thought she'd steeled herself for the conflagration of emotions Frankie invariably invoked, particularly that sense of nostalgia for those younger, simpler days when she didn't have to worry so much about getting a job, keeping a job, finding her own place and avoiding an ass-kicking from a ex-boyfriend who had valid reasons to be seriously pissed.

She'd thought wrong.

"I don't want to talk about it."

Lia slammed the drawer shut, catching the end of Marisela's favorite black cover-up. "Listen here, *chica*, I didn't get up early on my day off to take you to the beach and not get some serious dish. If you're not spilling all the gory details," she said, marching back to the bed and snapping the sheets tight, "then I'm going home to eat chocolate, lay out by the pool, and drink margaritas. Alone."

Marisela whipped her nightshirt over her head. "You're cruel. Bluffing, but cruel. You won't ditch me until you've heard every juicy detail."

She realized her error the minute Lia gasped, dropped the floral shams and rushed to her side. Lia planted her hands firmly on Marisela's shoulders and turned her, slowly, her winces increasing with each black and blue mark.

"Marisela, what happened? Did Frankie do this?"

With care born of her pain, Marisela gingerly moved out of Lia's reach. "*¿Estás loca?* Do you think he'd still be alive if he'd done this to me?"

Lia crossed her arms tightly, her size six-and-a-half foot tapping her hand-jeweled flip-flops on the carpeted floor. "If not him, then who?"

It had been a long time since Marisela had seen Lia's face so pinched and disapproving. The outwardly straight-laced Angelia Santorini knew nearly everything about Marisela's life, from her lovers to her jobs to her occasional run-ins with the law. But she'd disapproved only once—when Marisela had started hanging out with *las Reinas*. After Marisela finally decided to fight her way out of the gang, Lia had been her staunchest supporter. This morning, Marisela wanted to tell Lia about Nestor, about what he'd done, about what she'd done to stop him—but she kept her mouth shut. They weren't kids anymore and murder was too much of a burden, even for her best friend.

"Can we stop talking about last night? Trust me, the guy who did this looks a lot worse."

As in pale and dead.

Lia rolled her eyes, huffed and finished her project with the bed before turning her attention to Marisela's clothes-strewn floor. "You're in trouble again, aren't you? Don't deny it," she said, tossing her hands up. "I know and you're going to tell—"

At a knock on the door, they both jumped.

"Marisela, do you and Lia want *café con leche*? I'm turning off the stove. Papi's on his way to pick me up."

Marisela released the tight breath she'd been holding in her chest. "No, *Mami*. We'll stop at Starbucks."

As expected, her mother launched into a Spanish language rant on the less than acceptable brewing techniques of the Seattle coffee chain. As she retreated down the hall, back to the kitchen, her primary domain, her volume grew fainter. Lia covered her mouth to keep from laughing out loud, the humor erasing the picture of Nestor Rocha dead and bleeding on her mother's linoleum from Marisela's mind.

"You always know how to yank your mother's chain."

Marisela tugged her cover-up free and tossed it on the bed. "I just want to get out of here."

"And avoid telling me what happened last night."

Sooner or later, Lia deserved at least a portion of the truth, but right now, all Marisela wanted was to leave. She had a strong suspicion that her house would be Frankie's first stop after his court appearance. He'd promised to exact revenge after she'd left him handcuffed and horny last night. And Frankie kept his promises.

"When you came in, did *Mami* say anything about the neighbors this morning? You know, complaining about noise?"

"Neighbors? What, did you and Frankie get a little too loud last night?"

Marisela slipped out of her panties and squeezed the rest of her size eight body and 36D breasts into her Lycra suit.

She'd probably get Lia out of the house a whole lot faster if she lied and said that she and Frankie had fucked like bunnies all night long. That was, after all, what Lia expected to hear. Unfortunately, there was a hell of a lot more to the story.

"Let's take my car, okay?" Marisela said, opening her closet door and ignoring her friend's suspicious stare as she dug out her sandals and beach bag. Since Lia drove a choice Ford Mustang convertible, Marisela never volunteered to drive. But when leftover sand and shells spilled onto her carpet from her bag, Lia agreed to the change in normal procedure.

For once, Marisela would play smart. Smart people knew how to move ahead of trouble, not stand around and wait for angry, revenge-focused ex-boyfriends to charge into their bedrooms and demand retribution for the humiliation of being tied naked to a bed then left for his mother to find him. Before she'd headed back to the club, she'd hooked the handcuff key over the doorknob, right where Frankie's parents would find it. Didn't mean he'd be any less pissed just because she'd ensured his quick release. So to speak.

Sufficiently packed, Marisela shot to the door. "Let's blow."

Lia grabbed her arm. Marisela winced as pain shot through her. Lia's eyes widened with rage.

"He did hurt you!"

"No, *mija,* I swear it wasn't him."

"Then why are you so afraid of Frankie finding you today?"

Bravado was wasted on Lia, who thought Marisela was pretty darned awesome most of the time, for whatever unfathomable reason. "When I left him last night, he was not a happy camper."

Lia shifted her weight to one hip and tried to lighten the moment with a suspicious half-smile. "Didn't you satisfy your man, Marisela? I mean, I thought you took pride in that sort of thing."

Marisela grabbed Lia by the cover-up and yanked her toward the door. "Right now, I'm taking great pride in staying alive."

Marisela couldn't catch a break. Though her mother had gone out back to the lanai where her washer and dryer shared space with her plastic patio furniture and rusting hibachi grill, Marisela's father pushed through the side door from the driveway just as Marisela was about to grab the doorknob.

"Sneaking off again?"

"I'm twenty-eight years old, *Papi.* I don't sneak."

His expression, completely doubtful, softened when she smacked his leathery cheek with a kiss. The edge of his salt and pepper mustache tickled her lips. He smelled like Old Spice and dark, brewed coffee.

"*Sí,* and I'm Antonio Banderas," Ernesto Morales quipped, his trademark eye twinkle offsetting the gruff set of his square jaw. "Where are you two troublemakers going on a work day? Does the mayor know my daughter is corrupting his assistant, Angelia?"

Lia batted her lashes with that special little-girl finesse that all Latina daughters learned when dealing with their *muy macho* fathers. Technically, Lia wasn't Latina—her mother and father were second-generation Italian-American, but having grown up just two blocks over, Lia had balanced between the two distinct cultures with the skill of an Olympic gymnast. She spoke Castilian Spanish courtesy of the teachers at Tampa Catholic High School, Italian thanks to her parents and grandparents, and Ybor City Cuban picked up in various and sundry conversations with the Morales family, who considered her one of their own. Lia added diversity to Marisela's distinctly Cuban-American experience—not to mention the added value of having Lia's mother's fantasy-inducing meatballs every Sunday, followed with coffee and fig cookies that nearly caused spontaneous orgasms.

"It's my day off, Mr. Morales," Lia explained. "Even city employees deserve a vacation day every once and a while."

He sniffed derisively, but with a smile. Marisela wondered if her father understood the concept of time off for good behavior. For as long as she'd been alive, her father had missed work maybe three times—the day she was born, the day her sister Belinda was born and the day he'd had to bail Marisela out of jail. She winced, realizing that last event had actually happened on more than one occasion.

"What about you, Marisela?" He leveled his dark gaze on

62 Julie Leto

her, his black irises piercing. "A job isn't going to come looking for you."

"I have some leads on work, *Papi,* but today I'm working on my tan."

"Nonsense! You were born with a tan."

"I've been meaning to thank you for that."

"Where's your mother?"

"Right here, Ernesto." Aida Morales squeezed her petite body through the screen door, a pile of folded towels clutched in her thin arms. How her mother remained so skinny had been a topic of frustrated conversation between her and Belinda for years. Their mother didn't serve a meal that didn't include at least one fried item—from steaks to potatoes to *platanos.*

The only thing the sisters could figure was that their mother rarely remained still. She rose early every morning to fix breakfast for their father, then proceeded with the housework until sometime after nine-thirty, when their father came home from opening the store at six A.M. to collect his wife who ran the deli at their small but popular corner store. The Morales' bodega, on the corner of Habana and Tampania, provided sundry items from cold milk to fresh-baked Cuban bread alongside neighborhood gossip and local politics.

Aida plopped the towels onto a chair, knocked her fists onto her slim hips, and glanced around the kitchen with her lips turned down. "Something's wrong in here."

Uninterested, Ernesto shook open his newspaper. The hard crack of the newsprint nearly sent Marisela into the ceiling.

Her mother's eyes snapped on her, then narrowed into inky slits. "What aren't you telling me, Marisela?"

Marisela folded her lips inward and did her best "I'm innocent and didn't kill a criminal in your kitchen" imitation. She followed her bewildered expression with a quizzical look, shooting it first at her mother, then at Lia, then back.

Her mother wasn't buying. "Something is not right. I know my house. I can feel these things, and you," she said, pointing directly at Marisela, "know it."

Marisela fought the urge to shift her balance or offer denial too soon. Her mother was a sweet, loving, trusting woman, but her maternal radar could spot a lie with frightening accuracy. With a shrug, Marisela turned back toward Lia and lifted her eyebrows.

Her friend instantly took the hint.

"So, *señora,* how was your fancy dinner last night?"

Saved!

Aida launched into an excited and animated description of the entire night, causing Marisela to decide to buy the first round of drinks at the tiki bar at whatever beach she and Lia ended up at. Of course, she had been the one to tell Lia about her parent's wild night out in the first place, so she deserved a little credit.

Her father intruded on her thoughts of piña coladas with his deep, level voice. "Marisela, Manolo Diaz had some interesting news for me this morning."

He didn't look up from his paper—he didn't have to. Her father could scare the shit out of her from another room with that calm, controlled voice of his.

Manolo was the neighbor across the street. Marisela could only imagine what tale he'd come to tell her father. "Really?" She wandered to the counter and grabbed an apple from a bowl, then went to the fridge to score a glass of juice.

Her father continued, "When I went out for the paper, he stopped me, said he saw strange cars here last night. Were you home? Did you have company? I thought you were helping the Vegases find that son of theirs."

Marisela took a bite out of the apple, as if talking with her mouth full somehow lessened the impact of the lie. "Oh, I found him. After, I stopped by the house for a few minutes, but then Lia and I went back to her place, right?"

Lia was a reliable liar—a prerequisite for friendship with Marisela—but even she had her limits. One conversation at a time. She nodded automatically and Ernesto, only barely interested to begin with in neighborhood gossip, went back to his reading.

With a sigh of relief, Marisela slammed the refrigerator door, then noticed a new refrigerator magnet with an ad for some online service—only the Morales family didn't have a computer. Suspicious, she lifted it gingerly and caught sight of the jagged bullet hole in the metal underneath.

She slammed the business card–sized promo item back in place, covering the one clue Titan apparently hadn't been able to easily sweep away.

Her mother marched toward her. Marisela's hand felt glued to the refrigerator handle, but one arched eyebrow from her mother forced her to release her grip. If she noticed the magnet, her mother gave no indication, instead leaning in and retrieving the milk.

"So, what happened with Frankie? He gives his mother so much heartbreak."

"Not today," her father said, his tone paternally brusque

behind the Sports page. "Lucky bastard went to court and the judge dismissed the case."

Marisela's stomach dropped to her toes. "Dismissed? How do you know?"

Ernesto thumbed through the newsprint and found the horse-racing scores. He rarely bet the ponies, but he followed the industry since his father had been a jockey in Cuba.

"His brother, Roberto, came in just before I left. He came to play the Lotto. Figured it was a lucky day for the Vega family. The judge took less than five minutes to throw out the case."

Five minutes? That meant if Frankie wasn't knocking on her door in the next ten seconds, she was the luckiest *mujer* in West Central Florida.

"Good for him," Marisela said, her voice high-pitched. "Tell him I said congratulations if you see him, okay? We've gotta bolt, right, Lia?"

Her friend was already tossing out the obligatory kisses to Marisela's parents when the doorbell rang.

Marisela froze. She didn't want to have this confrontation. Not here. Then again, if she faced Frankie down in front of her parents instead of out in the open where anything could go wrong, she'd have a certain level of protection. He wouldn't dare pull anything with her father in the house. Her parents, however, were planning on leaving.

She could see the scenario clearly in her head.

No, no, Señora Morales. Don't let me keep you. I just want to properly thank Marisela for what she did for me last night.

Then they'd leave and bam, she was dead meat.

Or worse.

On the second ring, Aida headed toward the door. Ernesto, oblivious to the panic on Lia's face and the furtive exchange with Marisela, turned to the Business section.

"Lia! I forgot my beach towel," she said, glancing toward the door to the lanai. "I don't want to take *Mami*'s good ones for the beach."

"Oh, no. You shouldn't," Lia concurred. "Let's get another one."

"Right. See you later, *Papi.*"

He waved his hand dismissively and with that good-bye, the girls disappeared. By the time Lia had quickly closed the door from the kitchen to the lanai, Marisela had opened the squeaky screen exit. The last thing they heard before scooting into the backyard to vault the chain-link fence was, "Ernesto? Where did the girls go?"

Her father's oblivious reaction would buy them a few more seconds. If Frankie possessed any deference to her mother, they'd have a few minutes more while he managed a polite farewell.

Her body flush against the side of the house, Marisela scooted around Lia for a clear view of the front yard. Mr. Velasquez across the street was outside trimming his roses and his wife hacked at the weeds with a hoe. A good sign. With neighbors there to watch, Frankie wouldn't have messed with her car to keep her from taking off.

On three, Marisela and Lia scrambled for the car. Marisela disengaged the lock with moments to spare, and had their bags tossed in the backseat, the car started and in drive in record time. Without so much as a backward glance, she shot down the street and made a sharp right. When she hit the corner, she glanced back at her house. As expected, Frankie was tearing toward his mother's old Chevy.

"He's following us!" Marisela announced.

"I think you better tell me what you did to him last night."

Marisela flashed quick calculations in her mind. There was no way in hell her ten-year-old Toyota Corolla could outrun the Chevy. Her V-4 engine would sputter against his V-8, even with years of rust and neglect on the body. As she remembered from last night, his car was a piece of crap, but it was fast—and since Frankie's oldest brother, Miguel, was a mechanic, that baby likely purred like a cat when stroked the right way.

And Frankie was nothing if not an expert stroker.

"Marisela, he's right behind us!"

Luckily, Frankie hadn't been in town in a long time and Marisela knew this neighborhood like the back of her hand. He wasn't the first ticked-off *hombre* she'd eluded and likely, he wouldn't be the last.

She yanked the car into an unexpected left down an alley that ran behind a row of houses a few blocks up from hers. The car skidded in the uneven dirt, but Marisela kept her tires mostly on the ground and then slowed down, willing her charging emotions under control. At the first empty driveway, she cut through, maneuvering her tiny vehicle onto a main road. Moments later, they heard a screech and a crash behind them. As anticipated, Frankie's much larger vehicle wouldn't fit.

Marisela chuckled, easing the car to a confident and leisurely pace.

"What's he going to do if he catches up to us?" Lia asked. "Or do I want to know?"

"Probably make me suffer some grand humiliation. Remember the time he paid me back for spiking his soda with vinegar by tucking my skirt in my panties after feeling me up at school?"

Lia laughed at the memory, despite her usual attempts at decorum. "You were both twelve then."

"Yeah, well, Frankie's got a long memory."

"You gonna tell me what you did this time to piss him off?"

Marisela grabbed her seat belt and maneuvered it across her chest, then checked to find Lia already securely strapped in. In the background, she heard her cell phone trilling. No doubt, her mother was calling to find out what had sent Frankie running out of her house in such a hell-bent hurry.

"Remember how Frankie used to really hate how I'd tease him? You know, get him all hot and then not follow through."

"You did that?" Lia asked, startled. "When?"

She spared her friend a withering glance and Lia bit back a chuckle. "I can't believe you let him think you were going to do it last night when you were really out to return him to his parents."

"Yeah, well, I did more than just let him think it."

On the two-lane road, she swung around a slow-moving Honda Prelude. She saw no sign of Frankie behind her. Two more blocks and they'd hit Armenia Avenue, one of the main thoroughfares in West Tampa. The chances of running by a cop car improved on a busy street. If Frankie showed up again, she'd just get herself pulled over for speeding or careless driving. Except for the illegal gun she kept in the trunk—which the cops would have no reason to search for—a traffic ticket would be a small price to pay for a clean getaway.

Ahead, the traffic light flipped from green to gold. Marisela watched the traffic flow and had no choice but to stop. A truck already sat idling in the center lane, but as the first car on the side lane, she could take off the minute the intersection cleared, red light or not, if Frankie showed up again.

She cursed when a black SUV pulled into her path. She slammed on the brake. Not ten seconds later, Frankie's rusty Chevy pulled up behind her.

He'd cut through the parking lot of a strip mall, the son of a bitch. She shouted for Lia to lock the doors.

In the rearview mirror, Frankie's teeth gleamed. Not from a smile, but a sneer. He eased his car up until his front bumper tapped her back one. Lia yelped, but Marisela opted for a string of four-letter words instead.

"Shit, Marisela. When you piss guys off, you do a damned good job, don't you?"

Blocked in by the bloated SUV and Frankie's tank of a car, she had limited choices. She hated running, but hated being trapped even more. She could launch a preemptive strike and confront Frankie first, but what would that do except leave her open for him to exact his revenge? She was good, but Frankie was bigger—and badder.

Not to mention enraged. He knocked on her window with barely checked fury.

And the cell phone behind her, which had stopped ringing, renewed its high-pitched squeal.

"Get out of the car, Marisela," he said with surprising calm.

"Why? So you can get me back like you promised? I'm not stupid, Frankie."

"I just need to talk to you."

She glanced at the light. Would that sucker never change?

"Call me later. I'll be home around six. You got my number, right? 1-800-FUCK-YOU."

He shoved his hands into the pockets of his leather jacket. "Sounds like you want me to finish what you started last night."

"Shut up."

The cross traffic eased to a stop, followed a few seconds later by the cars turning north and south. A minute more and she'd be free.

The shrill cheep of her cell phone slipped beneath her skin and she shouted at Lia to answer the call, sending her friend stretching into the backseat to retrieve her bag. She had no doubt her mother was on the other end of the line.

"Tell *Mami* we're fine. Go away, Frankie. I did what I had to and you have every right to be pissed. But you'll have to deal with your anger without me."

"Oh, no, Marisela. I plan to deal with you. In the way you deserve."

Lia shoved the phone at Marisela. "Talk to him."

"Tell *Mami* I'm busy," she said, grinding the words out through her teeth.

Lia's olive skin had turned pasty white.

"Marisela, please, take the phone. It's not your mother. He says if you don't talk to him, this car will explode."

Six

"WHO IS THIS?"

"Calm down, Ms. Morales. Though I don't make a habit of offering idle threats, I simply wanted to emphasize to your friend that you shouldn't open your door to Mr. Vega. That wouldn't be wise."

She glanced at the caller ID, but as expected, the number was blocked. Still, the cultured voice seeped into her skin like warm, scented lotion—expensive and custom-blended with tiny threads of priceless silk. Even with Frankie now sitting on the hood of her car, looking like he was lounging seaside rather than annoying the hell out of her, Ian Blake's voice appealed to that shunted feminine part of her that loved a good rescue. The light had turned green, but the SUV hadn't moved—probably more interested in the show in the rearview mirror.

And just how did Ian Blake know what was happening to her on a busy West Tampa street? And how did he know Frankie?

"I don't suppose you have any brilliant plan for getting him off my ass? Or better yet, off my car?"

She turned her body, certain she didn't want Frankie reading her lips or guessing that she was up to her eyeballs in dangerous shit she still didn't understand. But with one phone call at the perfect time, the idea of working for Ian Blake grew even more appealing. Whatever job he wanted her for would undoubtedly take her out of town—and out of Frankie's vengeful reach.

"Your problem will be solved momentarily. In the meantime, we need to talk."

"Didn't I say I'd find you if I was interested?" She honked the horn. Frankie barely flinched and the SUV remained staunchly at a stop.

Blake sighed wearily. "A nice touch of bravado, Ms. Morales, but your claim was thoroughly impossible. You don't have the skills or contacts yet to find a man who doesn't want to be found. But if you come to work for me, you'll have a boundless opportunity to learn."

Marisela hooked the phone between her ear and shoulder, tearing off the minute an ambulance passed and the dark SUV finally cruised out of her way. Frankie's reflexes were agile, and as she'd known he would, he dismounted without getting himself run over.

She made a quick right at the intersection, then eased over the speed limit enough to create a distance between her and Frankie. By the time she glanced in the rearview mirror two blocks into her high-speed escape, he was nowhere to be seen.

"What do you want, Mr. Blake?"

"To discuss the details of my offer."

"I'm going to the beach."

"He'll find you there."

"We have a lot of beaches in the area, Boston-boy. No way will he know where I'm headed."

"I don't see why not. You really have only two choices, judging by the parking tickets you have collected over the years. Ben T. Davis or Clearwater Beach are your usual haunts, are they not? I suppose you could mix things up, head down to Sand Key for the first time in a long while, but the vibe there isn't really as social as you prefer, is it?"

Marisela, just about to turn onto the ramp at I-275, pulled instead down the access road, unnerved by the ease with which he'd delved into her life. At the first parking lot she saw, for a body shop, she stopped well out of sight from the road. She pointed at Lia so she'd remain in the car, then jumped out and slammed the door.

"You're thorough," she said, glancing over her shoulder as she marched a few feet away. Her friend was still white as a ghost, her arms braced on the dashboard as if her fear glued her palms to the cracked, vinyl surface.

"I'm consistently thorough when I'm in pursuit of something I want. Turn me down if you must, Ms. Morales, but don't delude yourself with thinking you can stay one step ahead of me or my associates. You can't. It reflects no weakness on your part. I am simply better equipped."

A few seconds later, a dark sedan identical to the one she'd ridden in last night parked not thirty yards away, on the opposite side of a bay where two mechanics were pounding out the dented side of a Ford truck. She didn't recognize the driver, but when the back window rolled down, she exchanged nods with Max, Ian Blake's right-hand man.

She couldn't contain an impressed grin. The man certainly knew how to illustrate his power. She wondered if his goons had taken care of Frankie, too, since he and his rusted Chevy were nowhere to be seen.

"Why are you following me? You obviously have my number. You could have just called."

"I'm on a bit of a time crunch, I'm afraid. I'd love to have the luxury of enticing you slowly into Titan, Ms. Morales, but I can't afford such seduction at the current time. So I'll cut to the chase."

The dollar amount he recited, double of what he'd promised last night, on top of his skillful use of words like *luxury* and *seduction* made Marisela drop her phone. Luckily, Lia had gotten out of the car and with quick reflexes, caught the cellular device before it crashed onto the asphalt.

But her friend didn't return the phone, even after Marisela stretched out her hand.

"Who are you talking to?"

Marisela snatched the phone from her friend and held the receiver to her breast. "If you don't want both of our asses kicked by guys who could easily dump our bodies where we'd never be found, get in the car. Now."

Terror froze Lia's eyes into a wide stare. Marisela stepped forward and gently laid her hand on Lia's arm. Her skin was clammy and hot, so she injected her friend with confidence courtesy of a wicked smile.

"*Chica,* we'll be fine. You just have to listen to me, okay?"

For some reason that Marisela had never been able to explain or understand since the day Sister Agnes placed Lia and Marisela at the same table in kindergarten, Lia trusted her. She managed a tiny nod, then sprung around to the passenger side of the car, got in, and buckled her seatbelt.

Marisela stepped back toward her car, opened her door, and leaned casually over the frame rather than sliding inside. No doubt, Max was reporting her every move to Blake. She didn't want to look like she was ready to take off.

"That's a generous offer, Mr. Blake. What am I supposed to do for this money?"

"Very simple. Rescue a missing child."

She laughed. No way was this guy altruistic. "How charitable of you."

"Charity has nothing to do with it, Ms. Morales. The girl's family is paying me a great deal of money to retrieve her from her father, a dangerous man who does not have legal custody. I will fill you in on the details once you accept my offer. You have to understand the value of discretion in these matters."

"The only thing I understand is the value of a dollar," she said, not sure her words were entirely honest. Marisela could always fire herself up with a benevolent cause. In such cases, her motto ran along the lines of the ends justifying the means. And while her outlook often landed her in trouble, taking the safe route in life often led absolutely nowhere except living with her parents and searching constantly for a perfect job that likely didn't exist.

Or maybe she'd finally found the ideal profession, in the least likely of places.

"I'm interested in your proposal, Mr. Blake, but I can't make a decision until I hear the details. In the meantime, you'll have to trust my ability to keep my mouth shut."

Marisela scanned the street and parking lot and saw no evidence that Frankie had followed after she'd ditched him at the light. Would he return to her parents' house and wait for her there . . . or did it matter, now that Blake's men were watching her back?

"In that case, we need to meet immediately."

She laughed. "Are you implying I can't keep quiet?"

"Do I have reason to believe otherwise?" he asked.

"Absolutely," Marisela responded. Keeping secrets and covering with lies was an art form to her. "But you'll have to trust me because I'm busy today. First, I have to bring my friend home and calm her down, which won't be so easy now that you've threatened to blow her up. I need time to smooth things over. If she blabs to my parents, your cover is blown. The last thing you need is the entire Morales clan descending on you like locusts, right?"

He cleared his throat. "I leave town on Sunday."

"Sunday it is. Where do you want to meet?"

"I'll have the directions delivered to your house."

The possibility of accepting the offer from Ian Blake added a swagger to her step that she hadn't realized was missing until right that moment. She waved at the guys in the sedan then practically hopped into her car seat.

"What do I bring with me?"

"Just your favorite workout clothes. Any weapons you prefer. We'll provide everything else you'll need, including a cover story for your parents."

"No shit? You're a full-service employer."

"We try to cover all our bases. Feel free to tell your parents about a job interview and training session you'll be attending in Boston for a Titan investigator position in our new Tampa office. As far as they are concerned, you'll be flown out Sunday morning and should return in two weeks. The trip is all expenses paid, of course."

"*Papi* will never believe it."

"I'm sure you can be convincing when properly motivated. When you return home later today, you'll find a packet of information on Titan's petty crimes division, as well as a flattering article from the *New York Times* on our part in exposing a major credit card fraud scheme. The indisputable facts will bolster your story."

Marisela started the car and did a U-turn so she could take an alternate route home. "I can tell my family that I work for Titan International?"

"Proudly. Our company has a long, respected history. Not all of our cases are featured in the public arena, but I think we'll pass your father's scrutiny. After you've convinced your family this opportunity is on the up-and-up, meet me at the arranged location and we'll complete the final phase of your recruitment."

"That sounds a little scary," she commented, though in all honesty, the possibilities excited her beyond belief.

Ian's chuckle on the other end of the line caused a field of gooseflesh over her bare arms. "Recruitment will be the easy part. Next comes training. Then, the mission."

After a brief good-bye, Marisela disconnected the call. Only after they were headed back toward her house did she even remember that the pale-faced woman in the seat beside her was her very best friend in the world.

"Marisela, what was that about?"

"A job. Looks like I finally have one."

"Doing what? Stunt driving?" Lia quipped.

Lying to her parents was one thing. Lying to Lia was something else.

"Stunt driving might be in the job description, actually," she answered. She wouldn't tell Lia about rescuing the kid—not until she had details.

"Who's your boss?" Lia asked.

"I can tell you that his sense of style is better than his sense of humor. He didn't mean his little threat, by the way."

At this, Lia let loose a string of curses that sounded more natural coming out of Marisela's mouth than her friend's.

"Marisela, this isn't funny. Those guys looked dangerous. For once in your life, *chica,* can't you follow a safer route?"

"Safer? And do what? Go back to working at Wal-Mart? Lia, I know you and my parents don't see it, but I actually have skills that other people will pay big money for."

"People like who? Criminals?"

"Well, the little stains on my record don't exactly make me appealing to the police academy. Besides, I think this guy is legit, relatively speaking. He owns a company called Titan International out of Boston. It's a top private investigation firm."

"And you know this because he told you?"

"I may be a fool about a lot of things, Lia, but I'm damned good at recognizing truths from lies. That claim is too easy to check out. In fact, instead of the beach, why don't we detour to your place? You can verify who he is for yourself."

Marisela knew just about every inch of Tampa, but the breezy, barren docksides near Rattlesnake Point was a whole new world. Just one day after she and Lia checked out Titan and decided they were for real, she turned into the cracked shell parking lot beside Riptide Marine and braced herself. From this point on, her old life would pale in comparison to what Titan offered. She couldn't wait.

Her tires crunched across the field, stirring up white dust that reflected off the Sunday morning sunshine. She'd had one day to put her affairs in order, as Blake had said, not so gently invoking the idea that she might not return home alive. The guy was slick, but could be painfully transparent. He wanted to intimidate her, possibly ensure her capitulation through the tried-and-true tradition of fear. Well, Marisela decided the first thing she'd do after she took his money was show him a thing or two about how she reacted when someone messed with her mind.

But right now, she had to concentrate on finding her way around this graveyard of rusted boats and dock equipment. She grabbed the map Ian had had delivered to her with the directions to their rendezvous point. For all her assets, Marisela's sense of direction sucked.

Once she'd traversed the junk yard, a monstrous warehouse loomed on the bleak landscape. She parked where Blake instructed her. The place looked entirely deserted. She turned off her engine and cracked her door, not surprised to hear a surly wind whistling across the warehouse's expanse of concrete and waxy glass.

From the trunk, she retrieved her gym bag, stuffed with her favorite sweats and lingerie, the only items her new boss had said she'd need. Of course, she'd also brought her favorite CDs, her must-have makeup, deodorant, nail polish, her gun cleaning kit, and last but not least, her gun, which technically wasn't in the bag, but safely tucked beneath her arm, hidden by the cropped denim jacket she wore over her hot pink halter. All identifying information—maxed out credit cards, driver's license, social security card—now lived with Lia, tucked away in her safety deposit box, along with a note to her parents and the police, just in case she didn't return from her first foray into covert operations.

She scanned the area with a scowl, her skin prickling with the sensation that something wasn't right. Slamming the car trunk, she shouldered her bag and climbed up the concrete stairs to the docking bays when a car engine revved behind her. Sand and shell shot into the air as tires spun in her direction.

For a moment, she squinted through her sunglasses trying to see who'd pulled in so fast, but the jolt up her spine told her to screw that and get the hell out of sight. The warehouse was long and open, with nothing but the bay doors to offer her haven— and the industrial-size padlocks wouldn't be giving way anytime soon. She turned, ran to the opposite end of the building and hurdled the railing to the ground below. The impact sent a hot jolt up her ankle, but the minute bullets sprayed across the building, denting the bay doors and crashing into the cement block, she had her weapon drawn.

The firepower from the car was semiautomatic. Nothing industrial like an AK-47. Was this another of Ian Blake's goddamned tests?

She shoved her bag beneath some underbrush, along with her anger and her fear. Right now, she had to concentrate on staying alive. She sped toward the back of the building, where the Inter-coastal waterway might provide an escape route. She spit out the grit coating the inside of her mouth and kept her back to the wall, her eyes darting behind her and in front of her, not knowing when or where to expect an attack.

She could hear the car spinning its tires in front of the building, the occupants whooping like kids pulling a prank. Thanks to a tall, chain-link fence, they couldn't get to her by following her route, not in the car anyway. But they could easily go around to the other side of the building and she'd be cornered.

Behind her, a man leaped to the ground precisely where she had, the black steel of a gun pointed in her direction. Adrenaline and self-preservation sent her running, feinting right and left just enough to make her a hard target to hit, but not enough to slow her down. Bullets screamed by, pinging off the building and exploding just behind the heels of her boots. She turned the corner in time to see the car that had followed her spin around the back of the warehouse. The front end crashed through a trio of metal drums, flinging them into the air like bowling pins.

Towers of metal crates, large enough to hold small cars, were stacked along the waterside. Marisela dove into the maze of enclosures, desperate for cover while bullets whizzed by.

One ripped through the sleeve of her jacket, searing her with white-hot pain and tripping her momentum. She swallowed a scream and shifted her weight so she didn't land on her injured arm. When she caught up to Ian Blake, she was going to rip his throat out. Where were his men? Where was he? Or were her attackers on his payroll yet again?

Bullets rent the steel and aluminum behind her. Marisela

struggled to catch her breath, boxed in by crates, her lungs squeezed by terror. Flattening herself to the crate's hot aluminum side, she gulped in air and checked the blood oozing from her bicep and soaking into her jacket. While the scorching pain of torn flesh watered her eyes, she trusted she would live, at least long enough to make sure she exacted a little payback on the *comemierda* who'd shot her.

She heard his footsteps before he whistled a sweet upbeat tune usually used to call a dog.

"Come on, baby. You can't hide. Your time is up."

The accent was unmistakable—too incredibly like her own to be someone who worked for Blake.

Marisela squeezed further into the maze of crates, one ear trained to hear if someone was approaching from the other side. This wasn't a test. This wasn't about Blake. Marisela could smell reality in the overpowering stench of her hunter's cologne.

She caught sight of a slim space between two crates across from her. In a dash, she folded herself into the suffocating darkness, willing her lungs to accept what little air she could give them, desperate not to pant and give herself away even when she brushed her wound and jolted her body with another explosion of pain. Not twenty yards away, where the crates opened up to reveal the hull of a large ship docked alongside the mooring, she could hear the continued whoop and victorious hollers of her stalker's *compadres*. She could, maybe, take this one. But what about the others?

She shook her head—forced away the treacherous thought of failure and focused on the here, the now. With one hand, she raised her weapon, prepared to kill or be killed.

Again.

This was wrong. She was supposed to meet Blake here. Where the hell was he?

"Come on, *puta*. We're just having fun. You know, we just want you to tell us where you put Nestor. He's our boy, you know. We can't let some bitch turn him in every time she needs new shoes."

Marisela grimaced. New shoes? Who was this asshole kidding? For the money she'd made bringing Nestor Rocha in, she could afford a whole fucking outfit.

She winced, certain she shouldn't joke about the dead, particularly when she'd pulled the trigger. She cleared her head and assessed the situation.

Apparently, his boys thought she'd only dragged him into custody somewhere. They weren't the brightest bulbs in the string of Christmas lights. Rocha had been gone for two days. Didn't they realize he would have made his one phone call by now?

She twisted her hips and wedged her shoulders between the walls of the crates for leverage, determined not to be taken down by such idiots. The minute she caught sight of a gun, she kicked out with her boot and sent the weapon flying. When he dived forward for his gun, she jumped out and kicked him hard in the small of his back, sending him flat to the ground.

She kept him there by jamming her gun into the exact spot where his spine met his skull.

"Don't," she warned, her eyes trained on the two inches between his fingers and his gun. She grabbed his hair and yanked back, glad to see the shells beneath their feet had sliced his cheek. Pain and fear could buy her the time she needed.

"You won't shoot me, you bitch."

She didn't have the time nor the inclination for a conversation and she had nothing to prove to this *pendejo*. The car that had been spinning around them now idled loudly, the passengers shouting for Miguelito to bring her out.

She pistol-whipped him to silence.

"Looks like you bought a few more hours of life, Miguelito," she whispered, then took his gun and proceeded forward, a deadly weapon in each hand.

"Two guns won't cut it, *vidita*. There are at least four of them out there, sniffing for your blood."

The voice twisted up her spine like a wild, determined vine. She didn't bother to turn around. Frankie Vega possessed an icy smooth timbre unlike that of any other man.

"Aren't they your *hombres*, Frankie?" she asked, careful not to move. "Did you come to help them out, maybe shoot me in the back?"

He chuckled, but she refused to let the sound relax her. She scanned her surroundings, but with less than two feet of space between the crates, a known enemy behind her and an unknown army of angry, possibly drunk Latinos seething for her blood somewhere around the corner not twenty yards away, she had nowhere to run or hide. She glanced up, but the crates were smooth and stacked three or four high.

"As much as I hate to admit it, I'm not here to shoot you, Marisela, I'm here to save you."

Footsteps chomped and skidded up ahead. Voices shouted in Spanish. Directions. Orders. They were coming for her. She spun to the side, pointing one gun in front of her—and one leveled on the threat that had snuck up from behind.

Frankie didn't have to move—his weapon, drawn and trained on her, glinted black in his leather-clad glove.

She swallowed, her legs quavering from a showdown she'd never intended to face today. "Make sure you tell my *Mami* how you saved me, okay?"

The corner of his mouth quirked beneath the thin strip of his moustache. "I will," he said, and then he fired.

Seven

SHE DIDN'T REALLY THINK he was going to shoot her. When crossed, Frankie Vega could be lethal, but if he'd wanted to kill her for what she'd done to him the other night, she'd be dead already. Instead, he fired at the *cabrón* with the .38 special who had just rounded the corner. Without a second glance at the jerk who'd dropped to the ground like a stone, Frankie shoved his gun in his waistband, hooked his hands together into a makeshift stirrup, and ordered Marisela to climb.

She hadn't thought there was space to move up the crates, but with Frankie's help, she hoisted herself out of the line of fire. The crates on top, slightly smaller than those on the base, allowed her a two-foot ledge to hide on. Before Marisela threw herself flat on the space between the two crates, the three gangbangers rushed to where their boy lay bleeding from a wound to his shoulder. With one glance at their injured buddy, three arms raised to fire.

Marisela twisted so she could fire blind, but one of the men yelled, *"¡Alto!"* stopping the violence before it began.

"Frankie? Frankie Vega? What the hell you doing here? Why'd you shoot Leo?"

Marisela willed herself completely still, lifting her face only enough to see the top of the three men's heads and a distorted, diagonal view of the action below. Frankie hadn't run with these boys for years. They had no loyalty to him and they outgunned him three to one.

"He came at me, José. Gun drawn. I didn't even know who he was. He's lucky I only popped him in the shoulder."

Judging by the guy's groaning, Marisela was fairly sure Frankie was right. Men on the verge of dying tended to stay relatively quiet.

"Why you here anyway?" José asked. "Where'd you come from?"

"I was looking for someone."

"That bitch, Morales? She grabbed Nestor, *¿comprendo?* He told us he had a line on paying her back for his stint in Starke, man, then he disappeared. Thursday night. We haven't seen him since. We think that *puta* got him locked up again and we gonna make her pay."

She heard Frankie sniff, as if the man's plea meant nothing to him one way or another.

"She ain't here."

"We followed her here, man!" a different guy objected. On the ground, Miguelito groaned. "We saw her."

"She's gone," Frankie said, emotionless.

Marisela heard someone cock a hammer on a gun. She hoped it was Frankie. God, she hoped it was Frankie.

"You let her go?"

"Put that away, *hombre*. I have no argument with you," Frankie said, his voice level and strong. "I didn't *let* her do anything. I'm here on business—my business. Not yours. Not hers. She left. End of story."

"She go on that fancy boat?"

"*Yo no sé*. But I don't think you want to follow her though, do you?"

From her perch, Marisela peered through a break in the tower of crates across from her and saw a large, luxury yacht tied to the dock, sparkling white with regal blue stripes slashing across the hull. She couldn't judge the full breadth of the vessel from this vantage point, but she could see what the gangbangers on the ground apparently could as well—a dozen men standing along the railing on several decks, armed with fierce looking automatic rifles.

About fucking time the cavalry showed up.

She rolled onto her back and waited while Rocha's boys gathered their injured men. Before they left, she heard Frankie speak to them, but she was too far away to hear his message. After they were gone, she braced herself against the burning pain in her bicep and lowered herself to the ground, straight into Frankie's waiting arms.

"You got shot."

She pushed away from his hot, musky scent and bone-melting tone. The last place she wanted to be right now was in

Frankie's powerful embrace. He might have saved her life just a few minutes ago, but he could easily change his mind and pay her back for her trick the other night.

"Just grazed me," she said.

"We'll see."

"Did you follow me, too, or was I only oblivious to one car trailing me?"

Frankie's subtle grin lessened the shooting pain in her arm. "You'll grow eyes behind your head soon enough."

"I used to have them," she spat, knowing she'd been so wrapped up in finding the marina that she'd left herself open to attack. She'd screwed up once. She wouldn't do it again.

"What did you tell them?" she asked.

"I told them you were gone."

"No, what did you tell them before they left?"

Frankie gestured toward the opening between the crates and Marisela had no choice but to follow. "They could hurt my family," she explained.

"They won't."

"How can you be so sure?"

"Because I told them Rocha was dead and that the crazy bastard deserved to die for double-crossing his boss, who happens to be the man who owns this yacht. I also told them that if one Morales family member so much as got a paper cut, I'd hunt all five of them down and slice their throats."

She nodded. Yeah, that ought to do it. Frankie never did beat around the bush.

"*Gracias,*" she said, then marched to a stop even as Frankie headed toward the gangplank that led up to the deck of the largest boat Marisela had ever seen, short of the cruise ships that docked in the Port of Tampa. "Wait a minute. How do you know what happened with Rocha?"

Frankie, juggling the guns he'd retrieved from the gang members, cursed and then threw all four weapons into the bay. Marisela had the fifth and followed suit, watching as the black snub-nosed sank to the bottom of the grayish, murky water.

"Cheap pieces of shit," Frankie said.

Marisela grabbed his wrist. "How did you know?"

He yanked away from her. "Damn, Marisela . . . haven't you figured it all out yet? You're supposed to be smart."

"Humor me," she snapped. She was in too much pain to think.

He rolled his eyes, stepped directly into her personal space and despite her squeal of protest, lifted her into his arms.

"I know because I'm the one who gave your name to Ian Blake. Welcome to Titan International, Marisela. I'm your new partner."

The armed sailors had disappeared by the time Frankie took one step on board. A good thing, since Frankie doubted Marisela would stay sedately in his arms if she knew other people were watching. He didn't doubt the woman couldn't board a frickin' multi-million dollar yacht without finding trouble. But he had no one to blame but himself for her presence. He'd given Ian Blake Marisela's name, even touted her quick-thinking and determined nature as a perfect combination for the job in Puerto Rico. If he'd kept his mouth shut, Marisela would not have killed Nestor Rocha, not yet anyway, and she definitely wouldn't have been shot.

Luckily for him, she didn't speak again until he'd squeezed them through the narrow door into his stateroom.

"You're shitting me, right?"

He laid her on the bed, then retrieved the first aid kit from the bathroom. He laid the kit on the bed beside Marisela and selected the surgical scissors first.

"Shitting you about what?" he asked.

She yanked her arm away, paying the price for her quick movement with a hiss of pain. "Cutting my jacket. Do you know how hard it is to find the perfect denim jacket? Bolero-style? In a size eight?"

He grabbed her sleeve and pulled, attempting to jab the sharp edge into the material so he could cut the denim away. "Check eBay next time."

"Fuck you," she snapped, scrambling to her feet and darting halfway across the room.

Coño. He really didn't have the patience for her attitude right now. If Frankie didn't gain control of the situation—and Marisela—quickly, all bets would be off when Ian Blake slid back into the picture. She was mad—and there was no negotiating with her when she was pissed off.

"You don't really want to go there with me, Marisela," Frankie warned. "Not now."

She wavered, despite her balanced stance. If the rusty stain on her jacket was a true indication, she'd lost a lot of blood. And seeing him again likely hadn't helped. Goddammit. Maybe if she passed out, he could dress her wound without dealing with any lip.

"I want to know what the hell is going on," she insisted.

"I'm trying to stop your bleeding. Two minutes ago, I was

hoping to take care of you before you fainted, but now, I'm thinking a little unconsciousness would be a good thing."

"Why? So you can cop a feel?"

At this, Frankie laughed. "Yeah, Marisela. That's it. Entertain yourself with that thought if the fantasy makes you feel important, but *verdad,* I've never stayed in such a nice room before. I'd rather you not bleed all over my carpet."

Furious, she took a step forward and nearly lost her footing. He caught her and helped her to the corner of the bed. She shook her head, but he knew the action wouldn't clear the fog from her brain as much as a good wound dressing and a belt of tequila.

"Why were you meeting me? Where is Blake?" she managed, forcing out the words while she stretched and gingerly unfolded herself out of her jacket.

"Blake's around. I told him I wanted to talk to you first. Before you boarded and heard him out."

"He told me not to talk to you."

"Yeah, well, after his goons picked me up, there was a change in plans."

She winced and hissed while he wiped away the blood, but otherwise contained her agony. He examined the wound as she balled the denim in her lap. It wasn't the worst gunshot he'd ever seen, but pain was pain. The bullet had torn a gulley through her skin, luckily leaving the muscle and bone unscathed. Too wide to stitch, she'd just earned herself another scar. Still, she'd recover relatively quickly, a good thing in their current circumstances.

He fished a square of cotton and gauze out of the kit, then doused the sterile pad with antiseptic.

"This might sting."

"It already stings."

He applied the sopping square to her arm. If not for the fact that he held her down with his other hand, she would have leaped right off the bed.

"Shit, Frankie!"

"I warned you."

"I ain't never been shot before."

"All those years with *las Reinas* and this is your first bullet?"

"It's an experience I tried to avoid."

"Smart thinking," he quipped.

"You think? Then why'd you get me into this?"

Her voice was barely a whisper, but her question punched through his chest and wrapped cold fingers around his heart. Did he really want to drag Marisela back into such a dangerous life? Did he have a choice?

No. Not any longer. From the minute she stepped foot on the deck of Blake's boat, the choice became entirely hers.

"You're right for the job."

"Tell me more about this kid I'm supposed to rescue."

He shrugged. "Not my place. Blake will fill you in on the details."

"Can you at least tell me why you thought I was so right for this work that I've had to face down killers for the second time since Thursday? How do you know Blake anyway?"

"From prison."

"Blake was in prison?"

He didn't like the way her voice sounded so disbelieving.

"Blake and Titan contract with the DEA, FBI, and CIA. They're a private investigation firm, but they're also independent contractors, so to speak."

"Mercenaries?"

"Nothing so skanky. They contract out their agents to do some of the dirty work the government can't. I was working a sting for the DEA when Titan sent operatives into the prison. They were my backup. I met Blake when he came in to check on his men."

Frankie gingerly lifted the saturated gauze and tossed it into a nearby garbage can. He applied a new strip, then directed her free hand to apply pressure while he fished out the rest of the supplies.

"I don't understand," Marisela said. "You were working with the DEA? You mean, you only went to prison to work undercover for the feds?"

Laughter burst from his gut. "Not by a long shot. I was one of the few guilty men in prison, *vidita*. Grand theft, assault, attempted murder. I did them all."

"Because of the gang," she said, attempting to rationalize, though why, he didn't have a clue.

Frankie had come to terms a long time ago with the fact that he didn't play by any rules except his own. He had no idea why he'd so easily gravitated away from the straight and narrow path his hardworking parents had charted for him, but he had no one to blame but himself. And he certainly hadn't gone to work for the feds out of any sense of good. Or more asinine, out of guilt. He'd worked for the feds because it beat staring at four walls twenty-three hours out of a day and provided a nice income for luxuries like cigarettes and deodorant.

"In the hole," Frankie explained, "the DEA sought me out, promised me a shorter stint if I helped bring down some asshole Columbian kingpin. I didn't have anything better to do, so I helped them out. They liked my work, so they started moving me from lockup to lockup, never keeping me in any joint long enough to get shanked or ratted out."

"You didn't mind being a snitch?"

"What the hell did I care? They never asked me for shit on my own boys. I was working the system."

"And after you got out?"

Frankie couldn't miss the expectation in her eyes. He glanced aside, hating the way one look from her reminded him of all the things he should say to her about his past, but couldn't.

"After I got out, I worked on the docks in Miami and kept my ears open. I did some more work with Titan when some Swedish smuggler set up shop in South Beach. After a while, I got bored, so I came home for a while, hoping to explore my options."

"By getting back in with *los Toros* and dealing drugs?"

"Don't fool yourself, Marisela. *Los Toros* were my boys. I called the shots, but I didn't want to be responsible for nobody else no more. I'd given up enough for the gang."

"Including me."

She didn't allow a wounded sound into her voice, but Frankie saw a glimmer of pain in her eyes that didn't stem from her injury.

"I had to do what I had to do, Marisela. You got out of the gang because you were tired of the life. Back then, I fed off the power, the violence."

Marisela glanced aside and inhaled sharply, handling her emotions with more control than he thought her capable. Or maybe, she just didn't give a shit anymore. "What do you feed off now?"

He grabbed surgical tape and more gauze and finished the last steps of dressing her wound. "The money. One more job and I can tell Ian Blake to stick his fancy organization up his ass. I'll be my own boss again. I'll answer to no one but me."

Voicing his dream out loud, even with spite searing his words, injected him with a euphoria more powerful than any drug he'd ever tried. He couldn't remember the last time he'd been truly in charge of more than what he had for dinner. For whatever naive reason, he'd thought his release from jail a few years ago would change his life, but the freedom had been just an illusion. He'd remained under the thumb of the DEA and NTSB, or whichever agency decided they needed him, addicted to the money they paid outside the joint—and the thrill. At first. But not anymore.

"Once you break with Titan, what are you going to do with all that free time?"

He shrugged. Beyond telling Blake to fuck himself, Frankie had no clue. "Haven't decided. What about you? You gonna work for Blake?"

"I don't know."

Frankie frowned. Once she heard the details of the mission, she'd likely break something in her haste to sign up. Marisela might be a ball-breaker, but she was still a woman.

"You're here because of me," he reminded her, wanting to make sure things were on the up and up. Not that she deserved the truth after what she'd pulled the other night, but after hearing the whole story from his mother and knowing everyone who loved him had been convinced he was jumping bail, thanks to Blake, he'd actually found Marisela's technique damn clever. "I'll stick around long enough to make sure you can still leave if you want to."

"Aren't you already signed on?"

Frankie growled. "Blake doesn't own me."

"Did you introduce him to Nestor Rocha?"

Frankie cursed. "Even I'm not that stupid. Everyone with ears knows that Rocha hated your guts. No, when I pulled a disappearing act on Blake, he decided he wanted you anyway. He knew I'd been in *los Toros,* figured whoever knew me knew you, so he found the gang. Nestor jumped at the chance to help him out."

"So he could kill me."

"After he raped you," Frankie reminded her.

Marisela half-grinned. "He should be so lucky. Now, he's dead. Is Blake why you were going to jump your bail?"

With a bitter laugh, he tossed the medical supplies back into the case and squeezed the clasps shut. "I wasn't going to abandon my parents, Marisela. You should have known that."

"I haven't seen you in ten years, Frankie. The last time we spoke, family loyalty wasn't exactly on the top of your list. I did what I had to."

Yes, she had. He had no doubt who'd leaked the news to his parents that Frankie was going to skip town. Ian Blake's power wasn't as far-reaching as he liked people to believe, but he could be a highly effective, manipulative pain in the ass when millions of dollars were on the line. The first minute Frankie had shown reluctance in accepting Blake's offer, the wheels had been set in motion. Blake and his operatives had set out to prove to Frankie that if he didn't pony up on their deal, he'd land right back in jail, courtesy of drugs planted in his car. Just as easily, Blake had retained the hotshot lawyer who wrangled his release in less than five minutes. For now, Frankie was in—no matter what he told Marisela.

"After the *pendejada* with Rocha, you still want to hear what Blake has to say?"

Marisela narrowed her eyes, clearly trying to pick up a clue from his expression, which he was careful to keep guarded. She had to make this decision for herself. His opinion of Marisela's potential effectiveness as a partner had not changed. With her on his side, they could complete this mission and he could milk Blake for the last cash injection he needed to kiss this life good-bye forever. She was smart and fast, and wouldn't screw him over unless he screwed her over first.

"Your old homeboys tried to kill me, Frankie, not Blake. And as for Rocha, he would have hunted me down at some point, so I'm just glad Blake's guys were there to clean up the mess. The only thing your rich friend has done for me so far is make my bank account fatter than it's ever been—and that's just a good faith deposit. My family is safe, thanks to you, and I've got a shot at something. . . ."

Her voice trailed off. She likely had no clue the level of danger their assignment would entail. And he wasn't entirely sure he wanted to tell her.

"Something what? This isn't the movies, Marisela. This isn't fake bullets or cartoon bad guys. This is the real world. I don't know if you're ready."

He cursed the minute the words spilled from his lips. *Shit.* Determination flashed in her eyes like fireworks.

She stood, tossed the bloodied jacket onto the bed and marched to the door, which she wrenched open with a powerful tug. "I'm up for anything you're up for."

Frankie clucked his tongue, certain the condescending sound would keep her from leaving. "Your competitiveness could get you killed, Marisela."

She spared a glance at her bandaged arm, then leveled her stare at him. "So could your cockiness, Frankie. Why don't we give this a go and see which one of us comes out alive?"

Eight

MARISELA RAISED HER FIST, but stopped mid-knock. She stared at the door—a plain, simply white slab of wood—and recognized the significance. She was about to walk into a whole new world. The shivers racking her body since her conversation with Frankie had subsided to barely noticeable quivers, but the emotional fallout of Frankie's long-standing involvement with Ian Blake would have to wait.

She focused on the essential information, starting with Blake wanting her enough for this operation to make a generous deposit in her bank account. The cash she'd withdrawn for emergencies prior to heading to the dock scratched at the tender skin of her left breast. But money wouldn't buy her out of trouble—instead, the lure of real life-and-death excitement was dragging her in.

She expelled a frustrated breath. Memories of her initiation into *las Reinas* flashed in her brain, causing her to lift her uninjured right arm and turn her hand so the tattoo on her wrist blazed like black fire. She'd been so young, so desperate for control over her life, hungry for danger and adventure. Was she headed in the wrong direction again for the same damned reason?

She had to hear Ian out before she made her choice, but deep down, she suspected the details didn't matter.

She wanted in.

She banged on the door, but didn't wait for a response before she charged inside. If she was rude, too bad. Nearly getting creamed by five hoods with loaded weapons tended to screw up her manners.

"Ms. Morales," Blake said, standing. Goddamn, but the man was stunning in a light colored linen suit, shirt, and tie that captured the sunlight pouring in from the windows. The crystal clear glass reflected nothing of the ugly warehouse or crates outside. Just the peacock blue sky.

"I'm pleased to see your injury isn't serious."

"No thanks to you or your heavily armed men. What took them so long to ride to the rescue?" She stomped over to his desk, rage propelling her forward. Handblown glass winked at her from a decanter filled with what she guessed to be a very expensive single-malt Scotch. "Seems to me your boys could use a little lesson in teamwork."

He arched one eyebrow, and then whispered to Max, who stood ever-present and oddly invisible at his side. The man sure could blend. Max nodded and moved to leave, but not before giving Marisela a quick once-over.

Was that respect she saw in his colorless eyes? She heard Max
close the doors behind them, but she didn't turn, determined to
retain eye contact with Ian Blake. She'd arrived at the showdown. How he responded to her questions—or how he avoided
straight answers—would make the difference in her decision.

Yeah, she wanted the money and she craved the excitement
and a chance at a job she could sink her teeth into—but she
couldn't very well enjoy her success if she was dead because her
boss double-crossed her.

"I can see how you would believe that Titan operatives don't
work well together. But you must understand that since our debacle the other night at your home, I've opted to take Mr. Vega's
lead on all matters pertaining to you. Perhaps your ire should be
directed at him."

His glance over her shoulder diverted her attention behind
her. Frankie leaned against the closed door, silent as a statue.

"You're not fooling anyone, Mr. Blake. You're calling the
shots here," Marisela said as she turned back to face the Brit.

His grin bordered on indulgent, which injected her blood
with the hot fire of intense annoyance. This man could push
her buttons with just an expression—and she suddenly suspected that had been his intention all along.

He tugged at his slacks and eased into his calf's leather chair,
inviting her to sit with the curve of his hand. She hooked her
thumbs in the belt loops of her low-riding jeans and waited for
his reply.

"You're entirely right, Ms. Morales. Mr. Vega is currently in
my employ, so the ultimate responsibility for your skirmish
today is in my hands. However, I must say, you handled yourself beautifully."

"If I thought this was another one of your tests, Mr. Blake, you'd be dead right now."

"If I thought you had real reason to kill me, I would have directed someone in my employ to confiscate your gun before you barged into my office. But as it is, you are still armed and I'm still in charge, so let's not ruin what we've established between us with empty threats."

She tilted her weight onto one hip. "So far, all we've established is a quick exchange of cash. What I want to know now is the specifics of this rescue mission, with all the details, start to finish."

Marisela glanced back at Frankie, but he stared straight forward, his gaze lost in the bright blue sky visible through the generous windows behind Ian Blake. His expression revealed nothing—not what he knew, not what he didn't know.

Suddenly, the room darkened. Marisela turned to see Blake engage a series of buttons that operated the window shades, blocking all light from outside, while a screen dropped from the ceiling.

Instinctively, she slipped into the nearby chair just as a photograph, a candid shot clearly taken from a distance, materialized on the screen.

"This is Javier Perez. He's a Puerto Rican national, born in San Juan on March 23, 1961. His father, Roberto Perez, operated a small hotel near Old Town in San Juan. His mother, Maria, ran the laundry and directed the housekeeping staff until her death in 1970. Roberto died ten years later, leaving the business, now a burgeoning hotel and resort catering to the elite, in Javier's hands."

The photograph changed. The subject was still Javier, but

now he was standing proudly in front of an illuminated hotel sign proclaiming the grand reopening of *Casa de la Mar.*

"*Casa de la Mar* is a five-star resort, complete with a world-class golf course and a casino that rakes in millions every night. Perez turned out to be quite the entrepreneur and the resort has allowed him to mingle with an incredibly diverse group of people."

The next picture, black and white and grainy as if repro-duced from a newspaper, showed a young couple frolicking on a sandy beach. The man was undoubtedly a younger Javier, in his twenties, with his shoulder-length curly hair tied back, his arms possessively encircling a strikingly thin young woman with cool, seductive eyes.

"Who is that?" Marisela asked. "Movie star?"

"Socialite," Ian answered. "Elise Barton-Ryce, though at the time, she was Elise Michele Barton. She spent her summer after finishing school in Puerto Rico at Perez's resort. Javier was twenty-five. Elise was seventeen. They had a wild affair. The so-ciety columnists of the time reported every salacious detail."

Marisela eyed Ian warily. "You mean like the tabloids?"

"Have you been to Boston, Ms. Morales?"

"You know I haven't," she sniped.

The left side of his mouth tilted up in a grin. "Yes, I do. You've never left Florida. Your travel experience will change soon enough. As you might have guessed, I was born in Lon-don, but spent a good deal of my formative years with my mother's family in Massachusetts. In Boston, polite society rules and they have their say in the legitimate press. At the time, Elise's dalliance was not exactly headline news, but gossip abounded. Unfortunately, this affair had long lasting effects."

Marisela wondered briefly why this mysterious man would offer personal information about himself, then figured he was trying to gain her trust. Couldn't blame him. But when the picture changed, this time showing a very poised, very posed portrait of an absolutely adorable baby decked out in yards of lace and ribbon, her attention was diverted. Marisela had to bite her lip to keep from cooing at the angelic little face. Not that Marisela saw herself having one of her own anytime soon, but she loved children. She always had. She figured it was cultural. In her neighborhood, even little girls who played cork ball in the streets with the boys or sported switchblades in their back pockets turned into *mamacitas* whenever babies were around.

"This is Jessica Margaret Barton, born April 2, 1988."

Marisela saw a certain darkness in the skin tone she hadn't noticed before. "Javier's kid?"

"Yes, though Elise didn't realize she was pregnant until she'd returned to Boston. When Russell Barton, her father, discovered her condition, he ordered a thorough background check into his daughter's lover. At this point, Javier was already dabbling in industries beyond the hotel—including the one that produces his income today. He's an arms dealer. Very rich and very dangerous."

A chill sneaked up Marisela's spine. "And he wants his daughter back?"

Ian chuckled. "Javier Perez is not our client. Elise Barton-Ryce is. She tried to keep her condition a secret, but too many of the Boston elite vacationed in Perez's resort. He found out about his daughter and tried to establish visitation. He was denied. Two years later, Jessica was kidnapped from her nursery. My father, who started Titan, worked on the original case.

They traced the baby to Javier Perez, but were unable to recover her."

Marisela watched Ian out of the corner of her eye. She witnessed no sign of disappointment or even the slightest hint of
irritation. He told the tale with cool professionalism, as if he
cared about nothing except dispensing the facts. So why did her
gut tell her differently?

"Perez lives in Puerto Rico, right? That's a U.S. Territory.
Why didn't the feds just go in and take the baby back, charge
Perez with kidnapping, and lock him away where he couldn't
sell any more cheap .38 specials?"

Ian's eyebrow arched. Undoubtedly, he was surprised by her
knowledge of the law—and of basic geography. Well, fuck him.
Just because earning her high school diploma had been a mon-
umental pain in the ass didn't mean she was uneducated.

"Perez vacated his home in Puerto Rico and ran the operation from various locations in South and Central America. For
several years, he avoided extradition to the United States. His
travel also gave him powerful contacts with terrorists and freedom fighters he might not have ever met otherwise. His arms
dealing business multiplied until he became one of the most
powerful suppliers of illegal weaponry in this hemisphere. I
doubt he deals in .38 specials."

Marisela shifted in her seat. Talk about a dangerous initiation into the world of international intrigue.

"Where is Perez now?"

"On his way to Miami for a meeting with his U.S. suppliers."

Marisela sat up. "His first trip to the States?"

"Not quite. Elise married not long after the kidnapping. Her new husband discouraged her from searching for her daughter and even pressured the authorities to forget about the warrants for Perez's arrest."

"Why?"

Ian shrugged. "That's unclear. About ten years ago, Javier moved back to Puerto Rico without incident. He owns most of the authorities down there, though he lives on a private island just off of Puerto Rico. Because Elise dropped the kidnapping charges earlier, the government refuses to expend the manpower and resources to intervene in a muddy custody dispute."

Ian changed the picture. Clearly shot from a distance, the photograph showed a young, dark-haired teenager flanked by bodyguards. The shot wasn't clear enough for Marisela to see a resemblance between the teen and the baby, but she figured a seventeen-year-old on an island of gunrunners wouldn't be hard to pick out.

"Elise recently divorced," Ian continued, "and she has renewed her efforts to retrieve Jessica before she turns eighteen. Elise still has legal custody, but she has no idea what lies Javier has told Jessica about why she has no mother. She wants to plead her case before her daughter has the legal right to—"

"—tell her to go to hell?"

That was from Frankie, who so far, had done nothing but lean against the door.

Ian frowned, animosity reaching the center points of his eyes. Marisela caught sight of Ian's hand, which had tightened into a ball.

Frankie looked no less angry, his hands pressed into his jacket so tightly, Marisela wondered if his fists were going to rip through the pockets.

Okay. Anger crackled between the two men, yet neither one breathed a word of discord. What was that about?

Ian tore his gaze from Frankie and focused his attention on her, his calm demeanor forced, but absolute.

"We have no idea how Jessica will react to her mother, but all our evidence so far points to a potentially joyous reunion."

Suddenly, Max was beside Ian, causing Marisela to yelp. She glanced aside, embarrassed, while the mysterious Max handed Ian a manila folder, which he presented to Marisela. Inside was a letter, written in what was obviously a child's hand. Marisela had to read no more than the first few lines to know that the child wanted her mother.

Dear Mommy,
Where are you? I miss you. Why haven't you visited me?

She flipped the file shut and held it over her shoulder, but Frankie waved the papers away. He likely didn't give a damn about the emotions of the case—which is precisely why Marisela didn't read beyond that first impassioned plea. She couldn't let her heart make this decision. Not when her life would be at stake in an arms dealer's nasty, violent world.

"So our job is to retrieve Jessica in Miami?" she asked.

"Not exactly," Ian replied.

"Then what exactly?" Frankie didn't even try to keep the irritation out of his voice.

He pushed off from the wall and stormed to Ian's desk. Slamming his palms flat on the polished teak, Frankie leaned forward just enough so his dark eyes were level with Ian's cool blue.

"Tell her straight, Blake. She needs to know what she's putting at risk. She needs to know she has a lot to lose."

Ian cleared his throat, but Marisela saw his spine harden, as if he'd rather die than back down one inch to Frankie's rough demand.

"In Miami, you'll infiltrate Perez's organization and finesse an invitation to his private enclave in Puerto Rico. Once there, you will contact Jessica, take her, and then utilize one of five exit strategies my team has created for a clean escape back to the mainland. Once you reach Florida with Jessica in your custody, I have assurances from the federal government that they will enforce the custody order Elise compelled the court to issue after the kidnapping."

Marisela listened, her mind swirling as she sought to put all the pieces together. "You want us to steal her back?"

"Yes."

"From an international arms dealer who has access to an arsenal equal to the United States Army?"

"Probably better than the U.S. Army, truth be told."

"And we'll be undercover?"

"Clearly," Ian answered. "Several Titan operatives will be on call as backup. Some of my best people are already in Miami setting down the groundwork. But this operation depends on you and Frankie. Perez trusts no one and he trusts non-Hispanics even less. We have created a cover for you that will at least garner you a face-to-face introduction. Once you're in, the rest of the team will follow your lead. You have two weeks to retrieve the girl. One week to train, one week to complete the mission. That's our time frame."

Marisela listened carefully, but her attention had not strayed

far from Blake and Frankie's standoff. Neither man had moved
an inch, save for the occasional twitch of the eye or tick in the
jaw. It was a real, old-fashioned Wild West showdown, without
the guns or the hot, noon sun.

Bored with their testosterone-enhanced animosity, Marisela
grabbed Frankie by the back of his jeans and tugged him away
from the desk.

"I need a few minutes to think," she said. "Just me and
Frankie."

Ian stood. "Of course." He glanced at his watch. "The
Oceanus must depart in no less than one hour."

Marisela nodded. "One hour it is."

"Please, avail yourself of anything in my office that will
make your stay more pleasant."

"Wait!" she said, suddenly wishing Blake hadn't ordered
her to leave her cell phone so she could call Lia and tell
her . . . what? That some rich dude on a yacht bigger than
city hall wanted her to go undercover with Frankie and steal
back the daughter of a man who sold rocket launchers and
surface-to-air missiles to killers like Osama bin Laden? Not
likely. "I left my bag on the side of the warehouse, stuffed
under the—"

"—already been retrieved," Max replied. "I had the steward
leave your bag in your stateroom."

The boss and his manservant left, closing the door behind
them. Frankie crossed his arms and stared at her, as if he expected her to make a decision instantaneously.

"I want in," she said.

"Of course you do."

She stretched, wincing when she raised her injured arm too

far over her head. "Why do you say that as if you know every-thing about me?"

"Because I do. Marisela, I know you think you're a different person now, but you aren't. You saw that baby and you wanted to scoop her in your arms and play dress-up for three hours."

"So? I like babies."

"This one ain't no baby no more, don't forget that."

"She's still a child stolen from her mother."

He nodded. "That's true. But don't sign on to this mission because you think it's a good cause. Don't sign on because you think your life is boring and this is just the thrill you need. And don't sign on for the money."

She stepped back, her eyes wide. "Then why the hell should I sign?" she asked, annoyed that he'd figured out her motiva-tions so easily.

A grin spread over his face, a bright curve amid dark, swarthy skin. "So you can be with me for the next two weeks."

She opened her mouth to tell him to go fuck himself, but re-alized she'd used that parting shot with him once already, with no discernable affect on his big head and cocky attitude. In-stead, she matched his smile, then sidled up to him and slid her good hand around his waist. "Ooh, Frankie. What girl could re-sist a temptation like you?"

Frankie laughed. "You."

"Damn straight. And don't you forget it."

"So, Max, think she's in?"

Ian eased onto the leather couch in his stateroom, giving a cursory glance out the porthole as the crew prepared the *Oceanus* for voyage. If Marisela Morales didn't agree to join this mission, there would be no need for a slow trip to Miami so she and Vega could train. In fact, if she didn't agree, there'd be no mission at all.

The current scheme to inject Marisela and Frankie into Javier Perez's dark world of violence and retribution had only a sixty-seven percent chance of success, according to his top operatives. The scheme exceeded their normal risk-ratio, but these weren't normal circumstances. The generous retainer would solve only part of his problem. The profit margin on this operation would be tight, in light of his current financial situation. He needed the million dollars Elise Barton-Ryce had offered to find and retrieve her missing child—and the additional two million she'd extract from her trust only after young Jessica was safe in her mother's arms.

Ian snorted. Safe wasn't the word he'd associate with a viper like Elise. The poor kid was probably going from bad to worse—but that wasn't his concern.

For now, he had only Marisela on his mind.

"She wants to take the offer," Max said, depositing a glass of iced Scotch on the table beside Ian before beelining for the computer on Ian's desk. He keyed in a few codes, then waited while a complicated schematic crisscrossed the screen. Max was a man of many talents, but give him something to blow up, he was like a child with a Gameboy. Ian didn't know if he was reviewing the blueprints to Perez's jet or triple-checking the controlled explosion Titan would detonate in Miami to further their cause. Either way, he toyed and fiddled every spare moment with every piece of information they'd gathered, upping his knowledge and perspective the way gamers accumulated points and higher levels.

"What makes you so confident about our newest operative?" Ian asked. Even though Max was only a decade older than Ian, the man possessed a wisdom that Ian had come to rely on, as if those ten years between them had been stuffed with a half-century of knowledge, experience, and heartbreak.

"Why would she say no?" Max replied, his brow arched as if the answer were so simple, he didn't know why they were bothering to discuss the matter.

"She might be killed."

Max shrugged, then slid his finger on the touch screen to change the perspective of the plans he'd been studying for over a week. "She strikes me as a very resourceful woman."

Ian seized his Scotch. "Resourceful women can die."

"So can you. So can I. We all make our choices, Mr. Blake. Sometimes, death is beyond our control. Doesn't matter if you're in the middle of a war zone or crossing the street."

Max's nonchalance came as no surprise. What alarmed Ian was not his assistant's assessment of Marisela and her courageous nature—he concurred—but that he couldn't shake a disconcerting sense of dread on the woman's behalf. Why did he care if she lived or died? He didn't make a habit of sacrificing his people for the bottom line, but most came out alive. Most, but not all. Still, they knew the potential risks. He imagined that each and every one of Titan's field agents had signed up precisely for that edge of excitement that challenged Fate to do her worst.

Marisela was the same as the rest.

The same, and yet entirely different.

She wasn't a former cop. She wasn't a former spy. And she only had a week to train for an assignment that none of his best people were qualified to handle. And yet, somehow, she'd gotten under his skin.

The woman was a walking testament to temptation. She dressed a little raunchy and swayed her hips with attitude, demonstrating that she could bring any man to his knees, any time. Unlike other females in Ian's not so distant past, Marisela Morales didn't hide who she was. She was right there—in his face, her sensuality too potent to ignore.

But if he had any sense, he'd turn away right now. Stick to business. Strictly business.

"Are Dionysus and Pan in Miami?" he asked.

"They've made contact as directed," Max answered, his fingertips flying over the keyboard. "Perez expects his assassins in one week."

Ian nodded. One week. If she agreed. The future of his company once again rested in the hands of a beautiful woman—only this time, Ian would be prepared. He'd learned his lesson with Eris. Betrayal wouldn't sneak up on him. Not this time. Not ever again.

Nine

"I CAN TAKE YOU, you know that, right?"

Frankie's inky gaze pierced Marisela's from only a few inches away. His lashes captured the sweat dripping down from his hair and her senses swam from the scent—decidedly male and infinitely determined. He had her exactly where he wanted her—and she could blame no one but herself.

"You could try," Marisela countered brashly, her own skin glistening, the moisture adding a barely perceptible slip to her position on the mat. Her arm, treated by the Titan physician, ached, but the liquid bandage and cloth wrappings held firm. Frankie had her pinned to the mat, her wrists shackled in his iron-banded hands. He'd gotten the drop on her for the first time in three days and the triumphant look in his eye guaranteed he wouldn't release her any time soon.

He shifted his body so that his trim abs slid over hers, his legs locked across her knees so that she couldn't move. She supposed she should feel embarrassed about falling victim to his attack, but she wasn't so sure she didn't appreciate her position. Frankie Vega might be an arrogant, infuriating prick most of the time, but he pulled the attitude off with such delicious style.

"And now that I have you," he said, his stare sweeping down her body with pure sexual appreciation, "what am I going to do with you?"

She arched an eyebrow. "You could try to seduce me, but you'd need your hands for that." She tugged at his hold, but barely managed an eighth-inch of movement.

"I don't know. My tongue is fairly talented, remember?" He swiped a lick over her lips and an electric current shot straight into her veins. Oh, yeah, she remembered his tongue. Intimately. "Besides, if I let go, you'll try to kick my ass for dropping you."

"There's that 'try' again."

He chuckled, hot and deep-throated, like the bass undertones of a sensual Spanish ballad, right before the guitarist increased the tempo to a frenetic pace. Baritone and primitive, the sound rippled through her, igniting the tickle in her belly that she'd been fighting since she'd signed on with Titan.

Frankie had warned her that working for Titan wouldn't be like the movies, but nothing she'd experienced so far convinced her otherwise. She was cruising to Miami on a two hundred-foot luxury yacht with gold-leafed fixtures in the bathroom, feasting on the most delicious, exotic foods she'd ever tasted and training with a man whose sexuality shimmered off him just like his sweat—raw and plentiful.

Besides, the most dangerous thing she'd encountered so far was Frankie and his magnetism. And now that he had her trapped, alone, in a main dining room that had been converted into a world-class gymnasium with sweet sea air teasing her nostrils and the vibrations from the engines and the waves rocking beneath her, she wasn't so sure she wanted to escape.

"Enjoying yourself?" she asked, sliding one leg free. "Because I'm getting bored."

Frankie grinned, then stretched languidly over her, making sure every inch of her body made contact with his and diverting her countermove. What had started as a practice session of kicks and punches had turned from purely physical to innately personal.

Training-wise, Marisela deserved a taste of this prone position for letting her guard down. She knew better, but he'd worn down her resistance. For three days, they'd been together nearly every minute—it wasn't entirely surprising that their old rhythms had reemerged. In the mornings, they ran laps around the deck, catching up on the gossip from the neighborhood. In the afternoons, they swam in the lap pool, pushing the limits of endurance. After lunch, they punched the bags and weight-trained, awakening muscles Marisela hadn't used in a while. At night, they studied codes and code names and acquainted themselves with the highly technical gadgets and gizmos dispensed to all Titan operatives. They also memorized the life and times of Javier Perez from the scant information other investigators already in the field had gathered through secondary sources and long-distance observation.

She and Frankie would be the first agents to infiltrate the arms dealer's organization. Yet despite their intense preparation, the key factors of this mission were still one big fat unknown. With so much going on, could Marisela be blamed for failing to resist a man that she'd found irresistible since puberty?

"I could think of more interesting things to be doing while on top of you," Frankie mused, writhing against her, "but you aren't ready yet." He straddled her and sat up, but didn't release her hands.

"Not ready?" she asked, disbelieving. "For what? For sex? Try 'not interested.' Been there, done that. Last week, as a matter of fact."

"I haven't forgotten," he said, his voice a throaty growl. "And believe me, *vidita,* neither have you."

No, she didn't suppose she had. "Is this your revenge?"

"Not by a long shot. I'm just taking a breather, wondering how long I can stand to feel you so wild and willing beneath me."

That did it. Frankie could tease and antagonize her all he wanted, but calling her willing went one step too far.

She bucked once to throw off his balance, then a second time to plant her feet close to her lifted knees. With the power of her hips, she twisted, unlocking her wrist from his grip. She dipped under his arm and threw her weight over his until he was the one with his back to the mat.

Ordinarily, she'd finish this move with a head butt and a knee to the groin. Instead, she kissed him.

Their mouths were salty, their lips tinged with the moisture of perspiration, power drinks, and desire. His tongue slashed into her mouth with hungry power and she matched his ravenous need taste for taste. Though she'd placed her hands firmly on his shoulders, he could have easily moved out of her way. But he hadn't—and she was glad.

Her spandex workout pants strangled her blood flow as the throbbing between her legs intensified. The telltale trickle of sensual cream seeped from her sex, announcing in no uncertain terms that she wanted Frankie physically even if her heart and her brain ordered her to back down. Ever since that night in the club, she'd experienced a powerful lust she wasn't sure she wanted to fight anymore. Not when there were so many other things to rail against.

He yanked his face away. "What's this?"

"A kiss, *cabrón.*"

"You just said, been there, done that."

"Don't you know when I'm just trying to be tough?"

His grin stoked the fire burning deep in her belly. "Yeah, I do."

She sat up on her haunches and despite the way the sports bra adhered to her skin, she yanked it over her head, freeing her breasts to his appreciative gaze. Her nipples were dark and hard and practically crackled for his touch.

"Let's go, then," she said. There was only one way to douse this flame. The old-fashioned way.

Frankie chuckled, but spread his hands benignly over her midsection. Then, in slow, possessive strokes that aroused her at the same time that they kept her at arm's length, he proved how talented his hands truly were. "Just like that, you want to screw me?"

"Why not? You want me," she said, leaning slightly forward so her nipples tantalized him from above. "I want you. What's stopping us?"

"Maybe good sense is stopping us," he guessed, pulling himself up until they sat face-to-face, legs entwined. "For once."

His words countered the message of his fingers, which tangled into her ponytail and freed her hair.

Her shoulders melted into her spine as he combed through the heavy strands. The residual soreness from the pounding her muscles had endured faded, replaced by the hazy half-awareness of sexual need. She guessed this might not turn out the way she wanted. Frankie was teasing her mercilessly so that when he pulled back, her frustration level would shoot through the roof.

She knew, but she didn't care. She had nothing to lose, but one hell of a good time to gain if she turned the tables.

"You're right," she murmured. "We shouldn't." With a stretch and a shift, she rubbed against his erection, invoking a strangled groan from deep in his chest. "We're working together now. I suppose it wouldn't be professional to get involved again after all this time, even just to feed our sexual urges."

She braced one hand on his shoulder, but with the other traced a tight circle around his nipple. Her nails tangled with the hair curling around the slick, dark knot, flashing red and sharp against his swarthy skin.

"You're driving me crazy," he admitted.

"That's the idea, isn't it?" She breathed the words against his skin as she traced a path of languid, liquid kisses up his pec to his shoulder, where she nipped him oh-so-lightly.

"You don't know what you're starting."

She continued her exploratory line of kisses across his shoulder to his neck. God, she loved how he tasted—hot with the elemental flavors of salt and skin. "Maybe not, but I know what I'm ending."

Mouth to mouth, their kiss breathed insatiable need into the desire arcing between them. Tongues clashed and dove and stroked.

He flipped her over and made quick work of removing her pants and thong. She managed a clear thought long enough to snatch her leggings out of the air when he tossed them aside. She'd prepared for this moment. As he stripped out of his tank top and tight biker shorts, she removed a condom from the tiny pocket that had been pressed against her hip all day, a constant reminder for the last twelve hours that she intended to seduce Frankie. Today.

With a magician's skill, he palmed the foil square. "We both had physicals yesterday, ¿sí? You have that patch thing. We don't need no rubbers. Besides, I'm not quite ready for what you want. Yet."

He was right about the clean bills of health and her birth control choice, but he was wrong about everything else—especially her ability to wait. "Think you're going to be a big tease or something?" She eyed his erection boldly. "You're ready now."

He shook his head, crawling across the mat until he was over her again, the muscles in his arms and legs undulating like the sinews of a large, ravenous cat.

"A hard-on is only part of the deal. I can get one of those just from looking at you. You do want me to do more than look, right?"

Flashes of their night together in his room over his mother's garage played in her mind. Not of how she'd handcuffed him to the bed, but how he'd brought her to orgasm with only his mouth—and left her completely and totally wanting more.

He desired revenge, but he probably didn't realize that his

retribution had been slashing into her ever since she'd turned her back on him and left him to deal with his parents.

Every moment in Frankie's presence, every touch while sparring, every laugh he'd tricked out of her was like another bite of a delicious, forbidden meal. The time for fasting was over.

"You can do whatever you want to me, Frankie, so long as in the end, you make me come."

His tilted grin assured her she had nothing to worry about. His first kiss, right between her legs, proved he was a man of his word.

The first orgasm racked her body only seconds after he plied his teeth and tongue to her sensitive labia and thrumming clit. He parted her with his fingers, delving deep into her sex, coaxing her to sensual overload with a dozen dirty phrases, all in Spanish, all speaking to the part of her soul she kept hidden behind a dozen types of armor. He flipped her onto her stomach, massaged her buttocks and spine then slipped his hands beneath her to pluck and arouse her breasts. Addicted to his skill, she lifted onto her hands and knees, desperate to give him more room to ply his trade. He chuckled triumphantly as she moved into what she remembered was his favorite position—and for today, she didn't care. He could have her any way he wanted her, so long as he didn't wait any longer.

But he did. The son of a bitch stroked her and played her, cooing kisses against her *culo,* stretching his strong chest over her back and slapping her with his thick sex. Her body wept for his and even when he pressed the head of his erection against her slick folds, he resisted the urge to drive inside her, even when she begged.

"Not yet, baby. There's so much I want to do to you. So much I want to see you do to me."

She read his mind and using a move not unlike the one that had laid her out flat on the mat a few minutes ago, she flipped Frankie with a thud, followed by a chorus of laughter that spurred her even farther. She'd begun her taste of him earlier, but the appetizer left her unsatisfied. Following the erotic path laid out by the hair coiling in a slim line from his chest to his groin, she explored until his erection teased her chin.

Flavors exploded on her tongue—bold and piquant. Coupled with the texture of his taut flesh over hard muscle, Marisela nearly devoured him. He'd tangled his fingers in her hair and begged her to never, ever stop.

But she had to. Her lungs screamed for unhampered air and she pulled away, her eyes nearly blinded by the light she hadn't realized until now surrounded them. Windows banked the wall on either side and despite the tinting, she suspected the crew on deck might have witnessed them getting it on.

The thought gave her pause, but Frankie instantly pushed her into fast forward the moment she realized he was ready to finish what they'd so frantically started. She struggled for words, but Frankie took a moment's pity on her and covered her mouth with two gentle fingers while he guided her onto the mat and kissed her until she forgot everything except reaching the end of this crazy, wild ride.

The minute he slid inside her, Marisela's brain burst into a million shards of light. Hard and thick, his sex melded with hers in one fluid glide, followed by a series of strokes that pushed both of them over the precipice. They collapsed onto the ground, panting more than either of them had during the height of their workout. Marisela found herself spent and exhausted—and oddly clearheaded.

She'd just screwed her ex-boyfriend, with the expressed purpose of putting to rest the big question—would sex still be as good with Frankie as it once had been?

Well, damn. She finally had her answer. Making love to him now had been a hell of a lot better.

"Not a wise choice, Ms. Morales."

Marisela jumped so high at the sound of Ian Blake's voice coming from her bed, she nearly dropped her towel. She'd just emerged from a long, hot, luxurious shower after a short, hot, and equally luxurious workout with Frankie. The last thing she expected was her boss perched against her pillows, his John Lobb of London loafers inches from crushing the blouse she'd picked out to wear for dinner.

She snagged the blouse with her left hand, since her right one was holding tight to the knot over her breast. After several days, she finally had her sea legs, but the gulf must have grown rougher. She had to brace her calf against the bed frame for balance.

"What the hell are you doing in here?"

"We need to talk."

"You need to get the hell out while I dress."

He gazed at her with a practiced, bored expression, but while Marisela may have been distracted, she wasn't a fool. He was as blasé about her nudity beneath her towel as she was thrilled that he'd come into her room without permission.

With a contained grunt, he swung his legs over the side of the bed and stood. He tugged at the cuffs of his sleeves and then shrugged into the jacket he'd casually draped over the wingback chair that stood beside her window.

Her knuckles whitened as she gripped the towel, but not because she was afraid to reveal her naked body to Blake. She didn't give a damn what he saw—in fact, served him right to catch a glimpse of what he'd never have. But dammit, just because he authorized her generous funds transfer didn't give him the right to invade her space—even if he owned that space from the woven carpets to the crystal light fixtures.

"I'm distressed with regard to your behavior this afternoon." His voice was checked, like a seething school principal determined to appear professional in front of the misbehaving kiddies.

Uh-oh. Had someone caught her and Frankie's action in the workout room? What did she care if they did? Celibacy was not a condition of her Titan contract.

She slicked back her dripping wet hair. "You don't expect me to care what you think, do you? What I do on my own time is my own business."

He stalked toward her slowly, casually. "And what time is that? I believe I made myself very clear, Ms. Morales. This entire trip, from start to finish, is about training for your assignment. There is no free time or play time."

"Shit, really? Does that mean I can't even go pee without messing up your carefully coordinated plan?"

He bristled at her crude reference, which was exactly why she'd said it. Ian Blake seemed a difficult man to ruffle, but she'd done pretty well so far. But the truth remained—he did own her for the time being. They were hundreds of miles out to sea and for the most part, out of contact.

For the most part. Only half an hour ago, she'd used the ship-to-shore system in the communications center to call Lia and fill her in on her afternoon delight with Frankie. Could that be what had Blake's boxers in a bunch?

"Taking care of private, physical needs is workable within the schedule," Ian verified. "Making phone calls to your civilian friends with our highly classified system is not."

Marisela leaned into the bathroom and grabbed a second towel, which she rubbed with brisk strokes on her hair. "I thought we were civilians."

His mouth tilted up on one side, but no one in their right mind would call the expression a grin. "Word play aside, Ms. Morales, please refrain from calling Ms. Santorini again until the mission is over. We have too much to lose if your cover is blown once you are in the theater of operation."

"Is that really what this is about? My phone call?" Maybe for once, she and Frankie had lucked out and no one had spied their carnal action?

"What else would I be here about?"

She yanked a stick of gum from her bag. She offered him one, which he predictably declined.

"Maybe you just wanted to sneak a peek at me in the shower."

That suggestion invoked the first real smile she'd seen on him in days. The expression did wonders for his face, which was so handsome, Marisela figured some women might find him hard to look at without staring. But despite his smooth, cultured voice, piercing blue eyes, sigh-inducing dimple, and tailored perfection that applied to everything from his clothes to his physique, Marisela couldn't shake the wariness that overcame her whenever he was near. As if he possessed a brand of danger she had no defense for—no strategy for survival.

"Who said I didn't peek?" he teased.

Marisela dropped the towel she was using on her hair and combed through the wet tangle with her fingers, drawing the strands over her shoulder. The man watching her with such lazy expectation was shameless and presumptuous. Scrumptious, too, but she wasn't in the mood to bestow any compliments. He clearly believed she didn't have the capacity to resist such a sexy and powerful man as he. Ian Blake needed a lesson in humility.

But then what fun would he be?

She eased up to him, breaking into his personal space with slow, deliberate steps. She might not break him, but she could always enjoy getting under his skin. "Nah, you're not the type to watch on the sly."

He countered by leaning closer, as if he'd welcomed her challenge. "What type am I?"

She grinned. "Oh, you know. The kind of guy who can make a woman think it was her idea to break in to your bedroom late at night and crawl into your bed wearing nothing but a smile."

Tentatively, she reached out and slid her finger up his lapel. The fabric was rich and expertly woven, without a single flaw. Just like the man who wore the suit—or at least, just like he wanted everyone to believe.

He watched her hand, then captured her stare with his. "I'm flattered that you've considered that scenario, but I assure you, the security around my bedroom is formidable. Should you attempt to turn your little fantasy into reality, I suggest you wait until Max isn't on duty. He's more dangerous than he appears."

She laughed, slapping him on the shoulder before pushing away. "You'd like to think I'm turned on by you, wouldn't you?"

"Your sexual preferences, Ms. Morales, are not my concern. However, your inexperience and cockiness are. I consider myself responsible for your actions and if you ruin this operation by blowing your cover, the fault will be mine. And I don't like to make mistakes. Ever."

He'd lost a measure of control; his voice was threaded with steel. Marisela caught sight of a vein bulging on the side of his neck. If he ever lost control completely, she figured Ian Blake would be one seriously unpredictable man.

But his potential danger wasn't her problem—staying on equal ground with him was. In her experience, a man like him would only respect her if she matched his intellect and strength—or at the very least, managed to put him in his place.

"If you wanted someone experienced, you should have hired someone experienced. You came looking for me, remember? I may not speak English with all the proper inflections, but I know when I can risk a chat with my best friend and when I can't. As for my cockiness, it will keep me alive. Has so far. Besides, my attitude is what most people love about me."

She smiled broadly, but he merely nodded and turned toward the door. He was a puzzle, Marisela decided. A man who liked to play games, though he'd never admit his preference, not even under extreme torture.

"I'll see you in thirty minutes," he said. "We have a special guest for dinner tonight." He glanced at the blouse she still held in her hand. "You might want to select something a bit dressier."

"Is the President here?"

"No."

"The Pope?"

"Not likely."

She held up the filmy red blouse she'd found in the collection of clothes that had been provided for her. She still hadn't been briefed on exactly whose identity she'd assume once they arrived—some hired gun or Cuban spygirl—but the clothes rocked. When she paired the shirt with the slim black slacks and spiky black sandals she'd also discovered in the generous trousseau, she'd look like one hot *mamacita*. "Then this will do."

Ten

THE MINUTE SHE STROLLED into Blake's private dining room, sliding past Max before she'd even realized he was standing stiffly in the shadows by the door, she caught sight of a cool, slender blonde dressed to the height of yachting chic from the tips of her needle-thin pumps to the luxurious cream crepe pants and coordinating silk blouse. Even the pearls dangling from her ears and draping her slim column of a neck coordinated with the setting. Light, breezy, and expensive.

Except her eyes. Although as blue as the gulf water churning in the white, frothy splash against the hull of the ship, even from a distance, her irises lacked any warmth, even after she caught sight of Marisela and with clear deliberateness, turned up the wattage on her smile.

"Ms. Morales!" The woman headed straight for her as if

Marisela had been holding the last Manolo Blahnik at Barney's in a size seven slim. "How utterly thrilling to finally meet you. Oh, Ian. You didn't exaggerate. How will Javier ever be able to resist her?"

Marisela sidestepped, avoiding the woman's outstretched hand. She was probably acting rudely, but too damned bad.

"Resist me?"

A new scenario played in Marisela's mind with lurid clarity, causing a slash of hot fire to ram up her spine. Nothing in the plans from the past three days included her acting as bait for some gunrunning kingpin. Either this woman knew something Marisela didn't, or she was off her Chippendale rocker.

"Well, you know what I mean," the woman said quickly, as if Marisela knew what the hell she was talking about, which she didn't. "Javier has an eye for beautiful women, particularly dark and mysterious ones like you. One look in your direction and he'll believe whatever cock-and-bull story Ian has cooked up for you."

She circled Marisela, eyeing her from head to toe as if she might offer a bid amount at any moment. When she completed her assessing rotation, she pressed her delicately manicured hand to her chest and released a rather soft, but effective sigh. "I feel so much more confident now. You have no idea what I've been through thanks to Javier Perez."

This time, Marisela didn't feint when the woman's hand shot out and grabbed hers. She didn't buy the intimacy of the move, but she could appreciate the way her body language added to the drama of the moment. She also appreciated the woman's barely contained expression of horror when she felt the calluses on Marisela's knuckles, courtesy of the punching bags in the gym.

"You will find my daughter for me, won't you? You'll bring her home to me?"

Marisela waited for the waterworks to start, but to the woman's credit, she kept her tears to a slight swelling that never rushed beyond her expertly lined eyelashes.

Oh, yeah. She was good.

"I'll do what I'm paid to do," Marisela answered. "What I've been trained to do."

"You see, Elise," Ian said, skillfully disengaging Elise and leading her out of Marisela's personal space, "you have nothing to worry about. Marisela and her partner will infiltrate Javier's compound, locate and extract your daughter. In no time at all, Jessica will be home with you in Boston."

With a quick flash of a smile, Elise Barton-Ryce rejoined Ian beside an exquisitely set table gleaming with gold-trimmed china and prismed crystal. A second later, Max appeared beside Marisela, holding a tray with a single drink—a mojito brimming with fresh mint leaves and a slushy service of ice. Marisela eyed the beverage warily.

"Did you get demoted to bartender?"

"I'm just bringing you your favorite drink."

"My favorite drink is a *Cuba Libre*. For once, you got something wrong."

Max's colorless eyes narrowed. "You order the *Cuba Libre* because most of the bars you frequent don't carry fresh mint. But when you go out somewhere special, you order one of these. Might be your last decent drink for a while."

Marisela frowned, unnerved by how much these people knew about her. Even Frankie wouldn't have known about her preference for the Cuban version of a mint julep. Rum, sugar, mint, and lime had only come to her attention a few years ago during one of her nights out with Lia. Despite her cultural background, no one she knew ever drank them. Lia and Marisela had laughed at the time, likening the experience to the fact that Lia, a born-and-bred Italian-American, had never heard of tiramisu until eating at one of those chain restaurants sometime after high school.

Marisela took the glass and sipped the icy drink. She smiled. Extra sweet, as she preferred.

"Max, you are an amazing font of information."

He shrugged humbly. "I know what I need to know."

"I'm assuming you find out what you need to know by blending into the woodwork. Care to share your secret?"

"Practice," he answered.

"Where's Frankie?" she asked.

"On his way."

She leaned forward so her whisper wouldn't be overheard. "So I met the lady with the checkbook. Do I have to stay?"

"You have to eat."

"I can eat in my room." Marisela didn't like the petulant sound in her voice, but she saw no reason to stay. She didn't like Blake. She didn't like Elise Barton-Ryce. And she wasn't entirely sure she liked Frankie at the moment, thanks to the way he stubbornly stayed on her mind when making love to him today was supposed to have exorcised her latent attraction to him.

Max handed the tray to a passing waiter, but otherwise hardly adjusted his rigid stance. "Mrs. Barton-Ryce expressed concern to Mr. Blake about the caliber of the agents assigned to her case. She's aware that you are entirely untried. Mr. Blake thought that a face-to-face meeting might alleviate her qualms."

Marisela snagged an hors d'oeuvre from a waiter's tray and popped the prosciutto-wrapped delicacy in her mouth, amazed when the cool sweetness of melon exploded on her tongue. Okay, maybe hanging out here wouldn't be so bad. At the moment, Mrs. Barton-Ryce seemed entirely more interested in flirting with Ian Blake than on further assessing the agents assigned to retrieve her daughter. After ten seconds of conversation, Marisela had been summarily dismissed. "Yeah, her maternal concern is overwhelming."

Max tilted his head slightly to the right, but otherwise controlled any reaction to Marisela's obvious doubt. "I didn't think you would judge another woman so quickly."

Marisela laughed, then swigged her drink heartily. "See, there is something you don't know about me."

The door opened behind them and Frankie walked in, looking like sin on a stick in slim black jeans, a black T-shirt, and his signature leather jacket. His eyes captured hers in a split second and caused a fluttering in Marisela's belly that she neither expected nor welcomed.

When Marisela turned back to Max, the guy was gone.

"How does he do that?"

Frankie answered her rhetorical question with a half-grin. "Never underestimate Max. He's not just some flunky."

"I never thought he was," she said, side-stepping out of Frankie's personal space, "but he's starting to creep me out."

Ian gestured them over, so Frankie placed his hand oh-so-subtly at the small of Marisela's back, renewing the tingle shooting through her veins. She was supposed to be over him, dammit. Immune. Satisfied enough to leave him alone for the duration of the mission.

Yeah, right.

Frankie guided her toward Elise and Ian. For God's sake, she could certainly cross a room without any help, couldn't she?

She tugged aside, then speared him with a warning glare. Maybe surrendering to that intimate itch with Frankie hadn't been such a wise idea. Not because, as Lia'd insisted, she'd simply renewed her addiction to a man who would never turn out to be more than a good lay, but because Frankie had that whole machismo thing going on. Sparking his protective instincts on the eve of their first mission together hadn't been the wisest move. He couldn't help himself. The need to protect and direct the female of the species had been bred into his blood, into his genetic code. With their history, his natural progression would be to protect her, rather than share the danger with her.

Well, that had to stop. She hadn't signed on this mission to be a liability to anyone.

"So, Ian," Marisela said, grinning with much more friendliness than she felt, "this is quite a spread. I sure hope you didn't put all the caviar on Mrs. Barton-Ryce's bill just for me."

Elise's smile was almost painful in its shape and stillness. Apparently, she didn't smile much—either because she wasn't good at grinning or perhaps, because shows of genuine amusement or warmth "weren't done" in her social circle. Though with her looks and cash flow, Elise Barton-Ryce probably had lots of reasons to be beaming from ear-to-ear 24/7, missing child or not.

"Sharing a meal with the people who will rescue my child is my privilege, Ms. Morales," she answered tactfully.

"Please, call her Marisela," Ian insisted, topping off Elise's glass with a golden Chardonnay and leveling a warning glance at Marisela to behave. "We're all friends here."

Frankie made a noise not unlike a snort, but with more subtlety. A sniff—with attitude.

"You don't agree, Frank?" he said, his gaze narrowing, but only for a split second. "Forgive me, Elise. This is Francisco Vega, the man who will accompany Marisela on this mission. He's a more experienced operative than Marisela, though we value them both, of course."

Elise's smile transformed, and Marisela, for one, was impressed. Elise's grin instantly morphed from feigned politeness to pure feminine huntress. She reached out with her finely boned hand and for a moment, Marisela thought she saw claws instead of French manicured nails.

Marisela finished the rest of her drink, then fiddled with the shoot of sugarcane used as garnish, crushing the mint and leftover ice into a cool, fragrant mash. She watched Frankie accept Elise's hand, smiling when he instantly released her, as if Elise's skin was too cold for prolonged touch. Too bad Frankie wasn't interested. This woman could use a real man to warm her up.

Marisela glanced up to catch Ian Blake staring at her with a keen focus that transformed the look into something nearly tangible, like the tip of an electrode activated against her skin, causing a resonant tingling to echo through her. She couldn't identify the sensation as either positive or negative—just . . . *there*. Strong and significant, and yet, completely abstract.

She started when Frankie's hand again slipped around the back of her waist. He moved her toward the table, under the guise of helping her politely into her chair.

"Don't fall for it, *vidita*," he whispered, his breath warm against her ear as he tucked in her chair. Where'd he learn such politeness anyway?

"Fall for what?"

His gaze flashed toward Ian. "He's not what he appears to be."

"Funny, all he appears to be is my boss." She snapped her napkin flat, then laid it across her lap. She leaned in close so only he could hear her. "Aren't you curious about why we're really all here? I'm betting Ian's guest has never shared a meal with people like you and me—except when the people like you and me were doing the serving."

Frankie grinned. "Do you know which fork to use?"

She winked and toyed with the edge of the appetizer fork, showing off her newfound knowledge. Max had taken the time to review table manners as part of their training. Apparently, the identities they would soon take belonged to people who moved flawlessly in and out of an upper crust world. Maybe dinner tonight was a simple test of her table manners and not something more nefarious.

Uh-huh.

Marisela might not know a lot about finger bowls and napkin rings, but she had a strong sense that there was more to this impromptu dinner than met the naked eye.

Ian helped Elise into her chair, and then slid into his own with a grace she'd never seen in a man before. She'd already pegged him as smooth as silk, but no matter how impressive an educated, cosmopolitan man like him should appear to an urban girl like her, she couldn't shake the persistent mistrust of him fueled by Frankie's warnings. Just what did her ex know about their boss that he hadn't shared?

Ian gestured for the server. A moment later, three white-jacketed crewmen popped into the room, carrying trays and refilling drinks. Ian approved the wine selection, and then turned his grin back to Marisela.

"I'm told you and Frank had quite the workout this afternoon. How gauche of me to delay our meal. You must have worked up quite the appetite."

Marisela raised one brow. "You should join us in the gym sometime," she said, determined not to let him unnerve her. "Might be interesting to spar with the boss."

Ian's grin was as intense as Frankie's steely glare.

"An interesting idea," Ian replied, "but I think I'll pass. I wouldn't want to intrude when your training is progressing just as Frankie assured me it would."

Marisela didn't know a damned thing about fishing, but she recognized bait when she saw it. She threw Frankie an intimate smile before meeting Ian's superior gaze directly. "Frankie certainly does know his stuff."

Ian cleared his throat. "So I've heard." With a snap of his napkin, Ian ended the conversation.

Marisela watched a silent battle ensue while the server placed small silver trays laden with individual servings of soft cheese, fruit, and warm, nutty bread in front of them. Ian attempting to look nonchalant and unaffected; Frankie doing his damnedest to keep from punching Blake in the face. She had to give Frankie credit for controlling his temper. In the old days, he would have called the guy out by now. Of course, maybe they'd already tangled sometime earlier, before Marisela was around. Maybe that was the animosity Marisela was picking up on.

"So, Marisela," Elise said, toying mindlessly with a gold

chain that dipped into her cleavage. "What do you know about my Jessica?"

"What do I need to know? You have custody and her father took her."

Elise looped her finger in the gold links, drawing Marisela's attention to a small locket peeking out from her neckline. "That's a rather simplistic assessment."

Marisela eyed the woman carefully. "Am I missing some complexity I should know about?"

Blake smeared cheese over his bread and Frankie, who'd pushed his plate away, concentrated on making quick work of his wine. Why did she have the feeling the men knew infinitely more than she did? Or that Elise wanted to say something she couldn't quite get out?

Elise took a brief sip of Chardonnay and then answered Marisela's question in a surprisingly straightforward tone. "My former lover is a cruel man who runs a dangerous empire. There is no telling how he's poisoned my daughter's mind against me."

Finally, Elise extracted the locket that she wore, unhooked the clasp and handed it across the table to Marisela.

"Open it," Elise ordered, her voice cool, but quavering.

Curious, Marisela complied. The minute she spied the angelic face she'd suspected she'd find inside, she clicked the tiny hinge shut and thrust the necklace back to its owner. "I've seen your daughter."

Elise sat up straighter, clearly offended, and made no move to retrieve her locket. "That's a picture. An old picture, faded by time. And it's all I've had for fifteen years."

Hot anger burbled in Marisela's chest. Did she look like

some bleeding-heart sap? Why was Elise pushing so hard, forcing her to feel some profound sadness for a cute little baby who was now all grown up? "That's not my concern."

"It should be."

"Why?"

As if on cue, a tear sprang from the corner of Elise's eye, which she quickly dabbed away with her napkin. "I'm terrified that Jessica will fight you if she knows who you really are. She'll run to her father and Javier will kill you both. Don't I have enough on my conscience already?"

She tore away from the table and Ian, after leveling an admonishing glance at Marisela, quickly followed his guest. In a dark corner by the window, they talked in hushed tones, leaving Frankie and Marisela alone while the waiters delivered the soup.

Marisela set the locket beside her bowl and eyed the pinkish cream concoction with a guilty appetite. She loved lobster bisque, but she'd just reduced their client to tears—something she was fairly certain Ian didn't appreciate. She hadn't meant to make the woman cry, but she was trying to stick to the facts. Of course the girl would resist if she knew the truth.

Frankie picked up his spoon and made short work of the lobster and caviar garnish. "You always did have a way with people, *vidita,* especially rich *gringas* who spend more on their shoes than you make in a year."

Marisela ignored the growl in her stomach, finished her wine, then waved at the waiter to bring more. "Than I *used* to make in a year, maybe. You don't believe those waterworks, do you? She should use some of her trust fund on acting lessons."

Frankie chuckled, grabbed a roll, and dunked a torn hunk into his soup. "You don't think she's sincere?"

With clenched teeth beneath tight lips, Marisela glanced over her shoulder. Ian had his arm draped over Elise's shoulder and their quiet conversation now included soft laughter.

"Not anymore than you think Ian can be trusted," she replied.

Frankie paused, then shrugged and dug into his soup with gusto. "Then we're both in a hell of a lot of trouble, aren't we?"

Suddenly, Marisela had lost her appetite.

Eleven

FRANKIE WATCHED ACROSS the table, noting how Marisela played with the gleaming gold locket Elise had given her. She'd ignored the trinket throughout the tense dinner, even tried to return it before Elise retired to her stateroom, but the woman insisted Marisela keep the charm. Now, she couldn't seem to stop touching it.

Frankie wouldn't care about what this Elise Something-or-Another did or didn't do to solidify Marisela's loyalty, except for one thing—Marisela's loyalty had to be to him. Or more accurately, to the team. He'd known her for a long time. If someone pushed Marisela's buttons, her temper could overcome her good sense. They'd all be a lot safer if Marisela's emotions stayed out of the mix. And nothing could stir Marisela up like an injustice to a child.

During their workout, she'd told him about how she'd lost her gig in the bond enforcement biz. Beat up a perp and used excessive force, all because the guy had been an asshole to his wife and kids. She'd had no stake in the jerk's crime or punishment, but she'd let the unfairness push her over the edge. If she pulled such a stupid stunt on this mission, they could both end up dead.

Frankie's gaze darted to Blake, who accepted a brandy from Max and thankfully had toned down his annoying charm. Blake was quiet and concentrated as he typed a series of codes into a cordless keyboard, which activated the flat screen on the wall across from them. A photograph of a man and woman boarding a charter plane flashed into view. Frankie pushed his concerns about Marisela aside. For now, he'd concentrate on making this mission work and keeping them alive.

"This is Dolores and Rogelio Tosca, exiled Cuban nationals who immigrated to Canada from Havana in 1987. They settled just outside of Toronto, though they spend most of their time traveling the world as high-paid assassins. Exactly three months ago, Javier Perez instructed one of his top lieutenants to contact the Toscas in order to eliminate a rival who's persisted in invading Perez's North American territory."

"Why didn't Perez do the dirty work himself?" Frankie asked. He'd crossed the paths of quite a few arms dealers during his stint in prison. They weren't the types to delegate deadly force outside their own organization.

Blake grinned wryly. "We're guessing he doesn't want to turn his problem into a turf war. He's not interested in sending a message to his rivals, he just wants to eradicate the immediate problem."

Made sense. If Perez did the hit himself, the rival's men would feel compelled to reciprocate with more violence. If the competitor was taken out by independent contractors, the source of the hit wouldn't be immediately clear. In the arms dealing business, deadly enemies were a dime a dozen.

"Where are the Toscas now?"

Frankie guessed the couple would provide the cover Blake had chosen for him and Marisela in order to infiltrate Perez's inner circle. Though Dolores and Rogelio appeared a bit older than he and Marisela were, assassins weren't generally high-profile people. Likely, the only thing known about them was that they were rich, Hispanic, and traveled in a pair.

But diverting paid assassins once money had exchanged hands would prove near to impossible unless they eliminated the real couple. Permanently.

"Already dead," Ian replied coolly. "Or at least, presumed so, thanks to a very reliable source."

Marisela's face blanched. "You had them killed?"

Ian quirked an eyebrow. "Nothing so dastardly, I assure you. Their specialty was execution by explosion. They particularly enjoyed blowing up boats. Last month, they were working for a drug kingpin in Brazil, eliminating a dealer who was skimming too much off the top. Apparently, something went wrong. They went down with the ship, so to speak. Had they lived, we simply would have detained them until our operation was complete."

Frankie glanced at Marisela. The locket, while still in her hand, seemed to no longer be a concern, though her thumb rubbed lightly over the smooth gold finish.

"Are you certain Perez doesn't know they died?" Frankie asked.

Ian grinned. "Oddly enough, yes. We had the good fortune to intercept the Toscas' moneyman shortly after the accident. They'd only received half their payment from the Brazilian and since they had completed their task, their accountant pretended they were alive in order to collect the rest. In the interest of earning some easy money, the accountant kept the fact that his bosses blew themselves up to himself."

Frankie chuckled at the guy's ingenuity and greed. Couldn't blame him for going for the big bucks since his meal tickets had just blasted themselves into a million fleshy pieces. "He took the money and ran."

"And then some," Ian verified. "But we discovered his secret. Since he's a great lover of cash, he's now on our payroll. During our initial surveillance of Perez, we'd intercepted the messages between the Toscas and Perez's men. We knew about his interest in hiring the assassins even before the Toscas died. We've promised the accountant one hundred percent of his boss's normal fee on the job for Javier Perez if he helped us orchestrate the hit in their stead."

Marisela leaned forward, her eyes wide, not so much out of surprise, but disgust. "So we're going to kill some dude just to get into Perez's good graces?"

"This 'dude' is a first-class killer, if it makes any difference to you." Ian tapped a few more keys, bringing another photograph onto the screen. "Ricky Ochoa. Razor Ricky, as he's called, for his practice of cutting the throats of anyone who displeases him, from hotel housekeepers to unruly dogs. He used to be the main enforcer for a drug dealer out of southern Venezuela. His brother, the head of the crime family, met with a rather gruesome death two years ago. Slashed across the neck, not surprisingly, by his younger sibling who then took over the operation himself. He's a ruthless, cold-blooded murderer with a long résumé of deaths at his hands."

Marisela shook her head, her eyes wide. "I didn't sign on with you to play avenging angel for a bunch of assholes who can't take care of their own nasty business."

Frankie leaned back into his chair, wondering how bad he'd screwed up by bringing Marisela to Titan. He finally recognized what had changed the most about her in the past decade. She was angry. Angrier than he'd ever seen her, even compared to when she'd signed on with the *las Reinas* years ago. But why? Marisela had family, friends. In his experience, only people who were alone held tight to their anger because rage was all they had.

Ian leaned slightly toward Marisela, and as Frankie expected, spoke in a keen whisper. Frankie rolled his eyes. He didn't really think she'd fall for such transparent seduction, did he?

"I don't ask my operatives to kill, Marisela."

"But they often have to, or we wouldn't be so well trained," she countered.

She put up a valiant fight, Frankie thought, observing how smoothly Marisela kept Blake on topic, ignoring his tempered voice and smooth gestures. But Frankie didn't fool himself. No woman could fight a guy like Blake forever once Blake determined that he wanted her. He'd seen this before with Tasha, code name Eris. Frankie had been new to the operation then and just like every male agent in Titan, he'd wanted a shot at the sleek, sexy operative. But after a cursory game of hard to get, she'd ended up with Ian. If Marisela wanted her boss in her bed as well, who the hell was Frankie to get in the way? He didn't own her. He didn't have the right to ask her to remain faithful to him, not when he had no promises to make in return.

But he didn't have to make Ian's inevitable seduction of Marisela easy.

"She's got a point," Frankie agreed. "You've made sure our workouts include all the skills the Toscas had, right down to the bang."

Ian's sneer only showed in his eyes, but it was there, causing Frankie to grin.

"I do not intend to sully Titan's reputation by taking on a murder for hire, not even to advance an important and lucrative case. You and Frankie will pose as the Toscas and we'll stage the assassination of Ochoa and then spirit the man away for a few weeks of rest and relaxation until the case is complete. The Tosca's moneyman has indicated to Perez that the Toscas are interested in taking on more work for him if he's satisfied with the outcome in Miami. That will facilitate a meeting after the hit is complete. Since Perez will be leaving soon for Puerto Rico, the meeting will likely occur at his private compound. If we're lucky, you'll then be in place to recover the girl."

He switched the screen again, this time displaying a map of the island of Puerto Rico, with a smaller remote island off the northwest coast highlighted with arrows and coordinates. "Once you are on *Isla de Piratas,* you'll find the girl and pick an exit strategy."

Blake's subtle flirting with Marisela was over. Back to business. Good.

"How will we contact you?" Marisela asked.

"Our agents have another yacht, which will cruise just out of range of Perez's security zone, which we're told includes radar. We'll move in at pre-set times to intercept communications from you. We've also devised a satellite phone jamming system that will keep Perez from picking up our exchanges so long as we keep them short. Max will provide you with a schedule. When the time for extraction comes, one of your assignments will include knocking out radar capabilities entirely so we can sweep in undetected on a smaller vessel, one built for stealth and speed. But we're a long way out from that. First, we've got to get you in."

For the next twenty minutes, Ian reviewed the plan for their arrival in Miami, with Max stepping in to provide all the specs regarding the fake assassination, which would hinge on the very real demolition of Ricky Ochoa's prized yacht, the prophetically named *Sharp's Destruction*. From there, Frankie figured they had fifty-fifty odds of infiltrating Perez's compound, and after that, a generous twenty-eight percent chance of getting out alive. The minute they moved to grab the girl, they'd be marked for execution, likely at Perez's own hand.

At least he knew that though Marisela drew the line at killing in cold blood for money or strategy, she'd kick, claw, shoot, or strangle anyone who tried to kill her first.

"You're awfully quiet, Frank."

He turned toward Blake, who eyed him with his usual cold assessment. Not that Frankie gave a flying fuck, but he'd like to remove Blake's expression of superiority—permanently.

"What's there to say?" Frankie replied. "Max has the whole plan worked out. All we have to do is follow through. Piece of cake."

Marisela snorted. "You work with explosives before?"

"Max has. He'll make sure we know what we need to."

Marisela quirked an eyebrow, surprised at the second showing of respect Frankie had paid to Ian's right-hand man. She wondered if the two of them had shared a past—perhaps a mission? Didn't matter. Right now, all she wanted was a few minutes alone with Blake. She had concerns she intended to voice without any witnesses, particularly a witness like Frankie who would undoubtedly interfere.

Ian finished the last of his brandy, then gestured to Max to join them again at the table.

"Your training tomorrow will focus on how we'll remove Ricky Ochoa from his yacht prior to blowing it up," Max assessed. "He's not a cooperative sort. He won't go quietly, even if his life is on the line."

Frankie nodded and Marisela noticed a dullness in his normally sharp eyes that testified to his exhaustion. This could also work to her advantage. She really didn't want to deal with the aftermath of their afternoon in the gym—if he insisted on an aftermath at all—tonight. And maybe by tomorrow, he'd forget that they'd surrendered once again to the lust they'd harbored since they'd become aware of the temptations of the opposite sex.

Yeah, right.

"In your rooms, you'll find dossiers on both Dolores and Rogelio Tosca," Ian added. "Study them. The Toscas didn't have a high profile, but I know Perez has checked them out. Before he makes the final payment or invites you to his private island per our plan, he'll demand a face-to-face. I want you both completely in character. Do you have any acting talent, Marisela?"

She bristled. "I act like I trust you, don't I?"

Ian disengaged the computer and projection screen. "Not in the least. I hope you'll do better with Javier Perez."

With that, they were dismissed and Marisela followed Frankie out of the room. Halfway down the hall, she touched Frankie's arm.

"I have something I want to run past Blake. See you in the morning?"

Frankie grunted. "Marisela, don't mess with things you don't understand."

"What don't I understand? This doesn't have anything to do with you. Go to bed. You're whipped."

His slanted grin responded to her accidental innuendo. "Not likely, *vidita*. I learned my lesson the first time."

She rolled her eyes. "You know what I mean."

He nodded, then grabbed her by the hand and reeled her flush against his body. Her breath caught, not so much because his move surprised her, but because the anticipation of what would happen next reignited the sexual awareness between them that never seemed to really cool, but had only settled into a steady simmer, ready to flare at the first intimate touch.

But he didn't kiss her, though her lips ached to press hard and hot against his. Instead, he seduced her with his half-closed bedroom eyes, so dark, they reflected the pure raw need swimming in the black depths.

Marisela pulled away, knowing her resistance wouldn't hold for long, not in light of the fact that following Frankie to his stateroom would be a hell of a lot more fun than confronting Ian Blake. But she'd had enough fun for one day. Tonight, she had to concentrate on work. On survival.

Without another word, Frankie disappeared down the hallway. She broke out of the mesmerizing aura he'd left in his wake and marched back into Ian's office.

She found him sitting on the leather couch near the window, sipping a cognac.

"Yes?" His smile was as silky and intoxicating as the liqueur in his snifter.

"Didn't you expect me?"

She pulled the locket Elise had given her out of her pocket and holding tight to the chain, let the charm drop and dangle.

"I've been trying all night to figure out why you brought Elise here in the first place and I decided that this little trinket answers my question."

She tossed the locket at him and he caught the charm in one easy snatch. "I have no idea what you're talking about."

"You brought her here to tug at the old heartstrings, to make me feel for her and use my well-known temper to keep me on task."

He popped the hinge on the locket and glanced at the picture inside, the one Marisela hadn't been able to ignore, no matter how hard she'd tried. A tiny angel with dark eyes the size of saucers, sweet, bowed lips, and skin not the Caribbean dark of her father, but the porcelain alabaster of her mother. Yet the beauty of the child hadn't been the clincher. Marisela had seen the young Jessica in the photos during the first briefing and frankly, she didn't care if the baby was pretty or not—she'd still care. What pushed this photo into unacceptable territory, beyond the means of delivery, was the inscription.

Return to Me.

Had Elise worn this trinket all these years, her silent wish pressed against her heart? Marisela couldn't imagine this gold charm coordinating with all the Ralph Lauren and Oscar de la Renta in Elise Barton-Ryce's closet, but then, accessorizing expensive clothes wasn't Marisela's concern. The fact that she'd come all the way from Boston to give Marisela the charm—that's what had her hackles up.

"Why would I need to manipulate you?" Ian asked, relatively unconcerned judging by the flippant way he tossed the necklace onto the table in front of him. "You've agreed to do the job. So far, you've trained hard and learned fast. I have no need to resort to emotional tricks in order to motivate you to perform."

Marisela listened to his claim and didn't buy a single word. She hadn't known Ian Blake long, but his type was easy enough to peg. His confidence ran deep and he demanded perfection from everyone around him, but he also went the extra mile to ensure success. And if that meant playing with the emotions of his underlings, then that's what he did.

Well, not with her.

She crossed her arms over her chest. "You're not so certain about what I'm going to find with Jessica, are you? You're thinking I need to be emotionally devoted to returning this child to her mother, just in case the kid hates her guts for never trying to find her in the first place."

"That's not true! I did try to find her!"

She turned and found Elise standing in a door that must have led to her private stateroom, still wearing her outfit from dinner, only without all the spit and polish. Her hair had loosened from the twisted upsweep and a few wisps dangled alongside her face, providing a natural softness that contrasted with the stricken look on her face.

"I'm sorry, Elise," Marisela offered. "I didn't mean to imply that you didn't search for your daughter. But think about Jessica. She'd had fifteen years to cook up scenarios where you hated her, maybe because of her black hair or because she cried too much as a baby. Maybe her father told her you took money as payment for her or that you begged him to take her away so you didn't have to live with the shame of raising a bastard child. Bottom line, whoever goes after your kid is walking into an emotional minefield that could prove deadly. So why not throw me in, not just as a competent agent," she turned back to Ian, spearing him with a glare that insisted that's all she wanted to be, "but as a woman on a mission involving a child ripped away from her mother? Go for the emotional jugular, you know? Make sure I know that if I fail, I'm not just jeopardizing the mission, but I'm leaving behind a young woman who was once a doe-eyed little girl clinging to her mother."

"And why not?" Elise shot back, beating Ian to the punch. She strode into the room with such venom in her eyes, Marisela had to fight all her instincts not to move into a defensive stance. "If you fail, that's exactly what will happen. This is my child we're talking about. My baby. She was torn away from me and if I have to appeal to your maternal instincts in order to make you care, then so be it."

Marisela didn't spare another word or look at Elise Barton-Ryce. She didn't blame the woman for her manipulations, not when Marisela knew that Elise Barton-Ryce never would have set foot on this yacht without Ian Blake's approval.

"Are all of your agents briefed this way?"

He put down the brandy and sat back, relaxed in the chair. "Of course not."

"Then I'll consider this a one-time lapse in judgment. I'll do my job because it's what you pay me to do, what I've trained to do, not because I'm some bleeding heart girlie-girl with an overactive supply of estrogen. I'm not going to get sucked in to every sob story that goes along with your missions. I did that once and the results weren't pretty." She pointed at Ian, jabbing the air with her finger to make sure he understood the intensity of her emotions now, because he wasn't going to see them again. "Don't fuck around with me. Treat me the same way you treat anyone else in your employ, got it?"

She didn't wait for an answer, but swept out of the room and slammed the door, careful not to look at Elise on her way out. It wasn't as if she didn't care. She did. She wasn't some coldhearted bitch with only her own paycheck on her mind. But she wouldn't let Ian use her heart against her—not without a fight.

She didn't take a normal breath again until she was locked in her stateroom. She scrubbed her makeup violently from her face, brushed her teeth, peed, and then settled under the silky covers with a bilingual curse. Yet before she clicked off the light, she retrieved the dossier Ian had, as promised, had delivered to her room.

Turning to the first page, she caught sight of the entry and slammed the folder shut. How could Ian send this after all she'd said? With a second curse, she realized her warning rant had obviously preceded the delivery of the documents. This one time, she'd give him the benefit of the doubt.

She opened the folder one more time and with a sense of heavy foreboding, read the complete letter written in a child's hand begging her mother to take her home.

Twelve

THREE DAYS LATER, Marisela and Frankie departed the *Oceanus* via a tender that slid them into the port of Miami unnoticed. Once there, a dark sedan met them, driven by someone Frankie referred to as Dion, a thick-muscled man with a sly smile. The men didn't chatter during the drive, but they exchanged enough conversation to allow Marisela to conclude that Dion was on the Titan payroll and would be instrumental in the abduction of Ricky Ochoa. They'd be briefed further after they checked into their hotel, changed clothes, and assumed the lethal roles of Dolores and Rogelio Tosca.

As they drove, Marisela couldn't help peering through the tinted window, wondering about the city outside, the one she'd never seen except in movies and television shows. Neon lights streaked by, as did the unmistakable silhouettes of tall, spiky palms. Cars whizzed alongside them on the highway, the thump of extreme bass from jacked-up stereos injecting into her veins. Here was a city that would welcome her, a city with the same soul as Marisela's—rhythmic, dangerous, and open to a million diverse wants, each contrasting to an equal number of different needs. She could lose herself here in Miami. She sat back into the seat. Perhaps she was better off locked inside the car.

"Roll it down," Frankie said, jerking his hand toward the window. "You know you want to."

"I'm fine."

Frankie arched a dark brow. "That I know."

God, how she'd resisted him during the last leg of their trip, she'd never figure out. Probably came down to the fact that they hadn't had one moment to themselves since Elise Barton-Ryce had been deposited at an unnamed port at dawn the next morning after her outburst in Ian's office and she, Frankie, and Max had set about to perfect the plan to retrieve Jessica Perez without further distraction. She and Frankie had memorized every minute fact about the Toscas from their preferred beverages to the bloody path they'd swept through the criminal underworld.

They'd learned about their childhoods in Castro's Cuba, including Rogelio's stint in the dictator's army. He'd passed his knowledge of explosives, learned in the service, to his wife, a clever communist spy with her own dark credentials. They'd defected young and with contacts to the mob made in Havana casinos, had started their own murder-for-hire business. With high fees and a keen investment strategy, the couple could have retired as multimillionaires years ago. But they liked their jobs—and had paid for that passion with their lives.

Marisela was determined not to make the same mistakes. If experts could blow themselves to kingdom come, she wasn't about to get cocky when it came to C-4. When she wasn't working out with Frankie or reviewing procedures with Max, she'd been studying the properties and weaknesses of the explosives until she could recite every word in her sleep.

She wasn't going to screw up. She wasn't going to end up in a million pieces. At least, not this early in the mission.

The quality of their hotel room left a lot to be desired, but Marisela figured if living in a hovel for a couple of nights was the worst thing she had to deal with on this mission, she was coming out on top. Musty-smelling and decorated with flamingo-themed bedspread and artwork—if the word "art" could be used to describe several ill-framed posters featuring flocks of pink, long-necked birds dancing down South Beach's Ocean Drive—the room contained all the paraphernalia they'd need to complete the final preparations for their mission. In the closet, she found two duffel bags. One contained stylish, but dark clothes in her size that wouldn't seem completely out of place at a top-dollar marina, a collection of high-tech gadgetry, and Marisela's favorite 9mm Taurus, complete with her old shoulder holster, which she lovingly strapped under a spangled black tank top.

"You could have requisitioned a new harness," Frankie said, snapping the worn leather that cut across her shoulder blade.

She swung around and shoved him back, though with a playful grin. God, she was pumped. Adrenaline seemed to accompany the presence of her weapon and with the night darkening and the time for the rendezvous nearing, she wasn't sure where her fear started and where the excitement ended. Even Frankie's smart-ass comments couldn't bring her down. "I like this one. It molds perfectly to my body."

She twisted seductively to prove her point and true to form, he grabbed her waist and tugged her flush against his taut silk T-shirt and slim black pants. His sex jutted hard against her belly and despite the ravenous look in his eyes, she knew not all of the lust coursing through him was because of her. She knew, because she felt it, too—the oncoming rush from what they were about to do.

Her senses were like trigger devices, sensitive to the slightest touch, primed to unleash an explosion of sensation at the least provocation. She tilted her neck and in seconds, Frankie's lips were on her, biting a sweet path of need from just below her ear to the corner of her mouth.

As much as she'd been avoiding their attraction over the past few days, she couldn't deny him any longer. She ran her hands up his back, then down so she could squeeze his amazing ass and hear him groan with appreciation.

"Is it always like this?" she asked, breathless.

His mouth quirked up in a half-grin. "Usually."

With tongues battling, they kissed until the sparring of lips wasn't enough. He dropped to his knees and placed his mouth directly over the crotch of her thin-fabric pants, firing her with his hot breath, teasing her with his fingers as they traced the tightening seams. She tore her hands through his hair, marveling at how silky the strands felt against her skin, how the air seemed rich with the musky scent of man. Crouched on his powerful legs, he'd started his ascent toward her breasts, his hands folding up the beaded blouse, when his watch beeped.

Fifteen minutes and counting to the first contact.

She slipped out of his grasp, panting.

"Later, *vidita?*"

She licked her lips, which still pulsed from their hungry exchange. "Will the rush last?"

His grin lent a sparkle to his shadowed eyes. "Depends on if we blow ourselves up. Sex is so sweet after you've faced death. And won."

Ignoring a brief sting of jealousy—wondering just who Frankie had been with when he discovered this little snippet of wisdom—Marisela turned back to the duffel bag, her nerve endings sizzling and her heart racing at a pace at least a half a beat faster than normal. A layer of perspiration had formed at the back of her neck, but she dispatched that telltale sweat by sweeping her hair into a tight ponytail. Behind her, Frankie rechecked his spare clips before shoving them into a belt he'd wear hidden beneath a custom leather blazer. She couldn't help but watch him dress. Down to his low-heeled boots and snug T-shirt, he looked every ounce the dangerous secret agent about to blend into the night.

"Who are we meeting again?" Marisela asked. Dion had briefed Frankie in the car, but she hadn't paid close attention. She's been too focused on the lure of the city.

"Dion and his partner, Pan."

"Don't these people have normal names?"

Frankie snorted. "Those aren't their real names. We're working with Titan operatives. They all have code names."

They'd briefly touched on that topic during their training, but since neither she nor Frankie were official agents, they hadn't bothered to take on Titan monikers.

"Can't they pick better names than a fifties rock star and a little boy who flies to Neverland and never grows up?"

Frankie tossed Marisela a small leather pouch. "That's not what the names mean. Dion is short for Dionysus."

That rang a bell. A school bell. "From mythology?"

"You paid attention in English class?"

She shrugged. "The teacher was a hottie."

Frankie shook his head and chuckled. "All the operatives for Titan have names from Greek or Roman mythology. It's a tradition or something."

She perked up, interested. "What's yours?"

"Don't have one."

"Come on," she said, disbelieving. "You've worked with this group before. You're telling me they never got around to giving you a name?"

Frankie dumped his pouch on the bed. Several miniature electronic devices spilled out, with hair-thin wires and feather-light power packs dangling from the ends. Marisela recognized the communications apparatus and slid onto the bed beside Frankie.

"I don't want a name," he answered.

"Why? Is Apollo already taken?" she quipped. She didn't remember much about mythology except the teacher had been a major hunk and the girls had taken to calling him Apollo because he was the god of hunks or something.

"Who?"

"Don't screw with me. If you know Dio-whatsis, you know Apollo."

"Dionysus. God of the vine."

"Does this agent drink?" she asked, concerned.

Frankie chuckled. "After a successful mission he might down a few, but he came from the wine country in Italy. He collects wine. That's his claim to fame."

"And Pan?"

Frankie's brow scrunched. "Don't remember. Something about getting into a lot of trouble."

"Do all the names reflect the agent's personality?" she asked, wondering if the Greeks or Romans ever conceived of anyone as screwed up as she was.

"Nah. There's a female agent named Nike and she runs like a duck."

Marisela laughed. "What's Blake's code name?"

Frankie frowned. "Zeus, of course."

"What was he, king of the gods?"

"Bingo."

Figured. "Why didn't we have to learn all these names?"

"It's need-to-know. You'll pick it up."

She untangled a tightly knotted line on one of the power cords, then handed it to him to attach to the correct device. Glancing under her lashes, she wondered if now was the time to broach a topic she'd wanted to bring up for days. "Why don't you work full-time for Blake? He seems to want you."

"For this mission."

Marisela shook her head. "No, I think he wants more. He acts all cool, but I think he wants you permanently on his payroll and that's why he set you up for that arrest back home."

He was half-way to inserting his earpiece when her claim arrested his attention.

"How did you know that?"

"I didn't."

"You guessed?"

"Seemed logical. Blake loves to show his power, like he did with me when he shanghaied my parents. You were about to tell him to shove his job offer up his ass, so he had you arrested just to show you who was boss."

"Yeah," he said with a grimace, then inserted the earpiece and connected the line to a power pack he then attached to the back of his collar. "He showed me, didn't he?"

She shrugged. "You still would have beat the rap because the charges were bogus. Even if his attorney hadn't gotten you out, your parents would have mortgaged their house a third time to hire a lawyer to spring you."

"They didn't bail me out when I got arrested the first time in eighty-nine."

"You were guilty then," she pointed out.

"Good point. Blake is power-hungry, Marisela. He's good at what he does, but his need to be in absolute control makes him dangerous to his agents. Remember that."

Marisela chased off a chill while she connected the wires of her earpiece to the power pack she'd stick in her bra. The last thing she needed right now was to doubt the man calling the shots only minutes before she departed on a potentially deadly mission.

"He's run Titan well so far," she ventured.

"He doesn't run Titan."

"Of course he does. Lia and I checked him out. He's all over the Boston and New York papers and trade magazines, accepting awards, testifying in court."

Frankie completed his communications task and turned to organizing his ammunition. "He's the top dog in the States, but his sister oversees the entire operation from Europe. The major action is across the ocean, babe. Don't let Ian fool you. If he screws up, Brynn will jerk the whole shebang out from under him without a second thought."

"No love lost?"

He shrugged. "They get along okay. But they're competitive."

Marisela couldn't imagine what kind of ball-breaker this Brynn would have to be to match her brother's intensity, but she decided she wanted to meet this chick someday. Maybe she could give Marisela some tips. Or vice versa.

"And you know all this . . . ?"

Frankie glanced sideways, a nearly imperceptible shift of avoidance. "I keep my ears open."

Yeah, and she was a natural blonde. Frankie had some personal connection to Ian Blake, possibly his sister, too. Maybe a love affair between him and Brynn? That sure would explain the animosity arcing between Ian and Frankie during nearly every interaction she'd witnessed.

"You only signed on with Blake this time because of me."

"Yeah, you're irresistible," he quipped.

"There is that," she agreed, "but you're the one who gave him my name, so you felt responsible for making sure I got out of this alive. Am I right?"

Frankie grunted in response.

"I can take care of myself, you know."

"So I've heard."

"So you've seen. You've trained with me, Frankie. All week. And you've known me practically all my life. I don't want you going into this mission tonight thinking it's your responsibility to save my ass. It's not."

"You're wrong, Marisela," he snapped, taking the rest of his equipment and heading to the wobbly table and chair beside the door. "It's my job to save your ass and it's your job to save mine. That's why we're partners."

Marisela grimaced. She'd obviously made some sort of secret agent faux pas, and with tensions running so high, there wasn't much she could do about Frankie's sudden anger. She checked the watch Max had given her, which had a mini-GPS system and tracking device inside. They had less than ten minutes before their ride to the marina arrived. She'd best concentrate on preparing her gear instead of chatting over old times.

She clipped a speaker to her neckline, constructed with the same beads that decorated her spangly top. The credit card–thin power pack attached to a line that edged her bra strap and then tucked beneath her cleavage. As she worked, she replayed the mission plan in her head. Ochoa and his family—his third wife and toddler son—were scheduled to leave Miami for Boca Raton in an hour with a small, four-man crew and three bodyguards. Two bodyguards and the wife and child, who had been visiting the woman's family in Ft. Lauderdale, would be detained shortly and held by Titan until the entire mission was complete. Ochoa and his personal bodyguard, however, were another matter entirely.

Attending a meeting in a well-guarded safe house, Ochoa and the bodyguard would remain untouchable until they boarded the boat. Intercepting him before that point would arouse the suspicions of Perez and his men, who were, reportedly, monitoring the Toscas' work from a safe distance. Though the crew of the *Sharp's Destruction* had already been replaced with trained Titan operatives—all of them former Navy

SEALs—taking down Ochoa and the bodyguard would be up to Marisela and Frankie. The crew had to concentrate on piloting the boat a safe distance from the marina before she and Frankie blew it up. Once Ochoa and the bodyguard were neutralized, they would hand the pair off to Dionysus and Pan, who would transfer them to individual small watercraft that could jet away undetected.

She and Frankie would remain aboard to set the charges, giving the Titan crew time to make a getaway. Frankie and Marisela would then board the *Sharp's Destruction* tender and depart, using a remote device to detonate the explosives. With the right timing, the explosion would cover the escape of the crew. Ochoa and the bodyguard would be transferred to the same safe house where the wife and child were being held and the mission to infiltrate Perez's inner circle would be complete.

Frankie's watch beeped again.

"Got everything?" he asked.

She checked her weapon, her ammunition, and her communication devices. Frankie went into the bathroom and they tested the equipment one last time.

"You there?" she whispered, talking into her neckline.

"I'll always be here, *vidita,*" Frankie answered.

She grinned. Good. He wasn't pissed anymore. She didn't want to go into the operation with things left unsaid or tense between them. When he emerged from the bathroom, one look told her she had nothing to worry about.

"Let's do it."

"The wife and child are secure," the agent reported, causing a quiver in Marisela's stomach. It had begun.

"Casualties?"

That voice Marisela recognized. Ian Blake. He and Max were coordinating the mission from the *Oceanus* and monitoring the conversation over their communications link. Funny how much sexier Blake's voice sounded when he wasn't in the room with her, looking at her with eyes that implied, ever so slightly, that she didn't measure up. She didn't know exactly where she got that impression—if he didn't think she was good enough, he never would have hired her. And yet, she couldn't shake the insecurity, no matter how much she hated it.

Hopefully, pulling off this plan would put her anxiety to rest . . . for good.

"One bodyguard wouldn't come along quietly and he got off a round before the darts took effect."

"Anyone call the cops?"

"Negative. We intercepted on the deserted highway as instructed. The body will be found by morning."

There was a pause, then Ian responded, "Forget about him. Ochoa considered him expendable, we'll do the same."

Marisela winced at the cavalier words, but she wasn't naive enough to think Blake was exaggerating. These gunrunners and arms dealers were ruthless people. For all anyone would guess, the guy was popped by his own people.

"Frank, what's your ETA?"

Frankie glanced out the window. "We're entering the marina now. Where's Ochoa?"

Another pause then Max's voice. "You have ten minutes on him."

Frankie acknowledged the information, then looked at Marisela with piercing eyes. "Ready?"

God, was she? Her heart suddenly leaped in her chest and lodged in her throat.

She managed a nod.

Frankie fisted his hand over his communicator. "You sure?" he whispered.

God damn him. Why did he have to be so frickin' concerned?

Again, she only nodded. If she spoke, either her voice would crack or she'd say something she'd regret later.

"Marisela, I'd like to hear your affirmation for myself," Blake said.

"Ready," she managed.

"Good."

The car pulled to a stop behind a small outbuilding just inside the marina. Frankie unloaded first, then came around to Marisela's side, opened her door and took her hand. With a large smile, she slipped her palm into his and exited the car, straight into his arms. She planted her lips on his and though their tongues clashed and Frankie slipped his hand around her waist and pressed her flush against his body, the kiss lacked intimacy, expectation. But to anyone watching, seen or unseen, they were two ravenous lovers headed for a carnal rendezvous on any one of the luxury yachts moored at the high-priced marina.

Frankie's chuckle quaked through his chest and into hers. "A shame this is all for show."

She swiped her tongue over her lips. "A crying shame."

With her head on his shoulder, her arm hooked around his waist, they laughed as they walked toward the docks. At nearly midnight, there weren't many people around, but lights and music spilled over the water from occupied yachts. They headed toward the largest boat docked in the last slip—*Sharp's Destruction*.

Frankie pretended to rub his nose, activating the tracking device on his watch. Marisela did the same, pressing the side of her watch against the hilt of Frankie's gun, tucked beneath his jacket. From this point on, Ian would have an electronic image of where they were at all times.

"We're approaching the *Destruction*," Frankie reported. "Are we clear?"

A man dressed in a white T-shirt and pants wandered onto the deck. He had a lit cigarette in his mouth, which he spit into the ocean, barely smoked.

The visual signal.

A second later, Ian broke in. "All clear. The crew and an additional unaccounted for bodyguard have been removed from the ship."

A chill slithered along the back of Marisela's neck. "What other surprises aren't we prepared for?" she asked, her voice soft.

Ian picked up her whisper. "Stay in the game, Marisela. You'll be ready for anything."

She glanced at Frankie, who merely shrugged. Not exactly an overwhelming vote of confidence, but she noticed that the closer they got to the gangplank, the quieter and more contemplative Frankie became. His gaze narrowed and his eyes dilated, the pitch center nearly overtaking the inky brown irises. With her arm around him, she could feel his muscles bunch and tense, like a panther, ready to strike at the first sign of prey. They stepped onto the boat seconds later and the instant they disappeared through the door that led to the main salon, they broke into action.

Frankie contacted the Titan crew and verified that the ship was under their control and ready for immediate departure. The cigarette-smoking crewman strolled back onto the deck and busied himself with casting off the lines. Marisela unzipped her light velvet jacket and dug into her blouse to readjust the credit card–sized power pack that had been jabbing her in the tits since they got out of the car. She rechecked the position of her speaker and then dressed again, turning to see Frankie staring at her with lust-filled eyes.

With Blake listening, she simply quirked an eyebrow. As if he hadn't seen her in less than a black lace bra before.

"I'll never get tired of looking," Frankie said, his eyes raking over her with enough fire to burn away the last of her nerves.

"I didn't copy, Frank. Repeat, please," Ian ordered.

"Never mind, bossman. We're preparing the hit."

"Understood," Ian answered, sounding more than mildly annoyed. "Ochoa is entering the marina as we speak. Radio silence until he's down."

"Copy."

Marisela pulled out her gun, not her cherished 9mm, but a special weapon she'd worn tucked in the back of her pants. She loaded her ammunition—a half dozen small darts filled with a sedative that would render the man unconscious until they transferred him off the boat. Frankie had the same weapon, as well as a 9mm semiautomatic and a backup Smith & Wesson. After one last check in the lamp light, Marisela slipped into a closet while Frankie took his place on the outer deck, prepared to take down the bodyguard while he did his initial sweep of the boat.

Inside the closet, the tattoo of Marisela's heartbeat echoed in the enclosed space, filling her ears with the music of her own fear. Her mouth dried and she clamped her lips, forcing her breath through her nose. Her eyes remained trained through the slit in the door, which she'd left ajar. If Ochoa didn't get suspicious and shoot first through the flimsy wood and metal, she might just get a clear shot.

She heard voices outside. Frankie answered in a flawless Venezuelan dialect. He'd just given Ochoa the all-clear to board the boat and apparently, he'd done a good enough job of mimicking a crewman's accent to pass the test. Soon after, two sets of footsteps clattered on the outer deck.

Ochoa burst into the salon and Marisela swallowed a gasp, not prepared for the man's size. She'd known he was big, of course, from the recognizance reports, but reality and adrenaline made him seem more like a giant. Easily six foot six and three hundred and fifty pounds, Ochoa lumbered into the stateroom and made the luxurious space seem very, very small.

A rough-edged scar sliced down his cheek from just above his left eye to the sharpest edge of his chin. She'd noticed the scar in the photograph, but he hadn't looked quite so menacing in a shot taken with a telephoto lens.

When he shouted for his wife, Marisela checked her gun again. When he marched across the room to the door that led to the head, she slipped the barrel through the crack in the door. Before he'd hooked his hand on the door handle, she fired. At close range, the sharp edge of the dart slid effortlessly into the muscle just between his shoulder blade and his neck. Because of his size, she fired a second round. He grunted, reached back in vain, then tumbled to the floor.

"Ochoa's down," she reported.

"Proceed to the engine room," Ian ordered.

"Where's Frankie?"

Before Ian could reply, Marisela heard the engines of the boat, which had been idling when they boarded, roar to life. The deck rocked beneath her boots and she had to grab a hand-hold to keep from tumbling backward into the collection of coats and jackets stored in the closet.

She burst out of her hiding place and pressed her finger lightly on her ear. "I didn't copy."

"Frank is on his way. Meet him in the engine room."

Marisela took a quick moment to check Ochoa, whose breathing was steady, if slightly labored. She checked his pulse. Strong. Good. He wouldn't die tonight.

In one last check, she pushed open an eyelid, but didn't like what she saw. The pupil was dilated. Same for the other eye. If he was coked out, two shots of the sedative wouldn't be enough. But the third could kill him.

A noise from behind sent her whirling around, her weapon aimed, adrenaline surging through her blood. The crewman threw up his hands and after a second, Marisela saw the telltale wire dangling behind his ear.

"You Pan?" she asked, eyeing the man up and down. He was no sprite-like boy, that was for sure. He was tall and well mus-cled, like a bantamweight boxer. Not bulky like a heavyweight, but stacked with enough power to move a mountain. Or more specifically, Ricky Ochoa.

"Guilty as charged. Thanks for not shooting me."

"My pleasure," she replied, holstering her gun.

He nodded and rushed to Ochoa's side. "He's out cold?"

She scowled. "His eyes aren't right. I think he's been using." She tugged the gun out, but Pan stayed her hand.

"I'm taking him out right now," he said, slipping behind the large man and sliding his hands underneath his beefy shoulders. "You need to hit the engine room, ASAP. I've got it from here."

Marisela hesitated, but deferred to the more experienced agent. *Sharp's Destruction* eased out of the marina as Marisela pictured the boat's schematics in her head and made her way below. She slid down the narrow steps until she was in the bowels of the yacht. Near the stern, she found the black bag, left for her by Pan. Inside were the explosives, ready for her and Frankie to set. Pan and Dionysus, somewhere above decks by now, would maneuver Ochoa and the bodyguard off the yacht while she and Frankie prepared the explosives.

She'd unpacked the C-4 and the detonating mechanism when Frankie finally vaulted down the steps.

"Sorry I'm late," he said without the least hint of sincere apology.

"What happened?"

"Brief delay. The bodyguard wasn't as stupid as I'd hoped he'd be."

"With criminals, you can never count on stupid," she said.

He only grunted and retrieved the detonator, which he keyed with the codes that would allow them to activate the bomb from a safe distance.

They worked in silence. Marisela placed four nodules of C-4, then ran the wires toward the signal receiver, which latched to the base of the fuel tank. Before she connected the last wire, Frankie executed a quick test of the remote ignition device. After a thumbs-up, she finished the job, repacked the bag, and headed for the stairs.

Marisela climbed first. She cleared the doorway and turned to check on Frankie when the boat lurched. They were heading out to sea and had picked up speed. She nearly lost her footing, but grabbed a rail and pulled herself out of the passageway— just in time for a big beefy hand to smash her across the face.

Thirteen

COLORS FLASHED AS PAIN exploded across Marisela's face, blinding her in a sickening swirl of reds, oranges, and blacks. Her eyes rattled in their sockets and she blinked desperately, trying to clear her sight. She finally regained her vision in time to deflect a second blow, then roll out of the way.

The assailant was huge. Even without the ability to focus on his face, she knew who he was.

Ochoa.

She grabbed her gun and aimed, but Frankie's shout of warning made her hold her fire. He rushed up the narrow stairs into the ruckus, gun drawn, threw the bag that had contained the explosives to Marisela, who barely grabbed a corner, then aimed his gun at the attacker and fired.

Marisela winced as the weapon discharged. Once. Twice.

The sound was soft and whooshing. She scrambled out of the way and said a silent prayer of thanks. Frankie had pulled the dart gun instead of the 9mm. He'd thought more clearly than she had.

Ochoa wavered, but didn't go down. He tore the darts from his shoulder and chest, then howled and charged Frankie again.

"You won't take my boat! *¡Piratas! ¡Ladrónes! ¡Eres es mi yate!*"

Marisela traded her 9mm for her dart gun and shot off two more rounds into his shoulder blades. Just as before, he couldn't reach them, though he grabbed wildly, screaming in guttural grunts about his goddamn yacht. He was now pumped with nearly six darts of sedative. How could two not have knocked him out for the count?

Frankie rammed his head into Ochoa's gut and used his entire weight to propel the huge man toward the opposite wall. Ochoa wailed when his back slammed against the wall, driving the darts deeper into his fatty flesh.

Frankie jumped back. "Move!" he shouted to Marisela, gesturing wildly for her to scramble to the next room.

Ochoa dropped to his knees. His eyes rolled up in his head and he collapsed to the floor like an iron barbell.

"We can't leave him here," Marisela shouted. She and Frankie were both strong, but hauling Ochoa up narrow stairways to the top deck would be near to impossible. Not with him completely unconscious. If he'd stayed on the main deck, Pan would only have had to drag him a few feet to the exit point.

"If he got down here, he must have taken out Pan somewhere along the way. Find him."

The static in Marisela's ear nearly drove her insane. At first, she heard nothing but feedback, and then she could hardly differentiate between noise and voices until Ian demanded radio silence. His agents immediately complied. Dion verified, at Blake's orders, that he and the bodyguard had already disembarked onto their escape boat when Ochoa woke up and overpowered Pan. His report to warn Frankie and Marisela must have been blocked by a signal too weak to reach their position in the innards of the boat. Now, they had one big dude to transport off the yacht and possibly, an agent down.

"Frank, report."

Marisela listened while she darted to the top deck and spotted Pan splayed and motionless on the ground, a deep gash across his forehead, blood pooling red on the polished deck. She gasped, then moved to him, grabbed his fabric hat and pressed it against the wound.

Frankie's voice crackled in her ear. "Ochoa's out for good this time. He must have been loaded. Heroin. Cocaine. No telling. The first few darts must not have knocked him out for more than a few minutes."

Marisela's stomach dropped. Pan had been hurt because she hadn't shot the bastard with enough sedative. She'd trusted his judgment. She should have had more faith in her own.

"Marisela, report."

She swallowed the thick lump of regret lodged in her throat. "Pan's unconscious. It's a head wound." She glanced up at the railing. Not only was the wood and brass covered in blood, there was a visible crack. "It's bad. Looks like Ochoa banged him hard against the railing to knock him out."

"What's his blood pressure?" Blake asked.

"I'm not a doctor!"

"Feel for his pulse."

Ian's voice didn't so much as raise or inflect, injecting Marisela with a sense of calm she wasn't sure she'd ever feel again once this mess was over with.

She complied, remembering that Max had given her a basic first aid course just a few days ago in case she or Frankie were hurt during the mission. Her hand slipped against the blood, so she had to feel around, closing her eyes and concentrating on finding the right spot on his neck. The sickening sweet scent seeping from his wound nearly made her gag.

The pulse was so faint, she missed it the first time.

"Not good," she reported. "I can barely feel anything."

"Can you lift him?"

Marisela's heart slammed against her chest. Her instincts screamed not to move the injured agent, but she knew they had no choice. If she demanded that Blake send in a second team to execute a rescue and abort this mission, Javier Perez would know he'd been set up. The rescue of Jessica Perez would fail before the mission truly began.

She moved Pan's body, arranging him for maximum leverage. Still, while she could lift him halfway to her shoulder, she'd never get him off the boat without dropping him into the water, where he'd surely sink before she could pull him out.

"Negative. Not alone. I need Frankie."

"Frank?"

"Ochoa smashed the remote device when he came at me and Marisela," Frankie informed them. "We'll have to go with the timer."

A crackle and pop broke into the communication stream, followed by Max's voice, so cool, a chill chased up Marisela's spine.

"Perez's men just drove onto the overlook. They're expecting an explosion soon. If they don't see one, the whole mission is a bust."

Silence ensued and Marisela's ears ached with the lack of information. Blake had a decision to make. With the clock ticking, they only had time to save one man.

"Frank, set the charge. Give yourself five minutes. Leave Ochoa. He sealed his own fate. Help Marisela get Pan off the yacht. We'll rendezvous at the prearranged point. Two cars, Max, see to it. Marisela, you return to the hotel for contact with Perez and Frank, you stay with Pan. Good luck."

Marisela shook her head, banishing all her regrets, all her fears, and concentrated on completing the mission and getting Pan to safety while Frankie set the explosive charge with a timer. She tossed the bag into the skiff tied below, then hoisted Pan halfway over the railing, keeping pressure on his wound and reassuring the unconscious man that he would survive. Despite his dead weight, she touched her hand to her chest and said a quick prayer. Against her better judgment, she'd worn the locket Elise had given her. Manipulative or not, the charm reminded her that she had a child to rescue.

Frankie burst out of the doorway. "Four minutes and counting."

Marisela transferred Pan's weight to Frankie, then vaulted over the side. The inflatable, tinted dark so that no light would reflect as they escaped into the night, rocked under her weight. She found her balance quickly, then motioned for Frankie to lower the injured man to her.

The operation wasn't pretty, but it was fast and with Pan unconscious, he wouldn't feel the pain of being dropped into the tender with only Marisela to cushion his fall. She shoved his body into the bubbled side, then covered him with a tarp, not only to fight off his shock, but to hide him in case Perez's men were watching their escape.

Frankie fired the engine to life while Marisela released the line that secured the dinghy to the yacht.

"Time?" she asked.

Frankie and Ian answered in unison. "One minute, eighteen seconds."

"Get down," Frankie ordered before he pushed the engine to the limit.

They roared over the waves, the choppy Intercoastal water bouncing them like children inside an inflatable bounce house. Marisela dove flat against the bottom and rolled next to Pan to protect his body against the coming explosion. "Sixty seconds," Blake said calmly.

Marisela raised her head. The yacht grew smaller as they moved away, but her heartbeat accelerated with every inch of distance between them and the bomb. She closed her eyes tight and said a prayer of eternal rest for Ricky Ochoa.

Damned fool. Loved his boat more than his own god-damned life.

When Ian counted down to three seconds, then two, then one, Frankie leaned low into the boat. The blast roared before the water heaved, but the heat of the fire reached out like the devil's fingers, scorching the back of their necks. Debris splashed around them and Frankie maneuvered their boat in a sharp angle toward shore.

The sickening sound of the sizzle would haunt her forever, she knew. A man had died because she'd screwed up. Not enough darts the first time. Not enough.

The chatter in her ears brought her to the present as Ian directed Frankie to the rendezvous point. Two agents waited on the shore, one of them Max. They splashed out to the boat and between Max and Frankie, unloaded Pan with maximum care and speed, the rescue hidden by sea oats and banyan trees. The third man, who identified himself as Romulus, spirited Marisela off to a dark sedan, giving her no time to speak to Frankie.

The minute the car sped out of the dense foliage, Marisela spun in the seat and watched the other car, an SUV, disappear in the opposite direction.

"Frankie, what is Pan's condition?" she shouted.

No response.

"Ian, what is Pan's condition?"

The silence deafened. She scooted to the front seat and slapped Romulus on the shoulder. "Why is there no radio contact?"

Romulus touched his earpiece. "The mission is complete. Communications are suspended."

"What about Pan?"

"He'll be all right."

"You don't know that."

"Blake makes agent safety a priority. He'll get the best medical care."

She slammed back into the seat, unwilling to share with this stranger that Pan wouldn't have needed medical care if she'd pumped Ochoa with more darts than she had. Per her training, two should have been more than enough, but Max had warned that someone on drugs, particularly heroin or cocaine, might need a higher dosage. When she'd shot Ochoa the last time after the attack, she'd turned him into a lump of lard too heavy for rescue.

She'd sentenced him to death.

She glanced out the window. They were on a bridge, but the reflection of the sliver of moon on the water revealed nothing of what had just happened less than ten minutes ago not a half a mile away. No wisp of smoke. No spark of fire. Nothing.

As if it had never happened. Only it had, and Marisela would never forget.

She should have known. Slamming the door behind her, Marisela marched two steps into the hotel room and stopped, her emotions a jumble of indignation and self-recrimination. And damn it, the last person she wanted to confront right now had propped himself into the chair beside the window, his face half-cast in shadow, with only his tight, square chin visible in the slats of light filtering through the blinds.

His fingers, steepled on the table, moved first. His hands slipped into the darkness, then reemerged with a small, black electronic device she recognized as GPS—synchronized to her tracking device, more than likely. In an anger she couldn't explain, she tore off her watch and tossed it on the bed.

She clenched her fists until her fingers ached, willing the shaking to stop long enough for her to talk to her boss without sounding like a, well, like a girl. A frightened girl. A regretful girl. A girl whose incompetence had just led to a man's violent death.

"How's Pan?" she finally managed.

Blake leaned forward so that a slash of neon from the sign outside ignited his aquamarine eyes. "Concussion, but so far, the swelling on his brain is under control." He toyed with the tracking device, tapping the pads of his fingers on the case. "He has the best care."

She stepped further into the room, certain he could see the way her muscles quivered uncontrollably, as they had from the minute she'd slid into the car with Romulus.

"You're so sure he'll recover?" she challenged.

Ian stood, grabbed her watch from the bed and examined the timepiece with a cursory glance. "He's a strong man with an equally strong will to live. All of my agents fit that description."

Marisela tossed her bag onto the bed, followed by her dart gun, which seemed to thud onto the mattress with more weight than it warranted. She twisted to remove her holster, but her shoulders balked with a numbing ache. Her cheek throbbed. She suddenly felt as if she had the weight of two men around her—and in a way, she figured she did.

But she'd be damned if she'd show that to Blake.

She propelled herself into the bathroom, doused a washcloth with cold water to wipe some of the salt spray and smoky grime from her face, hands, and neck. She'd had no idea the fire would trail so far, though a shift in wind had helped the blaze along. The putrid smell of burning fuel and congealing blood remained fused in her nostrils, in her mouth, and plastered to her skin. She turned on the water in the shower to the hottest setting, then ripped off her jacket and flung it on the bed.

"I'm taking a shower before Perez calls," she announced, hoping with uncharacteristic optimism that the information would compel Blake to leave. She haphazardly grabbed clothes from her suitcase, not entirely surprised when Ian strolled into the bathroom and turned off the scalding stream of water.

What did shock her was the way he came up behind her and slid his hands onto her shoulders.

"Pan's injury isn't your fault."

She wanted to shake him off. Every nerve ending from her neck to her forearms screamed for her to throw an elbow or a backfist so that he wouldn't touch her, wouldn't attempt to soothe her with that honeyed, cultured voice.

But she didn't move. Instead, she allowed his fingers to spear into the aching tendons in her neck and shoulders, massaging away the tension in slow, practiced strokes.

"I should have hit him with more juice from the start," she said, reciting the mantra her conscience had been chanting for the past half hour. "He shouldn't have had the strength to attack Pan. He shouldn't have gone below decks where we couldn't get him out."

Ian stretched his ministrations to her spine, pressing his thumbs along her discs, following the path downward to the middle of her shoulder blades. His touch, so like the man, was sure and decisive and strong. Everything about him was controlled precision, right down to the way his breath caressed her ear when he spoke.

"Too much sedative and he would have died anyway."

With tiny movements, she shook her head in denial, not wanting to do anything that would make him stop. She knew he wasn't lying, only oversimplifying. Her heart cracked at the thought that this man would seek to mollify her when her mistake had nearly cost him the life of one of his most valuable agents. Suddenly, he wasn't acting so superior toward her. There was equality in the way he touched her, as if for once, she possessed something he wanted. Maybe it was just sex. And maybe she didn't care.

The moment had grown intimate, but she couldn't harness the willpower to break free. His kneading lulled her muscles into sweet surrender, though her mind struggled with defiance.

"Killing doesn't bother you?" she asked, her throat dry and cottony.

He stepped closer, his chest and thighs nearly in complete contact with her body. With deep pressure, he rubbed his palms up and down her arms. She could hear the slight rasp in his breathing, a telltale hitch that revealed a vital clue about his aroused state, even more so than the increasing length of his erection against the small of her back.

"I'm bothered when one of my people dies, but otherwise, all's fair in love and war. These aren't boy scouts we're dealing with. They're conscienceless thieves and murderers."

Despite the sultry hum of his voice, she heard an indignation there that gave her the power to turn around and face him eye-to-eye. As she suspected, the centers of his irises were wide with the darkness and the tension of true, unbridled desire. He wanted her, and God help her, she wanted him back.

Sex is so sweet after you've faced death. And won.

Frankie's words slipped back into her brain, like a warning she was sure he'd never intended. The need coursing through her blood, lighting the tips of her breasts on fire even as they scraped against the cool, stiff cotton of Blake's shirt, wasn't real. It was adrenaline. Pure and inescapable. They'd succeeded in their mission, despite the unexpected turns. She couldn't deny her innate attraction to Blake, but her passion for him now was only a lack of resistance, born on the wave of her regret and his compassion, enhanced by a natural attraction she'd repressed up until this very moment.

His hands slipped down to her thighs. Her muscles were still shaking, still reacting to the overflow of hormones pumping through her body from the confrontation with death and destruction. His palms seemed to soothe the quaking to gentle trembles, even as her flesh ignited with unbearable heat.

This wasn't real—which was exactly why she could so easily tilt her head back so he could lock his lips on her neck.

The sensation exploded on her skin. Images of fire and wood hurling through the air and splashing into dark, unforgiving water faded from her mind. She concentrated on the silk assault of Ian's mouth, the moist pleasure of his tongue.

He caught her brief stumble by bracing his hand on her back. He tugged her closer so that the pressure of his hard sex against her body tripped her over to the next level of arousal. He murmured words she didn't even try to understand while his mouth dropped lower, teasing the nerve endings across her shoulder blades, forcing the world and reality farther into the darkness. Away from here. Away from any thought that could stop him and therefore stop this delectable pleasure. He curved his hand around her backside, then reached between her legs and pressed the seam of her pants until her blood thrummed with pounding need.

Then she made a mistake. She looked up. Even as his chin tilted and his eyes locked with hers to prepare her for an inevitable, potentially world-shattering kiss, she recognized the full breadth of what she'd been about to do and rolled slowly out of the way.

He didn't chase her.

She forced her fuddled brain to remember what they'd been talking about before lust and simple, bone-wringing need overwhelmed her senses and sent her spiraling into a fantasy world where she could screw her boss and not ruin her career.

Oh, yeah. *Death.* Her favorite topic.

"We aren't executioners, Blake. We don't get to pick who lives and who dies."

The words sounded entirely hollow, no matter how sure she was that at some point in her life, she'd believed them with all her soul. Right now, her mouth was spouting theories about life, death, and morality while her mind whirled with images of naked bodies and wet, intense kisses that banished the world to another realm. But the erotic images were relatively easy to push away. All she had to do was think about Pan lying semi-lifeless on the bottom of the skiff beside her.

Two men—almost three—had died this week because of her. She couldn't berate herself indefinitely, that she understood. Blake had a point. Men like Nestor Rocha and Ricky Ochoa made their choices and expected, some day, to die because of the lives they led.

But she suddenly realized that if she continued in the employ of Titan International she'd have to accept the possibility of her own inevitable death as well.

And that, she couldn't do. Not tonight. Not ever.

"I think you need to leave now," she said, digging her hands into the back pockets of her pants, knowing the heat effusing over her body was just an illusion, a crutch, a purely physical reaction to an emotional situation she'd been unprepared for. This time. But never again.

He looked at her with one tilted eyebrow, as if her reaction surprised him. "Are you sure?"

She nodded, then grinned wryly. "You're not the kind of guy who likes to take advantage of a woman who's just been through hell, are you?"

He matched her cynical expression. "Never. But I am the kind of guy who'd help you forget that hell, if only for a little while. No strings. No questions asked in the morning."

The idea tempted her more than she'd ever admit, even if he was her boss. Most of her lovers, Frankie included, subscribed to the machismo belief that they could satisfy any woman, any time, without even trying, and that they had the God-given right to prove their prowess to each and every attractive woman who caught their eye. Blake possessed the same self-assurance—but she imagined he didn't have to demonstrate his prowess to anyone. Not even himself.

So she was fairly certain he wasn't insulted when she glanced longingly at the door.

He smiled—only the second genuine grin she'd seen on him since they'd met—straightened, and walked toward the exit. When he spoke, the soft sound of compassion had slipped away, replaced by the clipped tone of professionalism. "Perez will contact you tonight." He removed a cell phone from his pocket and tossed it on the bed. "Use this monitored phone for all communications. Don't agree to go anywhere until Frank returns, which should be soon. I'm sure you're anxious to see him."

She nodded, but kept her face stoic. She'd let her guard down enough with him tonight, allowed herself a taste of temptation she couldn't afford. For once in her life, Frankie represented safety and security. How the hell had that happened?

Fourteen

THE BUZZ BROUGHT IAN awake instantaneously. With only the slightest fumble in the dark, he pressed the button on his nightstand without so much as rattling the crystal snifter he'd left there, untouched.

"Blake here."

Max's ever-present voice drifted into the darkness. "The call is in."

He rubbed the sleep from his eyes. He couldn't have been out for long. "What time is it?"

"Four A.M."

Barely three hours.

"Doesn't the man think his assassins deserve a little sleep?"

"Apparently, he's anxious to set up the meeting."

"Who's doing the talking?"

"Marisela."

Ian's chest tightened. "Pipe it in."

With a smooth transition devoid of crackles or pops or static, the conversation between Marisela, in the role of Dolores Tosca, and Javier Perez drifted into the room. Ian rolled back onto the pillow and hooked one arm behind his head. With the briefest nudge to his imagination, he could picture Marisela in the bed beside him talking to their client's ex-lover—a much more palatable image than dealing with the fact that by now, Frank Vega was the one lying beside her.

"You don't believe in sleep, *Señor* Perez?" Marisela asked, her voice appropriately thicker with the accent of her parent's native country, plus deeper and richer with her exhaustion.

"I do adore a good night's rest, *Señora* Tosca. But I was so pleased with your success that I wanted to share my congratulations. You and your husband have exceeded my expectations in every way."

Marisela sniffed. Yawned. Loudly. "We did what you paid us to do. No more, no less."

Over the phone line, Javier Perez's chuckle seemed extraordinarily hollow, raising the hackles along the back of Ian's neck.

"I wish to meet with you and your husband later this morning. I want to present the final payment personally, and of course, discuss further business dealings, as my man proposed to your associate."

"*¿Dónde?*" Marisela asked.

"At my hotel," Perez answered. "I'd like to invite you and your husband to be my guests for breakfast. I'll send a car."

"Make it lunch and we'll drive ourselves. What time?"

She sounded tired and bored, but Perez retained the smile in his voice—one that grated on the fine tune of Ian's nerves. "You name the time. I'm leaving the States in the early evening tomorrow, so—"

She cut him off with a curt, "One o'clock."

"Wonderful," he said, then named the hotel and provided the room number. "I look forward to—"

Marisela disconnected the call. A tense silence ensued until Max buzzed back in.

"I'll have Dion and Romulus tail them from the hotel."

"Do that," Ian snapped. He'd wanted Marisela to assume the part of Dolores Tosca, but if she'd gone too far . . .

"She did fine," Max reassured him, correctly interpreting Ian's mood.

"She was rude," Ian countered.

"By all accounts, Dolores Tosca was not Miss Congeniality. Don't forget what she did for a living."

Ian stretched, knowing Max was right. "Is everything in place to pursue Marisela and Frank if Perez takes them with him to Puerto Rico tomorrow?"

Max paused, but as expected, came up with an affirmative response. "The team that worked on the *Sharp's Destruction* is already en route to the island and will pick up a new boat by tomorrow that has all the equipment we'll need. The plane is fueled and ready to go. We won't let them out of sight."

"Good. Is there any news on Pan?"

"Stable. Doctor won't know about permanent damage until he wakes up."

"You contacted his wife?"

"She's there already."

"Cover story?"

"Mugging."

"Ochoa's family?"

"Under wraps. The wife is terrified. I don't expect she'll cause us any trouble so long as we keep her and the baby comfortable."

"The bodyguard?"

"Moved to another location."

"No complications, Max," Ian said by way of warning.

"Of course. Goodnight, sir."

Ian disconnected the link, rolled over, and opened the blinds on the window behind his bed. The moon was a sharp slice of light in the early morning sky, with no sign of the rising sun yet in the eastern waters. He couldn't remember the last night he'd slept more than three hours in one stretch, and yet he also couldn't dredge up the slightest memory of looking out the window or over the railing at a singularly spectacular view. Who had the time anymore? Who had the heart to give a damn?

He'd bet Marisela looked at the stars, probably every night if the mood suited her. Frank, too, if for no other reason than because he could after years in the pen.

The mental picture of his agents standing near a window while admiring the moon together drove a slim pin through the center of his brain. He speared his hands through his hair and rested his head in his palms, wondering what the hell had been going through his mind tonight. His first error in judgment had been going to her hotel room in the first place. He'd used the excuse that he was delivering the tapped cell phone, but any of his agents could have done that duty, including Max, who'd asked twice for the assignment. His friend undoubtedly sensed the growing fascination he had with Marisela and in his boundless insight, saw the train wreck that would occur if the dynamics of his interactions with Marisela skimmed anywhere near an intimate dalliance. Hadn't the disaster of his last affair with an agent taught him anything?

Women who made their living pretending to be other people never revealed their true selves.

Women who made their living by betrayal, lies, and death could not shift back into the civilized world without causing destruction.

Women who made their living as agents in his employ should remain, always, off-limits.

So why had he nearly destroyed the tentative hold he had on Titan by touching Marisela's skin in the privacy of a cheap motel room?

The buzzer broke into his thoughts.

"He called back?" he asked Max, surprised Javier Perez would be so insistent.

Max hesitated, then replied matter-of-factly. "Brynn would like to speak with you."

Ian's gut suddenly filled with burning hot lead.

"Is she here?"

"No, sir. Calling from an undisclosed location in Toronto, if my triangulation is correct."

Ian swallowed his annoyance. His sister rarely came back to North America. But so long as Brynn wasn't on the other side of his door, he didn't give a damn where she was.

"Patch her through. I've apparently had what little rest I'm getting tonight."

And what little peace of mind.

Ian shook his head and delivered the cheeriest hello he could summon to his twin. He anticipated that she'd chitchat a few minutes, then fill him in on her exploits in whatever case she'd undoubtedly made great progress on. And just after she'd lulled him to relax in their familiar sibling exchange, she'd slide in a loaded question—a query he couldn't avoid without outright lying. He'd done enough of that over the past few months and each mistruth chipped away at him. Still, he had to do whatever was necessary to keep Titan in his hands, where his legacy belonged.

Javier Perez's hotel, a tiny boutique establishment with a prime location on snowy white sand in the heart of South Beach encompassed everything Marisela had ever dreamed about Miami. From the salsa beat piped into the mirrored elevator to the pastel, art deco designs of the furnishings and tile floor, she half-expected to see Gloria Estefan sipping a mojito on the balcony as Perez's bodyguards ushered them through the luxurious penthouse. Instead, she found Javier Perez and a woman with a fake tan and vapid blue eyes sitting at a table set with fine china and crisp linens that fluttered in the ocean breeze.

Perez stood the minute his bodyguards stepped aside and Frankie and Marisela, as Rogelio and Dolores Tosca, walked through the impressive archway onto the terrace. The arms dealer looked exactly like his pictures, only more in focus. He was slim, but not tall. Elegant, and yet quick—just like a man who'd orchestrated his own rise to wealth and power should be.

He held out his hand, which Frankie accepted. *"Señor* Tosca. I'm honored. And *señora,"* he said to Marisela, offering his cool palm to her next, "you are indeed as beautiful as I've been told."

Marisela cocked an eyebrow. Either this was a lame compliment or Dolores's beauty had been highly exaggerated. Not that Marisela had seen more than the one grainy picture, but she wasn't exactly a classic beauty, Latina or not.

"You flatter me, *señor*."

"Yes, I do," he said, winking warmly. "But it is deserved. Please, sit down."

He spoke in rapid-fire Spanish to the blonde, who didn't even bother to look offended that she hadn't been introduced or that she'd been instantaneously dismissed. Arm candy. Once the bimbo left, they were alone, except, of course, for the two formidable bodyguards that flanked the entrance to the second-story suite.

Frankie cleared his throat, but otherwise remained silent, his gaze drifting over the balcony while his ears clearly remained trained on the conversation at the table. From all accounts, Rogelio Tosca allowed his wife to do most of the talking, especially the niceties and chitchat. He was the executioner; she the planner.

Secretly, Marisela couldn't help but enjoy the situation. If not for the Toscas' established roles, Frankie would never have allowed her to take the lead. She knew he had reservations about her inexperience, reservations she'd probably heightened thanks to her poor judgment the night before. And yet, when Frankie had slipped into their room last night, he'd said nothing except to report Pan's tentatively stable condition. While he'd showered, she'd taken Perez's call. With him nearby, she'd finally fallen asleep. During the night, he'd swung his arm possessively across her belly, and damn if the likely accidental gesture hadn't warmed her to the core.

Now, as he held out the chair for her, he glanced at her with eyes that revealed nothing—reminding her to do the same.

Perez snapped his fingers and one of the bodyguards fetched two silver carafes, one piping with hot coffee and the other with equally steamy milk. Marisela directed him in Spanish on the ratio she preferred. Frankie waved away the milk altogether.

"*Señor* Perez," she said, taking a sip from her coffee. "My husband and I appreciate your hospitality, but we are anxious to leave Miami. If you don't mind, we'd like to hear your proposal so we can consider our immediate options."

Perez watched her intently, as if every word crossing her lips contained a secret code. Luckily, she'd prepared for such scrutiny.

"I understand, of course," he assured her. His voice was rich and languid, not unlike the ocean breeze swirling through the palms on the terrace. "But my proposal is complicated and requires the input of my top associates, which is why I would like you to accompany me to Puerto Rico."

Marisela glanced at Frankie, who sullenly shook his head.

"My husband and I have other obligations, *señor*. Perhaps we can join you, let's say, in a week?"

Perez neither smiled nor frowned. He merely contemplated her suggestion. Marisela hoped their plan to not appear too anxious didn't backfire.

"I'm not a patient man, I'm afraid. But I am generous. If you join me now, you will enjoy a relatively uninterrupted vacation in the tropics, as a reward for the fine job you did last night."

Frankie rustled noncommittally in his chair while Marisela

carefully replaced her coffee cup on the delicate china saucer. "We're sure your home is lovely, *señor*, but we are independent contractors. Our business is lucrative. We have no need to limit our client base at this time."

Perez nodded thoughtfully, smoothly draping a napkin across his lap. A second later, two waiters arrived with three colorful plates laden with crispy greens, artfully cut vegetables, and a tangy mango-based salsa. Despite her concentration on the conversation, Marisela's mouth watered. They'd skipped breakfast and cluster-fuck or not, last night had built up a ravenous appetite—on too many levels to count.

She unfurled her napkin, but ignored the silverware. Food in her mouth—particularly delicious food—would undoubtedly derail her concentration.

"Please do not take our reluctance as a personal insult," she said earnestly. "We mean no disrespect."

Perez reached out and patted her hand, then gestured for her to pick up her fork. "I understand completely, *señora*. My needs are not long-term, but timing is of the essence. With careful planning, your services could ensure my continued domination in my field, which could benefit both of us, *¿sí?* However, I have personal reasons for returning to Puerto Rico *inmediatamente*. I assumed that a week or two on my private island, with fine food and ultimate luxury as an incentive, would lure you to listen to my proposal."

Frankie stabbed a few leaves of lettuce onto his fork. "You don't have to lure us, *señor*. If you pay, we'll listen."

Marisela smiled with an extra dose of patience to make up for Frankie's gruff, but practiced, tone. It wasn't such a stretch for him to act the reticent conversationalist, Marisela thought with a secret grin. Then again, she wasn't exactly earning an Academy award by playing the coldhearted bitch, either.

"What my husband means, *señor,* is that now that we've done business together, niceties are appreciated, but not necessary. We are at your disposal should the need arise."

Perez took his time to chew and swallow, his gaze never locking on either of them for long, but darting casually between his guests and the view—completely comfortable in his surroundings. And rightfully so. Chances were, if one of his holding companies didn't own this hotel, he at least owned every single person inside.

"I appreciate your trust. Which reminds me."

Another snap of fingers and a briefcase appeared at Marisela's feet. She checked to make sure the lock was secure and coded with the prearranged combination, but otherwise ignored the cash payment inside.

"We're happy you're satisfied with our work," she said with a solemn nod.

"I'm more than satisfied, *señora.* I'm thrilled. I had extreme reservations about destroying such a lovely family. The fact that the woman and child were inexplicably delayed was a stroke of genius, not to mention a show of true generosity of spirit."

A chill crept along Marisela's spine, a prelude to a shiver she tamped down with another sip of coffee. Was this some sort of trick question? "I cannot take credit where none is due, *señor.* We had nothing to do with the family not showing up. Rogelio and I guessed that you had been behind the change in plans."

Perez's eyebrows arched over wide hazelnut eyes. "Me? No, no. I have no taste for the blood of innocents, but my enemy cast his own lot when he brought his family with him into my territory."

Marisela decided to lay her cards on the line. Well, Dolores's cards, anyway.

"Is this a test?"

"*¿Perdone?*"

She shifted in her seat. "If you want to know something, *Señor* Perez, please, ask."

He didn't hesitate. "Have you killed a child before?"

"No."

"Would you?"

Marisela leaned forward. "Not as a target, no."

"Peripheral damage?"

She sat back in the cushioned wicker chair. "*Señor* Perez, my husband and I make no moral judgments. We do what you pay us to. I don't understand this line of questioning."

But in honesty, she could take an educated guess. He was inviting two world-renowned killers to his home—the home he shared with his daughter. The real Toscas likely wouldn't know that, but Marisela did and she figured he didn't want to expose his daughter to ruthless, cold-blooded assassins, even though she likely mingled with his cohorts and employees, no less murderous, on a daily basis. What an odd distinction he attempted to make. When he killed, he did so for power, money, and likely, revenge. When the Toscas killed, money alone drove them. Did that make them more ruthless in his mind?

"I apologize for dancing around a topic of great importance," he said. "I do not bring many people to my island, but as I said, I have no time to fly my associates here to meet you. I have credible information that three shipments of mine, already en route to their destinations, are being monitored by an upstart rival who intends to steal my product."

Credible information leaked to him by Titan operatives, no doubt. Ian had warned that he'd act quickly to force Perez home. Titan operatives knew the location of Perez's private island, but any attempt to take the girl without agents inside would result in a bloodbath—with Titan swirling down the drain. The only way to complete this operation was from the inside out.

"I need to regroup, meet with my people," he explained. "I can do that best from my home base."

"Where your family is," Marisela said. The comment was likely more intuitive than Dolores Tosca would ever speak aloud, but Marisela had to follow her instincts. Frankie ignored the conversation as if she'd made no error in judgment in turning the conversation so decidedly where it needed to go. Perez was a slippery character—obviously smart and suspicious. Better to finish this dialogue now and make their move rather than follow him to Puerto Rico under an air of suspicion.

"*Sí, señora.*"

"Rogelio and I do not work both sides of the coin, so to speak. Once we have been paid for our services, you have our loyalty. You have only our word, but we would do nothing to bring harm to your family."

She patted the briefcase for emphasis and was thankful that this claim was, surprisingly, true. The Toscas refused to work for rivals, which was why their murderous profession took them all over the globe.

Perez's expression softened. "I believe your sentiment, *señora,* but what you say is not entirely true, through no fault of your own. You might bring harm without intending to."

He'd given no verbal clue, but Marisela knew in her gut that Perez was worried about his daughter. Not his business associates or their secrets, not his money—his child.

"*Por favor, señor.* This is about trust, *¿sí?* You tell us where we are welcome and where we are not and we will respect your orders."

His eyes met hers in a stare that was at once inscrutable and painfully revealing. Marisela's mind swam with the incongruity of his response, wondering if his reaction was all an act, meant to illicit some response from her that would give their ruse away.

"I will give you no orders, *señora,* save those that would keep you safe. Please, join me in Puerto Rico. You will meet the men at the top level of my organization and perhaps help us plan the counterattack on my competitor. And of course, for your change in plans, I will make the trip worth your while."

In an instant, his uncertainty disappeared, replaced by the charming businessman Perez undoubtedly played most of the time.

Marisela matched his relaxed posture. They were in.

"I have no doubt we will be treated like royalty, *señor.* Your hospitality may be just what my husband and I need."

Fifteen

FROM ACROSS THE SEAT of the jetlike Agusta 109C helicopter, Frankie watched Marisela press her face to the bowed window like a child outside a candy store. God, had he ever been that wide-eyed? That green? Until this week, he'd barely taken the time to think back to his childhood, much less his misspent youth. He often thought about the wild, cocky *muchacho* he'd been, darting from scam to scam as someone else—someone whose curious, rebellious nature hadn't ended up propelling him into prison. Together, he and Marisela had experienced a hundred firsts—and here they were again. Just like old times.

Only she hadn't quite grasped that in reality, nothing was the same. Not him. Not her. Not their friendship. Especially not the sex. Even now, with Marisela no more than a foot away from him and the taste of her skin still fresh in his mind even though he hadn't touched her intimately for days, he couldn't help but suspect that he'd need a lifetime to know this woman completely.

But Frankie held his tongue on that point as they relaxed in the relative privacy on the last leg of their trip, sitting next to each other in the luxury cabin with just one guard in front with the pilot.

The copter jumped through a pocket of air and Marisela grabbed the brushed kid leather seat. Her eyes sought his instantly and he calmed her with a quirk of a grin. Just hinting that the flight didn't make him the least bit nervous was enough to bolster her courage. He chuckled, then reached down and patted her knee. She didn't balk at his touch. Instead, she rewarded him with a tiny, private smile that made his mouth water. They were, after all, pretending to be a married couple.

How he'd kept his hands to himself after all this time shocked the hell out of him—especially after last night. God, she'd played the pro from start to finish. She'd done her job, watched his back, reined in any fear or panic even after Ochoa had screwed up their plan and turned his fake execution into a very real one. Frankie had witnessed the smoldering fire in Marisela's eyes prior to their boarding the yacht and he'd felt the very real lust coursing through her when they'd kissed at the marina, even if the *beso* had been just for show. From that moment, he'd anticipated a wild night of post-mission sex upon their return to the hotel, but Pan's injury, Perez's call, and her complete exhaustion had waylaid his plans.

This morning, she'd brimmed with too much nervous energy. But now, an hour before sunset, dressed in a sinfully short miniskirt that rode up her thighs, he figured the time had finally come for them to work off the last of their pent-up sexual energy. He'd never done it in a helicopter. And who better to appreciate the unique experience than Marisela?

Still, he had more than a little trouble conjuring a picture of Rogelio and Dolores Tosca "doing it" in the sky.

"See anything yet?" he asked, his hand pressed to the left side of his earphones, which rattled against the hoop earring he'd adopted in true Rogelio-style.

"The most incredibly turquoise water I've ever seen!" she answered, with what Frankie guessed was a boatload more enthusiasm than Dolores Tosca would ever reveal. He decided not to worry about the lapse. Anyone listening in—and he was certain someone was—would expect a husband and wife, no matter their professions, to let down their guard.

Might as well give them something private to listen to.

"More colorful than the Sea of Cortez? Than that bay off the coast of Honduras?" he asked.

Marisela blinked twice, then rolled her eyes impatiently. The Toscas had traveled to just about every corner of the world, particularly in the Caribbean and Central and South America, where their services were particularly in demand.

"Much more," she said, then stuck out her tongue at him.

"Must be a trick of the sun," he said with a chuckle.

"Maybe Javier is right and this is his own private paradise."

Frankie glanced around, finally allowing the indulgences of the luxury around him to sink in—indulgences men like Javier Perez and Ian Blake probably took for granted as a privilege they earned simply because they breathed.

"*His* private paradise," Frankie said, scooting closer to

Marisela. Their long legs jockeyed for space. He let her win, but only because it meant her bare skin would now be easily accessible to his touch. "Not ours."

She eyed him from beneath thick, black lashes. "It could be ours, too. This is an opportunity, Rogelio. Perez wants us. He deals straight. We can trust him."

"For now," he said, adjusting the mouthpiece so that whoever might be listening heard every word.

"Maybe 'for now' will turn into something more."

They didn't have a lot of time to ingratiate themselves into Perez's organization. Since the moment they walked into Perez's hotel room, they'd focused on finding the opportunity to snatch Jessica. As soon as they accomplished that goal, they could get the hell out of Ian Blake's control.

Or at least, Frankie could. He wasn't so sure Marisela would be satisfied with only one mission in this seductive world. He'd watched her savor the fine food, admire the top-of-the-line training equipment, and covet the free supply of chic, designer clothes. And she'd performed exceptionally well last night under extreme pressure. And yet, she still had much to learn, though Frankie had no doubt that Ian Blake salivated at the chance to teach her himself.

Frankie shook the infuriating thought aside. For now, they had an idea to implant into Perez's ambitious mind—and this conversation was the perfect chance to move toward that goal.

"What are you talking about, *mi corazón?*" he asked, improvising the script they'd discussed earlier.

"I'm talking about working for Perez long-term," she answered, right on cue.

"He may not want us long-term."

"*Verdad,*" she said with a convincing nod. "*Pero,* we could change his mind. We're valuable, Rogelio. We know the alliances and blood feuds in the arms game. We've made friends with men who could further Perez's own operation. Or take him down."

He slipped his hand onto her thigh. "*Mi corazón,* what are thinking?"

Marisela's eyes flashed in warning, but with an even gaze, he convinced her there was no harm in surrendering to one slim thread of the desire that connected them with the tenacity of a spider's web.

"I'm not saying anything," she insisted. "I'm just thinking we should consider the value of Perez's power to our own ambitions. How rare is it that we meet a man like him?"

"You're weary of this life, aren't you, *mi amor?*"

"I don't know what you're talking about," she snapped.

She could be tough as nails and cold as ice and every other cliché of a kick-ass *mujer* she projected to the world, but damn it, he knew her better than to buy what she showed on the outside. She might have skillfully assumed the role of Dolores Tosca, but the real Marisela was never far from the surface.

He turned his hand over, laying his knuckles softly over her bare skin. "We live such isolated lives. You long to try something different. You want change."

Her gaze darted aside, but her hand inched closer to his. He broached the final distance and wrapped his fingers around hers.

"*Sí.* Change."

"Then I'll hear what Javier Perez has to say and then if you like what you see and hear, you can offer him what we know. *Nunca te olivides que eres mi reina."*

At this, Marisela rolled her eyes again and tugged her hand free and returned to looking out the window. Okay, so that was a little over the top, reminding her of her gang days while whoever was listening thought he was just claiming her to be the queen of his heart. Still, when their gazes met, she snickered, which elicited a smile from him despite his strong resistance. When was he going to learn? Resisting Marisela was a mission doomed for failure, no matter how hard he tried.

As they prepared to land on the ten square mile swatch of land Javier Perez had dubbed *Isla de Piratas* because cutthroats and privateers once used the land to hide and protect their booty, Marisela glanced over at Frankie, stunned. The aerial tour Marisela had convinced the pilot to give them made one point painfully clear—Javier Perez's stronghold was impenetrable.

Nearly entirely flat, the island boasted at least a half-dozen concrete block towers tucked behind slim sky-reaching palms. The guards posted in the third-story turrets made great show of their M-16s, waving them toward the pilot in greeting. Though Perez had stayed in San Juan to attend to a personal matter, his men had just made sure his guests understood what sort of home he ran here.

Taking Jessica Perez off this island was not going to be easy.

Marisela's stomach swirled about three seconds behind the chopper as it flew toward the landing pad within a Spanish tile complex some might call a grand *hacienda*. Marisela thought *fortress* was a much more accurate term.

The main house was stunning and seemingly precarious from a security standpoint with large open windows and grand archways. Slipping in and out would entail nothing more than a casual stroll. But to his security-minded credit, Javier Perez had surrounded the house with a single story, circular building which resembled a wall in shape and form—except this wall was about twelve-feet thick, hollow, with ten-foot ceilings and ample windows on either side, windows Marisela would bet were bulletproof.

As the copter landed, Marisela watched the guards inside the circular building stop and observe. With their three hundred and sixty degree view only thirty yards from the main house, they could easily monitor both the activities in the house and court-yard as well as any and all movement approaching the house from the sparse jungle or beach. She could see only one entrance through the circular outer building which boasted a rather spiky looking iron gate. Chances were, the painfully pitched roof of the protective structure was fitted with pressure-activated alarms. The only way to penetrate that building would be to somehow elude the guard towers and fly over in something much smaller and much quieter than a helicopter. Like bird's wings, maybe?

Shit. Shitshitshit.

"We'll be safe here, won't we, *mi amor?*"

Marisela spun toward Frankie, who grinned at her with the kind of verve reserved only for a man who relished a true and dangerous challenge. In an instant, the painful churning in her stomach subsided and the fiery spread of excitement rushed through her veins. He wasn't afraid. Why should she be? The worst that could happen was death, right?

"I'm very impressed," she replied. "It's been a long time since we've had a chance to truly relax. Enjoy each other."

She'd just removed her earphones and reached out to stroke Frankie's arm to counter his teasing when the pilot swung open the cabin door and invited them to disembark. The wind from the slowly churning blades tugged at Marisela's hair, despite the slick ponytail she wore. She couldn't help but duck, more out of instinct than necessity. In the past week, the girl who'd never gone anywhere had traveled by luxury yacht, private plane, and now in a helicopter that Perez told them once belonged to a sultan in the small but wealthy country of Brunei. But to counter the glamour of such travel, she'd also been nearly raped, shot at, smacked across the face so that her teeth still rattled with the memory and nearly blown up by a bomb she'd had a hand in setting. All in a day's work, she supposed.

A tall, dark-skinned man emerged from the house, dressed impeccably in a starched, long-sleeved tan *guayabera,* coordinating linen pants, and sandals. His grin reached his eyes, but didn't show his teeth. He greeted Frankie with a curt, efficient bow. He was apparently the tropical version of a rich man's perfect butler. He snapped a quick bow toward Marisela, then gestured toward the house, not bothering to try and shout over the dying but still deafening noise from the helicopter. After grabbing their own bags despite the wordless protest of their host, they followed him through the courtyard and into an open-air foyer that fluttered with thick-leaved banana plants and was perfumed by the distinct and sun-sweet scent of birds of paradise.

"Welcome to *Isla de Piratas, Señor y Señora* Tosca. *Me llamo Alfredo.*"

A butler named Alfred? No way.

"Mucho gusto, Alfredo," she greeted, offering her hand. He accepted, but not without a moment's hesitation. Though he was likely the most prized servant in the household, Marisela wondered if most guests even noticed his presence except when they wanted something. *"Muchas gracias por tu atenciones. Señor Perez es un hombre muy afortunado. Y generoso."*

Alfred's grin widened, but still failed to show anything more than lips that seemed lined in smoky khol. *"Señor* Perez has made his luck, *señora.* He takes care of the people who help him achieve his goals."

He grasped her hand quickly, but tightly, with both deference and confidence. Marisela immediately liked him.

Frankie must have sensed her softening because he took her by the elbow a little roughly when Alfred gestured them farther down the impressive, arched and airy breezeway.

"I've been instructed to offer you anything you need to make your stay here comfortable and relaxing. *Señor* Perez emphasized that you both deserve a rest."

Marisela and Frankie followed behind silently, Frankie's tight grip on her arm acting like a vise around her mouth. She didn't like submitting to his instructions, but she knew she'd nearly started down a wrong path. She'd allowed herself, even if momentarily, to forget she was Dolores Tosca—a reticent killer whose murderous profession had made her a woman unimpressed by wealth rather than a sheltered *mujer* who once thought a nineteen-inch color television with cable was the height of wealth and riches. Still, neither one of them bothered to hide their appreciative perusal of the dark, hand-carved teak furniture, junglelike collection of plants, and especially, the vast collection of art—from paintings to sculpture to hand-woven rugs—that filled every inch of the house with a distinctively Caribbean-flavored elegance. Marisela wondered if all men who made their billions selling arms to criminals and two-bit dictators surrounded themselves with such illusions of class and intellectual superiority. She supposed they must have or the stereotype wouldn't exist.

The bedroom suite Alfredo led them to was spacious and entirely self-contained, down to the gas-powered fireplace and a tiled bathroom that, if she wasn't mistaken, was bigger than her parent's entire house.

"This room is yours, but feel free to explore the *hacienda* as you wish. I will allow you to settle in and then would be honored to give you the, *¿cómo se dice?*, grand tour."

Marisela nodded as Frankie tossed their bags on the bed—a California king that seemed to have more pillows and shams on it than the entire linen section of Bed, Bath and Beyond.

Alfredo bowed, then backed toward an intimate table set for two. A colorful ceramic pitcher sweated with the icy, pinkish-red drink inside, which Alfredo poured into tall glasses and garnished with a long stick of cinnamon. "This is my own recipe. Very refreshing after a journey."

He handed Marisela a glass and the scent teased her nostrils with the promise of sweet wine and fruit juice. Sangria. She sipped and hummed her appreciation even as the cold nectar burst with flavor in her mouth and then slid smoothly down her throat.

"*Delicioso*, Alfredo."

"*Gracias, señora.*"

He fetched a second serving for Frankie, who accepted the glass but made no comment after he took a quick swig. With a slight frown, Alfredo took his leave, making a quick beeline for the door. "I'll return in half an hour. If you need anything, simply press the green button on the wall beside the bed."

With that, he disappeared, shutting the door soundly behind him.

Frankie took a second, more enthusiastic sip, his arched brow displaying his pleasure at the taste.

"Do the Toscas always have to be so rude?" she asked.

Frankie's gaze narrowed, but she stood her ground. Okay, so the room likely contained as many listening devices as potted plants and fresh flowers. In fact, the potted plants and fresh flowers probably hid top-of-the-line surveillance equipment. She stamped her foot in frustration. She supposed referring to herself in the third person wasn't the worst slip-up, but she had to be more careful.

"I'm not being rude, *mi corazón,*" he replied. "Just cautious."

Point taken.

She downed about half the drink while she walked around the room, exploring the beautiful knickknacks and looking for any sign of listening devices. She found none, but that meant nothing. Perez could have built the gadgetry into the walls. How were they going to plan a hostile kidnapping and a bloodless escape when they couldn't even speak freely?

"I want to explore the island," she announced, pushing back the soft, gauzy sheers that muted the view out the window. She tapped the glass. Just as she expected—bulletproof. The room was sultry with tropical warmth, but she shivered all the same.

Frankie slipped in behind her and snaked his hands around her waist while his mouth made subtle contact with the sensitive skin on her neck. She had to close her eyes to the point of inducing dizziness to expel the realization that the last man to assault her neck so deliciously had not been Frankie.

"A perfect idea, *mi amor,*" he said huskily. "I hope you packed a sexy swimsuit."

Marisela allowed herself to laugh, amazed at how his amorous attention, even if merely a ploy in his role as the devoted Rogelio, immediately dispersed the sense of dread thrumming through her body. Though there hadn't been much time between Javier's invitation to their departure to the island, she had made time to shop for a few extra things—items Titan wouldn't have thought to provide—at a South Beach boutique. The anticipation of Frankie's first glimpse of the grossly expensive suit shot a thrill through her that transformed the last of her fear into pure molten fire.

She reached over her shoulder and ran her hand through Frankie's hair, allowing herself to fully enjoy the sensation of the thick, soft strands against her hand. The stubble on his cheeks rubbed roughly against her neck and shoulder as he trailed wet, warm kisses across her skin. Even through her blouse, her flesh burned and she had to concentrate to remember that his suggestion of a beach-romp wasn't about seduction.

"You might not be able to control yourself when you see me," she teased.

"Who said I want to control myself?" he asked.

She spun around in his arms and caught the devilish flash in his infinitely deep and dark gaze. That was Frankie talking, not Rogelio. And for that, she was very, very glad.

"It's already too dark for a swim," she said.

"The ocean isn't the kind of wet I'm craving right now."

He pressed her completely flush against his body and the

feel of his hard sex against her belly dispersed any and all thoughts of listening devices and amorous bosses and secret plans from her mind. What would the mission suffer if they acted like the married couple they were pretending to be? The insatiable, eternally hot for each other married couple?

She grabbed his shirt, ripped the hem from his jeans, then flung the soft fabric over his head. He undressed her similarly, then stopped. With a wicked grin, he strolled to the table beside the bed and pressed the green button with a forceful jab.

"*Sí, señor?*" Alfred asked dutifully on the other end of the speaker. "You wish the tour now?"

"No. Give us an hour. Maybe two," he suggested, his dark brow arched.

Marisela licked her lips and surrendered to the buzz shooting through her veins. She unsnapped and unzipped her skirt, giving Frankie a flash of her bright red panties.

He swallowed thickly.

Alfredo's voice broke into the thick tension tugging between them. "I'll contact you when *Señor* Perez arrives."

"Perfect," Frankie finished, clicking off the intercom and then dropping to his knees at Marisela's feet to press his lips against the scarlet triangle. "Let's hope he takes his sweet time."

Sixteen

MARISELA KICKED OFF her sandals and in one bold flash, removed the chocolate brown sarong she'd tied artfully around her neck to conceal her body. Not that Frankie hadn't seen her body in multiple positions last night, but something about teasing him in the sunshine of a brand-new day appealed to her. With Frankie standing just a few feet behind her on Perez's private beach, she expected an immediate reaction to her barely-there choice of swimwear. But instead of a wolfish whistle or amorous growl, she heard a high-pitched girlish squeal.

"*¡Dios mio!* My father would faint if I ever bought something so wicked!"

Though still twenty paces away, there was no mistaking the source of what Marisela decided to take as a compliment. Jessica Perez marched across the sand, flanked on either side by two female bodyguards. Bodyguards who made no secret they were bodyguards, though they didn't exactly broadcast their gender. They wore their hair short, slicked back and out of their faces. They'd traded the requisite dark suit for simple light cotton shirts and slacks, but they wore their holsters and guns on the outside, within quick, intimidating reach.

"If my father were still alive," Marisela responded, slipping easily into Dolores-mode, "he'd faint, too. Right after he tore the eyes out of any boy who saw me and locked me in my room for thirty years."

"How long has your father been dead?" the girl asked, tempering her chuckle in light of the subject.

"Fifteen years. Doesn't matter. I still think he's why I bought it."

She winked and the young girl instantly lit up, her grin a serious rival for the morning sun. Just like in the picture in the locket, Jessica's hair gleamed black as night while her skin glowed pale and porcelain. She was a regular Snow White, Marisela decided, only with thugs at her side rather than dwarfs. Jessica pulled a woven beach mat out of her oversized bag, then without looking, handed the rolled pad to the guard on her left, who quickly placed it on the sand. The girl dropped her bag without so much as an acknowledgment.

Spoiled, Marisela decided, but she couldn't blame her. There was a price to pay for the combination of insane wealth and undoubtedly crazier isolation.

"I'm Jessica," she said, sliding her sunglasses down her nose so that Marisela caught a quick glimpse of the pale blue eyes she'd inherited from her mother. Just as keen as her mother's, too. Not much got past this *chiquita.*

"I guessed," Marisela answered.

"You're Dolores."

"Thanks to my parents."

"Your name doesn't suit you. You should change it."

The kid didn't mince words.

Jessica had turned her attention to Frankie, who'd ignored them both completely, wandering toward the water's edge where he'd whipped off his shirt and stretched toward the sun so that Marisela was the one inspired to whistle.

"Rogelio, venga aquí. Es Jessica, la hija de Señor Perez."

He spared her a quick but cautious glance. *"Hola."*

Jessica waved, but Frankie had already turned before she completed the gesture, which made the young girl sigh. The bodyguards attempted to more effectively hide their appreciation of Frankie's show, but Marisela would have bet all the money in Dolores's briefcase that under their reflective sunglasses, they were ogling her "husband."

"How'd you land such a *papichulo* with such a protective father?" Jessica asked.

Marisela watched as Frankie waded his impressive body into the water and then dove sleekly into the surf. "Actually, my father introduced us."

In fact, the former Dolores de los Reyes had been recruited into the service of Fidel Castro by her father, who served the dictator on his secret security forces. When Marisela had been talking about protective fathers, she'd been drawing from her own past, not the one she'd read about in Dolores's dossier. She distinctly remembered the day she announced to her family that she and Frankie were dating. Surprisingly, her father hadn't sent her to her room for thirty years—but he'd tried. Only Marisela's

concentrated skills in buttering up her *Papi* and the fact that
Frankie's family had known hers practically forever kept her
from being banished. Not that her father hadn't fought her romance with Frankie every step of the way, but at least she'd been
free, relatively speaking.

Jessica glanced at the bodyguards on either side of her, then
shooed one aside because she was blocking her sunlight. "You're
so lucky. My father doesn't let any boys near me."

Marisela lowered her sunglasses and gave the girl a quick
once-over. "Do you blame him?"

Jessica looked down at her one-piece suit, which while relatively modest, failed to hide the girl's rather impressive curves.
In fact, with the girl's neckline practically plunging to her ster-
num, Marisela could see why Jessica's father might be a tad
overprotective.

"He can't blame me for these," Jessica defended, buoying her
breasts with her hands. "I have his genes."

"And your mother's," Marisela said, pleased she had such an
immediate opportunity to inject the topic of Jessica's mother
into the conversation.

The girl sneered.

Not good.

"My mother was supposedly a skinny *gringa*. No, it's my
father's fault. You should see my tia Luli. She looks just like Angelina Jolie."

Marisela noted the same resemblance in her niece. Dark hair,
hypnotic light eyes, pouty lips, and a body that wouldn't quit.

"There are ways to hide your curves, you know."

Jessica leaned back on her elbows. "You don't look like the
kind of woman who hides her body."

Marisela smiled, watching as the bodyguards widened their perimeter, not surprisingly, bringing them closer to Frankie. He suggestively invited them to join him for a swim.

Marisela frowned. Cleared her throat. Loudly.

The bodyguards backed off.

Damned straight.

What she didn't know was if her jealous act was real or for show.

"Well," she said, saving that thought for another time, "I'm on a vacation on a tropical paradise with my *muy caliente* husband. I'm certainly not going to dress like a nun."

"Do you ever dress like a nun?" the girl asked, retrieving a fancy French brand of sunscreen from her tote and spraying the emollient lightly over her arms, chest, and legs.

"Not if I can help it. But, I do deal with men all the time. Sometimes, the curves come in handy, mostly with *Americanos.* But with Latino men, if you want to be taken seriously, you have to dress differently. De-emphasize those assets that bring their *machismo* to the surface, if you know what I mean."

Jessica scooted nearer, listening with the same intensity as she might have if Marisela had been imparting the grand secret to the meaning of life. Which, she guessed, in a way, she was.

"Do you know how to do that? Seriously. If my father maybe saw me more like a person rather than his under-aged *hijita* with the big boobs, he might loosen the leash a little bit."

Marisela doubted this so intensely, she'd bet her entire take from Titan that no change in Jessica Perez's wardrobe would make any difference, but she liked where this conversation was heading. In a few short minutes, she and Jessica were bonding over fashion—one of the few topics Marisela could discuss with authority.

"I can show you a few fashion tricks," Marisela said, trying to sound somewhat bored with the prospect. She was, after all, supposed to be an assassin vacationing with her husband. She couldn't seem too anxious to spend time with a teenager or she might blow her cover. "You got any magazines?"

"Magazines? I could open a stand with all the subscriptions I get! *Pero,* let's go one better. You're a friend of my father's, right?"

"I work with him."

"But he trusts you?"

"I can't say," Marisela answered, knowing Javier Perez would consider her suspect for a long time, even if the Toscas joined his organization soon, as they'd briefly spoken about at dinner the night before. Still, she couldn't ignore the obvious. "But he did invite us here."

"Right," Jessica said with a glowing smile. "And he, like, never does that. So what if you take me shopping?"

Marisela plastered a doubtful look on her face despite the leap in her chest from excitement. Shopping! How perfect was that? With Jessica out of the fortress that was this island, they'd have a better chance of snatching her.

"I don't know," Marisela said, gazing out toward the water as if the possibility wasn't the least bit appealing, while joining her "husband," who was swimming a rather sensual backstroke amid the turquoise waves, seemed forefront on her mind. "I don't know any of the stores around here."

Jessica leaped up from the ground. "Look, I'll find the stores if you'll come and show me what to buy. I never have anyone to shop with!"

"What about those two?" Marisela asked, leaning her head toward the increasingly annoying bodyguards, both of whom seemed more interested in Frankie's body than Jessica's, judging by how their tongues were practically wagging as Frankie swam in the surf.

The girl sneered. "They're protection, not company."

"Your friends from school?"

Jessica frowned, bent down, and retrieved a cold bottled water from her bag. "They're okay. They're afraid of me, you know? I only go to school when my father is in the country. The rest of the time, I have a tutor here at home."

Marisela pressed her lips together, weighing the situation, unable to imagine the isolation of this kid's life. Even when her family had moved into a new neighborhood, making her the outsider ripe for gang recruitment, Marisela had never been trapped on a tropical island with no one her age to talk to, surrounded by women who'd either taken vows of celibacy to God or those like her father's arm candy, who had strict orders to stay out of Jessica's way.

"That sucks," Marisela said.

"Sometimes. Alfredo has a granddaughter a little older than me," she said of the family butler. "She's older. Before she went to college, we used to hang out sometimes."

"When did she go away?"

"Three years ago," Jessica answered sadly. "She's almost done. She's studying physics at MIT in Boston. I've always wanted to visit her, but my father . . ."

She didn't finish the thought and from the look on her face and the knowledge Marisela had about Elise's location, she wasn't surprised. MIT was way too close to MOM.

"Okay," Marisela said, "you run the idea past your father. If he says it's okay, we'll go. I'm really loving this beach mat. I think I'll pick up a few."

Jessica's pale eyes lit up like roman candles. She squealed and hopped in the air, then waved hurriedly at her bodyguards so they could gather her belongings. Neither one seemed pleased with having to leave Frankie, who'd kept their attention rapt while Marisela and Jessica talked.

When one of them reached for the mat, Jessica shooed her away. "No, no. Dolores, you keep it. I have another one. In fact, I probably have a dozen. I'm going to go find my father."

The man didn't stand a chance. If she possessed half of the talent Marisela had at manipulating her own father when important desires were the topic, she and Jessica would be off the island in no time.

Jessica disappeared down the beach after reciting a half-dozen thank-yous. Marisela couldn't help but grin after her. When Frankie approached, cooling her overheated skin by pressing his salty wet body against hers, her ire at his friendliness finally gave way in to a victorious smile.

"What was that all about?" he asked.

"You'd know if you weren't so busy flirting with those two *machorras.*"

Frankie chuckled and nuzzled closer, bathing her skin in fragrant seawater. "Are you jealous?"

He'd know if she was lying, so she opted to change the subject. "I think I have a way to take the kid."

She explained quickly, snatching Frankie's hand and drawing him into the water to finish the tale while she cooled off in the deliciously calm water. The sun and salt tingled on her skin and made her want to splash and frolic, but she contained herself. Dolores might take a lonely young girl shopping as a favor to her new boss, but she certainly wouldn't whoop loudly in the surf.

"It's perfect, isn't it?" she asked, anxious to hear his assessment of her first-ever attempt at putting together a plan. She was sure the scheme had flaws—she'd only had a few minutes to arrange it—but whatever weaknesses he found, they could fix.

But Frankie had remained quiet as she'd laid out the plan, which included contacting Titan and giving them an approximate time and location of where they'd be shopping in San Juan. In a crowded mall or store, they could easily make the girl disappear and spirit her away before any of the bodyguards had a chance to report back to Perez. Yet despite Marisela's enthusiasm, Frankie said nothing, his gaze masked by sunglasses he'd snatched from the hidden pocket in his loose-fitting swimsuit. He glanced once over his shoulder, then finally rewarded her fervor with a sly grin.

"Only one problem, *vidita.*"

Just one? The water felt particularly buoyant, so she executed a rather impressive twirl, splashing Frankie in the process. Maybe she would turn out to be good at this secret agent stuff.

"I can handle one problem. Lay it on me."

"With your plan, one of us will end up dead."

"Where are you?"

Marisela turned so the nosy salesgirl couldn't eavesdrop on her cell phone call quite so easily. For what she was about to drop into the cash register in this trendy San Juan boutique, you'd think she'd earned a little privacy.

"A shop on Avenida Ashford."

From his location on Perez's island, Frankie repeated the information to someone nearby—more than likely, the man who was financing this protracted trip into hip fashion. She heard various voices in the background, guessing Frankie was still in Perez's war room, discussing the upcoming assault against Perez's newest enemy—one that didn't really exist, except in Titan's carefully placed evidence. Under the tense circumstances, Marisela had to give Jessica some credit. She never would have guessed the girl could orchestrate the trip so quickly and without strong protests from her father. With only Marisela and her two bodyguards in tow, they'd hit the shopping avenues of San Juan just after nine o'clock the morning the day after their first meeting. Now six hours later, Marisela's legs ached, but likely not so much as Perez's wallet would hurt when the bills arrived.

"*Señor* Perez wants to know if he has any money left," Frankie asked with a chuckle.

Marisela glanced over at Jessica, who giggled as she modeled a pretty floral skirt that fit her trim body snugly around the hips, but loose and fluttering just above her knees. Paired with a luscious halter-top brimming with short ruffles that downplayed the young girl's ample C-cups, the mixture of femininity and modesty elevated her from simply attractive to undeniably gorgeous. Marisela wasn't so sure Javier Perez would be pleased with the results.

"Just barely," Marisela answered. "I hope he doesn't regret turning over his credit card so willingly. He might have to sell that island and settle for a nice little cabana on the public beach."

Jessica slipped into a pair of slim-heeled sandals. A third salesgirl emerged triumphant from the back room with a matching purse. Her two cohorts applauded and Jessica beamed with delight.

A rustling sound alerted Marisela that the phone had changed hands.

"Is my daughter having a good time?"

"*Sí, señor,*" Marisela replied. "Spending your money does wonders for her attitude."

Perez chuckled. "Of course it does! She's a good girl. She deserves some fun, Dolores. So do you, *¿verdad?* But I didn't invite you to my island to baby-sit. You have no idea how much I appreciate your offer to take her shopping. She doesn't get enough female interaction."

The three salesgirls clucked around Jessica, offering a varied and impressive collection of earrings, necklaces, belts, and scarves. Nothing like a credit card with no limit to make Jessica the most popular girl in the shop.

"She's making up for lost time. You're a very generous father."

Marisela didn't know if Perez heard her as he'd handed the phone back to Frankie.

"Everything's okay, though, *¿sí?*" Frankie asked.

A subtle quaver in his voice caused a chill to snake up Marisela's spine. Was something wrong? Something Frankie couldn't discuss on the cell phone they now knew for certain was monitored? They'd spent a good portion of the afternoon yesterday touring Javier Perez's security complex, housed in the building that circled the *hacienda* within. All communications, from cell and satellite phones to all radio transmissions within a three-mile radius of the island, were routinely monitored by

Perez's sophisticated system. Even though Titan was skillfully blocking the signal at irregular intervals with static that sounded like normal satellite interference, for now, what they said could be heard by others.

Luckily, they'd prepared by setting up a simple code while they'd frolicked on the beach.

"I found a beautiful leather coat," she said.

Frankie mumbled as if he didn't believe her, not because she was talking about spending money, but because that was the code they'd established for an all-clear.

The afternoon before, Frankie had pointed out the not immediately obvious flaw in Marisela's kidnapping plan. Yes, a trip shopping in San Juan would provide the perfect opportunity for them to snatch Jessica and spirit her off to her mother, except for one detail—Frankie, as Rogelio, would have no reason to tag along. He and Javier Perez had already started plotting the first of three executions the Toscas would perform for the arms dealer and no amount of lies or manipulations would convince Perez that Rogelio preferred browsing for *bolsos* above planning a good hit. Leaving him on the island while Marisela kidnapped the daughter of their host would be nothing short of a death sentence for Frankie.

Even during their truncated communication with Ian courtesy of a timed system disruption in Perez's listening devices, their boss had nixed the idea. With the recognizance information they'd relayed during the brief three minutes that Titan had scrambled the signals to *Isla de Piratas,* Blake expected his experts to soon formulate another scenario that would ensure his agents not only succeeded in their mission, but returned home safely.

"You don't need another coat," Frankie said, the reply mean-
ingless. But his next words reinvigorated her initial chill. "I
could use a new backpack, though."

The message was clear. Watch your back.

Why was he so worried? Did he know something she didn't?
Something he couldn't share through coded language?

Unnerved, she walked toward the back of the store. Jessica
had disappeared inside a dressing room just a few seconds ago.
So why didn't she hear the rustling of clothes?

"Jessica? How's it going?"

Jessica opened the door a few inches and snatched a pair of
jeans that had been dangling on a hook just beside the three-
way mirror. "I'm going to try the casual look next. Could you
grab that pink top you showed me earlier? I think you're right.
It will look good with my hair."

Completely ensconced in her own world of fabrics and color
schemes, Jessica shut the door and after a second, Marisela
strolled back into the boutique and pointed to the pink blouse.
One of the salesgirls immediately fetched the shimmery confec-
tion off the mannequin, and then hurried into the back to deliver it.

"They don't sell backpacks here," she finally answered
Frankie. She had to pull herself together. She could have been
totally misreading Frankie's meaning, but she wouldn't be much
good at controlling the situation if she wasn't thinking clearly. "I
don't really think we need another backpack, but I'll keep an
eye out."

"*Bueno.* Call me if you find something you think I'll like,
okay?"

Marisela agreed, then disconnected the call and shoved the

phone in her pocket. Frankie didn't spook easily, but he had a vibe going that Marisela couldn't have misinterpreted.

Marisela glanced around, suddenly noticing that none of the salesgirls had circled her in the last few minutes. One stood behind the cash register tallying a sale, the other showed a new customer a collection of blouses in yellow, coral, and bubblegum pink. Marisela glanced back at the dressing area, then at the door to the back, which was ajar. Was salesgirl number three digging into the new inventory again, desperate for another item to add onto her sales commission?

And where was Jessica? How damned long did it take to try on a pair of jeans?

Marisela walked to the back of the store, determined to move to a new shop. This one was suddenly giving her a case of the willies. She knocked on the door and waited for Jessica's reply.

She heard nothing.

She didn't have to call the girl's name to know she wasn't on the other side. But she shouted Jessica's name loudly anyway, turning toward the front of the store to look for the bodyguard as she tugged her 9mm out of her purse.

The guard named Inma burst in from the sidewalk outside, gun drawn. Marisela shouted for her to secure the store while she shot off the lock on the dressing room door then kicked it open.

Empty.

The salesgirls and the other customers dove to the floor, screaming in fear. Inma was already shouting into a communication device she wore on her wrist, pleading with her partner, Dulce, who had been watching the back entrance, to report.

Marisela didn't wait for a reply, knowing again that they'd get none.

Marisela tore through the cluttered back room, her gun an extension of her arms and eyes, scanning the space ahead of her. Inma had entered behind her and quickly located the third salesgirl, who'd been pistol-whipped on the back of the head and shoved in a box of dresses. A scenario shot across Marisela's brain—someone paying the girl to lure Jessica to the backroom with a promise of some fashion find, then striking her unconscious and running off with Jessica. But what about the second bodyguard? Where was she?

At the back door, Marisela nearly stumbled over Dulce's body. Felled by a bullet through the forehead, death stared blankly through her dark eyes, taking no heed of the frippery around them.

Marisela swallowed the vomit burbling from her stomach and turned to Inma, who stared emotionlessly at the corpse on the floor.

"Call Perez," Marisela ordered in Spanish, her voice a harsh bark that snapped the woman out of the shock of seeing her partner dead on the floor. "We need backup."

The woman did as she was told. Marisela eased to the delivery door, aware that someone could be lying in wait on the other side, ready to pick off whoever might attempt to retrieve Jessica.

She led with her gun, squatting low to the ground. Seeing no one, she burst through the door and rolled behind a trash bin in the alley behind the store, searching for any sign that might signal danger. Inma followed a moment later, moving around the opposite side of the trash bin to cover both ends of the narrow passageway between buildings.

There was no room back here for a car. Jessica must have been transported on foot, at least until the alley spilled onto the sidewalk twenty yards away. Someone would have seen something.

Marisela shoved her gun into her waistband, but didn't release the grip. She wasn't about to go waving her illegally owned handgun around, but she needed her weapon close at hand. She blocked out a sudden flash of what Jessica was likely experiencing right now—sheer and utter terror—and focused on finding the girl.

Inma was close at her heels as they blasted out of the alley into the sunlight of the wide, busy street. Tourists and businessmen alike strolled up and down the sidewalk and cars sped by, but her eyes focused on the strip of concrete just outside the alley. Two vans were double-parked.

Two vans with dark windows.

She shouted to Inma, who rushed to the second vehicle. Marisela flattened herself against the door of the van by the sidewalk, gun drawn, only barely aware of the passersby scattering, some screaming for the police.

The door handle didn't give. She spun low under the tinted windows, then around toward the front of the vehicle where she aimed straight into the windshield. No one was inside.

Inma had done the same with the other van and now shook her head. Damn. Were the vans decoys?

Marisela lifted her gun sky-high and jogged into the street, glancing in both directions while cars swerved to avoid her. Down the block, a flash of sunlight caught her attention, reflecting off an enclosed cart, the kind caterers used to transport hot food. The kind large enough to move a teenage girl without anyone seeing. With no other lead, she lunged in that direction, yelling back for Inma to go in the opposite direction in case her hunch was dead wrong.

Mindful of the wide-eyed stares and startled cries of the people she passed, Marisela tucked the gun into her jeans and used her arms to pump her run to full speed. The two men pushing the cart, dressed in blue jackets and black pants like waiters, increased their speed when they caught sight of her behind them. She cursed. They wouldn't run if they weren't guilty as hell.

Ahead of them, Marisela spotted a large truck with the back door scrolled to the top and a ramp protruding from the bottom. No way could she catch them. No way.

Her lungs screamed with pain as she pushed her body to move faster. Her muscles cramped and she cursed the busy sidewalk and the assailants' head start. She watched in painful defeat as they pushed the cart up into the truck, kicked away the ramps, and jumped to grab the roll-down door.

Marisela pulled her gun, but too many people were around to fire. She couldn't risk a stray bullet. A few more yards and she could possibly damage the tires, slow their escape.

She cursed as her feet hit the pavement. A small sports car shrieked to a stop in front of her, blocking what might have been a wild and hopeless shot. She was tempted to pop the driver for getting in her way when he threw open the passenger side door and yelled for her to get in.

Max?

Bile rose in her throat as a horrifying possibility shot into her brain. She dove into the car and swung the door shut even as he peeled into traffic in pursuit of the van. After allowing herself to gulp air until the fire scalding her lungs subsided to an even steam, she turned and leveled her weapon at the man who'd trained her, the man who'd assured her that with Titan, she'd be in good hands.

"Tell me this isn't a Titan operation, Max, because I swear to God, if Frankie dies because we left him behind, I'll kill you myself."

Seventeen

MARISELA SLAMMED AGAINST the seat when Max threw the car into gear and peeled off in pursuit of the kidnappers. Her gun slipped in her sweaty palm, but she caught the grip and held tight.

She pressed the nozzle to Max's temple. "Tell me the truth."

"Don't aim a gun if you aren't prepared to use it," Max said evenly.

"If I have to sacrifice you to save Frankie, that's what I'll do."

He glanced at her briefly, but didn't move his head. However, when he swerved around a slow-moving taxi, the inertia threw her sideways. He had her gun in his hand before she could counter his move.

She opened her mouth to protest, but he tossed the 9mm

back in her lap with a smirk. "Keep that off me, understand? We've got a teenager to rescue."

She checked her weapon, then braced her hands on the dashboard as he maneuvered around another trio of cars.

"You didn't take her?" she demanded.

"Blake nixed that plan, Marisela. He'd never betray his own agents."

"Then what the hell are you doing here and who took Jessica?"

Max hopped a curb to avoid slamming into the back end of a car stopped at an intersection. Marisela braced her hands on the roof of the car to keep from banging her head.

"Your guess is as good as ours," he answered.

"Then why are you here? That's no coincidence!"

"We were watching you."

"Watching me? Why?"

"Standard procedure. Don't get paranoid."

"Too late," she snapped.

"Frank will not be harmed," Max assured her.

Marisela turned in the seat so she could see his face clearly, even if only in profile. Not that she expected to learn anything from a man with an uncanny ability to fade into the woodwork and hide his reactions.

"If we get Jessica back before Perez starts looking for someone to blame, maybe, just maybe, Frankie will get out of this alive," she told him. "The bodyguard called Perez. He'll be here any minute and might be tracking us right now." She leaned under the sun visor to check the bright afternoon sky for any sign of Perez's helicopter. So far, nothing. "Exactly who am I supposed to tell Perez you are anyway if he shows up? Just a friendly bystander I carjacked?"

"Sounds like a plan."

The truck turned abruptly, so Max threw the car into a controlled spin that brought them directly behind the escaping kidnappers. Marisela rolled down the window of the car and prepared to lean out to fire, but Max grabbed her arm and tugged her back in.

"Don't waste bullets. We're coming up on the marina. They'll have to stop once we reach the pier. Get ready. I'm guessing they didn't anticipate pursuit, but we can't be sure."

Marisela checked her gun clip. She'd fired only one shot at the locked door, so she was good to go with a full load of ammunition. Lot of help her trusty weapon and all her super-secret, intense training had done her and Jessica so far. Now that the kidnappers had returned to their van, there was no telling the firepower she and Max would face at the end of the narrow road. She glanced into the backseat, speechless when she caught sight of the weaponry Max had brought with him.

"You always come this prepared?"

"Of course," he said with a smirk.

"Is there backup?"

Max glanced up at the rearview mirror. Marisela followed his gaze and caught sight of the mini-camera attached to the mirror that could easily rotate and survey both the inside and outside of the car.

"*Hola,* Ian," she said, instinctively leaning to the left as Max swerved around a trash can knocked into the air by the speeding truck.

"Hello, Ms. Morales," Ian answered, his voice tinny and remote, and yet still annoyingly omniscient. "Max, the kidnappers are clearly heading for a boat moored at the end of the western side of the pier. The engine is idling and we see only one man aboard. We've moving in to intercept."

"Any sign of the police?" Marisela asked, not sure if she wanted the cops there or not. While she certainly wouldn't mind anyone and everyone with a gun working toward retrieving Jessica, there was the little matter of Marisela not being who she claimed to be, not to mention her criminal record whether the authorities thought her to be Dolores Tosca or Marisela Morales. She trusted that Ian would eventually extract her from the custody of the Puerto Rican officials, but not before her cover was blown.

"They've been alerted. Two helicopters left *Isla de Piratas* only moments after the bodyguard put in the call. Lie low, Max. We'll extract you at 5-21-876."

"Understood." He turned toward Marisela fast enough to unnerve her with a tiny smirk. "You'll be on your own soon. I'm an innocent bystander, remember?"

"Yeah, right."

The truck screeched to a stop, and Max stopped the car some five yards behind. The minute the car jerked to a halt, Marisela took her cue, threw open the side door and dove out of the car. Max had grabbed one of the rifles from the backseat and had taken a similar position on the driver's side. Until the authorities showed up, she had at least one other gun on her side.

The door of the truck rolled up and to Marisela's horror, one of the men had thrown a terrified Jessica in front of him as a shield. The girl clawed at his arm, pressed hard against her windpipe, her eyes hard with terror and rage. Fucking coward! Marisela wasted no time in picking off his compatriot, who fell to the ground in a spurt of blood and brain.

The return fire from the man holding Jessica sent Marisela ducking behind her passenger-side door. From the corner of her eye, she saw Max aim and fire, the sound immediately followed by a howl of pain on the other side of the truck. The driver. Two down, one to go.

The kidnapper traded his hold around Jessica's neck for an equally unyielding grasp around her waist. Holding her flush in front of him, he leaped down from the back of the truck, tucked against her like a parachute strapped to her back. Jessica screamed. On the tottering spiked heels she'd put on in the boutique, she couldn't support the weight of their combined fall. Her legs buckled, but the man yanked her painfully to her feet.

With her eyes trained over the sight of her gun, Marisela winced, but waited for an opening. A split second. One clear shot. She tuned out Jessica's ear-splitting pleas for help.

Beyond her concentration, she heard the deafening beat of helicopter blades. The cavalry had arrived, but could do no more than hover until Jessica was out of the line of fire.

Or so she thought. Somewhere on the other side of the truck, shots were fired, rapid, loud, and incessant until an explosion rent the air. The sound and vibration threw the last kidnapper off balance. He loosened his death grip on Jessica. She stomped backward with her spiky heel, slicing into the man's ankle. He howled and she answered by throwing her head back, slamming his chin with the full force of her skull. He staggered. She broke free and dove to the ground.

The man shook as Marisela's bullets pumped into him. Jessica crawled out of the way before his bloody body crumbled to the ground.

The helicopters swirled over them. Marisela looked around. Max was gone.

Marisela ran to Jessica, keeping her body low to the ground, her gun leveled ahead of her in case there was another kidnapper unaccounted for, one she hadn't seen in the mad chaos of the gunfight. Her face still flat to the ground, Jessica yelped when Marisela touched her shoulders.

"Are you okay?"

Jessica curled against Marisela's body, dragging her legs up close to her stomach and burying her head against Marisela's chest. She didn't answer, but simply wept, shaking as if the eighty-degree temperature had suddenly dropped below zero. Marisela forgot about the hovering helicopters, the second and third explosions of the boat burning on the other side of the truck, the whine of sirens moving closer and tucked her chin over Jessica's head, which was already beginning to swell. She touched the spot gently and made hushing noises, speaking in soft tones, assuring the young girl that she would be fine.

"You did great, *mija*. You fought them. You followed your instincts and that's why you're alive. Your father will be so proud of you."

Jessica shook her head, whimpered, but didn't reply. Marisela tried to steel herself against the wash of emotional connection to the girl, but she failed. Jessica, so spoiled, so coddled, had fought for her life—crudely, but she was still breathing. Marisela knew all too well what the fear of death smelled like, tasted like. It rattled the soul. And worst of all, she knew the shaking never really stopped.

Marisela accepted the drink from Alfredo and without a single glance to determine the contents, threw back her head and swallowed. She slammed the shot glass down on the table in front of her, and by the time the kick of the distilled fire had subsided and her eyesight cleared, the drink had been refilled.

From behind her, Frankie brushed his palm across her back. She turned and scrutinized his expression, a confounding mix of concern and something—if she didn't know better—she'd identify as fear. Didn't make sense. Now that Jessica had been retrieved and Marisela had played a key role in her rescue, the Toscas were even safer than before. Unless, of course, Perez decided to blame the newcomers for the abduction. The logic wasn't solid, but what frantic father didn't entertain conspiracy theories from time to time? And the bottom line remained—they weren't who they were claiming to be.

Javier Perez marched into the living room surrounded by a half-dozen of his top security men and lieutenants, all dressed in impeccable dark suits that clashed with both the climate and the casual elegance of the living room. Her host practically threw his body into the chair across from Marisela and with a violent wave of his hand, sent Alfredo and his whiskey away.

"How's Jessica?" Marisela asked.

Perez glanced away and dropped his hand limply to his side. "She's upset. The doctor wanted to give her something, but she refuses."

Frankie squeezed Marisela's shoulders, a fortified show of

support. She ached to lose herself in his touch, and fought to stay focused. On Jessica. On the mission.

"She'll be okay then?"

Javier glanced soulfully toward his daughter's room. Knowing teenaged girls the way Marisela did, having been one herself once, she figured Perez had been banished from his daughter's presence. Not because she was angry or blamed him for the terror she'd experienced today—though that could be the case—but most likely because Jessica didn't want to suffer a meltdown in front of the man who loved her so much, he'd kill for her.

"Her legs hurt from the fall off the truck," he continued. "She's got a bump on the back of her head. Otherwise, she'll recover quickly."

Marisela toyed with her empty glass, grateful to have something in her hands. "She was brave and strong, *señor*. You should be proud."

He speared his fingers through his hair, cursing under his breath. "How can I be proud when I am supposed to protect her? She's so young. So frightened. I've been very careful, *señora*, to see that my daughter was never dragged into my world. Today, she experienced all the ugliness I've sheltered her from for seventeen years."

Marisela forced herself to relax back into the couch. Frankie didn't take his hands off her and for this, she was glad. She couldn't help wondering if Perez suspected she and Frankie had been somehow involved in the kidnapping, but figured if he did, they'd both be dead by now. If nothing else, she'd earned his trust by saving his daughter. And the situation could have turned out so much worse.

Now more than ever, Marisela wanted this case completed.

She wanted Jessica out of here, safe in the United States where men wouldn't abduct her out of a boutique dressing room and spirit her off to God knew where to do God knew what, all on account of her father and his illegal business dealings.

"Who did this?" Marisela asked.

Javier glanced at the men that surrounded him, each one more silent and still than the other. Like beaten dogs, cowering. They clearly had no clue who orchestrated the kidnapping—and for their ignorance, they'd recently incurred their boss's wrath.

"I do not know. The police will identify the bodies, but there is no indication they are tied to any of my known enemies."

"What about this new threat? The one you've hired Dolores and me to handle?" Frankie asked, moving around the couch and sliding onto the leather cushion beside her.

Perez shook his head. "We have no proof they are anywhere near this island. Stealing a shipment and stealing my child are two different things."

"But you have to suspect someone," Frankie insisted. "Has anyone tried to take your daughter before?"

With a single-worded order, the room cleared.

"I am reluctant to speak of my personal life to business associates, but since you risked your life today to save my daughter, I believe I can share my suspicions with you. I do not believe the attempt to kidnap my daughter is related to my profession. There's hardly been time for Ochoa's men to retaliate, especially since I haven't yet made it known that his death was on my order. And the three men at the marina—no one recognized them."

Marisela watched Perez closely, alert to any sign that he wasn't telling the truth. "Is that so unusual? Your enemies come from around the world. How could you possibly know them all?"

"I can't, but these men were not professionals. The plan was weak at best, as if thrown together at the last minute. Opportunistic. They were sitting ducks in that truck once they reached the pier. They did not anticipate resistance."

"They nearly succeeded. You can't ignore that," Marisela countered.

"I have no intention of ignoring that I almost lost my daughter today, *señora,*" he snapped. "Security has been doubled on the island and for the time being, Jessica will remain on *Isla de Piratas,* even when school is back in session next week. She'll take her lessons here. I won't risk losing her."

Frankie broke in, his voice calm and deep. "You can't keep her prisoner forever. She's nearly an adult. She'll soon make her own choices, *¿verdad?*"

Javier sat forward, his hands folded loosely in his lap. "You both tell me things about my daughter that I already know. Can you tell me anything I do not—some wisdom you've learned during your extensive stay on my island?"

None of his sarcasm was lost on Marisela and she displayed the right amount of contrite apology in the tone of her voice and tilt of her head. "I'm sorry, *Señor* Perez. We shouldn't presume."

Javier nodded, then waved her apology away. "No, you shouldn't, but I'm honored that you do. Obviously, you care about my child."

Marisela crossed her legs, trying to look casual, trying not to appear as if she cared *too* much. "She's a special girl. I hope you don't take this the wrong way, but she reminds me of myself, when I was her age. Frivolous, but smart. Lonely. Desperate for her father's approval."

Javier shook his head, but Marisela could see his belief in his sad eyes.

"*Señor,*" Frankie said, "who would have something to gain from taking her? To date, you are the most powerful arms dealer in this part of the world. Antagonizing you will not weaken your power. Your enemies would know this. At this point, all but Ochoa are working to get into your good graces."

"*¡Exactamente,* Rogelio! Only one person would be so uncaring about Jessica's safety," Javier answered, disgust thick in his tone. "I've known ruthless people in my lifetime, but even you in your profession have never met anyone as cold and cruel as the person I suspect."

"And that is?" Frankie asked.

Perez grabbed the decanter of whiskey, poured a glassful, and downed the amber liquid in one choking swallow. "Her mother."

Marisela had to remember to act surprised. "Her mother is alive?" she asked, her voice halting. "I just assumed . . ."

"Yes, she's alive. She's *Americana,* lives in Boston. Elise Barton-Ryce, socialite and professional bitch. She likes people to think she has a lot of money, a lot of class, when in reality, she has neither."

Perez stood and refilled his glass again, glancing through the archway that separated the living room where they conversed from the hallway that led to Jessica's room. He undoubtedly did not want his daughter to overhear this discussion.

"I don't understand, *señor*. She doesn't have money?"

Frankie asked. "Then how could she pay someone to take your daughter?"

Perez glanced down the hall before he answered. "She has enough for *chapuceros* like the ones you encountered today. Her trust fund would give her that. But she has expensive tastes and my sources tell me her financial resources are limited. And for all her faults—and believe me, she has many—I doubt she has adequate contacts to find anyone better than she did."

Well, he was wrong there. Not that Marisela was going to point that out.

"Why would she try and kidnap her own daughter?"

"I don't allow her access to Jessica. She got pregnant by accident, I assure you. She was disgusted by her condition."

"Why didn't she have an abortion?" Marisela asked.

Javier shook his head. "Your guess is as good as mine. She's Catholic, but I doubt God has any influence over her. I can only thank *El Señor* that she didn't, because now my daughter is with me, where she belongs."

Marisela shifted forward. She'd never trusted the woman, and here was her chance to find out the scoop from someone who really knew Elise, even briefly—even if he had a clear bias against her.

"Maybe she really wanted the baby, but was too proud to let you know."

Javier spit on the floor, then made a gesture Marisela didn't recognize, but could easily interpret nonetheless.

"Or maybe not," she mumbled.

"Believe me, *señora,* there is not a maternal bone in that woman's body. I went to Boston when Jessica was born. I only had to watch Elise for a few days after she returned home from the hospital to know my daughter would not receive the care and supervision she deserved. Nannies and servants! That is not how you raise a child!"

Marisela and Frankie exchanged a look, but said nothing more. They knew the rest of the story. Javier took the child and so far as Marisela could see, had done a damned good job of raising her. He'd clearly had help, but Marisela had seen Jessica and Javier together. There was no stiff distance dividing them, just the to-be-expected high emotions of a teenaged daughter on the verge of womanhood and a father who wanted to keep her safe.

"Has this woman tried to take her before?" Frankie asked.

Javier shook his head, his nostrils flaring as he paced from the doorway.

"She never lifted a finger to get Jessica back, nor did she ever contact me, ask me for a visit. She wrote to Jessica once, asking her never to contact her, but I intercepted the letter. She didn't care about her child. She never cared."

"Then why would she care now?"

Marisela watched Javier stalk around the room like a caged animal. The veins in his neck and temples engorged as his muscles tightened. And yet, his voice was an even whisper when he finally spoke again. "Trust me, she has her reasons."

He knew something—something he wasn't willing to share.

"Then take care of her," Frankie suggested, crossing one leg casually on the other. A subtle change in his attitude drew Marisela's attention to his body language, to the lean cut of his slacks and the sharp polish and tapered heel on his ankle boots. From the grim line on his mouth to the square set of his shoulders, Frankie oozed cold intentions.

They were, after all, killers.

"You would do this?" Javier asked.

Marisela adopted Frankie's icy mien. Dolores and Rogelio wouldn't hesitate to offer this solution. The fact that Javier Perez didn't smile conspiratorially or jump on the opportunity cut like a hot knife through Marisela's heart. He was not the man she expected him to be when she'd signed on to the mission. Then again, how good or bad he was as a man or as a father shouldn't matter. She had a job to do. She had to keep her eyes on the prize.

Marisela slid a glance at Frankie, her tiny frown purposeful.

"The girl doesn't know her mother, ¿sí?" Javier mused. "She cannot miss a woman she's never known. . . ."

Javier's rationalization ended, stopped by his daughter's gasp. Behind him, Jessica stood, wide-eyed, her mouth frozen in a little O of shock.

"*Mija, por favor,*" Javier pleaded, crossing the room quickly to his daughter.

"No! You're talking about murdering my mother."

Marisela stood. "You misunderstood, Jessica."

"No! Inma told me. You're assassins. Both of you. Oh, my God! You'd kill my mother if he asked you to, wouldn't you? If he paid you. Wouldn't you?"

Her eyes glazed, thick with tears aimed directly at Marisela—at Dolores. At the woman she'd considered a friend.

Marisela's mouth dried and swelled, as if stuffed with cotton doused in a bitter swill. Instinct caused her to reach out to Jessica at precisely the same moment the girl's overwrought emotions sent her running from the room.

Javier caught Jessica's arm as she jostled past.

"Let go of me! You want them to kill my mother!"

"She's already dead to you, *mija.*"

"No! She's dead to you! To you, she's never been alive. But she's my mother! If you hire assassins to kill her, I swear, when I turn eighteen, I'll leave and I'll never come back." She panted and struggled, but once certain her father would not release her, she visibly drew her anger inward. She stood as tall as her petite frame would allow and Marisela watched as the girl's limbs froze and her eyes turned to clear blue ice. "I swear to God, Papa. If I have to move to the other side of the world, you'll never see me again."

With a sharp, deliberate tug, she shook her arm free and walked purposefully to the archway, as much a determined woman as the mother she'd never met, the mother she clearly didn't remember, but cared about nonetheless. The minute she was out of their sight, her footfalls pounded against the tiles in a frantic run. She finished her escape with a gut-wrenching sob and a slammed door.

Frankie shoved his hands in his pockets. Marisela would get no help from him. She had to undo the damage before Perez sent them packing simply to placate the daughter he loved so intensely.

"*Señor* Perez, I'm so sorry."

He shook his head, but didn't reply. She had to think quickly.

"I'll speak with her," she offered.

He held up his hand. "No! I should never . . ." His voice trailed off as he crossed his arms over his chest and leaned back, as if looking to heaven for guidance. "You saved her life today. I will not forget."

"And less than an hour ago, your daughter looked to me with respect. *Por favor,* allow me a chance to regain her trust."

Perez stared at her, weighing his options with every wordless moment. He no longer looked like the man she'd met on the terrace of that slick Miami hotel. She saw none of the infinite confidence, none of the limitless power.

With his daughter, he was just a man who didn't know what the hell to do.

Finally, he released his arms and crossed the room. "Are you a good liar? You'll have to be to placate my daughter."

Marisela fought the emotions churning inside her. Dolores would have undoubtedly grinned at such a question. Could she be so cocky when she wasn't sure that her efforts would placate a daughter who didn't know the full truth about either of her parents?

Marisela smiled and patted the man on the arm.

"Don't you worry, *Señor* Perez. When it comes to liars, I'm one of the best."

Eighteen

"MI CORAZÓN, IT'S LATE. You should wait until morning."

Frankie crossed the room and touched Marisela lightly on the arm. What he really wanted to do was shake some sense into her. Marisela was taking this role too far. Her emotions for the young girl were clouding her judgment. The real Dolores Tosca wouldn't give two shits if some hormone-crazed teen thought she was Jack the Ripper. In fact, the coldhearted bitch Marisela was pretending to be would probably relish destroying some girl's romantic fantasy about the world and the cruel people in it.

Of course, he doubted Javier Perez knew that much about the Toscas to see Marisela's concern as out of character. Their professional résumé didn't include much about their private lives and in Frankie's experience, most assassins weren't so different from the neighbor next door. They blended seamlessly into regular society when they needed to, not unlike most of the sociopaths he'd met in prison. And despite his misgivings, Perez seemed to be buying Marisela's concern hook, line, and sinker.

The man looked downright torn. When not surrounded by his butler and bodyguards, even Frankie could see the man's vulnerability where his daughter was concerned. Obviously, one of Perez's enemies had sensed the same weakness. Or perhaps, a traitor from within? Frankie should have seen this possibility from the beginning—when his daughter was in the mix, Perez didn't act predictably. The entreprenaur who ran a billion-dollar arms ring and the father who cared about the daughter he'd stolen from her crib were different sides of the same man. Chances were, Marisela had recognized that contradiction a long time ago—and she was using that knowledge right now.

Still, they had only so much time left tonight or they'd miss their scheduled communication with Titan—one Frankie was fairly sure they shouldn't miss. Not after what had gone down in San Juan.

Marisela patted Frankie's hand, but kept her eyes focused on Perez. "I know it's late . . . but I can't let her stay all night thinking such horrible thoughts about her father. *Por favor,* Rogelio, I need to speak to her tonight."

She turned. Her stare captured his and in the dark depths, he realized she knew exactly what she was doing. They had less than ten minutes until the scheduled communication with Titan. In eight minutes, the surveillance equipment on *Isla de Piratas* would begin experiencing quick, unexplained outages for no more than a few seconds at a time. Then, two minutes later, the equipment would go dead for precisely two minutes and four seconds. In that short time, he and Marisela would speak to their bosses about the current situation. And since only Marisela had been on scene during the kidnapping attempt and might have crucial information about whoever tried to beat them to the punch by taking Jessica, she needed to be on the satellite phone, not trapped in Jessica's room trying to smooth over a situation Frankie considered a lost cause.

"You need time to think, to figure out what you're going to say, *¿sí?* And the child, she is too emotional now to listen," Frankie reasoned.

She played her confusion like a pro, blinking as she listened, then slowly nodding in agreement. *"Verdad. Señor,"* she said, addressing Perez. "My husband is right. But I swear to you, I'll reach her."

"It is not your responsibility, *señora*. She's my daughter. I've raised her from a baby. I should never have made such a suggestion with even the slightest chance that she would overhear."

"Your anger is justified," Marisela insisted, glancing over at Frankie with panic in her eyes. "A mistake was made. I can repair this rift for you, and then we can continue our business as planned."

Javier cursed in Spanish, not at Marisela, but at the ceiling so that his words echoed around the room. "This has nothing to do with business, except that I shouldn't have exposed my daughter to the cruel realities of how men like me operate."

Finally, Frankie understood. If Marisela didn't help Perez with Jessica, he would send them away. As assassins, they represented the dark underbelly of Perez's empire. And with the increased security Perez had ordered, the chances of them completing the mission were zero if they didn't have inside access.

"*Señor,*" he said, stepping between Marisela and Perez, "my wife is not without a heart. To imply such . . ."

Perez's eyes widened, then narrowed. "I have made no implication."

"You deny her the chance to right a wrong she blames herself for," Frankie continued.

Perez turned to Marisela. "You have no reason to blame yourself, I . . ."

Marisela waved her hand in the air as if to dismiss his concern. She even let her eyes gloss over, as if tears were just a moment away. Frankie couldn't help but hold his breath, wondering if she'd taken the act too far.

"You are a man who cares about his daughter more than any father I've ever met. I agree that allowing Rogelio and me to come here might have been a mistake, but that damage is done. If I am ever to feel worthy of your trust, I must reach out to your daughter."

Frankie glanced at his watch. They had six minutes. The next window wouldn't come until just before dawn. By then, Perez could have them on his helicopter, heading for the main island.

After a long silence, Perez nodded. "I will allow you to speak to her, *señora*. But give Jessica time to calm down. If there is one thing I've learned after all these years is that she needs time before she can listen—especially when what you will say is not what she wants to hear."

Marisela grabbed Frankie's hand. "I promise you, *señor,* when I'm done, she'll want to have heard what I tell her."

They exited the room with quiet deference. The minute they hit the hallway toward their room, their pace increased but they didn't speak until they exited the house into the courtyard.

"Where's the phone?" she asked, her lips pressed close to his neck.

"I have it," he whispered back. A little louder he said, "Let's walk the beach, *mi amor.* The breeze will clear your head."

They exited the courtyard arm in arm, their pace hampered by the guards patrolling the inner sanctum. As they walked through the iron gate, Frankie wondered about the activity inside the outer building. Right about now, they were likely scrambling to figure out what interference was blocking their equipment, jamming their ability to listen in on conversations all over the island. He had no idea how Titan managed the technical sleight of hand and he didn't care. Before this case slid completely out of control, they needed to contact Titan—and hope like hell that Blake had a contingency plan to get them out alive.

"I want to talk to him now, Max," Marisela said, grabbing the phone from Frankie once the connection was established. They sat side by side on the sand, their backs to the *hacienda,* looking to anyone who watched like lovers sharing a private conversation.

"He's back in Florida. Pan took a turn for the worse."

Marisela pressed her eyes closed tightly and fought the wave of nausea that swam through her stomach. God, she'd forgotten all about Pan and his injuries—injuries her incompetence had caused.

"Is he dead?" she asked, not really wanting to know the answer.

"No, but it's touch and go. I'll relay any messages to Mr. Blake. I anticipate I'll have contact with him by morning."

Marisela bit her bottom lip, willing herself to gain control. Pan's injury was a regret she'd have to save for later. Right now, she had to figure out how to spirit Jessica off this now entirely fortified island without getting her and Frankie killed.

The events in the dress shop had been no random attack. She had suspicions, borne of the information about Elise provided by Javier, but would Max shoot her hunches down? Isolated on this island, she could never find out the information she needed on her own. With a deep breath, she decided to trust the organization she'd joined—or at least, the man who'd trained her for this mission. "Max, how well did Blake check out Elise Barton-Ryce before he took her case?"

"Extensively."

"Into her finances?"

"In an operation this expensive, we have to make sure the client has the ability to pay. Why?"

Marisela glanced up at Frankie, his head cocked as he listened to her side of the conversation. "Perez said something tonight—something about Elise not having all the money people thought she did."

"I can't see how that's possible," Max answered and she could hear the blatant insult in his voice. He'd likely investigated the client himself and now here she was, some rookie operative, questioning his thoroughness on a gut feeling that was based on the word of a man who was a known criminal.

And yet . . .

"Can you check again?"

Ever the professional, the affront in Max's voice disappeared. "What am I looking for?"

She sighed with relief. "When we met with her on the

Oceanus, Elise said that she wanted to get Jessica back before her eighteenth birthday because after that, she'd have no legal hold on the girl. That sounded so weird. Seems to me she'd wait until *after* her daughter turned eighteen to contact her because then, Jessica would be a legal adult. She could see whomever she wished, whenever she wished. For the record, Jessica believes that her mother *gave* her to her father. She'd testify to that in court, which would muddy any prosecution waters if Elise means to go after Javier for kidnapping. I can't help wondering then what the time constraint is. What if some other event is tied to Jessica's eighteenth birthday? Something financial."

She glanced at Frankie, who was staring at her as if she'd sprouted a new head. Well, too bad. From the start, she'd doubted Elise's motives for wanting to find her daughter. They had nothing to lose by digging a little deeper into the woman's situation, not after what they'd just learned from Perez.

"Like an inheritance?"

Marisela shook her head. "I have no idea, Max. The only thing I know about inheritances is what I see on the *novellas.*"

Max chuckled. "I'll trust your gut on this, Marisela. I'll check a little deeper. What's happening on the island?"

Frankie pressed the light on his watch. "Forty-five seconds."

"Jessica is distraught," Marisela explained quickly. "Perez will likely kick us off the island by morning if I can't talk her down."

"Any chance of an extraction before then?"

"Negative. He's brought a second wave of guards onto the grounds and Jessica won't be leaving anytime soon, not even for school. Any word on the guys who tried to grab her?"

"They were from Miami. Local thugs."

"When did they arrive in Puerto Rico?"

"Two days before we did. They'd been camped out at the pier, reportedly watching Perez's movements."

"And Jessica's."

"Apparently."

"Any closer to finding out who paid them?"

"There's no paper trail," Max admitted. "They paid cash for everything they bought while they were here and nobody's talking in Miami. It's a dead end."

"What are our orders?" Marisela asked.

Max didn't reply immediately and Marisela could hear his fingers flying over a keyboard on the other end of the phone. She hoped he was already looking into her request for more information about Elise's finances.

"Try not to get kicked off the island," he responded finally.

She grinned. "We're working on it."

"We'll talk again."

Max disconnected the call and Marisela handed the phone to Frankie, who pocketed the device.

"You're concerned about what Perez said," Frankie said. "Could be nothing but bad blood."

Marisela nodded. "But bad blood is all we have."

"You think Elise tried to snatch her kid today?"

"I don't know. Why would she? She already has us inserted into the organization. We've got the best shot. Those *pendejos* who took Jessica today could have gotten her killed."

"And you don't think she'd risk her daughter's life?"

Marisela snickered. "Of course I do. That woman is a viper,

no matter how much she tried to sway me with her crocodile tears."

"And the locket."

Marisela half-grinned. So he'd noticed that she still had the jewelry with her, tucked safely inside a tiny leather pouch she wore around her neck.

"I don't like to be manipulated."

"Never?"

The spicy scent of Frankie's cologne, so expertly intertwined with his natural musky scent, drew her awareness. The balmy breeze rustling the palm trees and the insistent, lapping waves provided a lush music that blocked out the cacophony of suspicions, fear, and plans flying through Marisela's brain. It was so easy to lean into his body and let his heat burn away her troubles for a few precious moments.

"Depends on who is doing the manipulating."

He took her invitation exactly as she intended, slipping his hands slowly down her back and then cupping her backside in his large, muscular hands.

"*Muchas gracias,*" he said, his words caressing the shell of her ear.

"For what?"

"I know what you did for me today."

"Oh, you mean putting your life in danger by letting Jessica get snatched when I wasn't looking? You're welcome."

He trailed a path of hot kisses down her neck, making her wish he'd stop wasting time and simply unzip her blouse, remove her bra, and get to work right here, right now.

With deft fingers, he fulfilled the first part of her wish. The sensation of each tooth of her zipper pulling apart from its partner reverberated against her. She concentrated so intensely on the delicious, anticipatory vibrations that she nearly missed what he said next.

"He wouldn't have killed me," Frankie claimed.

"If he'd thought you were involved? He would have strangled you with his own hands."

His tongue dipped low to the skin between her breasts. The heat of the night caught in her throat when her breath spiked in response.

"Me . . . or someone else."

Despite her overwhelming desire to surrender to his touch and forget all about the case and the danger for a few stolen moments, Marisela pulled back, her eyes hardly able to focus. "What are you talking about?"

"I understand your reason for suspecting Elise might have ulterior motives for wanting Jessica, but that doesn't mean she was behind today's attempt. What if one of Javier's lieutenants is attempting to stage a coup?"

"You mean a traitor?"

"I'm not sure. But someone within the organization could have used our presence here as a smokescreen. Taking Jessica would give them leverage. With Perez off-kilter, he'd let down his guard."

Marisela blew out a wavering breath, realizing that in their quest to infiltrate the Perez organization, they might have stepped into more trouble than they'd bargained for. "But the guys today were amateurs."

"And they also weren't known by anyone in Puerto Rico, which means if the plan failed, no one could trace the betrayal back to anyone here."

Marisela ambled away, immersed in the dangerous possibilities Frankie presented. His suggestion was clearly valid and with her concentration focused on making friends with Jessica, she hadn't paid a lick of attention to the men who followed Perez around like obedient puppies. Maybe one of them was tired of licking his boots. Maybe one of them wanted to be top dog.

"Do you suspect anyone in particular?"

Thunder suddenly rumbled above them. Great. A storm. At least Perez's security would have something to blame for the communications anomalies.

"No," Frankie answered. "They all act completely loyal, but that doesn't mean they are. While you're working on repairing the damage with Jessica, I'll make the rounds of the boys, see if I can find anything out, though I doubt anyone would be stupid enough to slip up to a stranger." The lightning flashed again, this time with a crack that seemed to break open the clouds. Thick drops of water splattered all around. Frankie pulled his jacket over his head and held out his hand. "Let's get inside."

She shook her head, then scanned the shoreline for anywhere they could go that wasn't under Perez's watchful eye.

"Not yet!"

She dashed in the direction she'd gone when she and Jessica had left the island that morning to shop. The boat ramp. Frankie followed, cursing all the way.

She guessed a guard would be posted at the boathouse, so she wasn't surprised when they confronted the man hulking under an awning barely large enough to shelter one person, much less three.

"*¿Qué pasa?*" he asked, his rifle tucked solidly beneath his arm.

"The rain!" she exclaimed. She let Frankie explain to the man that they'd been taking a romantic walk on the beach when the sky opened up and drenched them to the skin.

He offered them the inside of the boathouse, but only after making radio communication with his superior. He unlocked the door, clicked on a dim overhead light, directed them toward the kitchen where they might find towels, then made himself scarce.

The boathouse reeked with the stench of seaweed and fish and motor oil. A vast collection of rods and reels hooked onto the walls testified to Perez's obvious obsession with sport fishing. A boat, a good thirty-footer, hung suspended from a sturdy collection of winches and steel cables. For an instant, Marisela wondered about using the vessel to execute a quick getaway—until she noticed the gaping tear in the hull.

Besides, the boathouse, while situated on the edge of the water with a large bay door that allowed the ocean to splash beneath the boat, was fairly closed off. The minute they attempted to activate that door, she was certain the whole of Perez's security force would swarm down on them. And she couldn't ignore the fact that neither she nor Frankie were cowards. They had a job to finish, no matter the odds.

With ceiling fans swirling the tepid, moist air, Marisela peeled off her shirt and wrung the cotton material out onto the floor. Frankie removed his jacket and tossed it onto a barrel by the door.

"Trying to give the security guards a thrill?" he asked, glancing up at the security camera mounted in the corner of the room.

Marisela looked down at her sexy black bra, then spared the security device a glance. "If Perez's guards have any decency, they'll turn the cameras off while we're here. We are a married couple. Guests of their boss. I don't think *Señor* Perez would approve of his men peeping in on us instead of watching for real threats."

As if on cue, the tiny green light at the base of the camera faded to black.

"You don't trust that, do you?" Frankie asked, removing his shirt and then using the semi-dry material to wipe off his face and hands.

Marisela slipped her thumbs into her back pockets, arching her back until Frankie's eyes brimmed with hunger.

"If we can't trust the man who's hired us to eliminate his enemies, who can we trust?"

Nineteen

"MAYBE THIS WASN'T SUCH a good idea," Marisela said, her skin prickling despite the steamy heat in the boathouse.

His eyebrow quirked. A smile lit his eyes. *Damn.* In perfect keeping with the dance they'd established so many years ago, he closed in on her hesitation. He offered her his shirt and when she didn't accept, he balled it up tighter and proceeded to wipe the moisture off her face himself.

"Maybe what isn't a good idea? Drying off?"

He smoothed the cotton over her cheeks and she couldn't help but tilt her face into the fabric. His scent curled into her nostrils—a powerful elixir of male musk and fresh rain and body heat. When he patted the shirt lower, dabbing at the moisture glistening across the top of her breasts, her nipples hardened and ached for his touch.

"Making love," she said.

"Who said we're going to make love?"

He stepped closer, his erection brushing her belly, proving she wasn't mistaken. She and Frankie were alone, in the dark night, in a storm. What else would they do?

She cocked a brow.

He chuckled, the deep, throaty sound oozing over her skin like warmed honey. "We can't seem to keep our hands to ourselves, that's true."

After tossing the shirt aside, Frankie twined his fingers with hers even as she struggled to keep them at her sides. What was this force that drew them together? Chemistry? Familiarity? A little bit of both?

"Hands, lips, tongues, assorted private parts," she admitted, even as he coaxed her palms onto his butt where she could squeeze his tight muscles through snug, damp denim. "The minute we're alone, we go back to being teenagers again."

"Now that's where you're wrong. I never could do this so fast when we were kids."

In a split second, her bra popped free, his deft fingers working their magic even as she relished the feel of his strong body against hers. She shrugged her shoulders and the lingerie fell away, freeing her breasts for his hungry gaze. She stared at him wide-eyed—and aroused.

"If I remember correctly," she said, "you were faster than a speeding bullet in the backseat of your mother's car."

"That's just because I didn't want to get caught. I can take my sweet time when the incentive is right."

With a flash of lightning from outside, her arousal spiked. He pushed her up against a support beam for the boathouse, dropped to his knees, and proceeded to unsnap, unzip, and peel her jeans off her body.

She didn't resist. Couldn't resist. She had the strength to fight anyone but him. His power over her loomed like a bad omen of their past, but she couldn't form the words to tell him to stop, not when his mouth trailing up from her knee to her inner thigh, evoking all the sensations she craved. With Frankie, she'd do anything, because she knew intense pleasure would be her reward.

"You rescued Jessica to save my life today."

"Mmmm," she replied, concentrating so much more on the sensations of his breath and tongue across her heated flesh.

He shifted higher onto his knees so he could move his kisses upward, just along the edges of her black lace panties.

"You care about me that much?"

"I wouldn't want you to die on my account," she managed, but the long string of words cost her. With his hands sliding up and down her legs, she could hardly breathe. Her nipples tightened, and the pain stabbing through her body could be soothed only by Frankie's tongue. Yet his mouth was engaged elsewhere and she wasn't about to complain.

She tangled her fingers into his thick hair and eased his face closer to her *concha,* so she could feel his hot breath diffuse through the lace and enflame her creamy skin.

"You deserve a reward for your bravery," he murmured.

She swallowed deeply, nearly cooing when he pressed his tongue against her, delving into the cleft between her legs until she thought her knees might buckle. She might have whimpered. She wasn't sure. When his hands inched up and removed the lace barrier, she thought she'd scream in triumph, but instead she held her tongue until his assault pushed her over the edge.

And even then, he didn't stop. No matter how she begged, no matter how convinced she was that she had no more left to give, no more left to feel, he pushed harder. He drove his fingers deep within her and when that threw her into a spiraling orgasmic vortex, he shucked his pants and filled her completely.

He grabbed her hands and stretched them high over her head so he could suckle her breasts even as his thrusts milked her dry. Marisela tried to focus, tried to grab him, touch him, but he denied her, telling her in no uncertain terms that she was going to come again whether she liked it or not and he didn't need anything from her to make him hard but her complete and total surrender.

She gave it. God help her, but she couldn't resist him. Not now. Not ever.

The teddy bear sealed her fate. Marisela blew out a shaking breath and closed Jessica's door quietly behind her. She wasn't cut out for emotional scenes. No amount of training from Titan could prepare her for a confrontation with a vulnerable woman-child like Jessica. In the cool, dry dawn in her own room, wrapped in Frankie's strong, warm arms after a night of love-making, Marisela had made a decision.

One that could get them both killed—or save a mission that was dead in the water.

She strolled to the bed and with a light touch, moved a strand of hair that had tangled across the young girl's eyes. Jessica bolted upright, but Marisela remained steady and cool, even with narrow hatred slicing at her from Jessica's clear blue stare.

"Get out!"

"I came to talk to you."

She glanced at her watch. Right about now, Titan was jamming Perez's surveillance system yet again. This time, she had five full minutes to talk, though she knew she needed more. She decided to gamble that Perez didn't have his own daughter's room bugged. If he did, Marisela could be dead very, very soon.

"I don't want to hear anything you have to say!" Jessica spat, scrambling off the bed.

Marisela spun Jessica into a tight hold and blocked her mouth so she couldn't scream.

"Look in my pocket."

Jessica attempted to break free, but Marisela wrapped her foot tighter around the girl's ankle, then shifted to the side so she presented no target to Jessica's effective head-butt technique.

"Listen to me, *chiquita*. If you want to know what is really going on, you'll take what is in my jacket right now."

She felt the girl's capitulation in the way her shoulders sagged. Certain Marisela could regain control of the situation at any point, at least physically, she relaxed her hold so Jessica could do as she asked and slip her hand into Marisela's jacket.

She withdrew the letter, but the locket fell to the floor.

"Read it."

Jessica shook the folds until she could read at least the first few lines. In an instant, her muscles completely gave way. Now, Marisela wasn't restraining Jessica so much as she was holding her up. She took her hand away from the girl's mouth then led her gently back to her bed.

"This is a letter I sent my mother," she said, her voice quivering. "Oh, my God. Alfredo's granddaughter mailed it for me from her school. I found the address in my father's papers. He would have locked me up forever if he'd found out. I was only, I don't know, like eight."

"You were nine," Marisela answered, swooping down to retrieve the locket and chain from the floor. "Your mother gave me that letter only a week ago."

"My mother?" Jessica's honed instincts brought her voice to a whisper. "No, that can't be. My father would never allow . . ."

Her voice trailed off and Marisela watched her eyelids blink as she struggled to make sense of her admission. She shook her head, her hands quaking even as she pressed the sheet of paper onto the bed and tried to smooth out the wrinkles.

"Your father doesn't know," Marisela assured her.

"I don't believe you. He knows everything that goes on here. You're just playing with me! You're his assassin! You're trying to trick me so that I'll forgive him for asking you to kill my mother."

Marisela kneeled beside the bed as she glanced toward the door. Even though there might not be a listening device inside the room, there was no telling who was patrolling the hallway.

"*¡Silencio!* What I'm telling you could get me killed and I sort of like breathing. Think you can tone yourself down while I explain?"

Jessica's mouth tightened into a thin line, but she gripped the letter as if the paper had been glued to her fingertips.

"I'll hear you out, but I won't believe you."

"Don't make up your mind just yet. First, let's get one thing clear—your father did not order a hit on your mother. He was angry and frustrated and scared shitless when those thugs took you. He suspected your mother might have been behind the kidnapping and he was just thinking out loud. Those *pendejos* nearly got you killed. You can't blame him for wanting revenge."

"My mother would never try to kidnap me! She doesn't want me!"

Marisela rolled her eyes, placed her finger over Jessica's lips, and shushed her again. "Wrong again, *mija*. Your mother is the reason I'm here."

Even as the whole story poured from her lips, Marisela knew Frankie would kill her himself for telling Jessica the whole unadulterated truth. She didn't reveal her real name, fearing Jessica could inadvertently screw up, but she did promise to tell her once this whole situation ended.

If it ended with Marisela still alive, that was.

To seal her confession, she showed Jessica the locket, which the girl opened, then cradled in her palm as if the charm were made from spun glass instead of gold.

"So you're here to take me back to my mother?" Jessica asked, her voice raspy from all the unshed tears pouring down the back of her throat.

"I was. But you've been through so much and frankly, your father isn't the man I was told he was anymore than I'm guessing your mother is the woman you've been told she is. And now, there is a third player in this game and that's an unknown that could get you killed if I take you out of your father's protection. Besides, with the tightened security, I don't think we can get you off this island safely without your cooperation."

"Cooperation? What are you talking about?"

Marisela slid onto the bed beside Jessica and glanced quickly at the door. They'd been chatting for quite some time and no one had burst in or even so much as interrupted, which she hoped meant that her hunch about Perez keeping his daughter's bedroom off limits to his surveillance team had been on target. But this conversation couldn't go on forever. Sooner or later, her father was going to come in and check on his daughter. Frankie was supposed to run interference after he completed his call to Blake, but there was no guarantee he'd be able to keep the distraught father from his child.

"Do you want to meet your mother?"

"Yes! If she really wants me. I mean, of course."

"Will your father let you do that?"

"Are you kidding? You heard him. He hates her."

"I'm supposed to take you to her, back in the States, where she has custody, at least until you turn eighteen. But I don't want to do that anymore."

Jessica's brows shot up, then knotted over suspicious eyes. "Why not?"

"Because frankly, I don't trust your mother anymore than your father does. And I know you love your father and would be miserable if I took you away by force. I want you to meet your mother, but I'm not adverse to changing the terms in your favor. But only if you want me to. So until you decide, I'm putting my life in your hands."

A light rap on the door forced Marisela's heart into her throat for the split second it took her to realize that if she'd been found out, no one would be knocking at all. Jessica shoved the locket and the letter under her pillow and after pressing her hand softly on Marisela's, told whoever was on the other side of the door to come in.

Javier Perez leaned inside, his smile sheepish. "You're awake. *Señora* Tosca, have you had breakfast yet?"

Marisela inhaled deeply, then pushed her breath out with a friendly smile. "No, I'm starved. I was just going to ask Jessica to join me for some of Alfredo's amazing *huevos rancheros.*"

"He made the salsa fresh this morning. Your husband is already in the dining room. Why don't you go on? My daughter and I will join you."

Marisela glanced at Jessica, who was looking down in her lap, revealing nothing. If the kid gave her up, she and Frankie would be dead by lunchtime. Did Jessica really understand? Did she care?

With no other choice, Marisela stood. "Of course. Jessica, you remember what I said. Your father loves you very much."

And on that note, she left them alone. She caught up with Frankie on the terrace, where he was sipping an espresso and staring at the surf.

"How'd you do?"

Marisela stole his cup and took a sip of his drink. She blanched when she realized he hadn't added one speck of sugar. She shoved the demitasse back at him and swallowed a few times to erase the bitter flavor from her tongue.

"I made headway."

"What did you tell her?"

"The truth."

Frankie chuckled, but she killed his humor with one pointed look.

"What truth?"

"The real truth. Jessica Perez now holds our fate in her seventeen-year-old hands."

Frankie slammed the delicate cup onto the railing. It shattered, and he didn't seem to care.

"You're not shitting me," he said.

She crossed her arms over her chest. "Nope."

He cursed, a rather impressive long line of connected vulgarisms that spanned two languages and made his point. "Now what do we do?"

"We have breakfast. Might be our last meal, *¿verdad?*"

Twenty

FUNNY, Marisela didn't remember falling asleep outside. And hadn't the storm stopped hours ago? She vaguely remembered exiting the boathouse after the patter on the roof changed tempo from a raucous drumming to a slow, rhythmic beat. Wait. That wasn't last night—that was the night before. And yet, the moisture splashing on her face right now definitely felt like rainwater, even though she could also sense soft cotton sheets caressing her body as well as the searing heat of Frankie's skin against hers. She peeked open one eye to catch Jessica flicking water at her from a drinking glass.

She scrambled for the sheet, then elbowed Frankie awake. "What the hell are you doing in here?"

Marisela winced at Frankie's harshness, but Jessica merely

quirked an eyebrow, more interested by Frankie's naked chest than she was by his morning growl.

"Some greeting for the person who's about to save both your asses," Jessica quipped.

Marisela yanked at the sheet, making sure Frankie was covered. He hadn't gone to bed naked, but he'd ended up that way sometime around three o'clock.

"Keep your virgin eyes off his ass, okay?" Marisela warned. "I've corrupted you enough."

"Who said I was a virgin?"

Marisela's jaw dropped. "Like your father would leave you alone and unsupervised with any boy long enough for you to get busy."

Jessica set the glass on the bedside table with a splash and nodded in defeat. "Got me there. There's only one place my father ever lets me go alone."

The saucy tone in her voice brought Marisela fully awake. She shook her hand in the direction of her robe and the girl obediently fetched and retrieved. Marisela shrugged into the terry cloth just before Frankie swiped the entire top sheet from the bed and made a semi-modest escape to the bathroom.

"He doesn't stick around much when I show up," Jessica noted, disappointment barely hidden beneath her wry tone.

"Maybe because you keep showing up when he's half-naked?" Marisela offered.

"Well, I may be a virgin, but I'm not virginal. Big difference."

"Apparently. So why are you splashing me awake so early in the morning?"

"It's Sunday."

Marisela waited for the rest of the explanation, which didn't come.

"And that means . . ." Marisela prompted.

"Geez!" Jessica rolled her eyes. "Sunday? Hello? Church?"

"Oh," Marisela answered, suddenly guilty for not thinking of that herself. Funny how her life had changed so drastically over the past two weeks. Not only was she getting laid with incredible regularity, she'd become adept at dodging bullets and lying through her teeth. Okay, so the last two things weren't so unique to her life. Still, she wasn't looking forward to her first confession after her latest escapades.

Bless me, Father, for I have sinned. It's been three weeks since my last confession. Let me sum up—I'm nearly ten for ten on breaking the commandments.

A few novenas were not going to do the trick this time around.

"I think I'll skip mass, if you don't mind."

With exaggerated movement, Jessica skipped her gaze back and forth from Marisela to the door, her lips tight as she spoke. "You'd think you'd want to say a few prayers of thanks, you know? That we didn't get killed the other day?"

Marisela rubbed her face and eyes, trying to clear her head. The girl was trying to tell her something, but the message wasn't breaking through her early morning brain fog.

"Yeah, you'd think."

Jessica slapped her thighs in exasperation. "If you could stop being so stubborn and sarcastic, you'd realize that going to church with me, on the mainland, would be a great idea."

Click.

The child was brilliant. But why didn't Titan know about

this weekly excursion? They'd researched Jessica and her movements prior to her and Frankie's arrival.

"You do this every Sunday?"

Jessica shook her head. "No, I usually go on Fridays when I'm in school. But since *Papi* won't let me go to school, I convinced him to allow me a Sunday in church. The security will be very tight."

Marisela heeded the warning, but trusted Ian and Max could work out the details. "Your father wouldn't mind if we tagged along?"

Jessica grinned in relief. "Why would he? He won't go. My father is a lot of things, but a hypocrite isn't one of them. He has coffee at the café across the street while I go with my bodyguards."

"What about Inma?"

Jessica slid on to the bed beside Marisela, a frown underlining her knitted brow. "She's still on the job, along with a new girl named Carla. I think she was a man in another life. *Papi* isn't fooling around anymore."

Marisela smirked. "Like he ever was?"

Marisela pushed herself off the bed and stretched, invigorated by the opportunity Jessica had arranged for them. Only. *Oh, hell.* She'd promised Jessica a chance to meet her mother, not to run away. Marisela didn't even know if Elise Barton-Ryce was anywhere near Puerto Rico, much less available for a tête-à-tête with her long lost daughter in a little less than . . .

"What time do we have to leave?"

Jessica glanced at her watch. "I'd say we have to leave no later than eight. I usually attend the nine o'clock service."

Marisela hurried to her closet and threw open the doors, cer-

tain she didn't have anything in her current wardrobe appropriate for church. "What time is it now?"

"Ten."

Marisela spun around. "Ten? We missed it?"

Jessica's lips had folded inward. She was struggling to keep
from laughing, which made Marisela want to grab the girl and
shake her silly.

"Ha, ha," Marisela said. "The joke's on me. You had no intention of taking me with you to church, did you? What?
Afraid you'd get hit by lightning just by standing next to me?"

Jessica opened her mouth, probably to explain, but snapped
her lips shut with an audible pop a split second later. Her wide
gaze seemed locked on some spot over Marisela's shoulder and
in ten seconds flat, her skin went from seashell pink to ashen
white to fire engine red.

With her hands on her hips, Marisela turned and caught
sight of Frankie leaning against the doorway, dripping wet from
his shower and covered only around the waist in a very small
white towel.

"Have you no shame? She's just a kid. Put some clothes on."

"Clothes for church? *Vidita*, it's not Sunday. It's Saturday.
Seems our *pájarita* has given us a twenty-four hour head start."

By eight o'clock the next morning, a plan was in place, though
Marisela had had no idea how the scheme would progress until
they docked at the pier in San Juan and on the short walk to the
waiting limousine, caught sight of a jewelry-selling street ven-
dor who looked vaguely familiar. The disguise Dionysus had
donned made him look every inch the Puerto Rican entrepreneur, so when Frankie stopped to buy Marisela a lovely pair of

carved, mother of pearl earrings, none of Perez's men looked anything more than impatient. He bought a pair for Jessica as well, and in fine distracting perfection, the girl spent the rest of the walk and the first few miles of the drive squealing with delight over the five-dollar gift—just enough time for Marisela to put hers on and activate the listening device planted inside.

She pressed the tiny button on the clasp and a few seconds later, heard Max's voice buzz near her ear like a bug.

"Tap the earring three times if you can hear me clearly."

She winked at Frankie and did as she was told.

"Good. Elise is at the convent with Blake. If Perez follows his reported routine, he will have the limo drop his daughter, and the two of you, at the entrance to the church. The convent is in the back. Perez has ten bodyguards stationed around the inside of the sanctuary, but we can detain two without alerting anyone right away. Go with her to communion. On the way back, divert to the alcove off the west aisle where there's a statue of the Virgin Mary. Let the kid light a candle. Elise will meet you there."

Marisela tapped the earring three more times to signal that she understood and her heartbeat steadied as she replayed the plan in her head. Max and Ian seemed to have covered all the bases. She wasn't sure that Jessica would be able to make a life-altering decision about her mother after only a few minutes, but Marisela figured that was Elise's problem. In her last communication with Max yesterday, she'd made her point of view clear that in light of the mysterious third party possibly still working against them—Jessica needed to make the choice whether or not to go with her mother for herself. The kid had gone through too much for her and Frankie to swipe her now, mission or not, especially since she'd kept their secret. The mother had to do the convincing before Marisela made another move.

"Those earrings look quite beautiful on you, *señora*," Perez said, his eyes trained on how she continued to fiddle with the jewelry.

She reached over and grabbed Frankie's hand. "I don't usually let my husband buy me such presents, but I couldn't resist."

Perez chuckled, completely unaware of the threat that lay ahead. "My daughter's influence on you is undeniable, I'm afraid. I hope you won't regret making her acquaintance, *señor*."

Frankie managed a half-grin. Marisela couldn't believe they'd gotten this far. Or that in a few short hours, the entire mission would be over.

"Your daughter is charming, *Señor* Perez," Marisela said.

Charming and resourceful. For a kid, she had a sharp mind and good instincts. Marisela could only hope she'd be able to see beyond her childhood loneliness to judge her mother fairly. And accurately.

Jessica snuggled next to her father and from across the seat in the limousine, Marisela caught the look of uncertainty in the young girl's eyes, along with the clear, sharp reflection of determination. And trust. The young girl had put her future in the hands of a stranger, her, all because she wanted desperately to meet the mother who likely had an ulterior motive for wanting her home.

So far, Max had come up empty in his investigation of Elise Barton-Ryce's finances. And yet, something in his tone yesterday clued Marisela that he'd at least discovered some vague and unverifiable indication that maybe something wasn't quite right. Knowing that, Marisela decided she wasn't letting Jessica out of her sight for one minute. When Elise pleaded her case to her long-lost daughter, Marisela was going to be right there, watching the kid's back—and more importantly, her fragile, teenaged heart.

The drive to the church was noneventful, with Frankie staring sullenly out the window, having made Rogelio's displeasure at being dragged to church abundantly clear. Perez hung on every word his daughter chatted into his ear—and that was no small feat since the girl didn't stop talking. Marisela watched the driver and from time to time, checked out the traffic around them. Nothing unusual. Nothing out of place. Two cruise ships had come into port, so the streets of San Juan teemed with tourists. The convent and school were on an outer edge of the city on the way to the fort in the area known as Old San Juan. Little by little, the buildings grew smaller, the streets more narrow, the atmosphere decidedly more old world.

The cross on the top of the church thrust into the sky in simple wooden glory. Bricks washed white by the sun and wind curved and stacked into a building completely unremarkable except for kaleidoscopic stained glass windows. As the limousine pulled to a stop just outside the brittle concrete steps, Marisela immediately spotted the first of Perez's bodyguards.

God, she hoped Titan didn't fail them now—and that included not offing any of Perez's men. Jessica would never forgive Marisela if someone in her father's employ took a bullet because she couldn't resist the chance to meet her mother.

The bodyguard stepped forward to open the back door. Marisela had already started to scoot toward the exit when a loud pop sent her diving toward Jessica. Perez already had his daughter covered. Out the back window, Marisela saw the bodyguard stagger toward the church, gun drawn. He was hurt, but still standing.

"¡Dejame! ¡Dejame!" Perez shouted to the driver, who slammed his foot onto the gas. Tires screeched as they tore down the street, but a second explosion directly underneath the car jolted them all into the air. Jessica screamed, rolling herself into a tight ball. Her father tried to curve his body over her at the same time that he removed his gun from his jacket and yelled orders to the driver.

Only a few moments elapsed before Marisela realized that the driver couldn't comply. The explosion had locked up the steering and judging by their increasing speed as they hurtled down the hill, the brakes were gone, too. Frankie flung himself through the narrow opening into the front seat, but he could do nothing to stop the inevitable. They were going to crash.

Marisela grabbed Jessica and Javier and flung them to the floor seconds before the impact threw her into the opposite seat. Her shoulder smashed hard into the side panel, but not with enough force to knock her gun from her hand.

"Stay down!"

Frankie had flung open the passenger side door and Marisela did the same from the back.

"What's happening?" she shouted, aiming at the empty street behind them while Frankie covered the front. They'd crashed into the side of an abandoned store. The front end of the car tilted up onto a curb and broken glass sparkled around them in the stark white morning sun.

"Ambush!" Frankie shouted.

Their driver emerged from his side of the car with a wicked looking XM8 lightweight assault rifle clutched in his hands. He opened his mouth to speak, but a shot through his skull instantly silenced him. His body shuddered, then crumbled to the ground.

Marisela ducked back inside the car.

"Stay down. Your driver's dead."

Jessica's eyes were wide with terror.

Marisela had to trust that Javier could take care of Jessica until she and Frankie worked out a plan. This attack couldn't be a Titan operation. They wouldn't kill so indiscriminately. Would they? When she emerged from the car, she realized she had no time to work out the possibilities. An SUV with a tinted windshield veered down the street toward them, sleek black weapons dangling out of the passenger side doors, clearly meant to invoke fear. Was this an assassination attempt? Were they trying to kill Perez? Jessica, too? Or was this just another elaborate scheme to kidnap the girl? And if so, who was calling the shots?

Marisela tapped on her earring. She heard nothing and tried again until the rapid fire of bullets shifted her attention from communication to survival. She spun around in time to catch Frankie diving across the front seat and retrieving the driver's rifle. Their arsenal included two handguns—three if they counted Perez's—and a rifle against two men with automatic weapons and an unknown sniper. No backup from Titan and as of yet, nothing from Perez's men down the street at the church, either.

They had to get Jessica to safety. The limo wasn't going to move. They needed the closest vehicle—the attacking SUV.

Marisela yelled for Frankie to get into the car with Jessica and Perez and shut the doors. He was better trained, better able to protect two people rather than one. Besides, the limo was bulletproof. If they wanted them, they'd have to come in and get them.

Impulsively, Marisela ducked under the car, which was tilted up on the front end enough to allow her room to completely conceal herself. The stench of burning circuits and blood seeped into her nostrils, but she didn't dare breathe too loudly when the SUV slammed to a halt and the two men jumped out and proceeded to spray the car with bullets. They cursed, slammed the butts of their guns against the glass and fired into the door handles, then cursed more when they couldn't break through. From her shelter behind the tires, she could see a second SUV—same dark color and tinted windows—heading their way.

Shit. Reinforcements, but not from their side. She still heard no chatter in her earpiece, so she couldn't count on Titan to know what was going on. She had to make a move. Now.

With a quick roll, she leaned out from under the car and shot the first assailant. Her bullet blew apart his chin and she rolled again to avoid a dousing of blood and brain. The second assailant flattened himself to the ground and peppered the asphalt with bullets.

Marisela jumped onto the hood of the car and slid across, landing on the guy's back before he had a chance to stand. She aimed downward and pumped a bullet into his skull. She slammed her fist on the window and shouted for Frankie, Perez, and Jessica to get out while she ran to the SUV and commandeered the driver's seat. They had to escape before the second wave of killers arrived.

Frankie came out first, covering their exit with a wave of

gunfire from the automatic weapon. Perez pushed Jessica out next and Marisela leaned over to open the passenger side door. Jessica jumped in, her skin ashen gray.

"Who are they?" Jessica asked, nearly hysterical.

Marisela didn't have time to answer. The second SUV had screeched to a halt just a few feet behind. Perez and Frankie were exchanging gunfire and without cover, were sitting ducks.

"Open the back door!" Marisela ordered.

Jessica swiveled around and did what she was told while Marisela threw the car into reverse. Frankie shoved Perez toward the car, but he refused to get in.

"Take my daughter to safety!"

He grabbed Frankie's gun and shoved him toward the open door. The people in the church had spilled out onto the sidewalk and Perez's men were sprinting toward them. A Jeep spun around the corner a block away, sirens blaring.

"*Papi!*" Jessica yelled, reaching toward the open door.

Frankie pushed her back into her seat and ordered her down. "Get out of here!"

Marisela complied. Perez, taking his last stand against his enemies, ducked back behind the limo for cover. His guards were gaining ground, so the second SUV didn't stop, but spun into hot pursuit.

"They're following."

Frankie pulled a clip out of his pocket.

"Of course they are. They want Jessica."

"Me? Why?"

Marisela swerved around a corner. God, she had no idea where she was going. This time, she wasn't escaping an ex-boyfriend in the hometown she knew like the back of her hand. She was driving blind into an unknown city with narrow streets and gaggles of tourists.

"Frankie, call Max."

He rolled down the side window. "No time. Keep heading east. Once we get out of Old San Juan, there's open highway. Try to lose them!"

Marisela already had the gas pedal flush against the floor. She used every trick she knew to widen the distance between them and their pursuers, but nothing worked until Frankie leaned out and fired several shots into the windshield of the car following behind. They returned fire, but only seconds after Marisela flew through an intersection, clutching the steering wheel until her knuckles ached, the sports utility vehicle hit a bump and went airborne. The vehicle behind them crashed into a light pole and burst into flames.

Frankie pulled himself back into the car and for several long minutes, they drove in stunned silence. When a traffic light turned red in front of her, Marisela drew the car to a slow stop. Only then did she hear Jessica whimpering. She reached over with a shaky hand and gently patted her thigh.

"You're safe now."

Jessica drew in a long, shivering breath. "What about my father?"

Marisela glanced over her shoulder at Frankie, who was sitting straight against the seat, his neck tilted back, his breathing labored as he recuperated from the gunplay.

"I'm sure he's fine. He's a brave man. He gave us the cover we needed to escape."

"Who would want to kidnap me besides my mother?"

The light turned green. Marisela gingerly pressed her foot to the pedal and expertly blended them into traffic. She still didn't know where they were going, but at least they were no longer running for their lives.

"I don't know," she answered. "But we're going to find out."

Twenty-One

IAN MINGLED THROUGH the crowd, watching over his shoulder as Elise Barton-Ryce loitered by the baptismal font in the sanctuary just inside the church. Men had died trying to kidnap her daughter and she looked about as cool and unshaken as a stirred martini.

He tilted his wrist to his mouth. "Max, report."

Seconds ticked by and the delay unnerved him. Nothing had gone as planned. A third party was working against him, and he had no clue who was behind the attacks on Perez. Had Marisela and Frank entered the church, Titan would have Jessica in their possession by now, tucked away on his private jet, heading for the mainland of the United States where Elise's custody order would be enforced. How naive Marisela had been, thinking he'd let the child have a choice in this matter. The law had already decided which parent she belonged to—and besides, Ian wasn't about to give up on this case so easily—not with so much of Elise Barton-Ryce's cash on the line.

But while he didn't intend to give Marisela her way, he hadn't wanted her hurt. His chest tightened, thinking of how he'd spent the previous day, holding the hand of Pan's wife, a woman facing her husband's permanent disability. She'd had no idea how the man she loved had actually been hurt—or how the man showering her with platitudes in the hospital waiting room had been ultimately responsible for the injuries threatening her husband's life. He'd lost one agent too many already. Would he have to lose more before bringing the operation to a close?

"Max, report."

On the second try, the speaker in his ear crackled to life. "They got away."

"Are you in pursuit?"

"Negative, but neither are the shooters in the SUV. Traffic has jammed to a stop. They're somewhere up ahead."

"Is Marisela wearing her locator?"

"If she is, it's dead. I can't get a lock on her or Frank."

Ian tamped down a rumble from deep in his chest. "Find them," he ordered.

"Working on it."

In the meantime, Ian had to make sure that one player got out of this game permanently. He should have anticipated this development, but Marisela's personal interest in Jessica Perez had to end. She'd jeopardized the mission. But he'd deal with her later.

He broke through the sloppy police line and strolled over to

Javier Perez, who was fighting off the attention of a paramedic.

"Buenos días, Señor Perez. Yo soy Ian Blake, presidente de Titan International. Y tengo información muy importante con respecto a Jessica."

"I want to speak to my father!"

Marisela couldn't stand the tears. Her baby sister, Belinda, had always used waterworks to get her way. But dammit, there was a lot more at stake here than a new pair of jeans or the biggest piece of chocolate cake. Jessica had to shut up long enough for Marisela to think!

"Jessica, *por favor,* let me take us somewhere safe and I promise we'll call your father. The sooner he picks you up, the sooner I can figure out what the hell went wrong. Frankie, any suggestions?"

But Frankie didn't reply. In fact, he hadn't said a word in way too long. Marisela chanced a look in the backseat.

There was blood everywhere.

"Frankie!"

Marisela turned down a side street, pulling in to the nearest alley. She scrambled into the backseat. When Jessica finally turned to look at Frankie, she started to scream.

"Calm down!" Marisela ordered. She didn't need bystanders rushing toward them when they still couldn't distinguish friends from enemies. "Frankie, what happened? Frankie?"

He hadn't lost consciousness, but even when she pulled his chin down so their eyes met, a cloud had settled over his irises. Sweat beaded on his upper lip and forehead. The beginnings of shock?

With a mix of gentleness and panic, she searched his body

and found the wound. He'd been shot in the stomach, likely by a bullet that pierced through the car's chassis during the chase. With a curse and a wince, she placed her hand over the wound and tried to stop the bleeding.

"Jessica, get me something for the blood!"

"What?"

"Anything! Look in the glove compartment."

There was nothing. Tears flowed down Jessica's face as she frantically searched the car. She found a cache of weapons and ammunition, but nothing to press into Frankie's wound.

"Wait! Here!"

Jessica pulled a long lace mantilla she'd had folded in her pocket. The intricate fabric wasn't much, but would have to do.

"We need a hospital. Do you know where it is?"

As Jessica shook her head, Frankie roused himself long enough to move his hand over Marisela's and capture her watery gaze with his unsteady eyes. "No hospital."

"Why the hell not?"

Frankie shook his head, struggled to breathe through the pain. "Too many questions. If we stop the bleeding, I'll be fine long enough for Blake to get us out."

"I can't stop the bleeding here!"

Frankie forced himself to smile and Marisela could have killed him for managing even that small sense of humor—if he wasn't already well on his way to dying already. "Then get out of here, *vidita.*"

Out of pure personal need, Marisela stretched up on her knees and kissed Frankie squarely on the mouth. God help them all, but she wasn't about to let him die.

"Do you drive?" she asked Jessica.

The girl frantically shook her head.

"Then jump back here. You hold your hand against his wound, tight, while I find us somewhere to hole up."

To her credit, the terrified girl didn't hesitate. She switched places with Marisela, all the time reassuring Frankie that he'd be all right. If she could just contact her father, she was sure everything would turn out fine.

If only.

On a hunch, Marisela piloted the car to a rough edge of town. There, she traded the beaten and battered SUV and several of the guns Jessica had found under the seats for a scratched and dented cell phone and a room with a working bathroom. For the first fifteen minutes, Jessica and Marisela worked frantically, tearing sheets and bartering for antibiotic ointment and gauze to bandage Frankie's wounds. They couldn't stay here long, though. They'd bought quite a bit with their jewelry and trinkets, but they hadn't bought anyone's silence. And since they still didn't know who the enemy was exactly, they had to turn to those people they could count on as friends.

Jessica had the cell phone and was dialing her father while Marisela made sure Frankie was as comfortable as possible. She'd covered him with several blankets to chase off the possibility of shock and the bleeding had abated considerably. They'd bought time, but not much.

Marisela listened to Jessica's end of the conversation, translating the Spanish to English in her mind.

"I'm fine. No, I'm not hurt. But Frankie is. I mean, Rogelio. Yes, *Papi*, I know who they really are. No. No! No, you've got it all wrong. Who told you that? No. I don't believe it. You can't believe it. They saved my life. Twice now. They don't want to hurt me."

Marisela couldn't keep her distance or pretend she hadn't overheard every word Jessica spoke in this five-by-five closet of a room.

"What's going on?"

Jessica held the cell phone to her chest, her eyes wide and glossy, her cheeks streaked with trails of tears. She wasn't on the verge of crying again, but screaming with rage was a definite possibility.

"He says he's spoken with someone named Ian Blake. That he was your boss before you and Frankie went rogue. He says you have been conspiring with my mother to kidnap me, even though he refused to take her case when she tried to hire the company to retrieve me. Tell me it's not true, Marisela. Please, tell me."

Marisela's mouth dropped open. That son of a bitch.

"It's not true. I still work for Ian Blake. He's playing a game, Jessica, I swear."

"Why?"

Marisela spun around, jabbing her hands through her loose hair, pulling tight on the strands and hoping the pain would somehow kick her brain into working. What was Ian up to? What did he possibly have to gain by making Perez his ally?

No, that wasn't his motivation. He was destroying an ally, not building one. He was trying to put a wedge between Jessica and Marisela. But why?

"What does your father want you to do?"

She glanced guiltily at the phone. "He just wants to know where I am."

Marisela caught the thinning of Jessica's lips, the way her hands shook. "And what will happen to me and Frankie?"

Jessica was probably one of the strongest young women Marisela had ever met. Take away her sheltered childhood and her isolated adolescence and she would have made a great addition to *las Reinas*. At her heart, she was tough, though right now, the poor kid's confidence was fluttering in the wind.

"He didn't say, but you know. I know. I can't let that happen, Marisela. You saved my life. You've been honest with me, haven't you? You aren't some rogue agent trying to make a buck off me, are you?"

Marisela reached out and laid her palm on Jessica's arm. "No, *niña*, I'm not. I've told you the truth—all of it. Ian Blake is the one who is lying now and I suspect he's done that so I can't return you to your father without paying with my life. Your father is now a threat to me, not an ally, because you and I both know that even if I'm not some rogue agent, I'm still not who I convinced your father I was. Either way, I'm dead."

Jessica stepped back, her breathing ragged as she fought the greatest conflict the girl had probably had to face to date. If she ran home to the safety of her father, her new friends would die. If she stayed, she'd likely be returned to her mother against her will. Marisela stepped back to Frankie in the bed, where he slept fitfully. She checked his bandage. Blood was still seeping through. She touched his forehead. He was on fire.

She wasn't a doctor, but she knew she didn't have much time to sort all this out.

Luckily, Jessica sensed the dire situation and lifted the phone to her ear. "*Lo siento, Papi.* I can't tell you where I am. You'll kill them, I know you will."

Marisela couldn't hear Perez's response, but judging by the way Jessica jerked the phone away from her ear, he was furious.

"I do love you, *Papi*. More than anything. You need to trust that. You need to trust me."

With the same effort she might have used to lift a car off the street, Jessica pulled the phone away from her ear and disconnected the call. With a quavering hand, she offered the phone to Marisela. "I don't know how much time you have. He'll likely have the call traced."

Marisela took the cell and with a burst of emotion she knew she couldn't afford, pulled the girl into a tight and desperate embrace. "Thank you, *mija*. I swear, I won't let them take you. But we have to get Frankie help."

Moisture seeped through the material on Marisela's shoulder, though beyond a sniffle, Jessica contained her emotions, which helped Marisela hold herself together. But the surrender to sentimentality couldn't last. She pushed Jessica back, her hands clutching her arms.

"How safe do you feel in this neighborhood?"

Jessica eyed the window, fluttering with a pillowcase tacked over the splintered frame. "I'm pretty sure some of them know who I am, or at least, know my father."

Marisela nodded. This could be both good and bad. "Can you go out there? Make arrangements for someone to take us to the nearest hospital?"

Jessica's eyes widened. "But my father will find you! You'll be killed."

Rubbing her hands over the cell phone, Marisela glanced over at Frankie on the bed. "I thought Ian would get us out of this jam, but he obviously has his own agenda. Frankie will die if we don't act. The first thing we're going to need is a ride out of here before your father tracks us down. We've bartered nearly everything we have on us so we're going to have to depend on your influence as Javier Perez's daughter. No one knows that we're on the run from him. You go out there, let them think that they'll get a big reward for helping you, okay? It wouldn't hurt to imply that not helping you might get them trouble they don't want, too. Think you can pull it off?"

Jessica gnawed on her bottom lip, but nodded her head at the same time. "I'll do what I can."

"That's all I can ask. You didn't sign up for any of this, Jessica. I know you just wanted to meet your mother."

In a rush, Jessica grabbed for the door, turning at the last minute when Marisela had punched the first three numbers of Ian's cell phone. "Marisela," she said, laughing at the sound. "That suits you so much better than Dolores."

Marisela grinned.

Jessica's tentative smile melted away, replaced by a troubled frown. "Could my mother have done that? Have people shoot at us that way?"

Marisela had gone this far being honest with the kid, she couldn't stop now. "I don't know, but it's a definite possibility. That doesn't mean it's the truth. I don't know what the truth is yet, but I'm going to find out."

As soon as Jessica left, her face a streaked and pale picture of uncertainty and betrayal, Marisela finished pressing numbers until she heard Ian Blake's cool, collected voice on the other end of the line.

"Where are you?" he asked.

"Like I'd tell you, you snake. You betrayed us to Perez."

"No, Marisela. I simply ensured that you returned to our original plan."

"If you weren't going to meet me in the church, why didn't you just say so? You didn't have to send shooters after us. Frankie's been hit, you cock-sucking son of a bitch. I swear to God, if he dies, I'm going to slice your fucking heart out with my fingernails."

Ian clucked his tongue into the phone, but she also heard him move so that the noise she'd initially heard in the background faded. Good. He was taking her seriously.

"Frank is wounded?"

"Shot in the stomach during the car chase."

"Is he bleeding?"

"Yes, but I've slowed it down as much as I can. He needs real medical care."

"You know I'll arrange the best."

"No, I *don't* know that. If you would have kept your god-dammed mouth shut, I could have called Perez, reunited him with his daughter and played Frankie up to be the hero. We could have taken her another time."

"There couldn't be another time. I need the girl, now."

"Well, you royally screwed up, Ian, 'cause now, you're not getting her. Maybe not ever. She's terrified. As soon as I get Frankie help, I'm sending her back to her father. He's the only one that seems to have her safety in mind. You know, if you haven't figured it out, when bullets are fired, people die. Jessica could have been killed."

"I had nothing to do with those assailants. Despite my initial annoyance that you'd changed our strategy, I was at the church, with Elise, prepared to meet the daughter in the alcove. We weren't alerted to a change in plans until Perez's bodyguards suddenly left the building. I still don't know who orchestrated that debacle."

Marisela rolled her eyes, her rage increasing with every multi-syllable word he used. "Cut the crap. You know, or you'll know soon. I want to talk to Max."

The request caught him off-guard, she could tell. The truth remained that the only person she trusted in the Titan organization at this point was Ian's ever-present assistant. She doubted that he'd lie to her, even if Ian ordered him to.

"Max's been called away."

Had he found something on Elise? Or was he still investigating?

"Patch me through to him, damn it."

"I know what Max knows, Marisela. You should understand that by now. His loyalty is to me."

"No, his loyalty is to Titan. There's a difference."

"Semantics."

This argument wasn't worth the time. She changed the subject. "If you know what Max knows, then he's filled you in on my suspicions about Elise."

"Yes."

"And you know that so long as I suspect that ice queen of having a hand in the bloodshed that has freaked Jessica out, I'm not bringing her kid anywhere near her."

"You're too emotionally involved," Ian said, and Marisela could hear the words hissing through tightly clenched teeth. "You have a job to do. You work for Titan."

"And that means I leave my brain at the door? No such luck, Blake. You knew what you were getting when you signed me on. I am who I am and if working for you means leaving that behind, I fucking quit."

She was tempted to hang up, use that as her last parting shot, but there was so much that had yet to be said. The fact of the matter was, she couldn't get Frankie help without Titan's resources now that Ian had poisoned Perez's mind against them. Even if she found an emergency room, the minute Perez located them, they'd be dead.

"I do not accept your resignation. I want the girl. Bring her to me and I'll see that Frank is cared for."

"He's dying, damn you. You want me to trade Jessica's life for Frankie's?"

"You've given me no choice."

"Fuck you. You run this operation. You have a choice."

"Yes, I do. I choose to win. I choose to complete the original mission and collect the payment I'm owed for services rendered."

"You sure Elise has the cash? Or is she just yanking your chain? You'd better make sure, Ian. I swear to God, if I find out she double-crossed us, I'll take her out myself."

"You're full of threats, Ms. Morales, but you've proven you've got a soft heart where the child is concerned. Who's going to take you seriously now?"

Marisela swallowed, caught in the web of her own actions. He was right, dammit. With Jessica, she'd lost her edge. She'd acted because of a moral code she hadn't known she possessed. But she couldn't betray the kid now, not when she'd been through so much.

Behind her, Frankie groaned. He'd shifted on the bed, displacing his bandages. Marisela ran to the bed in time to watch the threadbare sheets saturate with blood and the last of the color drain from his skin.

"Oh my God," Marisela said, sliding gingerly onto the bed, tossing aside the cell phone while she struggled to press her hand against the wound and stop the bleeding. She could hear Ian Blake's voice echoing as if far away, and she could only hope he'd stay away long enough for her to figure out how to save Frankie's life and keep Jessica out of her mother's clutches.

Jessica rushed back into the room. "I've got someone!" She caught sight of Marisela on the bed with the moaning Frankie and she dashed toward them. "Is he all right?"

Marisela shook her head, overwhelmed by the realization that Frankie might not live. She'd confessed that truth to Blake, but the words had meant nothing until she could feel his life slipping away. Unwilling to wipe her bloody hands on his forehead, she leaned forward and placed her cheek on his. His skin scorched her.

"He's dying, Jessica. And Titan won't help unless I turn you over to them, to your mother."

Jessica staggered backward. "You can't!"

Marisela stared at the girl as if she'd never seen her before, trying with all her might to imagine that she was just some whiny, spoiled teenager with a father who was a killer and a mother who cared. Her eyes clouded, but the image simply wouldn't come.

She looked aside, listening as the voices beyond the door

raised. Whoever Jessica had wrangled to take them to the hospital had arrived. Frankie wouldn't survive without immediate medical attention. Time had run out.

"I'm sorry, Jessica," Marisela said, wrapped her fingers, sticky with Frankie's blood, tightly around Jessica's arm. "I can't let him die."

Twenty-Two

MAX CUPPED MARISELA'S elbow as he led her into the suite in the hotel across the street from the hospital. Frankie had survived surgery, but just barely. She'd had a scant moment to whisper in his ear before Max spirited her away for an emergency meeting with her boss. Or ex-boss, depending on how things went.

Ian Blake stood the minute she entered the room, not a wrinkle daring to mar his perfectly tailored pants. With his sable brown hair stylishly combed back and those devastating aquamarine eyes of his sparkling in unabashed triumph, he looked every inch the powerful, invulnerable mogul. But every man had a weakness and thanks to Max, Marisela now knew what Blake's was. She'd keep his secret—for now.

"I hear Frank will make a full recovery. We're very pleased."

Marisela glanced around the room. Elise Barton-Ryce stood sentry over her daughter, her French manicured nails curved over Jessica's defeated shoulders. Elise wore a tiny, polite smile, but her eyes remained cold as ice. Jessica, on the other hand, didn't bother to look up—or else, couldn't bear to. She stared into her palms cradled in her lap, broken and sad.

"Looks to me like no one around here gives a damn about anyone but themselves. Why is she still here?" Marisela said, nodding toward Jessica. "Aren't you playing with fire keeping her in the country so long? Her father is going to tear Puerto Rico apart looking for her."

Elise chuckled haughtily. "As far as he knows, Jessica has already arrived in Boston and is settling into a bedroom on my heavily guarded estate." She turned her gaze worshipfully at Ian, but the man didn't seem to notice. "Mr. Blake has Javier eating out of the palm of his hand. He'll never find Jessica."

"You better hope he doesn't," Marisela challenged. "If he finds her with you, he'll kill you. And no amount of begging from her will save you this time."

The *this time* caught her attention.

She tightened her hold on Jessica's shoulder so that the kid winced. "Javier wouldn't dare murder the mother of his child."

Marisela hooked her thumbs in the loops on her jeans, the same jeans that were stained with Frankie's blood. "You've been counting on that, haven't you? For a long time, you've based everything you've done, everything you've said on the confidence that no matter how far you went, Javier wouldn't order your death. Well, I think your 'get out of assassination free' card has expired, lady. I'm betting your daughter will agree."

If Jessica could have dipped her face lower, she would have.

Elise glanced down at her, trying not to look worried—and failing miserably.

Marisela afforded a half-grin.

"That is of no consequence," Ian said. "In a few minutes, Jessica and her mother will leave for the mainland and I don't think we'll have any trouble hiding her until she turns eighteen. At that point, she'll have her own decisions to make."

Jessica's gaze rose slowly. She locked stares with Ian, but almost instantaneously looked away. She spared her mother a cursory glance, but remained silent. Brave and resilient, Jessica would muddle through. For a few months, until her birthday. Marisela had to believe that Jessica could handle the heartbreak.

"Why am I here?" Marisela asked.

Elise's upper lip curled into a snarl. "Jessica insisted. She refused to leave until she knew your associate survived his injuries and she'd had a chance to talk to you."

Marisela quirked an eyebrow. Jessica could be headstrong and persuasive, but she didn't have the finesse to have altered Ian's plans. She glanced over her shoulder and caught the slight upturn of Max's mouth. He'd done this. Arranged the delay. He'd likely conspired with Jessica, too.

"So talk, kid."

Marisela caught the glimmer of energy in the young girl's eyes the minute she stood and put a few paces between her and her mother.

"I wanted to thank you."

"Thank me for what? For exposing you to your viper of a mother?"

"For exposing my mother to be a viper," Jessica retorted. "Did you get what you needed?"

Marisela dug into her pocket and retrieved the wad of papers Max had handed her shortly before they'd left the hospital.

"Just a few minutes ago. I'm glad you convinced everyone to wait around."

"You're not the only resourceful *sucia* around here, *mi amiga*."

Elise barged forward, positioning herself between Marisela and Jessica, her daughter at her back. "What are you talking about? I didn't come here to be insulted! And don't speak that horrible language. I don't understand."

"What a shame," Marisela said, feigning sincerity. "I've got a long list of names for you, lady. Some in Spanish, too, and they defy translation. But we'll start with your native tongue. How about trying on liar for size?"

Marisela unfolded the paper so Elise could see the legalese streaming across the page. Her eyes widened, but when she moved to snatch the codicil from Russell Barton's will out of her hands, Marisela easily yanked the document away.

"Have you seen this yet, Ian?" Marisela asked.

Ian had turned and was staring Max down.

"There wasn't time, sir," Max explained simply.

"No, Ms. Morales, I haven't had the pleasure."

She turned and walked over to him, her hips in full swing, her confidence spiking and her energy revitalized. That Ian had allowed Max to pursue her request for more information on the financial background of Elise Barton-Ryce earned him some credit. Apparently, he did have a modicum of trust in her instincts, even when all she'd had to go on was a flippant comment from a bitter ex-lover. And yet, he'd still done the one thing she'd warned him early on not to do—he'd toyed with her emotions. He'd pitted her loyalty to Frankie against success on a case. He'd forced her to betray an essentially fragile young woman.

For that, he'd pay.

She handed him the paper.

"This is from the recently probated will of Russell Barton, Elise's rich daddy," she explained. "Yes, he left his one and only daughter a shitload of money that should have kept her swimming in diamonds and furs for the rest of her life. But you'll notice in paragraph four," Marisela said, tapping her fingernail on the appropriate part of the page, "that Russell also willed a couple of billion dollars to various charities and foundations—money he would have given to his granddaughter, had she not been removed from Elise's care. This codicil also states in paragraph five that should Jessica return to the family fold before her eighteenth birthday, she'd inherit those billions instead of the charities—and every last cent would be administered by her mother until she turned thirty."

Because Marisela was standing so close to him, she noticed how Ian's lips tightened as he read, his eyes scanning quickly back and forth. The conclusion was simple—Elise Barton-Ryce had not hired Titan to reclaim her daughter because she loved her or missed her as she'd claimed. She'd arranged this operation out of pure, unadulterated greed.

Ian handed the paper over his shoulder and Max quickly retrieved it. "This changes nothing. Mrs. Barton-Ryce owes us no explanation of her motives."

Marisela shoved her hands in her pockets and nodded her head. "I can understand how you might see it that way, but you are not picking up the—oh, damn, what's the word, Max?"

"The nuance?"

Marisela pointed at him and then gave him a thumbs-up gesture for helping her out. "That's it. The nuance. You see, this proves Elise Barton-Ryce to be a greedy, lying bitch. I wanted to know who'd paid those Miami thugs to kidnap Jessica at the store and to try again at the church. Had one of those attacks succeeded, Perez would have had me and Frankie to blame. I'm guessing she hired cheap labor to beat us to the punch. Why pay Titan millions when she could buy amateurs for chump change and achieve the same results? Me and Frankie were just a smoke screen—a way to get information about Jessica and then exploit it."

"That's ludicrous. You have no proof!" Elise shouted.

"Don't I?"

Out of her back pocket, she retrieved the final nail in Elise's coffin. Ian Blake had been right about one thing—Max was top-of-the-line. Send him in the right direction and he could work miracles.

"This is from the very confidential, very private financial records of the attorney who transferred Elise's first payment to you, Mr. Blake. Seems he also authorized the release of a generous sum of money to a courier who then traveled to Miami. That money was laundered through a strip club in Liberty City." Marisela turned, piercing Elise's furious gaze with her own steady brand of steel. "Elise set us up. She'd hoped to retrieve her daughter herself and use Frankie and me as the scapegoats—and possibly, default on her final payment to Titan, which is no small chunk of change."

Ian turned to Max.

"Employing the Toscas' accountant was a brilliant move on

your part, Mr. Blake," Max confirmed. "He proved incredibly useful to me when you authorized my looking more deeply into Mrs. Barton-Ryce's financial dealings."

When Ian turned, all the anger he'd leveled at Marisela now shot directly at Elise.

Marisela's figured her smile as she delivered the last part of the story could have lit the whole goddamned room. "When the operation a few days ago didn't work, Elise arranged a second payment to the thugs in Miami, one Max was able to watch appear and disappear into the strip club's accounts. Elise knew the time and location of our meeting at the church. She might have even made it clear that if Javier died in the process, she wouldn't have been too sad. We'll find out soon enough. Not all of the assailants died when that SUV crashed. One is in surgery now, very heavily guarded by the Puerto Rican police and Javier Perez, who intends to find out who attacked him and his daughter. This witness has a relatively good prognosis for recovery, too. I'm betting your former lover will be very interested to hear what the injured man has to say about you, don't you agree?"

Marisela licked her lips, loving how Elise had started to shake.

"Jessica is mine. The courts will protect us."

"Are you sure? You're so busted. I don't think even a greedy son of a bitch like Mr. Blake will let you take Jessica now."

Marisela glanced in Ian's direction, certain that even if she'd read the man entirely wrong, she had a gun tucked into the back of her jeans that would ensure Jessica didn't go anywhere with her duplicitous mother. Luckily, Max's assurances that Ian wouldn't allow an injustice to go unpunished were not empty.

Fury drew Ian's lips into a thin, red line.

"Max, escort Mrs. Barton-Ryce to the plane that is waiting at the airport."

Elise's arm shot out and ensnared Jessica just above the elbow. "I'm not going anywhere without my daughter."

Marisela moved to break the hold the woman had on Jessica, but even her quick reflexes proved too slow. Jessica twisted out of her mother's grip and then slapped the bitch soundly across the face.

"You're not my mother. You never have been." Jessica stepped forward, straightening her spine until she was eye-to-eye with the woman who had given birth to her, had abandoned her, had tried to steal her back for money, and had almost gotten her killed in the process. "If you ever come near me again, I swear, I'll let him kill you. I'll even ask to watch."

Elise recoiled and only for a split second did she allow pain to mar her expression. Seconds later, she recovered, twirled on her expensive heels and marched out of the room.

Marisela was there to catch Jessica the minute the door slammed behind Elise. The girl crumbled into her arms and sobbed. Marisela could think of nothing more to say, except to whisper, *"Mija,* I'm so sorry. I'm so sorry," until Jessica recovered enough to accept a handkerchief from Ian.

"I'll arrange for you to be returned to your father immediately."

He turned to Max, who was already halfway out the door to make the arrangements, then faced Jessica again. Ian stood there, so cold, so stoic and waited for . . . what? A thank-you?

"What do you want from her, Blake?"

He looked askance. "Nothing, of course. Why don't you escort her into the adjoining suite. She can freshen up before we return her to her father."

Marisela seethed, but she did as Ian asked, then told Jessica to stay put until she came to fetch her. Which she would do, once she cleared up a few things with her so-called boss.

Ian was pouring himself a brandy when Marisela slipped back into the room.

"You drink too much."

Ian sniffed the fine liqueur, then took a worshipful sip. "Care to join me?"

"I don't drink with double-crossing *pendejos.*"

"You use that word quite a bit. It must be incredibly insulting."

"Try Berlitz. You have a lot to learn."

He crossed the room, slowing momentarily as he broke into her personal space. She was angry enough, finally, to have erected a wall against the powerful pull of attraction that had plagued her until now. He was still undeniably the most suave, sophisticated, and seductive man she'd ever met—but she said no with her eyes in a way that caused him to back away.

"You're angry."

"You bargained with Frankie's life. You think I'm just going to forget?"

He shrugged. "I did what I had to do after one of my agents allowed her emotions to interfere in a mission. You can't blame me for using those same emotions to achieve my objective."

"You think I can't? Watch me. I warned you not to manipulate me."

He stepped closer and challenged her eye-to-eye. "And I

warned you to do as you were told. I run Titan, Ms. Morales. My agents do as I say. I could fire you right here on the spot."

She narrowed her gaze. "I dare you."

He tilted his head back and laughed. "Fine then. I needed you for this case and this case only. You have outlived your usefulness. You're fired."

"No, she's not."

The door had swung open and in walked the leggiest redhead Marisela had ever seen. She wore a slim, pencil skirt, roach-killer pumps, and a silk blouse that draped lovingly over a bustline even Marisela envied for a few seconds before reminding herself that her own girls were nothing to sneeze at. With pure warmth in her cool, emerald gaze—one that matched Ian's with utter exactness except for the color—the woman extended her hand in greeting.

"Brynn Blake," she greeted. "I'm honored to meet you, Marisela."

Ian had stepped forward, seething. "This is not your operation, Brynn. You have no right to be here."

Marisela accepted the woman's hand and wasn't surprised to find a firm grip underneath her silky skin.

Ian was so screwed.

"No right? That's exactly the kind of misconception I came to clear up, brother, dear. Let's start with the idea that you run Titan. Technically, you are in charge of North American operations, but I don't need to remind you about who runs the rest, now do I?"

"You assured me you wouldn't interfere."

"So long as you had a firm grip, yes. But I received a call from Ms. Morales earlier today that made me doubt your leadership abilities. Seems I've arrived just in time to keep you from dismissing our most promising new agent."

Marisela had taken a risk in contacting Ian's twin shortly after Frankie had gone into the operating room for a six-hour surgery, but she'd been so furious at the way Ian had toyed with Frankie's life, she'd decided to deliver one parting shot before she quit or he fired her. Either way, she knew that her days at Titan had been numbered. She'd never imagined the woman would travel halfway around the world to save her job.

Things hadn't worked out as planned in any way, shape, or form. Marisela figured that on the surface, she'd actually failed in her first case. The objective had not been met, but the truth had come to light. Wasn't what she'd been paid to do, but hey, she'd take it.

"You can't interfere, Brynn. You have no idea how contrary Marisela is."

Brynn dramatically placed her hands onto her slim hips and sighed with exasperation. "I know! A woman with her own mind! How dare she think for herself."

He jabbed a finger at her. "That's not what I meant."

"Isn't it?"

Brynn turned her benevolent gaze toward Marisela, strode forward, and took her hand again, this time giving her a gentle pat. "My dear, you're probably a damned gorgeous babe when you've gotten some sleep, but right now, you look like hell."

Marisela shook her head wearily. "I'm too tired to take that as an insult."

"Good, because when I want you to be insulted," Brynn replied, "I'll be entirely more clever. Take Jessica home. Go see

Frank. Once Ian and I have settled our business, we'll get more acquainted, yes?"

Marisela would have loved to be a fly on the wall of the hotel suite, but she didn't have the energy. The most she could manage was a private smile as she crossed over the threshold into the hall. All in all, this hadn't turned out to be such a bad day. Sure, she'd blown the mission all to hell, had likely pissed off one of the most powerful arms dealers in the Western hemisphere, and had no idea what she was going to do about her ex now that she knew he'd live, but she'd kept her job.

For her, not a bad day at all.

Epilogue

THE PAIN IN HIS GUT was searing, but Frankie forced his eyes open, pushed the button on the edge of his hospital bed that released another dose of morphine into his system, and waited for his eyesight to clear. When the shadows and light stopped doing a sickening dance around the room, he focused on the woman sitting in the lounge chair by the window, her attention entirely engaged in a book.

"You read?"

Marisela looked up, her bright brown eyes filled with something he'd like to hope was relief. Maybe a little caring, too. He couldn't ask for her to love him, not now, but damn, having such an intimate showdown with death made him realize that he wanted something more from Marisela than an occasional roll in the hay. Though he wouldn't turn one down if she made the suggestion.

But not today.

"Smart ass," she quipped, closing the book and sweeping over to his bedside with that sultry, swinging walk that made his body ache in places that luckily hadn't been blown apart by a bullet or sliced open by a surgeon's scalpel. "I've been waiting for you to return to the world of the living."

He inhaled, bracing himself against the pain of forming words in his brain and actually speaking them with his lips, teeth, and tongue.

"Long wait?"

"Two days. Not so bad. Gave me a chance to study up on my mythology. I've got to pick a code name."

The sickening rock in his stomach plummeted another few feet into his sutured intestines. *Dios mio,* she wanted to work for Titan permanently?

"You're staying?"

"Of course! Okay, so our mission failed and we nearly got killed. Twice. But man," she said, sitting on the bed so hard and heavy that Frankie had to bite his tongue to keep from cursing, "what a rush! We were good together, too, don't you think? I mean," she said slyly, leaning forward and swiping her tongue over his parched lips. "In more ways than one."

Frankie cleared his throat. The thought of working for Ian Blake again rivaled the pain of moving in the bed after two days flat on his back, but the thought of leaving Marisela to work with Blake and him not around to run interference stung even worse. "He wants us back?"

Marisela shrugged and glanced aside, obviously withholding information. "Well, let's just say our jobs are available if we want them."

She propped the book back into her lap and flipped through the pages. "I got a list from Max. Unfortunately for you, Adonis and Atlas are already taken. However, I was thinking something dark and mysterious. Hades, maybe. He's the God of the Dead. Or maybe Hephe . . . Hepheas . . . oh, forget it. If I can't pronounce it, no one can."

With all the energy he could muster, Frankie reached out and took the book away from her. "*Vidita,* you're making my head hurt."

She leaned forward and kissed him on the nose, her gaze dipping downward. "Which one?"

"*Calienta polla.*"

"I killed the last man who called me that," she pointed out.

"Maybe, but you saved my life. I'm going to have to pay you back for that, you know?"

A tiny but wicked smile crossed her lips and she crawled nearer. "You've made that promise before, Francisco Vega. This time, I'm going to have to make sure you collect."

The scent of her perfume overpowered the medicinal smells of the hospital room. For an instant, he could almost imagine he was somewhere in paradise.

"*Por favor,* don't torture me, Marisela. I'm an injured man."

"Yes, but you're alive—and that's what matters most."

Silence hung there for a moment, a quiet that Frankie knew should be filled with some sort of private words between them, something to help classify what they were to each other. They were more than friends, but even lovers didn't seem to cut it. But he was too groggy to say more than, "Marisela."

The longing in his voice must have given him away, because instantly, she placed her soft fingers over his lips. "Don't, Frankie."

"Don't what?"

Tell me how much you care about me? Say that from now on, we should decide our futures together? Admit that being lovers after all we've been through is no longer enough?

She leaned back and popped open the book. "Don't call me Marisela. I've got a new code name, now."

Frankie groaned. He wasn't sure if he had the strength to hear.

"What is it?"

"Aphrodite, of course. The Goddess of Love." She strung out the last syllable, laughing at her own cleverness in a way that made Frankie's body, for an instant, pain-free.

"Mighty Aphrodite," came a voice from the doorway. "The world will never be the same."

Marisela snickered, waving Max into the room. He strolled inside, a hint of reluctance in his colorless eyes.

"Good to see you awake," he said to Frankie.

"Good to be awake." Frankie shifted in the bed and though he'd never admit it, Marisela could see the price he paid for moving around. The skin around his lips had paled and his eyelids drooped heavy over bloodshot eyes. The doctors warned her that he'd be back to his old bad-ass self in no time, but what Marisela didn't know was if she'd be there to help him through. All depended on Brynn Blake and whatever deal she offered.

"Marisela, you ready?" Max asked.

She grabbed the worn paperback Max had lent her and tried to stuff it into her back pocket. Her jeans, of course, were too tight. She tossed him back the mythology primer.

"As I'll ever be," she said.

"Ready for what?" Frankie asked.

Marisela brushed a quick kiss across Frankie's lips, and then bounded to the door without looking back. Frankie didn't ask again and if she wasn't imagining things, she could have sworn she heard him curse softly when she pulled shut his door. He was alive. She'd deal with him. Later.

Max gestured toward the elevator.

She followed, releasing a wide-mouthed yawn she'd been harnessing for hours. "You did good," she said to Max, realizing she hadn't had a chance to thank him for coming through with the information on Elise.

"So did you."

She shrugged, leaning her shoulder against the wall. "I broke the rules."

Max grinned as he punched the button and the automatic doors slid open. "That seems to be your forte. Might come in handy on your next case, too."

She laughed. Yes, it would. And for once in her life, she might have found a profession that not only appreciated her inability to do what she was told, but paid her handsomely for it. For once in her life, Marisela Morales might have found the true path to her future.

Up Close and Personal with the Author

WHEN I GOOGLE YOUR NAME, I CAME UP WITH SOME-ONE NAMED JULIE ELIZABETH LETO . . . IS THAT YOU?

Yes, it is. Julie Elizabeth Leto is my full maiden name, which I used when I started writing romances for Harlequin in 1998. I still use that name for my romance novels, but I decided to drop the Elizabeth for Marisela's books for several reasons. One, Julie Elizabeth Leto is so long! My hand cramps at booksignings. Two, my complete maiden name makes me feel like I'm in trouble for not cleaning my room or something. Three, with a shorter name, it can be bigger on the cover. All kidding aside, I thought I should differentiate for my readers between my romances and my mainstream action-adventures, so I did so simply by dropping my middle name.

THE HEROINE OF THIS BOOK IS LATINA, ARE YOU?

Yes, I'm one-quarter Latina thanks to my paternal grandmother, Velia Gonzalez, whose family was from Cuba and Spain. She encountered a lot of discrimination because of her ethnicity even though she was born and raised (like me) in Tampa, which is a very Hispanic-friendly town. Probably didn't help that she married into an Italian family. But since her family came to the United States before the turn of the last century (during the Spanish-American War), she considered herself entirely American. Because of this, the Cuban side of my roots was often ignored. This book gave me a chance to delve back into the culture I experienced mainly through my best friends growing up, who were all Latina. This gives me a chance to send special thanks to Denise Espinola, Lynn Saavedra, Marissa Cosio, and Yvette Castillo, among many, many others, who invited me into their homes on countless sleepovers and pajama parties. I also lived in a very Hispanic neighborhood growing up, so the culture was always around me, as well as the Italian-American culture that my mother's side (and half of my father's) brought into the mix.

SO YOU DON'T HAVE ANY CUBAN TRADITIONS LEFT IN YOUR FAMILY?

Oh, yes, we do! Luckily for me, most of them are about food. My uncle married a Latina, my Tia Anita, who if I remember correctly, was the one to inspire our fabulous *Noche Buena* celebration, which is a Cuban Christmas Eve. Since Tampa is a city that embraces the Cuban, Spanish, and Italian roots, it's easy for us to serve roast pork, black beans and rice, *platanos,* and flan on that holiday. Of course, on Christmas Day, it's manicotti, Italian sausage, and cassata. Best of both worlds. Tia also speaks Spanish and taught Spanish for many years in junior high. She made sure the grammar and syntax in this book is right, that's for sure!

HOW DID YOU COME UP WITH THE IDEA FOR MARISELA'S BOOK?

Over the years, I've become known for writing very strong heroines. I think this was my forte and I knew it was just a matter of time before I wrote a truly heroine-central book, especially with the increasing popularity of chick-lit and women's fiction. Romance novels tend to split their attention fifty-fifty between the man and the woman, but I knew that writing a mainstream book would give me a chance to focus even more on my heroine and her journey. I'm also a trend-watcher and I wasn't blind to the fact that Latina experiences were gaining attention thanks to actresses like Penelope Cruz and Jennifer Lopez and authors like Alisa Valdes-Rodriguez. The chance to explore that ignored part of my heritage really excited me, so I came up with the idea for Marisela. She definitely solidified in my mind long before the plot did, which isn't usually how things work for me. And of course, I wanted to make her really kick-ass. She never fails to entertain me with her tough *chica* attitude. I have a feeling we'll enjoy each other's company for quite some time.

DO YOU STUDY SELF-DEFENSE?

I don't, but I desperately want to. I simply need to carve out some time. I did quite a bit of research for this book, primarily regarding *krav maga,* which is the self-defense technique taught to the Israeli army and various law enforcement agencies around the United States. It's an incredibly practical form of defense and I'm hoping to actually try it very soon. Well, I did try it, but I was alone at the time. My knowledge about guns, knives, car chases, and the like comes from extensive research. Like I said in my Acknowledgements, I'm a Google junkie. If I can't find it on Google, I'm convinced the information doesn't exist.

IS THIS BOOK THE START OF A NEW SERIES?

I'm so excited to answer yes! I'm writing *Dirty Little Lies* (tentative title) right now. The book will once again put Marisela in the position of having to make a hard moral choice, which is diametrically opposed to the choice that will help her succeed in her mission. I don't want this spy stuff to be easy! With each book, Marisela will become better at what she does as an agent for Titan and her relationships with Frankie, Ian, Max, and Brynn will grow and change, not to mention her relationships with her family and friends like Lia.

SPEAKING OF LIA, WHAT CAN YOU TELL US ABOUT HER SINCE SHE'S NOT IN THE BOOK VERY MUCH, BUT IS CLEARLY AN IMPORTANT PART OF MARISELA'S LIFE?

I really wanted Lia to play a larger role, being Marisela's best friend in the world, but the plot simply didn't allow me to include her in more than just those two scenes. I like Lia, but then I should because she's more like me than Marisela is. I'd like to think I'm adventurous, tough, and resourceful like Marisela, but in reality, I'm more like efficient, caring, cautious Lia. And, of course, my ethnic background and experiences were more like Lia's. I do know she'll return in future books and, hopefully, will become more involved in Marisela's new job. She can't work for the mayor forever, not when her best friend has such a cool new career.

MARISELA AND FRANKIE HAVE STARTED SOMETHING REALLY HOT TOGETHER, BUT IAN SEEMS TO BE HANGING AROUND PRETTY CLOSELY. WHAT'S GOING ON WITH THE THREE OF THEM?

Well, I'm not entirely sure yet. When I first set out to write the books, I didn't expect Ian and Marisela to be so adversarial. I was hoping to have some really hot stuff happen between them. Unfortunately, characters often have a mind of their own and my opinion didn't mean much. There's a lot of sexual tension sizzling between them, especially since Ian is unlike any man Marisela has ever known, but they have issues. Frankie, the itinerate bad boy, has become her safety net and she doesn't know what to do with that, either. So I think you can look forward to a lot of exploring into the emotions and desires of this threesome, though probably not all at the same time. Of course, you never know with that either.

WHAT'S UP NEXT FOR MARISELA AND FRIENDS?

The next book is set in Boston and Tampa and I'm just starting to write it now (though by the time you are reading this interview, I should be through!). I can't tell you much except that Marisela will again get to kick some serious bad-guy ass and that she'll also have to deal with who she really wants to be when she grows up—or more appropriately for this book, who she doesn't want to be. And while she and Ian will connect on a deeper level, casting off some of their antagonism, her relationship with Frankie gets kicked up a notch through some incredibly hot sex, not to mention that whole life-death thing they have going. All in all, since this is the second book in the series and Marisela will be a Titan agent from page one, you can expect even more danger, thrills, and excitement. At least, that's the plan!

They're sexy, smart, and strong . . .
they're the

NAUGHTY GIRLS OF DOWNTOWN PRESS!

*Turn the page for excerpts
of the other Naughty Girls
of Downtown Press*

THE GIVENCHY CODE
Julie Kenner

LETHAL
Shari Shattuck

AWAKEN ME DARKLY
Gena Showalter

*Available from Downtown Press
Published by Pocket Books*

The Givenchy Code

JULIE KENNER

I felt fine, and I couldn't quite get my head around the idea that I'd been poisoned and had less than twenty-four hours to find the antidote. If this were a movie—or even an episode of *24*—I'd find the antidote in the last possible second, then I'd turn around and kick the shit out of the bad guy.

Would be nice, but I wasn't going to bank on it.

I shoved Kiefer out of my mind and focused instead on the man who was with me. The man who'd promised to help get me through this. I believed him, too, and already I'd come to rely on his strength, to anticipate his thoughts and suggestions. I'd only known him for a few hours, but my life was running in fast forward now, and Stryker was running right alongside me.

At the moment, though, he wasn't running anywhere. Instead, he'd parked himself back at the computer, and now he pulled up Google and typed in a search.

>>>*New York Prestige Park*<<<

About a million hits came up, all of them raving about the *prestigious* apartments/offices/restaurants on *Park* Avenue. So much for an easy answer.

We were running out of ideas. If we couldn't figure out Prestige Park, we couldn't find the next clue. And if we couldn't find the next clue, I was dead.

"Let me try," I said. I didn't care if there were two thousand pages of hits. We were going to look at every single one of them.

"Hold on," he said, then typed in a new search.

>>> *"New York" "Prestige Park"*<<<

He hit Enter, and *bingo.* A car park. "Well, hello," Stryker said. And I actually almost smiled.

We'd decided to stay in my apartment until we figured out the clue, since moving to some other location would take too much time. But we'd also decided to be quiet, just in case there were other eyes and ears watching us. I'd changed out of Todd's clothes and pulled on my Miss Sixty jeans and a Goretti tank top I'd scored off eBay.

Beside me, Stryker had his cell phone open and was dialing information. "Turn up the radio," he said.

I rushed to the stereo and complied, turning the volume higher and higher until he finally nodded, satisfied. How he'd hear his conversation, I didn't know. Didn't care, either, so long as he got it done. I knew he would, too. The man had it together, that was for sure. He'd told me that his earlier phone call was to a computer geek friend to try and figure out who posted that Web message. Nice to know he was on top of that. And now he'd solved the Prestige Park mystery. And the best part? He was on my side.

Behind me, Stryker muttered into his phone, then snapped it shut. He leaned onto the table, brushing my shoulder as he picked up the pen I'd been using earlier. He scribbled a note, then inched it toward me. *Prestige Car Park—downtown & Bronx.*

"Looks like we're going downtown," he said.

I nodded, trying to remember if the online version of the game extended to the boroughs. I didn't think it did. A plus for me, since, like so many Manhattanites, I was entirely clueless about life outside the island.

He snapped the screen shut on Jenn's laptop, then slid it into the case, balling the cords up and shoving them in, too. I thought about protesting—it was Jenn's computer, after all— but I didn't. Jenn would understand, and we might need the thing. Finally, he grabbed the original message and my notes interpreting it. "Let's go."

I stood up, then took the papers from him. I dumped

them and my pocketbook-sized purse into a tote bag that I regularly schlepped to class with me. "Are we coming back?"

"Not if I can help it."

I nodded, shifting my weight on the balls of my feet, now snugly encased in my Prada sneakers as I stalled in the doorway. What can I say? It was hard to leave. I hated the idea of abandoning all my shoes. Not to mention my handbags, clothes, photo albums, books, and favorite CDs.

"I'll buy you a change of underwear," Stryker said, since my thoughts were apparently transparent. "But we need to get moving. We've already wasted enough time, and—"

"Fine. You're right. Let's go." I told myself that this wasn't good-bye forever—just until we'd won the game.

I tugged the door closed and locked it, my worldly possessions now measured by the width and breadth of the Kate Spade tote I'd snagged last fall in a seventy-five-percent-off sale. "I'll be back soon," I said to the door. I hoped I was telling the truth.

Lethal

SHARI SHATTUCK

Through the silver rain dripping from the rim of my umbrella our eyes connected with a sharp magnetic click.

Boom.

I couldn't look away, didn't want to. He was gorgeously Japanese, tall and slim, about forty, dressed in a flawless black suit with a long overcoat. His straight dark hair had a deep glossiness that women would kill for, cut so that the front was long, meeting the shorter hair in the back, and moved over his brow in a sexy sweep as he walked with a smooth, sure, long-legged gait, with his black flashers fixed on my blue ones.

Ooh baby.

I entertained an arousing picture of him moving underneath me with that same grace, his hands firmly on my hips, mine pressed against his smooth bare chest, or sunk in that thick luxurious mane to give me a handhold, traction. If I hadn't been walking, I would have crossed my legs.

We were fifteen paces away and about to pass each other. Still his eyes held me, smiling a secret between us, and I felt that thrilling hook of a sexual jolt that I love so much, but that happens so rarely. I returned the smile knowingly and then continued past him and on into the open doorway of the bookstore, where I lowered my umbrella and shook off the rain.

I thought, He's watching me, waiting for me to turn. Arching my back just enough to accentuate my curves and opening my raincoat to reveal them, I turned flirtatiously and looked up.

But he was gone. Nasty little shock to my ego. Most likely he'd disappeared into one of the second-floor restaurants in the Little Tokyo Plaza in downtown L.A. Damn. Oh well. My dark green umbrella stood out from the several common black ones when I leaned it next to the door and turned to search for treasure in the Japanese-American bookstore.

I browsed in and out of the aisles for at least thirty minutes, picking out the biggest, most expensive picture books as well as some sexy paperback comics, selecting one with a sharp-eyed, dark-haired hero that reminded me of Evan. I flipped through a few pages and admired the artwork—the hero with a gun, the hero with a sexy half-naked blonde. Smiling to myself, I thought, It *is* us, and I anticipated showing it to him that evening. Turning another page I saw an illustration where the heroine stood over the body of a bad guy with a smoking gun, and I thought of how I had met Evan that way. Except I had been the one with the smoking gun.

Back on the street I continued on through the clean, sparsely populated shopping area. I wondered if it was the rain that made the place feel so deserted. As I crossed a concrete bridge over a subterranean shopping level, I leaned out a bit to try to see what was down there.

What was down there was a girl, a man, and an ugly confrontation.

A large man, in an ill-fitting suit and a baggy overcoat, had backed a pretty Asian girl up against a wall in an awkward niche behind the curved stairs. No one on the same level with them could have seen the two, hidden as they were by the wall.

The girl was turning her head away from the man as he pressed against her, talking to her fast and angrily. I froze and looked all around me. Nobody. I backed up a few steps to the top of the stairway, keeping my eyes on what was happening below me. Neither of them had seen me. The stairway curved slightly, and I would be out of sight for a few seconds. I started down the stairs as noisily as possible. Hoping that it would scare the man away.

I coughed. I cleared my throat. I stamped down the stairs with purpose. Instead of going the obvious, straight way into the shopping tunnel I turned right into the little nook, which reeked of urine, and coughed loudly again. But even a few feet away the man seemed oblivious. He was so focused on the girl and spewing his anger at her that he didn't even seem to hear me. The girl's eyes, however, shot to me, and there was a plea in them. *Don't leave me,* they begged.

The man noticed her glance and followed her gaze.

"Just keep going, it's none of your business," he snarled at me.

"See, it looks more like personal than business to me," I said. It was all I could think of.

"Keep walking, we're fine." He tried to smile. "Just a little disagreement, that's all. Isn't that right, sweetheart?" He shook the girl a little, prompting her to answer.

But I could see her answer as her eyes looked down between the two of them and then back up at me.

Instead I stepped in, almost casually, and smiled in what I hoped was a disarming and polite way.

"How about it 'sweetheart'?" I directed at the girl. "You think you two can work this out without counseling?"

"Take a fucking hike!" the man growled at me, raising the gun toward me, to scare me. It worked. The girl saw him aim at me, and with a scream, she grabbed at the weapon; I knew that was a mistake. With the umbrella in my left hand I swung down even as his arm came up, trying to point the gun and both their hands toward the ground, knowing it was hopeless, that his arm was far stronger than the flimsy aluminum and nylon. The man grabbed the girl by the hair with his other hand and threw her toward me. I heard the gun go off, felt a pressure against my stomach as the girl screamed and hit me, shoving me—books, umbrella, and all—to the ground. My left hand flew up, and the back of it smashed against the concrete wall. In my abdomen I felt a sharp, stabbing pain. I've been hit, I thought. Oh God, I've been shot.

"I don't see anything," she told me.

"Here," I gestured, pointing to where the pain was, low on my right side. Efficiently but gently, she pulled down the edge of my slacks, I was conscious of the rain, light now, falling on my bare skin.

"It's just a scratch," she said, "but it looks like a nasty bruise is coming up. Maybe some internal bleeding, we need to get you to a hospital."

"What?" I sputtered. "Where's the round?"

"I don't know," she said, shrugging, "maybe it bounced off you." She pulled the edges of my white mackintosh, now sadly limp and dingy, over me. Then she retrieved my dented umbrella and held it over my face.

Quite a crowd had gathered now, and I was disgusted to see several of them had video cameras running. What a world.

"By the way," said my capable nurse, "my name is Aya, Aya Aikosha."

"Nice to meet you, Aya. I'm Callaway Wilde."

"Thank you, Ms. Wilde." Her beautiful dark eyes searched mine. "That was very brave. Thank you."

"Oh, that." I dismissed it, for the second time that day thinking of the man who had tried to kill me a year ago and ended up dead on the sidewalk. "That was nothing." I waved a hand. "Call me Cally."

Awaken Me Darkly

GENA SHOWALTER

First rule of fighting: Stay calm.

Second rule: Never let your emotions overtake you.

I'd broken both rules the moment I began following him.

Kyrin swept out of my way, and I flew past him. The storm had died, but the sun hid behind angry gray clouds, offering hazy visibility. Because of the sheen of ice at my feet, I had trouble stopping and turning.

Definitely not optimal conditions; however, I wouldn't back down.

"You do not want to fight me, Mia."

I whipped around. "Wanna bet on that too?" I sprang forward again, intending to kick out my leg and knock him flat this time, but he reached me first. He grappled me to the ground, pinned my shoulders to the ice, and imprisoned me with his body. Cold at my back, pure heat on top. Neither was acceptable to me.

"Still want to fight?" he asked.

"Fuck yes." I quickly landed a blow to his groin. Yeah, I intended to fight dirty. He doubled over, and I shot to my feet, slipped, then steadied.

Using his prone position to my advantage, I was able to land a blow to his left side and knock the deoxygenated air from his lung. He grunted in pain and sudden breathlessness.

I darted to his right and gave a booted strike. This time, he grabbed my ankle and toppled me to the ground. I lost my satisfaction, felt a moment of desperation. We struggled there, rolling on top of each other, fighting for dominance.

Physically, he had me at a disadvantage, and we both knew it. He could have attempted to smother me, but he didn't.

"It doesn't have to be this way," he panted.

Think, Mia, think.

I still had full use of my legs, and I made total use of them. I gave a scissor-lock squeeze around his midsection, forcing him to release my arms and focus on my legs. That's all I needed. With a four-finger jab to his trachea, his air supply was momentarily cut off in a whoosh, giving me the perfect opportunity to spring free.

My old combat instructor would have been proud.

I took stock of my options. I had to render him unconscious if I hoped to win. He'd defeat me, otherwise. I would
have to be merciless, but stop short of killing him. I needed
his help, after all. His blood. I didn't want to spill a single
drop on this cold, hard ice.

"Concede, damn you," I growled, circling him like a ti-
gress locked on her prey.

"You first," he said, still on his knees.

"I am almost done playing with you," he said.

"Play with this." I launched a flying spin punt into his
side.

Quicker than I could blink, he advanced on me. He used
his weight to push into me, stumbling me backward. When
my body came into contact with his, the strength hidden beneath his clothing jolted me. He was made of solid muscle,
easily outweighing me by a hundred pounds, but he didn't
once use the power hidden in his fists to strike me down.
Why? I wondered, even as I punched him hard in the nose.
His head jerked to the side; he made no move to counter.
Why didn't he return attack? Why did he go out of his way
not to hurt me?

I circled him, but he surprised me by grabbing my jacket
and tugging. The ice at my feet aided him. Suddenly off balance, I tumbled into him, keeping a viselike grip. His warm
breath washed over my face as he leaned close.

"Now you will concede this victory to me," he ground out
low in his throat.

"When you haven't hit me once?" I said, a cocky edge to

my tone. I'd fought enough opponents to know Kyrin had had plenty of opportunities, but I wasn't going to admit *that* aloud.

His eyes darkened, revealing a hint of wickedness, and he leaned down until our lips brushed once, twice. Soft kisses, languid kisses. Innocent kisses.

NATIONWIDE AUTHOR SEARCH!

Be the
Next
Downtown
Girl!

Are you a downtown girl at heart and an aspiring writer with a story?

Ever dreamed of having that story published?

Downtown Press is looking for an author with a fresh, new voice whose story will be published in one of our future Downtown Press anthologies. The first prize winner will also receive $500 (for that new pair of stilettos!).

Before you start writing, visit **www.simonsaysthespot.com** to register your name for the contest. If you choose, we'll provide you with writing tips from our authors, hints from our senior editors, info on online chats, and a newsletter with the latest from Downtown Press.

The rest is up to you! Good Luck!

Stories must be received by July 31, 2005.

www.downtownpress.com • www.simonsaysthespot.com

11614

Be the Next Downtown Girl
Contest Rules

NO PURCHASE NECESSARY TO ENTER.

1) ENTRY REQUIREMENTS:

Register to enter the contest on www.simonsaysthespot.com. Enter by submitting your story as specified below.

2) CONTEST ELIGIBILITY:

This contest is open to nonprofessional writers who are legal residents of the United States and Canada (excluding Quebec) over the age of 18 as of December 7, 2004. Entrant must not have published any more than two short stories on a professional basis or in paid professional venues. Employees (or relatives of employees living in the same household) of Simon & Schuster, VIACOM, or any of their affiliates are not eligible. This contest is void in Puerto Rico, Quebec, and wherever prohibited or restricted by law.

3) FORMAT:

Entries must not be more than 7,500 words long and must not have been previously published. Entries must be typed or printed by word processor, double spaced, on one side of noncorrasable paper. Do not justify right-side margins. Along with a cover letter, the author's name, address, email address, and phone number must appear on the first page of the entry. The author's name, the story title, and the page number should appear on every page. Electronic submissions will be accepted and must be sent to downtowngirl@simonandschuster.com. All electronic submissions must be sent as an attachment in a Microsoft Word document. All entries must be original and the sole work of the Entrant and the sole property of the Entrant.

All submissions must be in English. Entries are void if they are in whole or in part illegible, incomplete, or damaged or if they do not conform to any of the requirements specified herein. Sponsor reserves the right, in its absolute and sole discretion, to reject any entries for any reason, including but not limited to based on sexual content, vulgarity, and/or promotion of violence.

4) ADDRESS:

Entries submitted by mail must be postmarked by July 31, 2005 and sent to:

**Be The Next Downtown Girl
Author Search**

Downtown Press Editorial Department
Pocket Books
1230 Sixth Avenue, 13th floor
New York, NY 10020

Or Emailed By July 31, 2005 at 11:59 PM EST as a Microsoft Word document to:

downtowngirl@simonandschuster.com

Each entry may be submitted only once. Please retain a copy of your submission. You may submit more than one story, but each submission must be mailed or emailed, as applicable, separately. Entries must be received by July 31, 2005. Not responsible for lost, late, stolen, illegible, mutilated, postage due, garbled, or misdirected mail/entries.

5) PRIZES:

One Grand Prize winner will receive:

Simon & Schuster's Downtown Press Publishing Contract for Publication of Winning Entry in a future Downtown Press Anthology, Five Hundred U.S. Dollars ($500.00), and

Downtown Press Library
(20 books valued at $260.00)

Grand Prize winner must sign the Publishing contract which contains additional terms and conditions in order to be published in the anthology.

Ten Second Prize winners will receive:

A Downtown Press Collection
(10 books valued at $130.00)

No contestant can win more than one prize.

6) STORY THEME

We are not restricting stories to any specific topic, however they should embody what all of our Downtown Press authors encompass—they should be smart, savvy, sexy stories that any Downtown Girl can relate to. We all know what uptown girls are like, but girls of the new millennium prefer the Downtown Scene. That's where it happens. The music, the shopping, the sex, the dating, the heartbreak, the family squabbles, the marriage, and the divorce. You name it. Downtown Girls have done it. Twice. We encourage you to register for the contest at www.simonsaysthespot.com in order to receive our monthly emails and updates from our authors and read about our titles on www.downtownpress.com to give you a better idea of what types of books we publish.

7) JUDGING:

Submissions will be judged on the equally weighted criteria of (a) basis of writing ability and (b) the originality of the story (which can be set in any time frame or location). Judging will take place on or about October 1, 2005. The judges will include a freelance editor, the editor of the future Anthology, and 5 employees of Sponsor. The decisions of the judges shall be final.

8) NOTIFICATION:

The winners will be notified by mail or phone on or about October 1, 2005. The Grand Prize Winner must sign the publishing contract in order to be awarded the prize. All federal, local, and state taxes are the responsibility of the winner. A list of the winners will be available after October 20, 2005 on:

http://www.downtownpress.com

http://www.simonsaysthespot.com

The winners' list can also be obtained

by sending a stamped self-addressed envelope to:

Be The Next Downtown Girl
Author Search
Downtown Press Editorial Department
Pocket Books
1230 Sixth Avenue, 13th floor
New York, NY 10020

9) PUBLICITY:

Each Winner grants to Sponsor the right to use his or her name, likeness, and entry for any advertising, promotion, and publicity purposes without further compensation to or permission from such winner, except where prohibited by law.

10) INTERNET:

If for any reason this Contest is not capable of running as planned due to an infection by a computer virus, bugs, tampering, unauthorized intervention, fraud, technical failures, or any other causes beyond the control of the Sponsor which corrupt or affect the administration, security, fairness, integrity, or proper conduct of this Contest, the Sponsor reserves the right in its sole discretion, to disqualify any individual who tampers with the entry process, and to cancel, terminate, modify, or suspend the Contest. The Sponsor assumes no responsibility for any error, omission, interruption, deletion, defect, delay in operation or transmission, communications line failure, theft or destruction or unauthorized access to, or alteration of, entries. The Sponsor is not responsible for any problems or technical malfunctions of any telephone network or telephone lines, computer on-line systems, servers, or providers, computer equipment, software, failure of any email or entry to be received by the Sponsor due to technical problems, human error or traffic congestion on the Internet or at any website, or any combination thereof, including any injury or damage to participant's or any other person's computer relating to or resulting from participating in this Contest or downloading any materials in this Contest. CAUTION: ANY ATTEMPT TO DELIBERATELY DAMAGE ANY WEBSITE OR UNDERMINE THE LEGITIMATE OPERATION OF THE CONTEST IS A VIOLATION OF CRIMINAL AND CIVIL LAWS AND SHOULD SUCH AN ATTEMPT BE MADE, THE SPONSOR RESERVES THE RIGHT TO SEEK DAMAGES OR OTHER REMEDIES FROM ANY SUCH PERSON(S) RESPONSIBLE FOR THE ATTEMPT TO THE FULLEST EXTENT PERMITTED BY LAW. In the event of a dispute as to the identity or eligibility of a winner based on an email address, the winning entry will be declared made by the "Authorized Account Holder" of the email address submitted at time of entry. "Authorized Account Holder" is defined as the natural person 18 years of age or older who is assigned to an email address by an Internet access provider, online service provider, or other organization (e.g., business, education institution, etc.) that is responsible for assigning email addresses for

the domain associated with the submitted email address. Use of automated devices are not valid for entry.

11) LEGAL Information:

All submissions become sole property of Sponsor and will not be acknowledged or returned. By submitting an entry, all entrants grant Sponsor the absolute and unconditional right and authority to copy, edit, publish, promote, broadcast, or otherwise use, in whole or in part, their entries, in perpetuity, in any manner without further permission, notice or compensation. Entries that contain copyrighted material must include a release from the copyright holder. Prizes are nontransferable. No substitutions or cash redemptions, except by Sponsor in the event of prize unavailability. Sponsor reserves the right at its sole discretion to not publish the winning entry for any reason whatsoever.

In the event that there is an insufficient number of entries received that meet the minimum standards determined by the judges, all prizes will not be awarded. Void in Quebec, Puerto Rico, and wherever prohibited or restricted by law. Winners will be required to complete and return an affidavit of eligibility and a liability/publicity release, within 15 days of winning notification, or an alternate winner will be selected. In the event any winner is considered a minor in his/her state of residence, such winner's parent/legal guardian will be required to sign and return all necessary paperwork.

By entering, entrants release the judges and Sponsor, and its parent company, subsidiaries, affiliates, divisions, advertising, production, and promotion agencies from any and all liability for any loss, harm, damages, costs, or expenses, including without limitation property damages, personal injury, and/or death arising out of participation in this contest, the acceptance, possession, use or misuse of any prize, claims based on publicity rights, defamation or invasion of privacy, merchandise delivery, or the violation of any intellectual property rights, including but not limited to copyright infringement and/or trademark infringement.

Sponsor:
Pocket Books,
an imprint of Simon & Schuster, Inc.
1230 Avenue of the Americas,
New York, NY 10020

Good books are like shoes...
You can never have too many.

Best of Friends
Cathy Kelly
Yes, you can have it all! Just be sure to share...

I'm With Cupid
Diane Stingley
What happens when Cupid wastes your arrow on a guy who isn't worthy of true like—let alone love?

Irish Girls
Are Back in Town
Cecelia Ahern, Patricia Scanlan, Gemma O'Connor, and many more of your favorite Irish writers!
Painting the town green was just the beginning...

The Diva's Guide to
Selling Your Soul
Kathleen O'Reilly
Sign on the dotted line—and get everything you *ever* wanted.

Exes and Ohs
Beth Kendrick
When new loves meet old flames, stand back and watch the fireworks.

Dixieland Sushi
Cara Lockwood
Love is always a culture shock.

Balancing in High Heels
Eileen Rendahl
It's called *falling* in love for a reason... and she's working without a net.

Cold Feet
Elise Juska, Tara McCarthy, Pamela Ribon, Heather Swain, and Lisa Ticker
Something old, something new, something borrowed—and a fast pair of running shoes.

Around the World in 80 Dates
Jennifer Cox
What if your heart's desire isn't in your own backyard? You go out and find him.

Great storytelling just got a new address.

DOWNTOWN PRESS
A Division of Simon & Schuster
A VIACOM COMPANY

Look for them wherever books are sold or visit us online at
www.downtownpress.com.

Published by Pocket Books

11910-1